THE SHILOH SISTERS

A HARRISON RAINES CIVIL WAR MYSTERY

The Harrison Raines Civil War Mysteries
by Michael Kilian

THE SHILOH SISTERS

A HARRISON RAINES CIVIL WAR MYSTERY

Michael Kilian

BERKLEY PRIME CRIME, NEW YORK

THE SHILOH SISTERS

A Berkley Prime Crime Book
Published by The Berkley Publishing Group
a division of Penguin Group (USA) Inc.
375 Hudson Street
New York, New York 10014

Visit our website at www.penguin.com

This book is an original publication of The Berkley Publishing Group.

PRINTING HISTORY
Berkley Prime Crime trade paperback edition / January 2004

Library of Congress Cataloging-in-Publication Data

Kilian, Michael.
    The shiloh sisters : a Harrison Raines Civil War mystery / Michael
Kilian.—1st ed.
        p.   cm.
    ISBN 0-425-19403-5 (trade pbk.)
    1. Raines, Harrison (Fictitious character)—Fiction.   2. United States—
History—Civil War, 1861–1865—Fiction.   3. Legislator's spouses—
Crimes against—Fiction.   4. Shiloh, Battle of, Tenn., 1862—Fiction.
5. Government investigators—Fiction.   6. Corinth (Miss.)—Fiction.
7. Sisters—Fiction.   I. Title.

PS3561.I368S54   2004
813'.54—dc22

                                                        2003062798

PRINTED IN THE UNITED STATES OF AMERICA

10 9 8 7 6 5 4 3 2 1

Author's Note

THOUGH this is a work of fiction, it has been my intent to recreate the battle of Shiloh and the subsequent advance on Corinth as authentically as possible, complete to using the principals' actual words where there is record of them, and having them in the actual places they were in during those memorable weeks in 1862—even as they become involved in the plot of this mystery.

I should like to thank historians William Seale and Roger Kennedy for background knowledge important to this book, and thank Sen. Mary Landrieu and former Mayor Moon Landrieu for their kind hospitality during my New Orleans visit. I am grateful to my editor, Gail Fortune, and my agent, Dominick Abel, for their excellent service, and to my wife, Pamela, and sons, Eric and Colin, as only they can know.

For Roger Poricky, Bob Devore, Doug Hejmal,
and Bruno Sadinowskas, with fond memories
of Fort Bragg and the Fighting 518th.

Chapter 1

"**WHISKEY**, General?"

Grant pondered the suggestion, and the flask that the young colonel, an Illinoisan named David York, was offering. There was a chill on the evening and Grant was feeling it, though there was a fire on every hearth here in Cherry Mansion, the house overlooking the Tennessee River he had taken as his headquarters.

Worse than the damp cold was the pain in his ankle. The previous night he'd taken a bad fall on his battle horse Fox, rushing toward the sound of Rebel firing in driving rain and on muddy ground. His leg had gone beneath the animal and only the softness of the soaked earth had spared him serious injury. But his ankle had been so badly hurt the surgeon had had to cut off his boot and he'd been walking on crutches all day.

Here in the parlor of Cherry Mansion, he'd propped his injured foot on a low stool, but otherwise was conducting business as usual and smoking a cigar.

Grant had left the door to this room open. Several officers were standing about in the hallway beyond, talking quietly. There was an aura of calm about the place, despite the masses of troops, ordnance, and equipment gathered on both sides of the river.

There had been that firing, and some bold displays by Confederate cavalry, but from all reports, the Rebel army was still some twenty or more miles to the south at Corinth, the rail junction that was the next goal of Grant's Army of the Tennessee after his twin successes at Forts Henry and Donelson. Grant was far from completely convinced they'd be free from attack in their present position, but confident enough to relax when he could.

His adjutant, Captain John A. Rawlins, was off on a lengthy errand. He'd been with Grant since Illinois, and had appointed himself the general's guardian against the temptations of John Barleycorn.

The general plucked up a coffee cup from the table next to him and extended it toward the flask. "I'm obliged, Colonel." He watched as the amber liquid came halfway up the inside of the cup, then raised his other hand to make the pouring stop. "Thank you, sir. Much obliged."

"It's fine Kentucky whiskey, General. We acquired a few cases at Clarksville." Despite his youth, Colonel York had been a congressman for a term before the war and was in the habit of taking liberties. He still harbored political ambitions for after the war, though he was a Democrat, a party in decline in Illinois with the Lincolnites in ascendancy.

Grant sipped, then took in a rolling mouthful of the good cigar smoke. These were simple pleasures but he knew of none greater, save the companionship of his wife, Julia, and his children. Were Julia here, he would have given no thought to whiskey whatsoever. Were she here, he'd not be working this late. Certainly not with things so quiet.

"It has my endorsement," Grant said, setting down the cup. "If you would, Colonel—that map?" He gestured toward his writing desk, which had been set up across the room.

"Yes, sir." York moved quickly, fetching the map and placing it in Grant's hands as a waiter in a restaurant might a menu.

Though Grant had established his main supply depot on the eastern shore of the Tennessee River here at Savannah, he'd placed most of his army on the other side, on ground that protected his base at Pittsburg Landing, a few miles to the south. There were five full divisions camped on the bluffs and in the woods over there, with flanks anchored on two creeks.

General Sherman held the westernmost position, starting at Owl Creek. Then came General McClernand's division, holding ground along the Hamburg-Purdy Road—with General W. H. L. Wallace's division to the east of him and General Hurlbut's troops to the east of Wallace's. Hurlbut's line extended almost to Lick Creek, a stream feeding into the Tennessee River.

General Prentiss had camped his division far out in front of the others, but he'd posted extra pickets and warned them to be alert.

The river was key to everything here. It was Grant's lifeline to the North, but could prove a death trap if his Federal troops were pushed back upon it, as had happened to a much smaller Union force in Virginia at a place on the Potomac called Ball's Bluff the previous fall. Grant had a small navy of transports and gunboats here on the Tennessee, but they'd be of small use in a fight as deeply inland as his army was camped.

Grant slept at Savannah, but spent every day on the opposite shore, visiting the troops and conferring with his commanders. He made a point of not leaving until an hour after darkness fell. Neither side had had any success with night attacks in this war.

"I have no doubt that nothing will occur today," Sherman had told him that morning. "I do not apprehend anything like an attack on our position."

Grant had taken his friend at his word, and certainly nothing had happened the rest of the day. Still, he worried. He intended to mount an attack himself as soon as reinforcements arrived. He was awaiting General Don Carlos Buell and the forty thousand men of his Army of the Ohio, who were expected to join him here at Savannah any day. Together, they'd have some eighty thousand men—enough to overwhelm the Confederates.

Corinth was the juncture of a railroad line running eastward from Memphis, another running south to the cotton country of lower Mississippi and Alabama, and yet another connecting with Jackson, Mississippi. Take Corinth and the only railway left to the Rebels in this reach of their "country" was the one running east from Vicksburg. Corinth was a linchpin needing only a yanking.

The general took another sip of whiskey and another puff of the delightful tobacco.

Unfortunately, the Army of the Ohio was an independent command not subject to Grant's direct orders. Buell had promised to join in this enterprise, but had made it clear he did not consider himself subordinate. And he was taking his time.

Their Rebel opponent was Albert Sidney Johnston, a West Pointer who had great courage and the absolute support of Jefferson Davis, though Johnston had never commanded anything larger than a regiment in the field before. Grant doubted him capable of wielding a large force in a major action. Still, Johnston was unpredictable, a trait that could be worth a division of troops.

Holding the map closer, Grant tried once again to think of any more advantageous place to position his force, but no alternative came to mind. Aside from the bluffs immediately along the river, there was a paucity of strategic points.

The only place name near his divisions was something called Shiloh Church, over on the Old Corinth Road. It was a peaceful name.

Grant could only hope Buell would be there in the morning. He wanted to move on. That was the only way to win this war. Push on. Grind away at the enemy. Knock him back. Destroy him, if possible. Keep on, no matter what.

He finished his whiskey, setting it aside.

"More, General?" Colonel York asked.

"I thank you, sir, but no."

"I can send a bottle. All you want, General."

"No, thank you." Grant's ankle still hurt, but not as much. Setting the map aside, he picked up a stack of correspondence. The most significant item was from Grant's immediate superior, the very political and pesky General Henry Halleck. "Old Brains," as the man was called, was becoming more than Grant could bear. Ever since his victories at Forts Henry and Donelson, in Halleck's frequently voiced view, it seemed Grant could do no right. No matter that the newspapers were calling him a hero. Perhaps the harassment was because of that.

There was a sudden commotion outside the house, moving up onto the first-floor veranda. Grant could hear a woman's voice. She went from anger to pleading to anger again, without lessening the degree of her hysteria.

The open parlor door gave him a view of the foyer by the front entrance.

"Would you see what that's about, Colonel?"

The officer rose, uncertainly. "I'm not sure I want to know, sir."

"Well, I do," said Grant. He went back to the letters, which he'd not yet answered, pleased when the ruckus outside abruptly ceased.

York returned with a bemused grin on his face. "It's a woman, sir."

"That much I could apprehend, Colonel. Who is she?"

"Claims she's Congressman Abbott's wife."

Grant winced. That man was a member of the Congress's newly formed Committee on the Conduct of the War, which was to the U.S. Army what flies were to a horse.

"Do you believe that?"

"The lady is very firm in her conviction, sir."

"Very well. Guess I'd better talk to her."

"You sure, sir? She's in quite a state."

"Sooner I listen to her, the sooner I won't have to."

The woman swept inside in a billow of black hoop skirt and crimson cloak, causing one of Grant's young aides to totter backward. She looked wildly about her, then down at Grant.

"I'd rise, madam," he said, "but an injury prevents it."

Her gaze was imperious as she looked to affirm that claim, but then softened. "Please, General. I must get across the river. I must do so tonight."

Grant pushed himself higher in his chair. "Please, madam. Seat yourself."

She pulled up a small chair, sitting on its edge and leaning forward imploringly. "Do you know who I am, sir? I am May Abbott. Mrs. May Abbott."

"You've been announced. I shall take you at your word that you are."

She was an attractive woman, slender and finely boned, with light brown hair and large, somewhat sad brown eyes. Though her clothes were muddy, they appeared to be expensive and finely made.

Reaching within her red cloak, she brought forth a locket, which she hastily opened. It contained a Daguerreotype of a man with black hair and mustache, though Grant could not make him out well enough to identify him as the congressman, whom he knew only through newspaper articles.

"This is he," she said, leaning close.

"Yes, indeed," said Grant, a trifle uncomfortable to be in such close proximity with a handsome woman not his wife. He inched back. "Tell me please why you must cross the river?"

"I'm bound for Corinth, to find my sister."

"Mrs. Abbott, that place is occupied by the enemy."

"I know. My sister's husband is a Confederate officer—Colonel Townsend."

Grant nodded. He had known Townsend when both were at West Point and later in Mexico. The man had served competently but was distinguished mostly by his extreme views on the question of slavery—which he'd espoused with great passion.

"You've come all the way from Washington?"

"No. I've been in Cincinnati—and Louisville."

"And now here, just to see your sister?"

"Yes. As soon as I can."

"Why such urgency?"

"I fear her life is in danger."

"And why is that?"

"I cannot say." A tear came into her eye, then more.

Grant sighed. He wanted to take a puff of his cigar, but feared he would offend—and at an obviously awkward time.

"Madam, if I am reluctant to grant your request, it is not because I do not believe you are who you say or doubt the seriousness of your concern. It's because there's a Rebel army sitting where you want to go. They've sent infantry probes and cavalry raids this way. There've been some brisk exchanges of fire. And it's night. In the dark, you could get shot by either side. You could get lost—"

"I know this country, General. Perhaps better than you. I grew up here." She slid to her knees, clutching her hands together in plea. "Please, General Grant. You've no idea how much this means to me."

"I do not believe your husband would appreciate my letting you do this."

"I do believe he will not forgive your refusal." She wiped at an eye. "General, have you a wife?"

"I do."

"If her life were in danger, would you let yourself be stayed by"—she paused—"by some officer standing on regulations?"

Grant was more accurately sitting on regulations. And they did not forbid what she asked. It was entirely at his discretion. He'd written passes for wives seeking to cross the lines several times in his advance along the Tennessee.

But those ladies had been going north. Mrs. Abbott wished to go into enemy country.

Still, there was no immediate prospect of battle. There were several habitations where she might take shelter between Savannah and Corinth. And he could see to her safety at least part of the way.

"Please rise, madam. I am going to do the same." He

reached for one of his crutches and used it to stand erect without too much clumsiness. She was by then on her feet as well. He nodded to her, then hobbled over to his desk.

"Are you going to let me through?"

Seating himself, Grant took pen and paper in hand, then paused. "I will write you a pass that will provide you safe conduct coming and going," he said. "But I must ask something in return." He handed the pen and paper to her. "If you would put your request in writing, please."

"Are you really that much afraid for me?" she said.

"Yes, ma'am."

"And for yourself, I suspect, if I should meet misfortune?"

"I am, madam, in this regard. I mean to invade Mississippi and push these people back all the way to the Gulf of Mexico, if I can. I will be sorely inhibited in this effort if I am being called to account by a member of Congress for an ill-advised action you are asking on his implied authority."

"I understand." She took the paper from him and began to write. He did the same.

They exchanged their papers upon completion. "Would you care for some refreshment, madam?"

"No, thank you, sir. I must make haste. I hope to be in Corinth by tomorrow."

"Have you baggage? A servant?"

"A small portmanteau. In your anteroom. I have a maid traveling with me. She is outside."

"A maid?"

She sensed what he meant. "Not a slave, General. She is paid wages."

"And you're taking her into Confederate territory?"

"She will not be molested."

"How did you get here?"

"By public coach and farm wagon. I was hoping to hire horses on the other side of the river."

"At the moment, I think that would be most difficult." He called to Colonel York, who appeared in the doorway an instant later—no doubt having been standing just outside to better hear the peculiar conversation.

"Sir?"

"I want this lady taken across the river and given an escort of cavalry as far south as the military situation permits. Provide her and her servant with mounts."

"Yes, sir."

"There is to be no contact made with the enemy. If that happens, she must be brought back. I don't want her injured in some fool skirmish on a night so dark."

Mrs. Abbott stood listening to this without comment. Her expression was a strange mixture of relief, gratitude, and continuing anxiety.

"I would be happy to lead the escort party myself," said York, making a gallant bow. Grant was a little irritated. She was indeed a comely woman, and the officer was married.

"I fear I cannot spare you tonight, sir. There are able enough officers to be found in the cavalry for this task. But you may accompany her across the river to make arrangements. Don't tarry coming back."

The colonel came stiffly to attention. "Yes, sir."

Mrs. Abbott smiled for the first time since she had burst in on him. "Thank you, General. I shall be forever grateful."

When she had gone, Grant went back to his soft chair. The whiskey flask was standing by his empty cup. He thought briefly of another refreshment, then discarded the notion.

He needed a clear head. The nagging worries had prompted a decision. He would reposition his divisions in the morning. It would not suffice just to sit and wait for Buell.

Chapter 2

HARRY Raines called himself a Union Army "scout," though his actual status was as a captain in Allan Pinkerton's U.S. secret service. Raines was proving a very poor scout now. He sat upon his one-eyed horse at the edge of a high Texas mesa, contemplating the crossroads that was the principal feature of the broad, arid valley below, wondering which way he should go.

He had no map and could only guess where these two tracks led—if anywhere. They might just peter out somewhere in the Texas vastness. But it was into that vastness he had to go.

Harry had been sent out West ostensibly to observe Confederate moves and designs on the New Mexico Territory, but also because Mr. Pinkerton feared he had exposed himself too much as a Federal agent in the Eastern Theater and was liable to be captured.

The Rebels had been thwarted in their attempted conquest of New Mexico and been sent yipping back into Texas, but Raines had played no great part in that federal success. He had little to report on the situation in the West that hadn't been telegraphed to Washington through regular military channels. His only consolation was that, while in Santa Fe, he'd made the amorous acquaintance of a beautiful, highborn Spanish lady, but she'd gone off to Mexico with her father, who thoroughly disapproved of Harry at all events.

In sum, he'd been left with no reason to linger in the territory any longer. Notorious as he might be among Confederate agents in Washington City and Jefferson Davis's secret police in his native Virginia, he figured returning home would be well worth the risk. He missed the greenery and the good whiskey, his horse trading business in Washington, his small farm up the Potomac, his friends and gambling acquaintances, and the eastern ladies, of both Northern and Southern persuasion. He also missed his family, especially his sister. His father and brother, unfortunately, were fervent believers in the Confederate cause and serving officers in its military. He had barely spoken to them since the war began.

Harrison Grenville Raines had been brought up a member of what was called "the Chivalry" of Old Virginia. Belle Haven, the family plantation, was one of the largest on the James River, and home to no fewer than a hundred slaves owned by his father, now a Confederate colonel serving under General James Longstreet. Harry had grown to manhood as something of an idler, passing his days at nothing more industrious than reading books or going for walks with young ladies of the Tidewater. He would have been content to continue that pleasant existence were it not for the one great disagreement he had with his father and all his father's kind.

Harry hated slavery. He despised it as much as any evil extant in the world. His best friend through childhood, named Caesar Augustus, had been a slave born on the family plantation. His father had treated him as something less than human, and had given him to Harry as he might a horse. Thanks to Harry, Caesar Augustus was now a free man and a partner in Harry's livestock business in Washington City.

And they were still the best of friends, while Harry and his father were estranged—a mild term for the bitter enmity the elder Raines now bore him.

For all his strong feelings about "the peculiar institution," as his father and others who profited from slavery liked to describe it, Harry had not initially been an ardent supporter of the war. As a Southerner, he had many friends on the Rebel side. And he could foresee nothing to come of the internecine struggle but political impasse and endless, massive slaughter.

But it was not a struggle in which a man who harbored any kind of principle could long remain neutral. With some initial reluctance, he'd allowed himself to become recruited into Pinkerton's web of agents. Now, more than a year into the war, he might not be Pinkerton's most competent operative, but he was certainly among the most dedicated.

The Stars and Stripes had been restored to New Mexico. The main war was still raging to the east, with the Union cause still much in doubt. That was where he belonged. The only question was how to get there—starting with which of the roads below to take.

Harry guessed one would lead south, to the rough country around Fort Bliss, now a Confederate stronghold. There was no knowing where the other went, but he hoped it might be to the coast, where with luck he might find a Federal warship or a neutral steamship bound for eastern ports.

He took his spectacles from the case in his frock coat and put them on, as though clearly seeing the two dusty tracks would assist in the decision. Though no narcissist, Harry was somewhat vain about his looks, or at least of the impression they made on young ladies when he wasn't wearing his glasses. If not as handsome as the actor John Wilkes Booth, his chief rival for the affections of a Washington actress he had long admired, Harry had an agreeable countenance, with soft brown eyes, sandy colored hair, and a long cavalier's mustache. He was tall, slender, and, when bristling with his navy Colt revolver and the other arms of his new profession, presented something of a buccaneering figure. But with his spectacles on, he looked more a schoolteacher or preacher.

There were no young ladies here.

"What are you thinking, Harry Raines?"

It was his companion on this journey who spoke—a half Indian, half French Canadian Métis named Jacques Tantou. Harry had met Jack, as he called him, on the way to Santa Fe, and they'd been through much together, including two gunfights and one full-fledged army battle.

Tantou had gotten himself in trouble in Canada and was wanted for killing a Mounted Policeman. He'd fled south into U.S. territory, working his way down into California and U.S. Army service as a scout. In this capacity, he'd gotten in more trouble still, and now was willing to accompany Harry anywhere he wished to go, as long as it was many miles from where they were now.

Harry turned to look at him. Tantou also was tall— muscular but lean, with a scarred, somewhat malevolent-looking, weather-worn face. He had long black hair he wore gathered in the back. In contrast to Harry's gentlemanly finery, Tantou wore dusty brown boots, a cavalry trooper's trousers, a grimy gray shirt, and a fringed yellow leather jacket. His hat was dark brown, with an extremely wide brim. He carried a dragoon pistol in his wide belt, a long

Bowie knife at his side, and a long-barreled rifle on his pommel. Whatever lay ahead of them, Tantou would always be ready.

"I'm thinking about which way to go," Harry said.

"It's all hard country," the Métis said. "Unless you want to double back and take the road north to Denver."

"Denver's away from the war," Raines said. "I need to get to an active military command where I can telegraph Washington for instructions."

"You take the south road and you will run into Rebels around El Paso. You are known now and they will hang you."

"They will hang both of us."

"No, because I will not take that road with you."

"The other one may go to the Gulf Coast. From there we can go to Louisiana."

"We know nothing of Louisiana."

"You speak French."

"Oui. Bien sur. Comme vous savez."

"That will be a help."

"We could forget these roads and go due east—go straight to Mississippi or Tennessee."

"I don't know what part of either state the Union Army holds—if any. But I am sure there are Union Navy ships in the gulf."

"Louisiana," Tantou said.

"Louisiana. And New Orleans."

"I am told it is dangerous."

"It is other things besides."

"I fear you are taking us into trouble."

Harry clicked his one-eyed horse forward. "Then why do you follow?"

"Because trouble is better than hanging."

Chapter 3

GRANT slept fitfully and awoke before sunup. There'd been dreams and Mrs. Abbott had been in one of them, appearing as a wraithlike figure amid the smoke and confusion of a battlefield, among trees, calling out to him for help. He tried to reach her, but could never get near enough with his injured limb.

He sat up, reminding himself of where he was and why, and then swung his legs over the edge of his bed, rubbing his ankle. It felt better now, but he wasn't sure how long that would last if he started walking on it. He'd stay in the saddle as much as possible this day. He was sorely tired of the crutches.

After a washup, he put on clean underdrawers, socks, and shirt, but chose the same rumpled uniform trousers and coat he'd worn the day before. There were a number of officers in this command who were fond of disporting themselves like parade ground peacocks, but Grant was not one of them. He now had major general's stars on his shoulder straps. That was peacock enough.

Everyone on his staff was there at breakfast except the handsome Colonel York.

"Where's York?" he grumbled, seating himself.

"Not seen him this morning," said Major Hawkins, another aide.

The general turned to his meal, but had barely taken a mouthful of it when Captain Rawlins entered the room, marched up, and saluted. "General Nelson's compliments, sir. He asks if you want him to move out now. He asks if you aren't worried about Johnston attacking."

"There will be no fight here or at Pittsburg Landing," Grant said. "We will have to go to Corinth for that, where the Rebels are fortified. Tell him to wait. General Buell should be here today, surely tomorrow."

"Yes, sir."

The imposing General William Nelson was part of Buell's command and had come in with a division the previous day, the first of Buell's troops to do so. He was a huge man with a neat beard but unruly, curly hair. Fond of ornate uniforms, he was given to a strange quivering of his great bulk when agitated, which made his epaulets quiver as well. He was called "Bull" Nelson, and it was appropriate.

Grant began to eat more rapidly, but was interrupted again. He set down his fork and listened raptly.

Cannon fire. Across the river. A vigorous artillery exchange. He regretted the irony of his words on the prospects of a Johnston attack.

All the officers at the table had ceased their conversation and were looking to him. Grant rose, holding to the back of the chair.

"Gentlemen," he said, "it would appear the ball is in

motion. Let's be off." Limping toward the door with that slouching, almost shuffling gait of his, Grant stopped beside Hawkins. "Send someone to catch up with Rawlins. I want General Nelson to ready his division and move it down the river to a point opposite Pittsburg Landing, there to wait for further orders."

"Move up there by boat?" the colonel asked.

"No, a march overland. I want to keep the boats here in case General Buell arrives with the rest."

"Do you think we need Nelson's division, sir?" The cannon fire was louder.

"I'm going over there to find out."

A more truthful answer would have been a simple "yes."

GRANT'S steamer, the *Tigress,* seemed to take longer on the voyage to Pittsburg Landing than usual, clanking and clattering along beneath its canopy of smoke as though on some pleasure excursion, with no mind to the urgency of the moment. The cannon fire had increased in depth, some of it sounding from the far distance, some of it booming quite close. It struck Grant that the enemy may well have engaged his force all along the line.

The numbers possibly favored the Federals, but the circumstance did not. Attacking at breakfasttime, just after first light, was a move to catch his troops unprepared—as they undoubtedly were. Bill Sherman's camp in particular had been worrisomely at leisure the previous day.

Rawlins had returned from Nelson in time to catch *Tigress.* The captain came up to where Grant was standing on the foredeck.

"You're feeling well this morning, General?" he asked.

"Better, John. What do you think?"

"I think we're in for a big fight."

"I wasn't expecting it."

"None of us was."

"It's the other end of this battle that matters now."

A round of solid shot struck the top of a tree and then sailed down into the river, sending up a huge plume of water. It missed the *Tigress* by a good hundred yards or so, but several aboard ducked.

Grant remained where he was standing, thinking hard. He doubted that the Rebels could turn either of his flanks, but they could well exploit the gaps and lax arrangements of the three divisions in the center—especially Prentiss's, which was so much nearer the enemy. Judging from the noise, they'd thrown a large force against the Federal positions, possibly some of their reserves as well. Grant was shortly going to be a very busy general—though all he could do for the moment was listen and think.

A few miles shy of Pittsburg Landing was a smaller debarkation point called Crump's Landing. As they neared it, Grant saw a steamboat with its prow against the shore. Coming nearer still, he recognized it as the headquarters boat used by General Lew Wallace, a former Indiana newspaper reporter and politician whose able service in the Mexican War had commended him for high rank in this one. A major general now after the Donelson fight, he had a division under his command. They were reserves, a long way from the fight. Grant would need them, though, and soon.

He sent an officer to the wheelhouse to tell the *Tigress*'s captain to change course toward shore but not to stop. As they drew nigh, Grant leaned over the rail and called for Wallace. The other general appeared almost instantly on the main deck of the other vessel.

"General, get your troops under arms and have them ready to move immediately."

"Done that, sir," came the reply over the murky brown water. "Where's the fight?"

"Can't you hear? Pittsburg Landing!"

"When do you want us to move?"

"As soon as is convenient. And to Pittsburg Landing."

"I will, General."

The *Tigress* moved on, clanking and thumping. The artillery fire was louder still, not simply because he was coming closer but also because more cannons were being added to the combat. That much was very clear.

By the time they rounded a wide curve in the river and caught sight of the Pittsburg bluffs, the sounds of war had become a din—as though both sides were going to use up every artillery round in North America, and do so before lunchtime.

An unhappy sight greeted Grant as they turned from the channel and headed toward the landing. A ribbon of blue was visible along the shoreline—long and thick.

Grant lighted a cigar, clenching his teeth down hard on it. Shirkers—hundreds of them. They must have run at the first Rebel musketry. He shook his head. His impulse was to see to their punishment, but there was no time for that. At least, with the river, they could run no farther.

The steamboat mushed against the shallows by the landing between two other vessels, and a plank was run out off the bow onto the shore. Grant called for his horse, Fox, to be brought to him on deck and, with help, mounted. His crutch was put into his saddle's rifle scabbard.

Without waiting for his staff, he walked the animal down the plank. The landing was literally aswarm with skulking soldiers, sheltering in the lee of the bluffs from the artillery barrage atop. Grant estimated more than a thousand of them. Doubtless with more to come.

There were officers among them—as scared and inexperienced as the privates.

"What's your division?" Grant asked one, a second lieutenant.

"General Prentiss's, sir. It's hell up there."

Grant shook his head again, sadly. Prentiss had held the most forward position. Now some of his troops were in the extreme rear. Was this a rout?

Paying no further mind to the lieutenant, he moved his horse away, looking down the line of beached steamboats. The sight of a woman standing at the rail of one of them made him pause. Julia had written that she might join him when there was opportunity. He could not believe she would come on ahead without his declaring it permissible. As much as he desired her company, this was the last place he wanted her to be.

Despite his ankle, he put his horse into a trot and went up to the lady, halting the animal at the bank.

It was not Julia. She was Anne Dickey Wallace, General W. H. L. Wallace's wife. A lovely woman of considerable gentility, she also had her father, two brothers, and two brothers-in-law in Grant's Federal army here.

Grant removed his hat. "I fear your husband is occupied, Mrs. Wallace," he said.

She smiled, but it quickly passed. Her eyes went to the top of the bluff. "I fear that also, General Grant."

"You have just arrived?"

"Less than an hour ago. I was going to join Will at his camp, but I'm told that's not possible now. I shall wait here, I suppose."

It seemed as safe a place as any. "If you would, madam. I must take my leave of you now and rejoin my army."

She looked to the mob of shirkers, whose numbers were growing with reinforcements. "It would seem it is rejoining you."

"My place is with those who are fighting. I look forward to talking with you later, Mrs. Wallace."

"Please tell my husband I am here and that I wish him well."

"Of course, madam."

He pressed his horse hard to reach the top of the bluff. This pained his ankle, compelling him to shift most of his weight to the other stirrup, but he didn't slow until he reached the crest. Then he came to a stop.

Until that moment, Grant had not been certain of where the Confederate attack was directed. Now he realized he was at the very spot that was the object of their ambitions. They were pressing all along his line—if the disposition of his forces could be described as anything that organized—looking for a place to break through and cut his army off from the river.

Grant was depending on his flanks. The water was running high in both Snake and Lick Creeks, making them all but impassable for an attacking force. Sherman's troops on the right had never been in an engagement before, but their general's skills as a commander were compensation for this. Grant had great faith as well in his fellow Illinoisan General W. H. L. Wallace.

He took out his pocket watch. Eight o'clock. There was a long day ahead of them.

There were two Iowa regiments idling atop the bluff—awaiting orders, according to the colonel on command. Grant had them form a straggler line to turn back other skedaddlers, and added an artillery battery with guns trained on the road that led into the woods and the fighting.

Grant pulled up his horse, waiting for Major Hawkins to come up.

"I want reports from every division," Grant said, clenching down harder on his cigar. "Now."

"Yes, sir."

RAINES and Tantou had traveled nearly forty miles along the Texas road that day, and it was still daylight. If the cool, dry weather continued, there was every reason to think they could keep up that pace. They might well arrive in Louisiana before the Federal army and navy did. Lacking newspapers in this wilderness, Harry had no idea what the war's progress might be. He'd have to play that hand when it was dealt.

In the meantime, there was the matter of getting there alive. What had remained of the Rebel army had run back to El Paso, and the Union forces were all clustered around the New Mexico towns and forts along the Rio Grande. There would be no authority representing either government out in this wild country.

Harry and Tantou were carrying a considerable amount of Federal gold on them and had only two rifles and four pistols to defend it with. They'd had one nasty brush with Indians while riding into New Mexico. Had it not been for Tantou, Harry would not have gotten any farther than that.

"Do you think we're clear of Apache country yet?" Harry asked his companion, who was riding with his hat pulled down so far he looked asleep.

Tantou raised his head, squinting. *"Presque."*

"I don't know what that means."

"It means almost."

They rode on, walking their horses. Harry's great hero
and fellow Virginian George Washington—the finest horseman of his time—had a regimen for moving long distances
on horseback: a rotation of walk, trot, and canter, with a
sensitivity to when the animal needed to change its gait.
Harry had become good at this, but Tantou was better.

Taking advantage of the walk, Harry again fetched up his
spectacles from their case and put them on. There was a line
of scrubby little hills on the far side of the wide, flat valley
they were traversing. The sky hadn't a shred of cloud, and
the lowering sun was very bright behind them, illuminating
everything to the horizon sharply. Harry could see individual
pine trees miles ahead of them.

"I'm feeling a trifle exposed out here," Harry said.

"You should," Tantou said. "We are."

There was a hawk or an eagle circling to the southeast,
but no buzzards. Doubtless every carrion in the West had
gone to the New Mexico's Rio Grande Valley, picking over
the remains of the retreating Confederate column.

"We haven't even a map," Harry observed.

"We're army scouts. We don't need maps."

"I'm not a scout. I'm a secret service agent."

Tantou snorted, sounding much like his horse. "If you
want a safe, well-marked road back to the East, Harry Raines,
we should go to Denver. There are Federal troops moving
up and down the Colorado road, and many forts. In Denver,
there may be a railroad."

"Why do you say that?"

"There is a telegraph. They go with railroads."

"Well, it's too late now."

They went another hundred yards. "Why do you want to
go to New Orleans?" Tantou asked.

"I've never seen it."

"You have never seen Hell."

"I think our fastest way back to Washington City is by ship."

"The railroad is faster."

"Damnation, Tantou, I just want to go there."

"Why?"

"I'm curious about something."

"General Kearny, when I was working for him, he said something about Louisiana. He said it has the most dead of any state."

"You mean in cemeteries?"

"No, I mean more people die there than anywhere else."

"The mortality rate? It has the highest mortality rate?"

"Yes. That is what he said. Yellow fever. Other dangers. A very dangerous place."

"No more so than anywhere else with this war on." Harry looked to the circling predator again, just in time to see it swoop toward the ground.

"What are you curious about in New Orleans, Harry Raines?"

Harry sighed. "A woman, if you must know."

"Women are curious, *vraiment*."

"Her name is Louise Devereux. She's an actress. And French, like you. Mostly."

"She is Creole, maybe?"

"What do you mean?"

"Creoles are part African, as we Métis are French but part Indian."

"Actually, Jack, you have touched on the very thing. When I knew her in Washington, she had this document. She kept it secret, but let me see it. From Louisiana, it was. Freedom papers, for an African woman—maybe a mulatto— whom I took to be Louise's mother."

"Did she say this was so?"

"No. She kept me guessing. But it was a manumission paper, and she was taking great care to preserve it."

"When did you last see this woman?"

"In February."

"Where?"

"Richmond, Virginia."

"Then why are we going to New Orleans?"

"Someone there may know what she has for a year refused to tell me."

"If you learned that she is part Negro, would it make a difference?"

"Yes!"

Tantou frowned, and pulled down his hat even farther. "I think maybe you are on the wrong side in this war," he said.

"No, Jack. You don't understand. It's quite the contrary. I would welcome such news."

"Why?"

"Because then I would know for certain she is not a Confederate agent."

There was a gunshot, and a bullet came whizzing high overhead. It had been fired at long range from the line of scrubby hills in front of them. It missed by so much, Harry was uncertain whether the shooter was trying to kill them or stop them from going any farther.

Tantou broke into a gallop. He was heading straight for those hills.

WITH his staff trailing behind him, Grant rode south on the Corinth Road, allowing his horse a canter, which he found tolerable, but not a trot, which was now impossible with the pain in his injured ankle.

The ground around him was good for defense—undulating and in large part wooded, providing good cover. The firing ahead was so intense, though, he wasn't sure cover made any difference. With so much lead flying, a soldier was liable to get hit if he were to expose a single finger to the enemy.

Grant was not worried—not yet. His flanks were holding. That much was clear. His troops were giving way only in the middle, and that rearward lurch would soon be stemmed by his straggler line. Soon he would have General Nelson across the river with his division. Don Carlos Buell was en route. Grant had only to hold his position and prepare a counterattack. His mind was working on that.

But he needed more information. He needed a lot. Happily, he just then saw what appeared to be a general's party trotting up the road toward him. It was General W. H. L. Wallace, coming back from the fight.

"What are you doing here, Will?" Grant asked when the two groups had mingled into one.

"Orders from your Colonel McPherson," Wallace said. "He took command when the Rebs hit us—in your absence."

McPherson was Grant's senior staff officer. He'd spent the night on this side of the river as Grant's representative to the various commands. Instead of waiting for his superior's arrival, he'd issued orders to deal with the emergency—orders he'd doubtless assumed Grant would have made. He'd done the right thing.

"What's the situation?" Grant asked Wallace, a thin, clean-shaven man as handsome as his wife was pretty.

"They've hit us hard, sir. Damnably hard. Prentiss was way out in front, and I think he may be flanked. Sherman's falling back—McClernand with him. Hurlbut's holding—for now. My orders from McPherson were to stand by as reserve to plug whatever holes may appear. He took one of my brigades and is posting it now on the right. I was riding back to look for you."

Grant lighted a cigar and puffed on it a moment. Here and there in the woods he could see blue-jacketed men flitting through the trees—moving too quickly to be wounded. Grant hadn't been at First Manassas, but he'd heard and read all about that Union rout. Preventing that kind of panic among the troops might be his biggest task here, straggler line or not.

He chomped down hard on his cigar and signaled Rawlins to join him.

"Send a rider back down to the *Tigress*. I want them to steam back to Lew Wallace and tell him to march up here on the double quick."

"Double quick?"

"As fast as he can. I want a message to General Nelson to get across the river just as fast, if he hasn't got there already. There should be transports enough at the landing."

"Yes, sir."

"Wait, John." The other halted. "Ammunition. I want all ammunition wagons forward at once. From the sound of it, we may lick the Rebels just because we have more cartridges than they do."

"Do we, General?"

"Take care of it, John."

Rawlins took off as though he were in a horse race. Grant moved his horse forward, troubled to see the skedaddlers increasing in volume.

"Can this be stopped, Will?" he asked Wallace.

"A lot of the men are green."

"Sherman's troops are green, and they're holding firm."

"The main Rebel attack's not directed at him, sir. It's headed this way."

"Very well, Will. Get back to your command. Do what you can to keep them fighting."

Wallace saluted, and started to turn.

"General," Grant said, his words halting the other, "forgive me for not telling you. Your wife is here—on a steamboat at Pittsburg Landing."

Wallace looked stricken. "How can she be here? We are in the middle of a battle."

Grant frowned. "She was expecting it no more than we were. She's safe, Will. She'll be there waiting for you when we finish this fight."

"Thank you, sir."

"General? You haven't come across a woman named Abbott in your sector? Tall woman, married to a congressman. She was headed for Corinth."

"No, sir. I would wish her someplace other than this."

"Thank you, Will. I'll be sending orders directly."

As the general and his party moved away, another skulker came running by. Grant stopped him.

"Who are you, boy? What division?"

The youth seemed almost as afraid of Grant as he was of the Confederates. He looked furtively toward the battle, which now seemed just the other side of the trees.

"General Prentiss's, sir. The Rebs—they're in our camp."

"What's his position now?"

"Not sure, sir. Some of the boys are strung out along this road, and holdin' 'em back. But I think a lot of the Rebs are busy lootin' the camp. When they're done, they'll be comin' again. My company, we were on the left flank. They hit us there—even got behind us. My captain says to fall back, and that's what I've been doin'." He turned his head away, looking sheepish.

"You may stop falling back now, Private. We're going to need every man."

"Yes, General."

He left the boy standing by the road. He had no musket. Grant supposed there'd be ample supplies of those available soon.

Grant flicked his reins against his horse's flank, easing the animal forward. The smoke ahead was rising from the tree-tops like a great curtain. The road was becoming crowded, not with skulkers and cowards now, but with wounded. He could only wonder how many lay ahead upon the ground, unable to walk—or move ever again.

TANTOU was heading for the line of hills, but obliquely, toward the right. "Other way!" he shouted back at Harry. "Meet you in the middle!"

Without hesitating, Harry emulated Tantou's example, but turning his galloping one-eyed mount toward the left. Tantou's tactic presented their foe with two diverging targets, gaining them time from the shooter's indecision. It was a clever move, impaired by only one lamentable fact: There were two shooters, and they immediately took to harassing both Harry and Tantou, with ever nearer bullets.

Riding low and keeping his head to the side of his horse's neck, Harry thundered on, his mind working as fast as he could make it.

Whether Indians, Confederate soldiers, or banditos, the enemy had made a serious error—opening fire when Harry and Tantou were effectively out of range and, in so doing, throwing away the element of surprise. More sensible assailants would have waited until their prey were almost upon them, killing them swiftly with accurate fire, minimal expenditure of ammunition, and little risk to themselves.

Harry thus assumed that Indians and regular soldiery were not part of this. That left banditry, or travelers who were simply interested in making Harry and Tantou go away. Harry would have been most happy to go away, giving this place a wide berth and proceeding on to Louisiana in a wide detour. But it was too late for that. Tantou was charging madly on with his flanking movement, as though he had a regiment of cavalry behind him.

Leaping over a shallow gully, Harry swerved One-Eye back and forth to the right and left as more whizzing balls came at him—low enough now, but passing behind him. Raising his head slightly, he saw a cleft between two hills just ahead. Jabbing at One-Eye's ribs with his heels, he raced toward it, pulling the horse up some two hundred feet within the ravine's shelter.

Turning around to make a quick reconnaissance and collect his thoughts, he saw a piñon tree halfway up the slope and urged his horse to it, tying the animal fast to a branch and dropping to the ground. Hearing and seeing nothing here in the way of threat, he took his rifle from its scabbard and some extra cartridges from his saddlebag. With the long gun and his navy Colt in his belt, he trudged up the slope and slipped into more trees, heading toward the place where he thought the shots had been fired. With luck, he'd come up behind them. What he'd do then, he knew not.

Moving as quietly as possible over the rocky ground, stepping where possible on sandy patches or beds of fallen pine needles, he followed the undulating ridgeline cautiously, excusing his slowness as stealth, though it was borne of apprehension.

Once again, Louise Devereux was the cause of his troubles. It had been on her account that he'd gone to Manassas and found himself within range of Rebel muskets when the Federal army had turned tail and run. She was responsible for sparing him a hangman's noose in Richmond, but also for a mad duel he'd had to fight there in which a Confederate officer of his long prewar acquaintance had come close to killing him because of her.

Now he was bound for New Orleans to learn her secrets, and this dalliance with bushwhackers was the result.

Something flitted in the blur of his side vision—off to the right. He shrank behind a tree, lowering himself to peer through the branches.

The figure was a man with a rifle. He moved again, abandoning one tree for another, passing near Harry without noticing him. Harry realized he now had a clear shot at the man's back, but he could not bring himself to do that, self-preservation or no.

He eased himself backside first to the ground, keeping his rifle at the ready but doing nothing to impede his adversary as he moved away. What worried Harry most at this moment was the silence in the other direction. The gunfire had ceased. Had the other shooter finally succeeded with his marksmanship? Was the resourceful Tantou now dead?

Harry pondered his course: Go back to the right, to overtake the man who'd just gone by him? Or go left, to try to rescue his friend from the other foe? Harry chose the left, suddenly as certain in this decision as he was uncertain about what lay ahead of him.

Hurrying on, with weapon cocked, he went around the rear of a grassy hillock, reentering the trees on its other side and taking cover in the thickest of them. Hearing only the wind, he crept forward until he could glimpse through the branches the wide plain he and Tantou had been crossing. In the distance out there, he could see a solitary mounted figure. It was hard to make out much about him, but the rider seemed too small to be Tantou, and he was on a different-colored horse.

Harry inched forward still, wishing now that he hadn't the clumsy rifle to drag along. Reaching a clump of large boulders, he sought their farther side. He was about to raise himself up, when he suddenly noticed a man who was not Jacques Tantou crouched by the face of the largest boulder. He wore a battered hat and had white hair and a scraggly gray beard. His clothes looked ragged. The only sign of prosperity about him was the gleaming, long-barreled rifle he held—from the look of it, a buffalo gun.

Gently, Harry laid down his own long rifle. Creeping forward, he extended his Navy Colt and took aim with it. Fully in his sights was the head of the old man. A single pull of the trigger and their odds would improve enormously.

Again, he could not make himself do it—even as the man abruptly turned around and stood up, looking back across the top of the boulder. He seemed not to notice Harry, but was frantically trying to raise up the buffalo gun, scraping the stock against rock. There was a shot from behind Harry. As if shoved by some powerful hand, the old man went reeling and rolling down the hill, his splendid firearm falling with a clatter behind him.

Tantou came up beside Harry, his own rifle smoking. He eyed the now motionless body, then examined Harry's position. "Did you not see him, Harry Raines?"

Still holding his revolver, Harry brushed off the knees of his trousers. The figure out on the plain hadn't moved. "Didn't have a clear shot."

Just after his last word, they heard a rustle of leaves or

branches to the right. Tantou had not reloaded his weapon, and his revolver was still holstered. It was up to Harry. He dropped to one knee as he brought up the Colt, firing without aim but on instinct, not quite sure who he was trying to kill.

Whoever it was, he succeeded. The man dropped where he stood. Harry had somehow managed to hit him in the head. They stood there silently, Harry staring at the bleeding body, Tantou watching him.

"Is that all of them?" Harry asked.

"Yes. I think so."

"I saw someone out there—on the plain—on horseback."

The Métis came forward to the edge of the slope, then waved his arm back and forth, twice, in a beckoning manner. The rider called out something neither of them could hear, and began coming toward them.

Tantou set down his own rifle and picked up the buffalo gun, checking to see if it was loaded. Harry pushed down the barrel.

"These men fired on us, Harry Raines," the Métis protested.

"Let him get closer, please."

They waited. The rider reached the bottom of the hill, peering up. "Pa?"

GRANT drew up at the edge of the fighting. The center of his line seemed to be holding, but only because of the scrap Prentiss had gotten himself in forward of the other positions. That, and the Confederates' looting of the Federal camps, had slowed the Rebel drive. If they had instead pressed on without pause, they might have pushed Grant's entire army to the river.

Riders were bringing in a stream of reports, all saying

much the same thing: Under heavy attack. Send reinforcements. Grant sent a courier to Will Wallace, urging him to support Prentiss at all costs.

In the way of many successful generals, Grant had a way of holding a picture of a battle in his mind, altering it as its tides ebbed and flowed. Listening to the gunfire now, he sensed a shift in the Confederate effort. One of his big worries was that the Rebels would concentrate on his left flank and try to push his divisions away from the river and their source of supply and reinforcement. According to McPherson, they had showed signs of trying this in the beginning.

But now, perhaps because they had run into Prentiss so unexpectedly far forward, they were easing away from the left. Grant could hear it. He also could hear much more firing on his right. The Rebels were now piling on Sherman.

He signaled to Rawlins. "We're going up to Sherman. Have someone inform me directly when Lew Wallace is up."

"YOU killed my pa," said the youth, looking down at the bodies that still lay where they had fallen.

"They were firing on us," Harry said. "This is what comes of it."

"Who are you?" said Tantou. "Why were you shooting at us?"

The youth continued to stare at the dead men. He was perhaps sixteen, and had yellow hair and pale blue eyes. He might have been handsome, were his nose not so large and his mouth not pinched and small. There were tears forming in his eyes, but he held them back.

"We were bringing a string of horses back to Texas," the

youth said finally. "Indians caught us and took the mounts—all but that Appaloosa pony I got." He wiped at his eye.

"Do we look like Indians?" Harry asked.

"He does," the boy said, pointing to Tantou.

"Why did you shoot us at such long range?" Harry asked. "Why not wait to see whether we meant any harm? Or were you after our horses?

"I wasn't. I got a horse. My Uncle Caleb—he started shooting at you."

"And the other man?"

"That's my pa."

"Who was using the buffalo gun?"

"Uncle Caleb. He was a good shooter. He could have hit you with that gun."

"But he missed high and wide."

"My pa tried to stop him from firing. It threw off the shot. And then you started ridin' fast." The boy began crying in earnest.

"How old are you, boy?" Tantou asked.

"Seventeen, sir." It was a word he doubtless would not have used were he not so afraid. Harry saw that the youth's hand was trembling.

"I am sorry that your father and your uncle have been killed, and I'm sorry that we were the ones who did it," Harry said. "But you must understand that they gave us no choice."

"You could have run away."

"That's advice you all should have given yourself," Harry said.

"Yes, sir."

"Now you will help us bury them. We must move on."

He set the boy to digging first. Tantou pulled him aside.

"We should put him into the hole, too, Harry Raines."

"No. We'll take him with us."

"We killed his kin. You're asking for trouble."

"If we run into Indians, he'll be of help."

GRANT found Sherman ignoring the intense fire, taking time from the fight to show some of his artillerymen the proper length to cut their shell fuses. An enemy ball cut the top of a nearby tree as Grant came up, sending it to the ground in a great crash that in the midst of this carnage and chaos fazed no one.

Grant handed Sherman a cigar, then lighted a fresh one for himself. "How goes it, General?" he asked.

"It's pure hell, Grant. As bad as it can get. These boys are green, but they're fighting well. Won't be another Bull Run."

Grant took note of the bandage around Sherman's hand and the bullet tear in the shoulder of his subordinate's coat. "You all right, Bill?"

"I'm fine. Worried about Prentiss, though."

"Lew Wallace is on this side of the river. I've sent orders for him to bring his division up fast as he can. Nelson's marching for the transports opposite Pittsburg Landing and should be shipping his troops over soon. I have ammunition wagons rolling and Buell's due in Savannah."

"That's all good news."

"Can you hold?"

Sherman looked to the front, where the artillery battery he'd been assisting had gone back into action. He shook his head. "Not all day. We'll have to fall back. McClernand, too. But we can do it orderly. Maybe find some better ground. Maybe throw 'em back."

Grant nodded. He needn't tarry here, where everything was so well in hand.

"I'm going back down the line," he said. "See you tonight."

A shell landed not a hundred feet away, killing one artillery horse and ripping out the belly of another. It began to walk in circles, screaming.

Grant returned Sherman's salute and turned his own horse. Rawlins and McPherson drew up beside him.

HARRY had grown up with horses and was counted among the very best horsemen in Charles City County, Virginia. It was obvious to him after a mile or so that the boy was something of a stranger to his pony.

"You all came out here for horses?" Harry asked. "Coming into the territory from Texas, we found fresh mounts as scarce as water holes. Where'd your father and uncle get that string?"

"From the Confederate Army—after a battle. Someplace called Peralta."

Harry had been at that fight. It had been a month before, and, after their defeat, the Rebels had ridden out of the town on everything short of prairie dogs. He guessed the boy's father and uncle were in some way connected to the invading Texans, but that they had liberated some local rancher's stock on the way back.

"Were your father and uncle with the Rebel army?" he asked.

They had put the line of hills and the now-buried bodies some five miles behind them.

"Got mixed up with them, but we weren't soldiers. We

come out with the army. Pa said there'd be business to do."

"What was the buffalo gun for?"

"Killing game. Killing Indians."

And maybe loyal New Mexican settlers.

"You stay close to us," Harry said.

GRANT had ridden down the line to the center, where the state of affairs was better than he'd expected. McClernand had closed up with both Sherman and what was left of Prentiss's division. Though shot up, Prentiss's force had taken up a position in a sunken road that made a natural trench, fronting a wide, cleared field. The Rebels coming across it could count on being torn up badly. Will Wallace's division was just to the left, some of his troops mingling with the others.

Prentiss saw Grant and came back to speak to him, Prentiss's grimy face adrip in sweat. He was an Illinois lawyer whose military experience amounted to schooling at a military academy and serving in a state militia fighting insurgent Illinois Mormons during the Mexican War. He'd entered this war between the states at the same time Grant had, becoming a colonel and brigadier general at just about the same time. He was a good officer. Grant knew generals who would have run if placed in the circumstance Prentiss had been.

"Can you hold, Ben?" Grant asked.

"For a time." Prentiss looked at the bodies already accumulating in the sunken road. "My division's pretty well shot up."

"Reinforcements are on the way," Grant said, wondering where in blazes Lew Wallace was. "You and Will Wallace have got to keep your flanks in contact with Hurlbut and McClernand."

Prentiss nodded. "This is good ground."

"Maintain it at all hazards."

The other general looked a bit perplexed, then grinned. "All hazards. That's what we're up against."

THE extremity of Grant's left flank down near the river was held by a lone brigade commanded by a General David Stuart, once a congressman from Michigan. Amazingly, there was only desultory firing there. The Rebels' earlier attack in that sector had been abandoned completely.

"Are you all right here, General?" Grant asked.

"Quiet as a church, for now."

"There's a Shiloh Church over Sherman's way. It is not quiet at the moment."

"I do believe that's where Albert Sidney Johnston wants to go," said Stuart. "Sherman's way."

Stuart's brigade had been detached from Sherman's division to help hold this flank. Grant could not tell if the congressman preferred to be here or there. The firing to the center and right was now so furious it was no longer possible to discern individual cannon or musket shots. It was all one continuous roar.

"Keep a hard eye to your front, General," Grant said. "Lew Wallace'll be up presently."

"Are we going to attack?"

"Not yet."

A rider came up at the gallop, reining in before McPherson, who listened to his message and hurried to Grant.

"The right flank's been turned, sir. Sherman and McClernand are falling back, but in good order."

"Very well. I'm going back to the center."

By the time he reached that position, the firing on the right was subsiding. Grant supposed that, with Sherman's withdrawal, the Confederates were regrouping—or perhaps indulging in more looting of stores. If Nelson and Lew Wallace would turn up, he'd have an opportunity to redress this unhappy situation.

He asked Rawlins for notepaper and quickly wrote a message to Nelson:

"The appearance of fresh troops would have a powerful effect, both by inspiring our men and disheartening the enemy. If you will get upon the field, leaving all your baggage on the east bank of the river, it will be more to our advantage, and possibly save the day for us."

There was a desperate need for reinforcements here. Lacking Nelson's and Lew Wallace's troops, Grant had only the two Iowa regiments he'd left near Pittsburg Landing as a straggler line. He sent a rider to order them forward to McClernand's position. The river would have to serve as a straggler line now.

Another messenger. Sherman was taking advantage of the Rebel pause before him to launch a counterattack. Grant did not object.

He dismounted, needing to attend to the requirements of nature. When he returned, he found his staff distributing rations.

"Will you take some food, General?"

"Yes." Grant dropped his cigar and accepted a mess tin. Couriers arrived from Prentiss and Will Wallace, warning that the Rebels were throwing everything at the sunken road and that they could not hold much longer. Another rider brought good news. Buell had arrived.

"He's at Pittsburg Landing," said Rawlins.

"With his army?"

"No, General. Just his staff."

"I'll go meet him."

* * *

THE scene at the landing was infuriating. Literally thousands of shirkers and skulkers had now taken shelter along the base of the bluff. If Grant could get them into the line, there'd be no need of Buell, Nelson, or Lew Wallace.

He hadn't time for that. "Good afternoon, General Buell. Where is your army?"

"Arriving at Savannah, General. I will have them up as soon as I can get them aboard the steamboats, but"—he gestured at the mob of malingerers—"have you made preparations for a retreat?"

"I have not despaired of whipping the enemy yet," Grant said.

Buell looked at Grant as though he had gone mad. Grant lighted another cigar and rode away.

Returning to the fight, he again found no sign of Lew Wallace. He summoned Rawlins and McPherson. Along with Sherman, he trusted these two most.

"Both of you, if you would, ride to Lew Wallace and get him moving. He could decide the day. Impress this upon him."

"Yes, sir."

As they thundered off, Colonel York came up, looking as though he had spent the night with his bottle, his handsome face so wearied one would have thought he'd been on a fifty-mile march.

"Where in blazes have you been, Colonel? We have been engaged with enemy since eight o'clock this morning."

"I know. I got caught behind them."

"Did you get an escort for the Abbott woman?"

"Yes, sir. A six-man detachment from Colonel Ingersoll's brigade. A Lieutenant Riordan commanding."

"And where is Mrs. Abbott now?"

"I don't know, sir. I presume in Corinth."

"Has the Riordan detail reported back?"

"Don't know, sir."

"I would be pleased to know."

"Yes, sir. I'll see to it."

"But where were you?"

"I was worried about Mrs. Abbott, sir. I set out after them to make certain she got through all right."

"And you failed to find them?"

"Yes, sir."

"Did you have any ken of the enemy's forward movement? They got their whole army up without anyone noticing. Hit us hard."

"Yes, sir. By the time I ran into them, the fight was under way."

"How'd you avoid getting shot or captured?"

"I guess I'm lucky, General."

"I hope so, because I'm going to need you. Stay close."

"Yes, sir. Is the fight going our way?"

"Not yet," Grant said.

"You seem calm, General."

"Not quite the word for it."

Grant trotted his horse up to a low ridge that gave a view of Prentiss's and Will Wallace's troops. He looked at his watch. The time had somehow gotten to midafternoon.

Couriers were now bringing bad news with the frequency of artillery shells. The Confederates were pressing Prentiss on both his flanks, driving wedges in the line. Sherman and McClernand had counterattacked, briefly regaining their lost ground, but eventually had been pushed back once again. Stuart reported that he was now under attack on the left. All this at the same time.

Grant could only wonder where the Rebels were finding the men. Several times now he'd thought they were putting in the last of their reserves, but more kept coming. Johnston must have been using every cook and orderly. Grant guessed he might be up against as many as a hundred thousand men, though he could not understand where they were coming from.

He realized then that he was close to losing it all. The reasons were obvious, and he'd have small defense in a court of inquiry. He had been caught by surprise, made perhaps too confident by his earlier victories. His forces had not been concentrated, even though they had camped within some twenty miles of the enemy. He had not been able to work in concert with Buell's army, which was coming much too late to the field.

But he was not about to panic, and certainly not about to give up.

Everything depended now on his line. Short of being pushed into the river, it did not matter so much where it ran. The important thing was to keep it intact. They were well into the afternoon. If they held until nightfall, they could live to fight another day.

There were too many men on both sides who would not. Grant had passed several field hospitals. They had filled quickly. There had been grotesque piles of severed limbs at first. Now there were rows of the dead.

He could not now count on Lew Wallace bringing his men up in time to do any good. He removed that chessboard piece from his calculations. Sherman was falling back to high ground. Though it was dangerously close to the river bluffs and the landing, it was far more defensible than the ground he'd briefly won back. And Sherman was Sherman. He would be dependable to the end.

Stuart had not budged much. The problem was the center. The Rebels had shifted back and forth from flank to flank, but were fixed now on the beleaguered middle of his line, a scene of as much chaos as there was carnage.

Grant turned to another man on his staff, Colonel Joseph Webster, who'd deferred thus far to Rawlins and McPherson, reflecting Grant's partiality toward them. Webster would be given his chance.

"Webster," Grant said, turning his horse toward him.

"Yes, sir."

"You are now this army's chief of artillery."

"Sir?"

"I want you to lay hands on every available gun and bring them up to the center. Position them just behind the line. If it breaks, you and these guns are to keep the enemy from cutting us in two and reaching the landing."

"Yes, sir!"

More riders. More bad news. Now Stuart and Hurlbut were falling back. Sherman and McClernand were getting hit again on the right. Prentiss's division had been cutting down the Confederate charges as they might mow wheat, but the Rebels were to either side of him now. And Will Wallace's division, Prentiss's chief support, was coming under furious assault.

The salient Prentiss occupied was of little use now to Grant, and he wished there was a way to pull Prentiss out of it. He had to stop the drain of shirkers. He had cavalry on hand, as useless as a third leg in the fighting. He sent orders to the horseman to form a line across the road, then gathered his staff and rode forward toward Hurlbut, Wallace, and Prentiss.

Colonel York rode close alongside, but he did not speak.

"Something amiss, Colonel?"

The young officer reached behind him and took from his

saddle a crimson fold of cloth. Grant, horrified, recognized it instantly.

"Is that Mrs. Abbott's cloak?"

"Yes, sir."

"You're sure?"

"Yes, sir. Lieutenant Riordan had one of his men bring it to me. He just now came up with it."

"Riordan?"

"Her escort, sir. The man said he found it hanging from the branch of a tree near the Corinth Road."

Grant took it in hand. He hadn't the slightest doubt it was as York said.

"Riordan's with Ingersoll's brigade?"

"Yes, sir."

"Did the lady get to Corinth safely?"

"Riordan sent no message, sir."

"Where are they? Ingersoll's brigade?"

"Somewhere over near Sherman. Not much use on this kind of ground."

"Send a rider. If it's convenient, I'd like a word with Lieutenant Riordan."

"Yes, sir."

"Keep this safe," Grant said, giving the garment back to the colonel. "We shall return it to her when we reach Corinth."

"Do you think we will do that, sir?"

"Not today." Grant urged his horse into a canter, heading once again to the shambles that was Prentiss's line, not knowing what to do about it.

HARRY turned in the saddle to make certain that the youth was still riding with them. They had disarmed him, and Harry didn't think him much of a threat. But Tantou was still worried about him.

"You all right?" Harry asked.

The boy nodded, glumly.

"Your horse holding up?"

"Yep."

Tantou looked disdainfully to the youth and then to Harry. "This is a mistake."

"He's done no harm to us, and we've done plenty to him. Let him be."

"How long you plan to let him tag along?"

"We'll drop him at the first town we get to."

"I do not like Texas. It is like its own country."

"It was—from 1836 to 1845."

"Full of slavekeepers," Tantou grumbled.

"A few."

"No slavers in Colorado."

"Jack, our goal is Louisiana. You will like it there."

The sun was getting low in the west. There was nothing ahead that looked like a good place to camp.

WHATEVER the outcome of this fight, however he coped with Albert Sidney Johnston, Grant would have to face another foe when the firing stopped and the battle smoke cleared: General Henry Halleck.

He'd been chiding Grant after his two clean and clear-cut victories at Forts Henry and Donelson. What he'd do after this mess was nothing Grant now wanted to contemplate.

It was five o'clock. Grant returned his watch to his pocket and examined the western sky, trying to gauge how much light and how much battle he had left. He ardently wished it was less.

A courier from the center, his right arm hanging useless with a bandage around it, galloped up, the horse nearly throwing him with the abruptness of his halt. The man was breathless.

"General Hurlbut's compliments, sir. Bad news. General Prentiss and his command have been captured."

Grant chewed on his cigar twice, then tossed it onto the ground. "How?"

"Outflanked and cut off from behind, sir. General Hurlbut said to tell you General Prentiss put up a hell of a fight. Turned his sector into a regular hornets' nest. General Wallace's division is in retreat and he is missing."

Grant's thoughts went to the woman waiting on the steamboat at the landing, but that would have to wait until later.

"My compliments to General Hurlbut. He is to hold his position at all costs."

The young officer saluted with his left hand, then gathered up his reins and charged back toward the fray.

Another messenger, this time from the landing. And this time good news. Nelson had finally arrived with his troops. Grant turned back to go and greet him.

The big general had taken the time to put on his best uniform, which made him look like one of the marshals in Napoleon's Grande Armée. He ascended the bluff from the landing on horseback, his presence announced by regimental bands playing patriotic airs. His first words to Grant were in denunciation of the mob of skulkers huddled at the base of the bluff.

Grant didn't ask what had taken him so long. He explained the situation to Nelson calmly. If worse came to worst and his line gave way at any farther point before nightfall, there'd be a Confederate rush to the landing. He was forming a sort of last redoubt, extending a line across the top of the bluff—creating a position the other divisions could fall back to. Bolstering it were sixty or more pieces of artillery Webster had gathered together, plus the cannons on the gunboats *Lexington* and *Tyler,* anchored just off the landing.

The band music prompted cheers from the men who'd been up on the bluff all day. Grant helped Nelson position his troops in a line running almost down to the riverbank. The last of them were in place by the time the sun sank behind the trees that marked Sherman's new position on the right.

Whatever ill feeling Grant had been harboring toward Nelson for his late arrival now vanished. Late or no, he might well have saved the day.

Grant snapped his head around as, out of the gathering dusk, came a storm of musketry and wild Rebel yells. The Confederates were making one last charge against the part of the line where Grant had been most vulnerable all day.

There was no need to order his massed guns into action. The batteries opened fire as soon as the first of the Rebels came into view.

Grant urged his horse forward. The noise was the worst of the day, so loud as to be almost palpable, enveloping him like a heavy, suffocating weight. There was no speaking to his aides. He had no useful order to give at this point anyway. The success or failure of this mad, desperate, last Rebel charge would be decided solely by the will and courage of the cannoneers and the men with muskets. His troops were fighting for their lives and their honorable cause. Grant could not understand this heroic, vainglorious, nearly suicidal effort by Johnston's men—giving their all for the dubious right to own Negroes.

Grant's wife's family owned slaves in Missouri, and when he and Julia were living there, in large part dependent on her father, some of them had labored for their household. Grant had hated that. He loved his wife above all else, but when he'd moved his family to Illinois to take work at his father's harness and leather goods shop in Galena, he persuaded Julia to leave the black folks behind. He would have preferred taking them to Illinois and setting them free, but that would have sorely riled her father, who'd been more than disappointed in her choice of husband.

Lighting another cigar, Grant moved in close to the fighting, merely a spectator now, coming near enough to see individual hand-to-hand combat by the infantry and the terrible slaughter ceaselessly visited upon the oncoming Rebels by the massed guns.

Colonel York came up beside him and began to gesture forward excitedly, smiling. Grant could not figure out what he was trying to communicate, but nodded, puffing on his cigar.

And then he saw it. On the edges at first, and then all along the line, the Confederates were peeling away. In a few minutes, they had disappeared into the darkness. The quiet began to spread over the countryside as the darkness deepened. The Rebels were pulling back, reorganizing, settling down for the night—doubtless in the camps in which so many Federal troops had abided the night before.

"Not beaten yet," Grant said.

"Sir?" said Colonel York.

Grant turned his horse. "There's much to do before the morning. Let us see to it."

He headed back toward the landing. His ankle had begun to hurt again. It hadn't for hours.

TANTOU had strongly suggested they'd sleep better if they tied the youth up for the night, but Harry was feeling so sorry for what had been done to the lad he would not allow it.

They'd found a steep-sided arroyo in which to camp. There were enough pieces of old dead piñon lying about to make a fire, which the high walls would mask from view. They had water and food, which Harry was happy to share. Tantou was not.

"We have a long way to go, Harry Raines."

"We have that long buffalo gun. You can shoot some game."

"Not much game here. Unless you like snake."

"You're half Indian. You know how to live off the land."

"On my own."

"Be of better cheer, Jack. We have survived a parade of calamities. We'll do it again."

Tantou said nothing, then took up his blanket, rolled himself up in it, and went to sleep.

"You'll be among friends soon," Harry said to the boy.

The youth looked sadly at the ground, then finished his scrap of corn bread and followed Tantou's example.

Harry had been hoarding a small flask of whiskey toward a time when he'd be really grateful for it. Leaning back against the side of the arroyo, he lighted yet another thin cigar and then carefully uncorked the vessel, allowing himself one pleasant swallow.

He tried to think of Louise Devereux' last words to him, spoken outside of a Richmond hospital. He failed, though he still remembered the look in her eyes as she had leaned forward to give him a farewell kiss.

It was a lovely memory to go to sleep by.

ONCE sure that the Confederates had disengaged all along the line, Grant made a tour of his division commanders—

those he could find—then rode back to his new field head-quarters, where tents had been put up and a fire started.

He hesitated. "I must go to Anne Dickey Wallace and tell her of her husband."

"There's no need, General," said York. "Her brother has gone down to the landing to give her the news."

"And what is the news?"

"General Wallace was seen to fall, General Grant. Shot through the head."

A camp chair was brought up, and Grant wearily lowered himself onto it, stretching out his injured leg and propping it on a log.

"Whiskey, General?" York had refilled his flask.

Grant shook his head. All his staff was there now except for McPherson, who was still out searching for Lew Wallace. "Let's hear it," Grant said to the others.

They made their reports. Prentiss's and Will Wallace's divisions had ceased to exist, and Prentiss was still missing. Estimates were of as many as ten thousand men killed, wounded, or missing in action—and many of the wounded would join the "killed" list in a day or two. Four of Grant's five forward division camps had been captured, with all their equipment and supplies. His line had been pushed back to less than a mile from Pittsburg Landing. Several thousand men—at least a division in strength—were cowering beneath the bluff to either side of the landing. He'd had some forty-two thousand men at the start of this, not counting Nelson's division. Now he had something between two thirds and three quarters of that fit for duty.

Grant's mind was on the morrow. The Rebels had done their worst and doubtless had suffered casualties as appalling as his. They would be as exhausted as Grant's force as well, and would be in a disorganized state from all the looting that must have gone on in the captured camps. Counting Nelson, Buell's force numbered some twenty thousand. If he and Lew Wallace would ever come up, Grant would have a large reinforcement of fresh troops. Even so, he had Nelson, whose division had seen little combat.

McPherson came galloping up, with news of Lew Wallace. "He took the wrong road, General. Marched due west from Crump's Landing instead of joining up with you. Just kept on into the woods."

"You spoke with him?"

"Yes, sir. He is redirecting his division and will be here by morning."

"I needed him this afternoon."

"He is now aware of that, General. Says he got a late start so his men could get some dinner."

Lew Wallace fancied himself a writer. Perhaps he was in the wrong calling. Grant sighed.

"Shall I set about organizing the retreat?" McPherson asked.

"Retreat?"

"Yes, sir. In this position—"

"No retreat." There were a few newspaper reporters skulking around his headquarters here, though they'd been scarce enough when the air was full of shell, shot, and minié balls. He could see three of them passing a bottle of whiskey around in some trees just at the edge of the firelight. "Send those men over to me," he said to McPherson. "I'll speak to them this once."

They brought a few of their colleagues along, and stood in a small semicircle around Grant, their eyes beady with anticipation, like rats who'd found a way into a kitchen.

"The battle's not over," Grant pronounced. He spoke

with them for another ten or fifteen minutes but told them
little else.

It began to rain.

GRANT ate, then tried to sleep beneath the sodden canvas of his tent, but could not. He moved to the shelter of a
nearby tree. The pain in his ankle had become simply mon-
strous, the worst of his ordeal. After midnight, he gave up
and, with help, hobbled down to the bottom of the bluff
and a log house he remembered being there.

The rude dwelling place was being used as a hospital and
was filled with wounded and dying men. Grant found a
bench out of the way in a corner and leaned back against the
wall, stretching out his injured limb.

It was there that Sherman came upon him. He'd been
searching through the darkness and the downpour.

"Well, Grant," he said, "we've had the devil's own day."

"Yes." Grant lighted a cigar. "Lick 'em tomorrow, though."

Chapter 4

"**WAKE** up, Harry Raines."

Harry opened his eyes to a faint gray sky and a glowering Jacques Tantou towering over him. He sat up, stiffly, for it had been a cold night and his blanket was thin. "What time is it?"

"Time to get up. The boy is gone."

Harry rubbed his eyes, then blinked. "Our horses?"

"He left the horses. Maybe he thought they'd slow him down. He took the gold."

"That gold is Federal property."

"I don't think he cared." He reached down to help Harry to his feet.

"What do we do now?" Harry asked.

"Do you want to find him?"

"Yes. Of course."

"We should have tied him up. I said we should do this."

"I shall henceforth defer to your superior judgment of human nature, Jack. Right now, I am deferring to your superior judgment of tracks left by fugitives in the wilderness."

Tantou looked to the east. "We should have breakfast."

"Jack, I need to retrieve that gold. I can't tell Mr. Pinkerton that I let a seventeen-year-old boy steal it from me while I slept."

Tantou grinned. "We should eat. I need more light if I'm going to track him."

Harry scuffed at the gray, grainy dirt. "All right."

"We want him to feel safe—that maybe he's going to get away from us with no trouble. That way, he'll keep on—instead of stopping in some rocks somewhere and waiting to bushwhack us."

"You think he'd do that?"

"He took the buffalo gun."

GRANT slept little during the night. He'd ordered the gunboats on the river to fire shells at the known Confederate positions every fifteen minutes, and he was unable to keep a hold on sleep. Worse, the sight and sounds of the wounded and dying around him in the log house was proving more than he could bear. It was his fault—not theirs—that they'd been taken unawares and mauled so badly.

Wearily, he went back to the top of the bluff, seeking the shelter of his tree. It was past two o'clock in the morning. Instead of attempting sleep, he roused his staff and started issuing orders.

He would surprise the Rebels much as they had surprised him the previous morning. They had come close to pushing him into the river and would think him in no shape to mount an attack. The Confederate troops would be preoccupied with the loot they'd taken from the Federal camps—loot, and food and drink.

With Buell's arrival, Grant now had about the same

number of troops with which he'd started the previous day. Johnston must have suffered losses equal to his own—if Johnston was still in command. Some Confederate prisoners who had been brought in during the night said they'd heard Albert Sidney had been hit and was down and that General Pierre Beauregard had taken over command.

Beauregard was more cautious than Johnston. And, with the rain and heavy darkness, there was a good chance the Rebels did not yet know that Buell had arrived on the field.

Grant called to York. "I want a rider to take this to General Nelson," he said, writing out a note. "I'd like him to move out on our left flank, staying near the river. I want him to move out by five A.M."

"Yes, sir."

Grant sent for fresh cigars, ate a little, then mounted his horse. He visited the four division commanders he had now readied for the day's assault—Hurlbut, McClernand, Sherman, and Lew Wallace, whom he'd put on the right flank. It was to Wallace that Grant went to wait for the commencement of the attack.

"About yesterday, General . . ." Wallace began.

"I've received your report, sir. No more need be said." He nodded to Wallace to ride forward with him. They halted in a line of trees atop a small knoll. Soldiers were moving past them. The sky was lightening, and the rain had slacked off.

"Presuming General Nelson is punctual today, he'll move out first with the rest of Buell's divisions behind him. You, Sherman, McClernand, and Hurlbut will roll forward together after he starts. Keep close to that creek in case they try to flank you. Hit 'em hard, Lew. By jig, I mean to do to them today what they did to us yesterday."

Wallace looked to the sky. The dawn was turning to morning. "Rain's stopped."

"Your men have eaten?"

"Yes, sir. No fires. Cold meat. But they've got it in their bellies."

Grant nodded, puffing on his cigar. He took out his watch, holding it close to the red glow of the ash. It was time.

Nelson was indeed punctual. His artillery began a brisk fire. His troops would be moving forward just behind the barrage.

"General?" Grant said to Wallace.

The other pulled on his gauntlets. "Your orders, sir. What formation for the march?"

"I leave that to you, sir."

THIS time the birds were buzzards. They would rise and circle and fall and then rise again, all this happening less than a mile ahead near what looked to be rude stone dwelling places.

"Do you suppose that has something to do with him?" Harry asked.

"I hope so," Tantou replied.

Those stone dwelling places turned out to be ancient Indian ruins, which Harry found odd so far from what he'd thought was Pueblo country. Turning One-Eye onto a rocky alley that led among them, he came to what he'd expected to find.

The buzzards would take flight when squabbling with each other but stood their ground at Harry and Tantou's approach. Harry had to kick two of them off the boy's body, which lay face down in the dust.

He'd been stripped of his boots, most of his clothes, and a considerable portion of his scalp. There were three arrows in his back—all deep—and one that had entered the back of his right knee. He had taken the long buffalo gun with him. The Indians for some reason had left it behind, though they'd taken the boy's pistol.

Tantou looked about the ground, then went over to a low wall by one of the ruins. He shook his head in amazement and picked up the leather bag.

"They left the gold," he said.

"Truly so?"

"Yes, Harry Raines. This is the gold."

Harry went over, dipping his hand into the bag and bringing out a fistful of gold coins. "I don't understand."

"Weighs a lot. Not much use to 'em."

"You told me we were clear of the Apaches."

"These are Kiowa. Texas Indians."

Harry looked to the eastern horizon. "We'd best get out of here—after we bury him."

Tantou shook his head. "I don't want to be here that long. Let us cover him with some of these rocks and be gone."

Harry assented. They worked hard and fast, but took longer than Harry wished. He muttered a sort of biblical incantation, then returned his hat to his head and got on his horse. Tantou had already done that.

As they moved out onto the open plain again, Harry checked the loads of all his weapons.

THE advance was moving steadily all across his front. Grant could tell he'd taken the Rebel army by surprise. There'd be bursts of firing that would quickly diminish as the foe ran back, seeking better ground and cover. The Confederate retreat was greatest in the center. The Rebels were clinging to their flanks more firmly. Grant and his staff kept pace with the rear of Sherman's division, halting when it did, keeping close when it moved on.

Here and there were fresh Confederate dead—some of them obviously pickets who'd been cut down trying to fall back. Others, laden with Yankee ammunition, food, and supplies, had been caught in fresh looting. One dead Rebel lay clutching a small keg of molasses.

A rider came up from Sherman, reporting to Rawlins, who hurried up to Grant.

"It's official, sir. General Sherman took some prisoners. Albert Sidney Johnston was killed yesterday—shot through the leg and bled to death. Beauregard's in command for certain."

Grant lighted a cigar, listening. There was a brassy rattling off to his right. "They're counterattacking on the right flank."

"Should I call for the reserves?"

Grant listened further, then shook his head. "I don't think so. It's not working." He gave a very slight grin. Despite his hurting ankle, he felt a certain elation he was hard put to restrain, though he did so. "By jig, John, I think we've got 'em. I do believe this day will be ours."

Rawlins made no reply. It was too early for such pronouncements.

GRANT was right. The enemy counterattacks failed. They'd proved as effectual as feather dusters. The battle continued to be general all along the line, and the Union push kept on steadily. The Confederates fought back stubbornly but in vain. Grant could almost feel their line straining, near to breaking. It took well into the afternoon, but all the ground his army had lost the day before was recaptured—yard by yard but inexorably. Many Rebels were taken prisoner.

McPherson came galloping up. He had been over with Sherman. "The general reports resistance stiffening, sir."

"Let's go on up there."

McPherson wheeled his horse about and commenced a trot toward the front. Grant called him back.

"Colonel McPherson, I want to bring some troops with us."

"Yes, sir."

Grant sent him over to the right to gather up two regiments that had been ambling along behind the fighting as a reserve. He dispatched Rawlins to muster up another regiment taking its rest on the ground to the left. York he sent to the rear to find whatever loose troops might be loitering among the ammunition and supply wagons.

Within twenty minutes, Grant had a fair-sized scratch body at hand. He moved out in front of them to preclude any premature firing by these troops that might hit Sherman's men.

The Rebels were holding a section of the Corinth Road on the other side of a clearing about as wide as the effective range of musket shot. Grant halted at its edge. There was a hole in the Union line here between Sherman and McClernand that the regiments he'd brought up now effectively plugged.

Grant wanted more out of this situation than that. If he could break the Secesh at this point, the game might be up.

He looked to either side of him, and behind. The men in blue seemed eager enough.

"Sound the charge," he said to McPherson.

It was given over and over—"Charge! Charge!"—until drowned out by a rising chorus of cheers and shouts. The men began running past him, one regiment with fixed bayonets.

The Confederates fired a volley and then two more. By

the time the Union troops were halfway across the clearing, the Rebels began to turn and run. In a few minutes they had disappeared from the trees on the other side completely. By three in the afternoon, the foe was gone from the field.

Grant expected that some of them might not stop until they reached Corinth.

He had been sitting his horse next to Colonel McPherson, who had Major Hawkins to his side—the latter having lost his hat, but nothing else, to a bullet. McPherson's horse had been panting, and now gave out a moaning grunt and began to sag. The colonel flung himself from the saddle just as the animal went to his knees, then slowly keeled over. He'd been shot in the right flank just behind the saddle. Looking down at him, Grant noticed that his own sword scabbard was severely bent. Lifting it, he saw that it had been shot nearly in two.

"We are each of us fortunate, gentlemen," Grant said.

"It is the army that's fortunate," said McPherson, whose eyes were on the battlefield.

Grant noticed a horse standing out on the field, and could not understand why it had not run with the rest of the Rebel army. Leaving the others, he trotted Fox out into the clearing, ignoring a warning from McPherson not to expose himself.

The reason for the animal's immobility became clear: Its rider, a Confederate officer, had fallen dead beside it with the reins still wound around his hand. Dismounting painfully, Grant limped up to the man and freed the animal, a raw-boned, skinny, saddle-worn nag who seemed on the last of legs. No one would have objected had he shot it to prevent further suffering.

But Grant was not a man to do any such thing to a horse, and certainly not this one. He'd been ill treated and showed it, but he was a Thoroughbred. Some care might achieve a transformation.

Keeping hold of the animal's reins, Grant remounted and trotted back to the others. "I have recruited this animal to the cause of Union." He looked to the colonel. "If you would see to it that he is cared for, sir. Well cared for."

"Do you mean to keep him for yourself, General?" McPherson asked. "I fear he'd be a poor specimen for the parade ground."

"I do. We shall see what sort of specimen he may become. We are a long way from any parade ground."

"What will you name him, sir?"

Grant looked over the animal's configuration. The legs were dainty, but there was power in the haunch.

"Kangaroo," he said.

"WELL, Grant, you were right," said Sherman, when Grant caught up with him. "We have whipped 'em good today."

"Should we pursue, sir?" asked McPherson.

Grant surveyed the troops around him, finding happiness and exultation, even among some of the wounded. But there also was exhaustion. Some of the men had just slumped where they had stopped firing.

They'd just been through two days of what had to have been the fiercest fighting of the war—certainly in the Western Theater. They'd endured that through a cold driving rain and when it seemed they would all be driven into the river and slaughtered.

Grant wasn't certain he could order Buell's independent command to go forward with him. Probably not, at all events, without consulting General Halleck.

Perhaps in a day or two. Grant could not imagine where

Beauregard was going to find reinforcements to counter the now numerically superior Federal force.

"No, Colonel," Grant said. "We've won. We'll let the men rest for the remainder of the day. That's small enough reward."

Riding back toward the bluff, he came upon another clearing in Sherman's sector that the Rebels had charged across repeatedly the day before in an unsuccessful attempt at breaking that Union division. The grass was so carpeted with bodies one might have walked across the clearing in any direction without a foot touching the actual ground.

He shook his head sadly—not simply in remorse but also in the melancholy realization that the rest of the war, however long it took, was going to be like this. The Rebels would fight for every inch. There would be no single, decisive victory, such as the Northern newspapers kept clamoring for. There would be Shiloh after Shiloh, until the last Rebel was killed or captured.

The Rebels had kept coming. This was their message. And their strategy and tactic. If the North became sick enough of such slaughter, the politicians might call a halt to the struggle. He doubted Abraham Lincoln was of that mind. He'd seen too much blood already invested to abandon the work. But there were others of more fragile convictions. Grant had seen Indiana and Ohio newspapers that were calling Lincoln a bloodthirsty baboon.

Reaching the bluff that directly overlooked Pittsburg Landing, he received extraordinary news. Will Wallace had been found and was still alive—though barely. He'd been taken to the steamboat that had brought his wife.

Grant went aboard at once. The stricken general had been taken to the main salon, which had been converted to use as a hospital. He'd been laid on a cot by a window. His wife, Anne, sat upon a stool at his side, holding him in a comforting embrace.

"It's an amazement, General," said the surgeon, coming beside him. "The ball went through his temple and came out at the base of his skull, and yet he lives."

The doctor's apron was so covered with blood he looked like a British soldier.

"Can he survive long?" Grant asked, lowering his voice.

"I leave that to God, sir. There's little we can do but keep him comfortable."

"If you deem it warrantable, have him moved to Cherry Mansion at Savannah—my headquarters."

"Yes, sir."

Grant went up to the cot and placed his hand on Mrs. Wallace's shoulder. She looked up at him with tearful eyes, but an almost worshipful smile came over her face. She had believed her husband dead, like everyone else. To have him here, even like this, was a gift.

"We'll do everything we can, Mrs. Wallace."

She put her hand on his, but only briefly, returning it to her ashen-faced husband's arm. It was as though her touch were all that was keeping him alive.

BACK on the bluff by his tree, Grant took a chair, propping up his injured leg, to wait for his division commanders to come in.

Colonel York came up first—with his ubiquitous flask.

"No, thank you, Colonel." Grant lighted a cigar.

"Is there anything else I can get you, General?"

Grant started to shake his head but thought better of it.

"That Lieutenant Riordan—the fellow who escorted Mrs. Abbott through the lines. I asked for him."

"Yes, sir. And I sent for him." York looked toward what had until recently been the front line. "He was killed, General. Apparently in today's fighting."

Chapter 5

THE day turned hot and by afternoon had become intolerably so. Harry removed his frock coat, then his waistcoat, then his cravat. Had it not been for the strictures of his Virginia gentleman upbringing, he would have removed his shirt. Tantou, inexplicably, stayed dressed as he had been in the cooler weather, removing only his leather gloves. Harry could not decide whether this was the stoicism of the Indian at play or the Canadian's relish for warmth of any kind. But he was impressed.

The soldiers in this war fought in such heat in wool jackets, some of them lugging as much as fifty pounds of equipment and weaponry. As a Southerner, Harry could not comprehend it. Civilized people stayed inside in such heat, or found a place with cooling breezes, such as the veranda of Belle Haven, his family's plantation, which overlooked the James River from a high, breezy bluff at a point where it widened into its estuary.

There was a wind blowing here on the plains of West

Texas, but it was the draft of a furnace. Harry supposed they'd be suffering no less if they were traveling stark naked.

He tried to keep his mind on Louise—on her incomparable face and bewitching dark eyes, and on other parts a true gentleman should not be contemplating even in reverie. He needed to keep his thoughts from his misery if he was to complete this journey, and no other image served so well. She had a penchant and a talent for rubbing his back in relaxing, pain-relieving ways. He yearned for her merest touch.

In some quarters of Eastern society, actresses were considered only slightly more elevated than common prostitutes. He would have shot the man who said that of the love of his life, the British actress Caitlin Howard, but with Louise he had sometimes wondered. She was so artful and so full of artifice.

She'd killed a Union officer, almost before Harry's very eyes, because she had feared he was about to expose her as a Southern agent.

Yet in Richmond, enjoying such esteem that she was invited to President Jefferson Davis's own table, she had gone to great lengths to rescue Harry from being hanged as a Federal spy. Which she knew very well he was.

She was back there in the East, somewhere. He was certain that, whether he returned to Washington City or continued to ply his trade behind Confederate lines in Virginia, he would encounter her again. He would hold her in his arms again, hold her tightly, bury his face in her long, cascading, dark hair. He loved Caitlin more, but this Louisiana woman was in his blood.

"There is a town near," said Tantou, riding to the right of him.

"How do you know that?"

They had no map, and no familiarity at all with this part of Texas.

The Métis pointed to the sky. "There is an eagle over there, and they are mostly fish eaters, so I think there is a river. This is a wide valley, and valleys are made by very old rivers. And there is grass. And cattle bones. And there are more tracks upon this trail. I think it will soon become a road. All this says there must be a town."

"Over the next ridge?"

"Or the one after that."

Harry wiped his brow with a now sodden handkerchief. "Who would live here?"

"Cattle raisers. Mexicans. They can live anywhere, or so I have seen."

One-Eye's head was drooping. Harry wasn't sure the horse would make it to the next ridge.

"I would give all this federal gold to be in New Orleans now," Harry said.

"You may have to."

"What do you mean?"

Tantou shrugged, a white man's habit. "Bandits, maybe Confederate soldiers. Who knows what we will encounter on the trail ahead—or in the town?"

"I'll surrender this gold to no one but Allan Pinkerton."

Tantou looked past him and smiled. "Maybe not, Harry Raines."

Harry turned to see what he was talking about. A long, thin, yellowish line was rising from the northeastern horizon. As Harry stared, it became thicker—and wider. "What is it?"

"Riders," said Tantou.

It seemed another dust storm to Harry. He put on his spectacles to better see it. By the time he could make out the horsemen, Tantou had spurred his horse and was racing southeast, toward the ridge.

Harry followed, but One-Eye had trouble keeping up, and Tantou was over the ridge before Harry could reach it. Finally, attaining that landmark, he looked to the northeast again to see the line of galloping horseman coming on straight for him. Worse, he saw now that they were Indians.

Dead ahead, at the bottom of the slope along a meandering creek, was the town that Tantou had predicted would be there and toward which the Métis was galloping at a furious rate.

Knowing that his very life depended on it, Harry whipped his horse into a frenzy of exertion, careening down the rocky grade and making a last dash across the flats beyond into the little jumble of buildings.

If Tantou had thought this was sanctuary, he was mistaken. The dusty street was littered with corpses—arrows sticking up from some of them. The Indians had been this way before.

Harry hadn't time to examine them, or look for any who might still be living. If he wished to remain in that state himself, he needed to find Tantou, who had vanished.

Cantering up and down what appeared to be the town's only street, he was at last halted by a shout. "Harry Raines! In here!"

He saw Tantou in a window of the second story of a rude hotel. As the horse was not in view, Harry presumed it was inside and led One-Eye into the building, too. Taking his breech-loading rifle with him, he mounted the stairs, stepping over the body of a young Mexican woman who wrenchingly reminded him of the lady he had left behind in New Mexico.

Halting, he saw that it was not she—as it could not possibly have been.

"Harry Raines! Come up here!"

He hurried to the next floor, where Tantou had moved to a back room that had a view of the ridgeline they'd galloped over. Harry joined him, squinting. The Indians were moving just as fast, but sticking to the ridge, continuing past the town.

"Are they trying to get behind us?" Harry asked.

"Pretty much every place is behind us." Tantou pulled up a chair just to the side of the window opening and sat on the chair, holding the buffalo gun on his lap. "You best go to the other side. Maybe they will come back that way."

Harry nodded and crossed the hall, sticking his head out the window there and looking up and down the street. Nothing moved, except those damnable birds. He could hear a faint rumble, getting fainter. He took it to be the Indians.

Presently the sound was heard again, but from the opposite direction.

"Harry Raines! Come over here!"

Obedient again, Harry went to Tantou's window. The rumble was louder still, but he could see no source for it. Then at once he did. A long file of riders as numerous as the Kiowa, if that's who the Indians were.

These mounted men were white.

IT was two hours before they came back. In their absence, confident that the Indians were bound elsewhere, Harry and Tantou had undertaken the labor of gathering the dead and laying them in a military-style row outside the hotel. Harry counted nineteen, including three women and a child. There was little mutilation of the bodies, and none of the structures had been fired, but the Indians had taken the time to loot the town of horses and weapons.

They were in the cantina, drinking bad whiskey, when the mounted party of white men returned, several of them pulling up just outside the bar.

A large, older man with a neatly trimmed gray beard entered, flanked by two much younger fellows and looking to be in command. All three wore circular badges with stars in the middle.

"Are you the sheriff?" Harry asked, standing.

"We are Texas Rangers," said the older man, as though that fact should have been immediately obvious. "And who be you, sir?"

Harry almost introduced himself as Captain Harry Raines, out of a wish to be treated as this man's equal. Doubtless the fellow would have taken a more dubious view of Harry's association with U.S. Secret Service.

"My name is Harry Raines. This is my friend Jacques Tantou."

The man took a step forward, then gestured toward the street. "That you who laid out all those poor folks?"

"Yes, sir. Hoped you might be coming back here. Thought that was the least we could do."

"What are you doing here?"

"Running for our lives."

"From where?"

"We were in New Mexico, until the Yankees took it back."

The Ranger leader looked Tantou over, not happily. "Where're you bound?"

"Louisiana." He nodded to Tantou. "He lives there. I have friends there."

"He Cajun?"

"*Oui,*" said Tantou, drinking down his whiskey.

"He looks like he could be one of that Kiowa band we were chasing."

"Well, he isn't. Did you get them?"

"One or two. Wished it had been more." One of the younger Texans went behind the bar. Harry noticed he was missing an ear.

"Whiskey, Captain?"

The older man nodded. "I'm Captain Stollenwerke. I command this Ranger company. We're going to take care of those folks in the street and then we'll be moving out in the morning for Austin. You're welcome to come along."

"I would be most grateful," Harry said.

"You oughta know that there may be Yankees in New Orleans by the time you get there, if that's where you're going."

"That cannot be."

"Yes, it can. They're deep into Tennessee and in the gulf and heading up the Mississippi." He drank. "Never take Texas, though."

THEY left early the next morning, forty-seven Rangers, Harry and Tantou, and the bodies of a man and a woman who apparently had been Texas citizens of consequence. The other victims of the Indians were left buried in the town.

"You Rangers are going to abandon the place?" Harry asked as they rode out, heading southeast. "There must be other people who live here."

"They'd be best advised to stay where they are—for the duration."

"The duration of the Indian troubles?"

"The duration of this war between the states. The Indian troubles will go on until that ends."

"I don't understand."

"I have only a score of men fit and of full age. The rest, as you've seen, are old men and boys. We patrol a hundred and fifty miles. Sometimes more. The Kiowa ain't much bothered by us. We were lucky to get close to this band. And we didn't catch 'em."

"So back to Austin."

"Need supplies and ammunition." The captain gave Harry another look-over. "You don't sound like you're from Louisiana."

"I'm not. From Virginia, originally."

"How come you're not in the army?"

"Rode into New Mexico with the army." A half-lie. They'd been a day behind it, and had been careful to stay that way.

"Hoping to turn a Yankee dollar?" said the captain.

Harry had put the gold into the bag of flour he carried on his saddle. "No luck at that."

The captain frowned, then spurred his horse on ahead. Harry fell back with Tantou at the end of the column.

The day was as clear as the one previous but not so hot. Harry thought they'd make good progress and do it in safety. Once across the border into Louisiana, returned to civilization, there'd be nothing to fear but a continuing brawl between hundreds of thousands of well-armed men, laboring to kill one another from the Mississippi to the Potomac.

Chapter 6

GRANT made no official report to General Halleck about the battle, save to send a brief letter stating that there had been an engagement near Pittsburg Landing and that Federal forces had prevailed in two days of fighting.

A reply had swiftly followed by telegraph. He was to avoid another battle until reinforcements arrived. As his main reinforcement—General Buell's Army of the Ohio—had already been employed in the Shiloh fight, Grant was perplexed. He had no idea from where these new reinforcements of Halleck's would come.

It made no sense to wait for them. Grant had wanted to give his bloodied army a day's rest and time to refit and reorganize, but there was no reason for delay beyond that. If Beauregard was still in Corinth, as Grant's scouts were reporting, he could be fought there handily with the forty thousand able men Grant now had at hand. If it came to a siege, it wouldn't last long.

Depending on the success of the Union navy in its effort to

take New Orleans, the North had an opportunity here to seize control of the entire Mississippi and cut the Confederacy into two pieces. But it required celerity. His mind's eye was on the town of Vicksburg.

POOR Will Wallace died in his wife's arms. The surgeon reported to Grant that his last words were that he and she would meet again in Heaven and that she had accepted that in full belief. Grant himself was not quite so devout, but if he had to perish on the battlefield, dying in Julia's arms would be Heaven enough.

He hadn't time for such thoughts. More bad news came in the form of another telegraph message from Halleck, saying he was arriving at Pittsburg Landing shortly to make his headquarters and take command in the field. Halleck was a desk general who had never led troops in battle, though he'd been third in his class at West Point and had authored a textbook, *Elements of Military Art and Science,* and a translation of Jomini's *Vie de Napoléon.*

As Grant recalled, Halleck had spent his time in the Mexican War in California, as a captain performing administrative duties for the local military government. After the war he'd become a wealthy lawyer, just like the president, who'd seen fit to make his fellow member of the bar a major general at the outbreak of hostilities.

Now the lawyer was descending upon Grant, armed no doubt with tons of paper. He'd not been as bad at running the Missouri Department as his predecessor, the flamboyant John C. Frémont, had been. Halleck had organized the command to within an inch of its life. There'd been a noticeable improvement in the flow of supplies and fresh mounts.

But having Halleck on the scene here would retard all movement as effectively as a blizzard or a flood.

Grant had another, nonmilitary reason for wanting to get to Corinth quickly. After seeing Wallace's widow and the general's body off on the steamboat that would take them back to Ottawa, Illinois, Grant repaired to Cherry Mansion and his private parlor.

He'd folded Mrs. Abbott's cloak and set it on a side table, debating whether to send it on to her husband. He had felt uneasy about doing that. There was a finality to the gesture. She was only missing.

Standing a moment by the table, he'd put his hand on the garment, but disturbed it no further. With a sigh, he went to his writing desk and began a letter. Dissatisfied halfway through it, he crumpled the paper and tried again, without success. He was commencing his third attempt when there came a knock at his door.

"Yes?"

Colonel York's response was to open the door and step inside. "Message from General Halleck, sir. He arrives to-morrow."

Grant stared hard at the paper before him. "Very well. Thank you, Colonel."

"He arrives at Pittsburg Landing. We're to greet him there."

Grant tore up the unfinished letter. He'd wait for better news before setting to it again. "And so we shall, Colonel."

"Whiskey, General?" Again the flask.

"No, thank you." Grant wondered how to discourage this continuing generosity. He turned in his chair. "The troopers who were part of the escort with Lieutenant Riordan. Have you found them?"

"I didn't know I was to look for them, General."

"Perhaps I neglected to inform you of my wishes. Would you have Captain Rawlins attend to it?"

"Yes, sir."

HALLECK arrived on schedule, bringing with him an enormous staff and enough clerical supplies to run the entire War Department. Grant was there to greet him on the landing. He'd failed to button his coat and waistcoat, and Halleck looked askance at that. The commanding general's own uniform was freshly cleaned and fully buttoned, its brass buttons and fittings polished to rival the sun. But it failed to make of him a military figure. Stuffed into that starched perfection, he seemed all the more less so.

Grant had concentrated his officers' efforts on retrieving the wounded, securing the front, and posting patrols to ascertain the enemy's whereabouts. As a consequence, he'd neglected the disorder in his rear, which was what one would expect of an army that had been taken by surprise and fought a two-day savage battle.

The riverbank was littered with equipment and supplies, including arms and ammunition brought there by the shirkers, some of whom remained as well. Furniture had been taken off the steamers to make room for the wounded still being brought aboard. Animals were wandering at large—pigs, camp dogs, surviving horses from knocked-out artillery batteries.

Halleck's pale eyes looked on all this with dismay, an expression that remained fixed upon his face as, with Grant in tow, he ascended to the top of the bluff.

"I gather you have been otherwise engaged," he said, staring at a scattered pile of tent poles lying near Grant's tree.

"Sir?"

"To attend to this disorder."

"We have just fought a major engagement, General Halleck. The casualties have been heavy."

"That lamentable fact has been noted in every quarter, General Grant. It was my unhappy task to inform Secretary of War Stanton of our losses. There is a great concern for the effect of such grievous news on the general public."

"The Rebels suffered as well, sir."

Halleck moved on, stepping over the tongue of an abandoned ammunition wagon. "Perhaps they have, General. And we have regained the field. I do not disregard that fact." He turned, his frown now replaced with something akin to eagerness. "But now we must attend to our defenses."

"Defenses, sir? I intend to move on the enemy as soon as possible—and attend to his defenses at Corinth."

"And so we shall, General Grant. In due course. But right now I want entrenchments all along our forward positions. And I want this ground cleaned up and the army organized into orderly camps."

"General Halleck. I propose to move forward tomorrow."

"No, General Grant. We must wait for reinforcements."

"I have General Buell—"

Halleck raised his hand to halt the line of discussion. "General Buell's Army of the Ohio is under my command, sir, as is your Army of the Tennessee. I propose to wait for General Pope. He has taken Island No. 10 up the Mississippi and is now available to join in our enterprise. When he is here, we may proceed. But I shall require entrenchments whenever we stop. As we are very much stopped now, I want the digging to begin."

"Shouldn't this be at the discretion of the field commander?" Grant asked—meaning, of course, himself.

"But I now am the field commander," Halleck said. He bent his head, as though to see Grant's face the better. "Do not look so disheartened, General. I am making you second in command."

"Second in command, sir?"

"Yes. I shall have overall command, here in the field, of your army, Buell's, and Pope's. You shall be my deputy. I will give your army over to General Thomas, transferring him and his division from Buell's command."

Major General George Thomas had fought in the Seminole Indian War, in Mexico, and on the western frontier in the cavalry under Albert Johnston and Robert E. Lee. He'd also taught at West Point and had survived a hostile Indian arrow in the face. A large man—six feet tall and weighing two hundred pounds—he'd been called "Old Tom," "Slow Trot," and "Pap Thomas." Grant liked him, but saw no need of this rearrangement.

"As you wish, General," Grant said.

"Not merely my wish, sir. This all has the approval of the War Department, rest assured of that." He patted Grant's stooped shoulder. "But be of good cheer, General. As deputy commander, you will have a lot to do. Now, is there anything else I need to know about what happened here?"

For a brief moment, Grant considered bringing up the matter of Mrs. Abbott—as though doing so would transfer the responsibility to Halleck and free him of this melancholy preoccupation. But he knew Halleck too well. Avoiding responsibility for things gone wrong was one of his great talents.

Chapter 7

CROSSING into Louisiana, Harry and Tantou came not so much into civilization as into a soggy land of mossy trees, large birds, gigantic insects, moist air, and swamp. There were snakes in the water and snakes hanging from the branches. And there were scaly-backed reptiles of astounding size and ferocity. Harry had had to shoot one that burst forth from the murk and snapped at One-Eye's rear leg while they were fording a river.

"Alligators," said Tantou.

"You've been here before?" Harry asked.

"No."

"Then how—"

"I read about them in the newspaper."

It was the first Harry knew of the Métis' ability to read. "Do you read much?"

"I read when I need to read, Harry Raines."

"I have a book with me."

"I know."

"It is *Les Misérables*."

"I saw it."

"Do you want to read it?"

"Is it in French?"

"No."

"Books are better in French."

"I suppose that's quite possible."

"I will buy a book in New Orleans." He moved his horse ahead of Harry's. "A book in French."

THE cavalry sergeant had been wounded, and stood at attention awkwardly, his arm too stiff to properly salute.

Grant waved away that formality. "Seat yourself, Sergeant Bishop. Please."

"Yes, sir."

"I sent for you—"

"Some days ago, sir. I know. I was in the hospital. I only just yesterday got word you was looking for me. Came as soon as I could."

"Are you all right, son?"

"Yes, sir. Mighty lucky. The ball hit no bone. Just tore out a bit of flesh. They was fixing to amputate till they took a second look."

"Always advisable—a second look."

"Yes, sir."

"You were on the escort duty with Lieutenant Riordan?"

"Yes, sir. The congressman's wife."

"What happened?"

"We met her at Pittsburg Landing as Colonel York arranged and took her down the Corinth Road. It was hard going. Muddy, you know. And dark."

"Did you encounter the enemy?"

"Yes, sir. Once. Couple of pickets, or maybe scouts. We exchanged fire. One of them had a shotgun, so maybe they was cavalry scouts. Nobody got hurt. After our second volley they turned tail and run."

"And then?"

"We took her as far as this creek we came to farther down the road. I don't know the name of it. Had a bridge over it. Lieutenant Riordan took her to the other side and then came back."

"Were you close to Corinth?"

"No, sir. But we was close to the Rebs. We could see some campfires through the trees. That's why we turned back."

"And she kept on going?"

"Yes, sir. The lieutenant said she told him she knew the way from there and that we'd be risking our lives to go with her any farther."

"And that's all?"

"Yes, sir."

"Was she wearing a cloak?" He got up and went to a chest at the side of his tent. "This cloak?"

The sergeant examined a turn of the cloth. "She was wearing a cloak. Maybe this one. Hard to tell in the dark."

"This was found over in General Sherman's section of the line. Pretty far from where I think you left her."

The sergeant shrugged, wincing from the effort. "Don't know, sir."

"And the rest of the men in your outfit?"

"Three killed in the big battle, along with Lieutenant Riordan. Three of us wounded. The other two wounded died."

"Colonel Ingersoll's brigade is still intact?"

"There's a trooper or two left, sir."

"Thank you for you time, Sergeant. I'm much obliged."
He opened a wooden box and withdrew two cigars. "Please,
take these."

"Thank you, sir." He started to salute with the cigars in
his hand. Grant smiled.

"Are you sure you are fit for duty, son?"

"Yes, sir."

"Well then, I'm obliged for that as well." As the sergeant
limped away, he carefully returned the cloak to the chest.

HARRY and Tantou passed by a small Confederate military encampment at some distance, were stopped twice
by Rebel sentries and passed on, and encountered a few
butternut-garbed stragglers in the rude taverns where they
paused for food and drink. The Southern army was not otherwise much in evidence. If the Yankee army had landed in
Louisiana, as the tavern rumors had it, there was no Rebel
line before it. Only swamps and small lakes that the road
wound among or crossed by means of more muddy fords.

It was not until they reached the Mississippi itself that
they saw their first sign of the Federals—a small, steam-
powered gunboat chugging upstream, flying the stars and
stripes.

Harry sat his horse, watching the boat's progress and taking in the breadth of the great river, which he had not seen
since accompanying his father on a trip to the cotton states
while still a boy. The eastern rivers were this wide only in
their estuaries. The Mississippi was broad for nearly all its
incredible length. Unbridged, it effectively cut the nation
in two. If the U.S. flag had indeed been hoisted at New
Orleans, then all that was needed to sever the Confederacy
was for gunboats like the one Harry was watching to keep

pushing north until they made contact with the Union forces pressing south.

Unhappily, Harry wasn't sure if they had come upon the river above or below New Orleans. If above, they'd need only turn south and eventually they'd come to the city. If below, the small gunboat might merely be a courier vessel serving a Union fleet still laying siege to the city. They'd not be able to attain their goal without getting mixed up in a fight.

Unless they wished to wait.

"I'm not sure which way to turn," Harry said. "North could take us into a battle. South could merely deposit us on the seashore."

"Go south, Harry Raines."

"Why."

"Because we have been traveling directly east, and the sea has always been much to the south of us."

"I'd say that, in these swamps, we've been traveling in just about every direction there is."

"The sun has been before us in the morning and behind us at day's end."

"And if you're wrong?"

"It is better to miss a battle than to miss New Orleans."

Harry pondered that pronouncement. Whether he might ever be able to answer his question about Louise was apparently a matter of luck.

"We'll go south," Harry said.

There was a good road to the south, following the river at varying distances. They encountered no soldiery of either persuasion for many miles but saw increasing numbers of Union naval vessels moving in both directions.

Finally, near the end of the day, they came to a dreary waterfront town called Algiers. Approaching the river along one of its dusty streets, Harry spotted a distant church steeple above the tree line on the opposite bank. Finally, reaching the embankment with its sweeping view of the wide river, he saw steamboats, and wharves and warehouses. One of the warehouses was burning.

THE only ferry the Union navy was allowing to make the crossing from Algiers to New Orleans stopped running at sunset, compelling them to camp overnight with other travelers and some U.S. Marines, who kept a sort of guard. They made the first trip across just at sunrise, setting foot and hoof on the levee at the foot of a broad avenue called Canal Street.

As the river was crowded with naval traffic, the streets were full of soldiery. Harry and Tantou kept out of their way as much as possible, nodding to the occasional officer. This respect spared them the kind of trouble and abuse that the troops seemed otherwise happy to inflict on the civilian population. Apparently a number of warehouses and thousands of bales of cotton on the waterfront had been fired in contemptuous welcome to the Federals, and this hostility was being returned with great ill humor, if with little violence.

They rode up Canal Street to a large and very grand statue that proved to be of the great Henry Clay, whose grand compromises had so dramatically failed to prevent this war. To the right, along Royal Street, Harry spotted the welcome sign of a tavern and turned toward it, finding a place to secure their horses in a narrow alley and paying an African boy a dime to watch them.

Most of the customers were in blue uniform and none paid any mind to Tantou's fearsome and very western appearance. The barkeep served both of them without comment. He had no Old Overholtz in stock, but the whiskey he poured was passable. The menu was limited. Harry ordered a spicy stew called étouffée for them both. It was the first food Tantou showed any indication of enjoying since they had met.

Harry got small news from the bartender. The mere arrival of seven Union gunboats a few days before had sufficed to send the governor of the state and New Orleans' entire Confederate garrison into flight. Mayor John Monroe had remained behind but had been deposed by the Union army commander and put into jail. A week-old newspaper was on the bar. There were stories full of alarm about the Yankee progress up the Mississippi from the Delta, coupled with others about the impregnability of the city's defenses and the great fighting spirit of the Rebel troops manning them.

One article suggested that General Beauregard might be marching south down the Mississippi to succor them.

Stepping outside, Harry inquired of a young lieutenant who was standing idly by a hitching rail as to where he might find the army's general headquarters. He was told that one had been established at the Customs House and another at City Hall. The young officer said that he did not know which being used by the new military commander of the city, General Benjamin Butler.

Retrieving their horses, Harry and Tantou followed directions to the Customs House, where the quartermaster of the Union army had established himself. A sergeant told them Butler was at City Hall.

Setting out again, keeping out of the way of blue-coated cavalry patrols, they reached this second destination with some difficulty, finding it aswarm with what looked to be Butler's entire army.

Making their way inside, Harry went to a sergeant seated

behind a desk. Taking the risk of identifying himself as a Union army scout returning from a foray into Texas, he asked if he might report to the commander. The sergeant studied him for a few seconds, shook his head, and then pointed across the room to another desk, where an officer was seated.

Harry went before the man, a lieutenant colonel in very clean uniform, and repeated his introduction and request.

"Impossible, sir," said the officer. "General Butler is extremely busy."

Harry needed to take another risk. "I am in the service of Major A. E. Allen, in Washington. You may telegraph the War Department to confirm that."

"Major A. E. Allen" was the *nomme de guerre* Allan Pinkerton employed for his clandestine work.

"Your name again?"

"Raines. Captain Raines."

The officer made a notation. "Come back tomorrow."

"**WHAT** now, Harry Raines?" asked Tantou when they were back outside.

"We acquire some more suitable clothes and some decent lodgings, and then I pursue my inquiries after Miss Devereux. Tomorrow we'll see General Butler."

"If you wish him to believe you a scout coming in from Texas, you'd best keep on the clothes you have."

"Perhaps you're right. But I am going to obtain some decent lodgings. I have been dreaming of them all these many miles."

"I wish you well in finding them." Tantou climbed aboard his horse.

"Are you leaving me?"

"For now." He started moving off.

"When will you come back?"

"Soon."

"But how will you find me?"

"I am a scout."

"Tantou, where will you go?"

"To buy a book in French."

He turned the corner.

HARRY asked what was the best hotel in New Orleans and was told it was the St. Charles. Following the directions given him, he came to a long, imposing structure with high colonnades that might have been a federal building in Washington. Actually, it was grander than any building in the Federal City save the President's House and the U.S. Capitol.

They had no rooms available, not for any price, for all had been taken by Union army officers. He was referred to the Verandah Hotel, not quite so elegant as the St. Charles but certainly acceptable for a gentleman. He was declined again—not, Harry figured, because it was full up with bluecoats but because, judging by the desk clerk's disdainful glance, his appearance was no longer very gentlemanly.

He settled for the Florance House Hotel, a small but agreeable establishment with side galleries running the length and width of the building on every floor.

Though it cost him a Federal dollar, he was able to obtain a hot bath and shave. Disregarding Tantou's advice, he acquired a new suit of clothes and several changes of shirt and linen, as well as new boots, two new cravats, and a wide-brimmed hat.

Feeling himself again, he inquired at the Florance's desk

as to what theaters might be open in town and was handed a circular advertising them.

Leaving One-Eye in the livery stable behind his hotel, he tried the palatial French Opera House first, where he found preparations under way for some sort of Creole musicale that evening. The black majordomo at the stage door said he never heard of an actress named Louise Devereux and so could not say where she lived.

The Orleans Theatre was closed, and seemed too small a place for an actress of Louise's talents and reputation at all events. The American Theatre, also closed, was far too wretched. Placide's Varieties Theatre at Canal and Carondelet had burned down. The nearby St. Charles Theatre, at St. Charles and Poydras Streets, was up and running with two comedies on the bill, but the cast credits failed to list her name. Finding the box office unattended, he went around to the stage door, where he discovered two actors, still in costume from a matinee, sitting on the wooden steps and sharing a bottle of whiskey.

"Excuse me, gentlemen," Harry said. "I'm trying to locate the abode of Louise Devereux."

"Do you mean the actress Louise Devereux?" said the older of the two, still wearing his stage whiskers.

"Yes. A lady of considerable charm and beauty, given to wearing her hair loose."

"More than that," said the other, a younger man who was either wearing a wig or had dyed his hair yellow.

"She has not, sir, played these boards since 1859," said his companion.

"She went to the East, I believe," said the younger. "Washington City, or Richmond."

"Richmond is where I left her," Harry said. "I am looking

for her residence here. I wish to call upon her mother."

"Her mother?" asked the older. "And who be you, sir?"

Harry produced a *carte de visite,* one bearing his Pennsylvania Avenue address. "Harrison Raines," he said. "I deal in horses."

The bearded one squinted at the card. "You're from Washington?"

"I'm from Virginia."

"What brings you to this city?"

"The shifting fortunes of war. I was in New Mexico, until the Yankees took it back."

"You're not a Yankee?" said the older one.

"I am a man of business—*un homme d'affaires*—and I conduct my business on both sides of the line."

"What is your business with Louise's mother?"

"A matter concerning Louise's welfare and safety."

The older man spat, then took a large swallow of whiskey. "Her mother is dead."

"Dead?" Harry considered this. It was altogether reasonable that she might be dead—especially in such a city.

"The yellow fever," said the younger. He drained the bottle.

"I am fond of the theater and people of your calling," Harry said quickly, "and would like to stand you a drink. I unfortunately haven't the time to join you but would be honored if you would accept this from me and raise a glass on my behalf." He tossed the older one a Yankee dollar.

The man examined it as if it might not be real. Satisfied that it was, he pocketed it.

"I need to proceed with my inquiry concerning Miss Devereux," Harry continued. "If you would be so kind as to direct me to her home."

"Can't miss it," said the older man, getting to his feet. "Find the Pontalba row houses on Jackson Square. It's one of them."

"Which one?"

"You must inquire, sir. We were never invited there."

RETURNING to Canal Street, whose unusual breadth was dictated by an actual waterway running most of its length, Harry noted a crowd gathering to the north. Curiosity overcame caution. He halted half a block from the gathering but was drawn nearer, until he stood at the periphery of the assemblage—better described as a mob.

The issue under discussion was not clear to Harry, but the crowd was much agitated by it. Many of the men there seemed fresh out of the taverns. To Harry's surprise, some of them were armed. He saw a few skirts among overalls and frock coats, though he was uncertain whether they belonged to ladies or tavern wenches. After a year of war, sometimes it was hard to tell the difference.

Their complaint seemed to have something to do with general orders being issued by the new federal military command, one of them having been interpreted to be a call to slaves to rise against their masters. Copies of it were being thrown about and brandished. Snatching one up, Harry saw that it was actually addressed to the laborers and mechanics of the city, urging them to throw off their status as serfs to the moneyed classes. He was unsure whether the mob's rising fury was directed at these moneyed classes or the U.S. government, but that question was quickly answered when he saw a company-size contingent of cavalry, sabers drawn and in broad formation, coming up Canal Street from the river levee.

Harry ducked into the nearest side street—it was named Dauphine—and hurried along it as the crowd turned to face their adversaries. He was in the Vieux Carré district, an old quarter of decidedly French flavor. It was badly run down and, in places, malodorous. After liquor, its chief industry seemed to be prostitution—though the same could be said about Washington and Richmond at this stage of the war.

Two Union officers stumbled out of a grog shop just ahead and began weaving their way along the wooden walk in the same direction Harry was heading. He kept his distance from them, and was glad he did, when a woman stepped out on a gallery above and, with great deliberation, emptied the contents of a large chamber pot on them.

One of the officers pulled out his revolver and loosed a shot into the air, though he aimed straight up to avoid inflicting injury. The woman swore, made a rude gesture, and returned to her apartments. Harry crossed the street.

He reached Jackson Square by way of St. Peter Street, pausing by a row of shuttered shops to make his reconnaissance. To the left was a cathedral with an imposing steeple and two large government buildings that appeared to date well into the city's colonial past. On the opposite side of the square was a block of large row houses.

The name on the manumission paper Louise had carried had been Betty Mercier. In Virginia, it would have been unusual for a slave woman to have a last name, but it occurred to Harry that Louisiana might have a different custom. The authorities also might have allowed her to sign the papers with the name she had chosen to use as a free woman. But then, her owners might have been named Mercier, though that did not explain Louise's having the name of Devereux.

Given the expensive nature of the dwelling places here, it

was likely the Mercier woman lived here as a house servant.

One of the shops on his side of the square was not shuttered. Harry entered and found himself in a small bakery.

"Excuse me," he said to the man at the counter. "I am looking for a woman named Betty—possibly Elizabeth—Mercier. I'm told she lives in one of the houses on the square, but I don't know which one." He reminded himself of her unhappy bout with yellow fever. "Actually, I think she's dead."

The baker was eyeing him as though he were mad. The man said nothing, possibly because he spoke only French. Harry wished he had Tantou with him.

"She is not dead," he said finally, in English.

"Not dead?" Harry asked.

"No. She lives in the house at the center there." He came around the counter and to the door, pointing. "There. That is the house of Baroness de Pontalba. Ask for her there."

"She is not dead?"

"*Non.*"

"Very well. Thank you."

"*Est-ce-que vous voulez acheter quelque chose?*"

Harry recognized the word *acheter*.

" 'Buy'? Yes, I would like to buy something." He pointed to a little square cake covered with powdered sugar. "What is that?"

"*Un beignet, monsieur.*"

"I'll have one."

There were many people in the square, and Harry had to weave his way among them, glancing up to admire the equestrian statue of General Jackson as he passed it and wondering how the war might now be proceeding if it had that fiery, half-mad old Indian-killer running in it. There was no telling which side he'd be on. Jackson had kept slaves, but he had wanted to hang John C. Calhoun for preaching secession back in 1832.

Coming before the house, he stepped back onto the paving stones to make certain he had the right one, then went to the door and rapped three times on it with the knocker, munching the remains of his delicious pastry as quickly as possible.

A white woman answered. Richly dressed, dark-haired, and of remarkable beauty for a lady of middle age, she did not admit him, but stood in the open doorway. *"Monsieur?"*

He quickly used his handkerchief to remove the powdered sugar from his face. "My apologies for the intrusion, madam," he said, removing his hat in a sweeping gesture. "I am seeking a woman of color named Betty Mercier."

"She is not of color. She has the same color as I."

"I was told she works for the Baroness de Pontalba."

"I am the Baroness de Pontalba," she said. Her hand went to her chest, and Harry saw that the hand possessed only two fingers. "Betty Mercier does not work for me. She works for the Countess de Lachaise-Valérie. It is in the next block up from the square. A tall red house with white galleries."

Harry bowed. "I thank you, madam."

"What do you want of her?"

"I am a friend of her daughter's."

"Her daughter's?" She stepped back into the darkness of the hall.

"Yes." The door closed. "Thank you, madam."

He found the red house easily enough, but felt something amiss. There was a dark-skinned man with a horse and cart at the curb.

"Excuse me, sir," he asked. "Is this the house of Betty Mercier?"

The man was old, and turned slowly. "This is the house of la Comtesse de Lachaise-Valérie."

"And Betty Mercier?"

The other shrugged. Harry did the same, then went to the door. There was a bell rope extending from a hole above the frame. He pulled it twice and stepped back, hat in hand.

At length, an older woman who might have been African but had very light-colored skin answered the door, opening it only a little. "Yes?"

"I am seeking a Betty Mercier. Would you be her?"

"What do you want? Are you with the soldiers?"

"No, ma'am. This has nothing to do with them."

"If faut que vous parler à la comtesse, monsieur."

"You want me to speak to the countess?"

"Yes. I will go fetch her."

She did not invite him in but left the door ajar. He heard her footsteps ascending wooden stairs and, after a few moments, heard hers or another's descending.

The door opened wider, and there stood Louise.

Chapter 8

GRANT was sitting idly in his tent, which had both flaps tied back. He was contemplating the horizon beyond the camp, as though he could see beyond the trees all the way south to Corinth.

Beauregard had had more than a week to gather reinforcements. Union cavalry scouts had reported that the rail center sat on elevated ground behind a broad swamp. It would not be easy to take it with a frontal assault. Each passing day would only increase the difficulty.

Halleck had organized the sprawling Northern army into a neat encampment, and entrenched its borders to withstand attack by every soldier in the South.

"If you had entrenched at Shiloh Church, General," he'd said, as though lecturing a class of West Point cadets, "you would not have suffered the casualties you did. You would have won the battle the first day."

Grant had not argued, though he could have done. It had

not been his intention to fortify at Pittsburg Landing. His intention was to gather his and Buell's armies together there and move on Corinth. He'd been taken by surprise, but that had had nothing to do with entrenchments.

Except for cavalry patrols and a few probes by skirmishers, Halleck hadn't budged his force but an inch. And he'd given Grant absolutely nothing to do except join him in his compulsive tours and inspections of the camps. Arguing his still lame leg, Grant declined the invitation.

York and his ever-present flask were absent. Had he been at hand, Grant might now have taken him up on his perpetual offer of refreshment. Grant could, of course, order up a barrel of whiskey for himself, if he chose. But he knew of the rumors about him and did not want to feed them, not with Halleck hovering so near.

Instead, he turned to his correspondence. He was writing to his wife daily and had already sent his letter of the morning. But there were things he'd failed to say, emotions he'd not expressed, decisions he was about to make. If this idleness became any more protracted, he was prepared to resign. Grant was a fighting man, and fighting was the only avenue leading to an end to this war. Halleck was an entrencher.

Major Hawkins appeared at his tent opening. "Got news, General. Good news, I guess."

Grant looked up from his still half-empty page. "From General Halleck?"

"From General Pope. He has arrived, sir. His troops will be up directly."

Grant turned around in his chair. There was still pain in his ankle. "Then we march at last." He frowned. "Anything from General Halleck?"

"No, sir."

* * *

LOUISE pulled Harry into the corridor and down it to the doorway of a parlor. It had dark, filigreed wallpaper and darker curtains, which made the red velvet furniture seem all the brighter.

She came very near him, looking up into his face. "Harrison Raines, what in hell are you doing here?"

"I might ask the same of you—'Countess.'"

She ignored that last, turning away from him. "Richmond has become more than a little dangerous. It seemed an excellent time to come home."

Harry gestured at the elegant room. "This is 'home'?"

Louise went to a chaise lounge, seating herself demurely. "How did you find this house?"

"By making inquiries."

"Am I so well known to the Yankee army?"

"I didn't inquire of the Union Army. I asked some of your fellow actors."

"I've not been on the stage in New Orleans in years."

"As always, you left an indelible impression."

"Do be seated, Captain Raines." She reclined, stretching out her legs and crossing her pretty ankles. Her beauty was in no way diminished from his memory of it.

Harry went to one of the red velvet chairs. He was heartily glad he had bathed and acquired new finery.

"I left you in Richmond as the amour of my friend Palmer Mills."

"He is not your friend. He tried to kill you. I am happy to see that you have survived his wound."

"He said he made a point of not killing me—to please you, though your fondness for me decidedly displeased him."

"A boorish fellow, Palmer. I am well rid of him."

"But why?"

"It was not amour, you dolt. He was of use, but then he was no longer. And that dreadful policeman Nestor McCubbin and his plug-uglies commenced following me about the town. It was time to depart. Had I taken a later train than I did, I might well have been detained."

"Are you trying to tell me you're a Union agent?"

"If you speak those words aloud within my hearing, Harry, I will gladly shoot you." She reached within a pocket of her dress and pulled forth a double-barreled derringer pistol, being careful, however, not to aim it at him.

He sat perfectly still, not knowing what to say.

"Would you like some sherry?" she asked.

"Why, yes. Thank you."

She called in Betty and requested the refreshment.

"She is your slave?" Harry asked, when the woman had gone to complete her mission.

"Betty is a free woman and my housekeeper. I pay her wages."

"I recall seeing her name on a document in your possession."

"I recall asking you not to ask me about that."

"Very well. Are you a countess?"

"I've no idea. My mother was a countess, but she married my father, who was only a cotton broker."

"Named Devereux?"

"Yes."

"You're mother . . ."

"Was la Comtesse de Lachaise-Valérie. She is dead now."

"Of yellow fever."

"How did you know that?"

Harry ignored the question. "The title has fallen to you?"

"As you should know as an educated man, sir, the United

States Constitution forbids the conferring of titles. What the Emperor of France has made of my mother's passing I do not know. Nor care. I have never been to France."

Betty entered, bearing a silver tray with two crystal glasses and a crystal decanter, quite full. She set it before Louise, who poured. Waiting, Betty then brought Harry his glass.

"To you," he said, raising it.

"To your swift departure from this city," Louise said, raising her own glass and draining it in a few swallows.

Betty withdrew. Harry had looked at her face very closely, but found no particular resemblance to Louise, except perhaps for the dark eyes.

"I just got here," Harry said.

"It was foolish of you. This is a dangerous place. Where were you?"

"Out West."

"West of here? Out among the barbarians?"

"Yes."

"Whatever for?"

"The same reason as for everything. The war."

She refilled her glass, then stared at him over its rim. "Are you really a Union agent, Harry?"

"It isn't obvious?"

"Too obvious, I suppose." She sipped the sherry now. "Why have you come? You had no idea I would be here."

"I found myself in this city. I thought I would take a chance on finding you."

"Balderdash and tommyrot, Harry. You could not possibly have expected to find me here."

"I wanted to find out more about you."

Her eyes narrowed. "Why?"

"I am very fond of you, Louise."

"You love Caitlin Howard."

"And she loves John Wilkes Booth."

Her face colored. "And so you turn to me."

"We have turned to each other."

She sat up. "This is an unseemly turn of conversation, sir."

"My apologies if I have given offense."

Louise stood up. "You have not given offense. But you must go. I fear you will compromise me."

"But no one in this city knows me."

"But they know *me*. And there is surmise. Dangerous surmise." She came to him and pulled on his arm, compelling him to rise. "Do go, Harry. Where have you taken lodgings?"

"At the Florance House."

"I should have thought better for a Virginia gentleman."

"The town is full up, with all these soldiers."

"I will call upon you."

"When?"

She gave him a gentle shove toward the door. "At a discreet hour."

"After dark?"

"*Monsieur,* please. Just do not go a-wandering." She stood on tiptoes and kissed him, putting her arms around his neck and holding him very tightly.

"*Adieu,*" she said, pulling herself away and darting up the stairs. Harry hurried to the street, finding himself wary now about who might be watching him. Also a little dizzy from her kiss.

THERE was a saloon on the river side of the square in an old wooden building that seemed to lean toward the water. Harry entered the tavern, thinking he might enjoy some refreshment while considering what to do next. There were only Union soldiers at the bar, most of them officers, and they eyed Harry with some suspicion.

He nodded and smiled, ordering a whiskey.

"Are you a resident of this city, sir?" a lieutenant asked.

"Temporarily," Harry said.

"We are looking for friendly ladies."

"We have encountered only the hostile kind," said the lieutenant's companion, a sergeant.

Harry had passed by bawdy houses in seemingly every district of the town. "There are establishments for such pleasure."

"Establishments for the pock and clap," said the sergeant.

"I believe I mentioned 'ladies'—not bawds," the lieutenant said. "This city is famous for the beauty and refinement of its ladies. But they will not even speak to us."

"One of them emptied a chamber pot on Admiral Farragut," said the sergeant. "Can you figure that?"

"I fear it has become the fashion," Harry said.

As if to illustrate his remark, a small mob of soldiery came thumping along the wooden sidewalk outside, a woman in their midst being dragged along most unwillingly. Harry caught only a glimpse of her as they went by the doorway. He blinked, uncertain, then put on his spectacles and went to the door.

It was Louise, swearing magnificently—in French.

Harry came stomping toward them, arm outstretched. "You there! Officer! Unhand that woman!" It occurred to him that sounded much like a line from a play.

A captain stepped forward. "This woman is under arrest."

"What for?"

"For spitting in the face of a Federal officer."

"But she's the Countess de Lachaise-Valérie!"

"I don't care if she's the Queen of Sheba. She conducted herself like a woman of the town." The captain took her arm and moved her away.

Chapter 9

HARRY sat in the anteroom for more than an hour before he was finally admitted to see the colonel in charge. A portly man, he was doing battle with piles of paper—and losing.

"You are the provost marshal?" Harry asked.

"You should know that, as you've asked to see me."

"Yes, sir."

The colonel glanced at a piece of notepaper. "You are Harrison Raines?"

"Harrison Grenville Raines, yes, sir."

"You claim to be a government scout?"

"Yes, sir. Formerly of the Eastern Theater and General McClellan's command. Recently in New Mexico Territory."

"You come here out of the West?"

"Yes, sir. Heading back East."

"And you seek the release of this French woman?" He crumpled up the note, having exhausted its supply of information.

"She's American. When she's not being a countess, she's

Louise Devereux, the actress. President Lincoln has been to her plays."

"But she's Secesh. She spat on an officer."

"He may have given offense. She's very proud."

The portly colonel adjusted himself in his chair. "She's conducted herself openly and flagrantly as a Rebel. Women all over New Orleans are behaving in this outrageous manner. We've got to put a stop to it, and the best way is to set an example."

"The result could be the opposite of what you desire, Colonel. You make martyrs of southern ladies—you only rally the men to the cause."

"Who are you again?"

Harry had only one ace, and the time had come to play it. He set his foot on the edge of a wooden chair and, with his Bowie knife, sliced a thread at the top of his boot, pulling forth a carefully folded piece of paper. It was a pass through all Union lines, signed "A. Lincoln." He handed it over.

"This is genuine?"

"You may telegraph Washington if you like. Ask for a Major A. E. Allen."

The colonel frowned. "You were by earlier."

"Yes, sir."

"Return to the anteroom, if you would. I'll talk to the general—if he's free."

"And my pass?"

"It will be returned to you—maybe."

Harry went back to outer chamber, feeling the weight of his fatigue and apparent defeat, slumping into his chair. On the bench opposite were two brigadier generals and a fat man in a checkered suit who might have been a drummer, though Harry suspected he had grander commercial ambitions in mind for this newly conquered city. Such men followed close on the heels of every Federal army.

He was made to wait another hour, and most of yet another. Finally he took a piece of paper from his pocket and wrote his name and that of his hotel on it. He went to the sergeant at the desk.

"Please give this to your colonel. It's for General Butler. I have an answer to his problem with the women of New Orleans."

Harry turned and put on his hat, heading for the door.

"You better wait," said the sergeant.

GENERAL Butler was a turtle of a man, severely balding and with eyes so crossed it was disorienting to look upon him. He talked as a turtle might—in snaps of words. He was busy—and impatient.

"Sit down. Sit down." He fumbled among the papers on his desk and then handed Harry back his all-important pass. "This seems legitimate. You've asked us to telegraph Major Allen. I know who that is. I had dealings with Mr. Pinkerton when I was in command on the North Carolina islands. As he reports to General McClellan, it seems strange that he would have an agent out here."

"I'm in transit, General Butler. Heading East."

"Yes, yes. You'll have to wait for a ship. The river is still contested. The Rebels have that fortress town—Vicksburg." He sat down, rubbing his stubby-fingered hands together as though washing them. "Now, what about this woman? This 'countess'?"

"I knew her in Washington. She's an actress. Louise Devereux."

"Never had the pleasure. Colonel Morton says she's a

banshee when it comes to Federal officers. For all I know, she's a Confederate agent."

"Begging your pardon, General, but that hardly seems the conduct of someone trying to gain the confidence of an enemy."

"You may be right. Maybe so. But what am I to do with them? These ladies?"

"I think one of your officers has already hit upon their weak spot. If you jail them, as you have Miss Devereux, you only encourage their pride and willfulness and worse, make martyrs of them. Their vulnerability lies in their social station. Spittle and chamber pots are not associated with refinement. Seize upon that to deny them their stature, and they will be undone."

"I don't get your meaning."

"Don't jail them. Simply cease treating them as ladies."

Butler stared at his cluttered desktop for a moment, as well as he could stare at anything with his ocular affliction, then smacked the wooden surface with his fist. "Aha!"

"Sir?"

" 'Ladies,' eh? They're no better than ladies of the evening, women of the town, women of the street. And that, sir, is how we'll treat them."

Harry wasn't quite certain what Butler had in mind—nor how much he himself had contributed to it. But he appeared to have achieved his purpose. "You will let Miss Devereux go?"

"What? Yes. Of course. Damned captain she spat on overstepped himself. You're quite right. We'll have more riots on our hands if we go too far with 'em. But if this harassment continues, I'll have an answer. You're quite right. We'll hit 'em where it hurts." He squinted at Harry, creating a most peculiar expression. "Very well." He stood up. "Captain Raines? Captain, is it?"

"Yes, sir."

"Captain Raines, do not tell anyone of this conversation. Have I your word?"

"Yes, sir."

"Very good. Go fetch your actress and get her out of here. I'll attend to the rest." He fluttered his hands. "Go."

Harry went to the door, anxious to fetch his actress within the fewest number of minutes and seconds possible.

"Raines! Wait!"

He turned warily, wondering if the previous remark was to be rescinded. "Sir?"

"If anything is missing from the house of the countess, inform me, and I will see to restitution."

"Missing, sir?"

"Plunder, Captain Raines. Soldiers come to view victory as the right to load their pockets with spoons."

"Yes, sir. We'll count her spoons."

LOUISE had been taken to an office, where she'd been made to sit on a bench while two enlisted men kept watch over her. Harry entered in the company of the colonel who was provost marshal. If the enlisted men had any mischief in mind, it quickly vanished from their immediate plans.

"She is being released on the order of General Butler," said the colonel. "This gentleman will escort her."

Louise's dark eyes settled on Harry unhappily. One would have thought he was there to carry out a death sentence.

"Come, Louise," he said.

"I'm not apologizing to these Yankee bastards."

"An apology is not required," Harry said. "Only your departure. Now, if you please."

He extended his hand. She took it almost reluctantly, rather limply allowing him to pull her to her feet.

"Come, my sweet," he said, putting his arm around her. "A better audience awaits."

"Be warned, madam," said the colonel. "The behavior you exhibited will not be tolerated."

Louise hissed as they passed into the hallway.

"You have no shoes," Harry said, looking down at her stocking feet.

"They took them."

"Let me get them back for you."

"No. Let us leave this place, now that you've ruined everything."

Perplexed, Harry continued on, saying nothing until they were out on the street and moving along the sidewalk. Dark gray clouds were boiling up to the south.

"Why are you so unhappy?" he asked when they had turned the corner. "I have delivered you from their clutches."

"Their clutches were precisely where I wanted to be," she said. "Now it will be wondered how I've come to be released in such a short time."

"But—"

"And you, imbecile. Now a similar question will be asked about you. How did you, a Southerner and a civilian, manage my freedom so quickly? And at the hand of the commanding general. You might just as well wear a sign around your neck saying, 'Yankee spy.'"

She stepped on something and came close against him. He held her while she examined her foot, wincing.

"Are you injured?"

"No."

"I'll hire a hansom."

"No. Just turn the next corner."

When they had accomplished that, she pressed back against the wall, pulling him toward her in an embrace. Rather than seek his lips, however, she was keeping her eyes on the building corner. They remained that way for several minutes.

"We've not been followed," she said. "Yet."

"Who would follow us?"

"This city is acrawl with Confederate agents. I was hoping to allay their suspicions. But now—"

"I'm sorry."

She kissed him, warmly but quickly. "That's all right, dear man. Go to your hotel. I will come to you. As I promised."

"When?"

"Soon enough." Without another word, she left him, moving swiftly down the walk, though with a hopping limp. The rain was coming down in thuds by the time he reached the Florance House.

THERE was no word at the hotel desk of any visit by Tantou nor of anyone else making inquiries. Harry took a quick meal and bought a bottle of whiskey to bring to his room. He moved the one armchair there away from the window and settled into it. Sleep came long before Louise.

BUT she kept her promise. He awoke to her lovely face, very near him, long, dark hair falling over her eyes.

"You're here," he said.

"I am."

"How did you get in?"

"I picked the lock."

"Remind me to remember that you can do that."

"It is very uncomfortable leaning over you like this."

"I'm sorry."

"This chair is very small."

"It's all the furniture I have."

"No. It is not. There is the bed."

"Louise."

"I trust that is not chastisement."

"No." She rose, and so did he.

As they slipped beneath the sheets and into each other's warmth, he held her back a moment, looking at her face again.

"In the West, in the desert, I thought of you—of us, like this."

"I trust you don't only think of me in deserts."

"Oh, no."

She came nearer now, very near. "Promise me that when you close your eyes you won't think of Caitlin Howard."

"*Chère Comtesse.* How could I do that?"

HARRY awoke again to the sight of another face, but it was not Louise's.

"Tantou?"

"Get up and get dressed, Harry Raines. There is big trouble."

Harry sat up. Light was coming through the window. He was alone in the bed. He put his hand to where Louise had gone to sleep in his arms and found the sheet cool to the touch.

"Where is Louise?"

"There is no woman here. There is a man, and he is dead."

Blinking, Harry looked around the room. "There's no one."

"Not in here. Just outside, in the hall. By your door."

Harry set feet to floor and stood up, rubbing his eyes. Then he went to the door, pulling it all the way open.

A bearded man in a brown suit lay face up, mouth agape. He had two mouths, actually. Someone had cut his throat.

Chapter 10

HARRY stared in wonderment at the corpse, as though it were some marvel, like the fabled mastodon. Tantou finally broke his trance by putting his boot toe under the man's back and rolling him over.

"Roll him back, Jack. I want to look through his pockets."

"We don't have much time, Harry Raines."

"Patience." Harry found the man's wallet. There was nothing in it to indicate he was any kind of policeman—as Harry had suspected—only some money of both Federal and Confederate issue, a letter, a Masonic card of some sort, and a cardboard *carte de visite* bearing the picture of a naked woman, such as were in wide currency in both armies.

He went through the other pockets, finding nothing else of interest but a small five-shot pistol, fully loaded. Harry put that into his own pocket, but returned the other items. He'd gotten blood on his hand and wiped it on the man's coat.

His room was near the hotel's back stairs. He could hear someone with a bucket on the floor below.

"We have to move him—away from my room."

"There's blood on the hall rug."

"The rug, too."

"Where?"

Harry looked up and down the hall, and then back into his own room. "Out on the gallery. Him and the rug. Now."

"He'll be seen."

"Not for a while."

Harry felt confident enough of his newfound relationship with General Butler to stand up to any official inquiry in this matter—though possibly not if the dead man turned out to be Federal. But Rebel or Federal, the corpse was a complication he could do without. His most pressing need was to find out what had happened to Louise.

"We must hurry."

"Yes. Take an end of the rug."

They carried and dragged the man into Harry's room, then out the rear door leading to the gallery and the cool morning air. His room, unfortunately, faced a side street, and in growing light the body would be noticed. The back of the hotel overlooked only a narrow gangway and small courtyard.

"Come on," Harry said.

Tantou shook his head, but obediently lifted his end of the rug. When they'd gotten the body to the other side of the building, they covered it with the bloody rug and stood up. Harry realized he was still entirely undressed.

"We should leave this place soon, Harry Raines."

"Just give me time to shave."

THEY were ready to depart, but for one detail—the Federal gold from New Mexico Harry was taking back to

Pinkerton. He and Tantou had better than a thousand dollars secreted in their belts, linings, boots, and elsewhere. But the larger sum—three thousand dollars—Harry had hidden in a place that had seemed perfect: beneath the dusty, cobweb-covered coil of fire escape rope in the corner by the gallery door.

Three bags there were—now gone.

"Louise," he said quietly.

"She took the gold?"

"My horse is in the livery around the corner," Harry said. "Where's yours?"

"Tied up in front."

"Get them both, please. Meet me by the side entrance."

He gathered up his clothing and saddlebags and descended to the lobby. The clerk on duty at the desk was asleep. Harry roused him with two dings of the small round bell on the counter.

"I must leave early," Harry said. "My bill, please."

"On your way back to—Virginia?" said the clerk, looking at the registry.

"Yes. Is the railroad open?"

"It's running. But the Yankee army's using it. Steamboats'll take you to Baton Rouge, now that the Union's got that. From there . . ." He shrugged.

Harry tipped him a dollar, hoping that would buy some discretion.

"**WHERE** do we go, Harry Raines?" said Tantou from atop his horse. He held the reins of One-Eye loosely.

"To the Vieux Carré—Jackson Square." He climbed into the saddle in haste, taking the reins and turning the animal before he had his feet fully in the stirrups. With Tantou behind him, he trotted down the street, then broke into a canter when they reached a broad avenue.

BETTY the housekeeper was the only one at home—or so she said. Harry nodded politely to her and smiled, then moved past her into the house, gesturing to Tantou to follow. "Search everything," Harry said.

"For what?"

"For the gold. For anything."

They wasted no time. Harry went to the bedroom Betty said was Louise's. He found nothing that might implicate her in crime or treason—nothing of value or interest at all, really, save a packet of small glass Daguerreotypes of herself. Four were all in the same demure pose, and he was led to wonder if they might be prizes she handed out to male personages useful to her. The fifth was of her in the nude. This he put in his own pocket.

"Where did she go?" he asked Betty, who had not left the open front door.

"She go away."

"I can see that. Where? Back East? How?"

"She go. She come back in a few days. But now I go back to Baroness de Pontalbo's. I close this house."

Tantou took a step in front of her, glaring down at her menacingly. *"Où va la comtesse?"*

"Leave her," Harry said. They returned to their horses. "To the levee. We'll ask among the steamboats at the foot of Canal Street."

They went off at a mad gallop.

* * *

"THERE was a boat to Baton Rouge this morning—more'n an hour ago," said the harbormaster. A Union navy petty officer was seated beside him, and there were perhaps half a dozen U.S. Marines on the dock.

"Was there a woman on it? Very pretty?" Harry could have showed the man the Daguerreotype, but thought better of it.

"This boat was commandeered by the U.S. Navy. Strictly military."

"No civilians aboard?"

"A few."

"A woman? Dark hair, worn down."

"What name?" He consulted a list.

"Louise Devereux. May have used Lachaise-Valérie."

The harbormaster read all the way to the bottom of the list, then shook his head. "No Devereux. No Lachaise-Valérie."

Harry grimaced. "You're sure?"

"There was a damned good-looking woman with long hair," said the petty officer. "She was traveling with a large black man. Had a military pass."

"Had to have a military pass to get on that boat," said the harbormaster.

"Who are you?" said the petty officer to Harry.

"A friend of hers. She left something behind." He turned his attention to the harbormaster. "What name did she use—the woman with the black man?"

"Mercier," the man said, putting his finger to the place on the list. "Elizabeth Mercier."

"What is the next boat?"

"The *Pascagoula*. Leaves this afternoon at two o'clock. Unless they change the orders. And if you want to go aboard you have to have a military pass." He gestured toward a large Navy gunboat tied up at the wharf. "Try them."

"And tickets?"

"No tickets. Get a military pass."

"Can we take our horses?"

"If you get a military pass," said the harbormaster.

Harry started toward the gunboat, then thought better of it. "Wait here, Jack."

Tantou grumbled and went to a piling to seat himself. Harry swung back into One-Eye's saddle, and pounded away up the street toward City Hall.

"**W**HAT now?" said the portly colonel.

"I need a pass to go upriver aboard the steamboat *Pascagoula.* For me; for my associate, Jack Tantou, an army scout late of General Kearney's army of California; and our two horses."

"And why would you be needing that?"

Harry took a deep breath. "Someone wanted back East as a Confederate agent turned up here, killed a man, and escaped on an upriver boat bound for Baton Rouge this morning."

"You should have reported this incident."

"I just did."

The colonel clenched his teeth in frustration. "I mean on paper. Here." He started to look for something in a desk drawer.

"There isn't time, sir."

The colonel stared at him dubiously, then took up a pencil. "Very well. What is the name of this Rebel agent?"

Now he'd done it. He wanted desperately to see Louise again, but not hanging from a gallows.

"Not sure. She went by aliases. The last one was 'Heloise Abelard.'" He spelled it carefully. Fortunately, the colonel was not a literary man. He wrote it down without pause or comment.

"Wait here." He rose and left the room. He was back soon, with a slip of paper in hand. "General Butler himself," he said, handing the pass to Harry. "It's only good for a week. He wants you back here."

"Yes, sir." Harry put the all-important paper in his wallet and then fled.

GRANT wrote the note while in the saddle, afterward looking for Rawlins, who was unfortunately not in view. Colonel York was there, but Grant wasn't sure he wanted to entrust this missive to him.

"Where's Rawlins?" Grant asked.

"He saw one of Sherman's cavalry patrols coming back from a reconnoitering party and went to get their report."

Grant nodded, lighting a cigar. His position as second in command of this grand army of the West amounted to observing it and its commander as though an audience watching a theatrical performance. Halleck sent orders all day, none of them going through Grant. Halleck had met with Pope, Buell, Sherman, and other major officers without inviting or consulting Grant.

That day, with fine weather at last, Halleck had taken all morning to get the army up and organized for the advance, marched it forward about a mile, then halted it to prepare for the night. These exhaustive preparations included felling trees to build new corduroy roads running diagonally across the front to enable the concentration of troops at vital points.

Deep entrenchments were dug from one flank to the other, though the previous night's entrenchments were just behind them.

It seemed Halleck meant to scare Beauregard out of Corinth with the might of his shovels. If he meant to dig his way to Corinth, he should have attempted a tunnel. Then he might at least catch the enemy by surprise. As it was, Grant could not think of an advance in all military history that had advertised itself so flagrantly.

"Whiskey, General?"

"Not now, Colonel. Thank you."

Grant's eyes were on the road ahead, along which Captain Rawlins was approaching at a fast trot.

"What news, John?" Grant asked when the man drew near.

"Beauregard is being reinforced and is fortifying."

"Don't know why. We're more on the defensive than he is."

"Yes, sir. Guess we'll get there eventually."

"Not all of us." He handed Rawlins his carefully folded note. "I'd like you to take this to General Halleck. Deliver it personally. I don't want it to go astray in the chain of command."

"Yes, sir." The captain took the note and placed it carefully in a pocket, buttoning it afterward. "Where will I find General Halleck at the moment?"

"He's always in the same place. Over on the right. Pope's on the left, and seldom gets to talk to him."

"And you, sir?"

"I'm enjoying the fine day."

Rawlins gave him a peculiar look, the kind that came over him when he suspected his general might have refreshed himself from a bottle.

"Best be off, John."

"Yes, sir." He nudged his horse forward, but stopped after a few paces. "What's in this note, sir?"

"My request to be relieved from this position of second in command."

Chapter 11

LEAVING Tantou to watch over the horses on the aft deck, Harry went forward in search of one of the steamboat's officers, finding a long-bearded U.S. Navy ensign standing at the bow rail, his eyes on the floating debris that seemed everywhere on the river.

"How long will it take to get to Natchez?" Harry asked.

"Who said we were going to Natchez?" replied the aging ensign, his eyes still fixed on the oncoming water.

"They said on the New Orleans wharf that the river was clear all the way to Natchez."

"The river may indeed be clear of Rebels all the way to Natchez, and beyond. They've lost many vessels sunk and the rest are probably now near Vicksburg. But the shoreline is likely crawling with Rebels. Admiral Farragut is way ahead of the army. It may take the soldiers weeks to get that far upriver, unless we take them up there."

The man should have been careful with his talk. Harry had General Butler's pass carefully folded in his pocket, but the ensign hadn't asked to see any papers or even inquired as to who Harry might be.

"How far up will we go?"

"Depends on how far upriver Farragut's fleet is. We're bringing victuals and supplies to it. Where it is, that's how far we go."

"Above Baton Rouge?"

"Don't know, sir. We'll know when we get to Baton Rouge."

"There was another steamboat that went upriver this morning—the *Crawford.* How far could it get?"

The ensign shrugged, his gaze still fixed ahead. "Depends on what she was asked to do."

"Might she put people ashore?"

Another shrug.

"How about this boat?"

"Have to ask the captain, only he's too busy. So am I." The officer stepped aside, discontinuing the conversation.

Harry went to the rail, still marveling at the abundance of flotsam on the water. There was no telling how it all got into the river, but it was an amazing variety of things— half-burned cotton bales, wooden boards, dead horses, the occasional dead sailor or soldier, a badly damaged small boat or two, floating streamers of bandages, empty ammunition boxes, and what appeared to be a few unsuccessful fire rafts, one of them still smoldering.

It was difficult to tell if this debris was simply effluent of the Confederate flotilla that had turned tail and run upriver from New Orleans, or the result of some new battle brought on by Admiral Farragut's advance. Harry hoped not the latter. He was as worried about Louise as he was furious with her.

Someone on the Texas deck above called out a warning. Harry looked to see what appeared to be a small vessel headed directly toward them, its mast leaning to port.

His own steamboat gave a lurch as the captain abruptly stopped one of the side wheels and turned the rudder to starboard, frantically steering the river craft toward shore. Harry had read that the Confederates sometimes loaded boats with gunpowder and mounted torpedoes in their prow, set to go off on contact, and shoved them into the current simply in the hope they'd find a Yankee victim.

If Harry's boat was going to evade the menace, it would be at the risk of running aground on one of the Mississippi shoals that lay off the main channel. A worse predicament would be running aground and then being struck by the boat.

He headed back toward Tantou and the horses.

"What has made you afraid, Harry Raines?"

"Why do you say that?" Harry went to One-Eye and began stroking his neck.

"Because you look afraid."

Harry gestured at a plank floating by the rail. "There's a lot of debris floating downriver."

"You are afraid of that plank?"

"Very well, Jack. There's a rogue vessel bearing down on us. Could be a Confederate torpedo boat."

"What is that, Harry Raines?"

"They fill a craft with explosives and extend a torpedo from the bow."

"Torpedo?"

"A tube full of powder with a contact fuse."

"You people fight war strangely."

"You've no idea. Back East, they're directing artillery fire from balloons."

"Balloons?"

Before Harry could answer, there was another lurch, this time to port, and then a gigantic crash that sent them both tumbling to the deck. The horses skittered backward, Tantou's sliding against the rail but keeping his feet.

Harry clumsily regained his footing. Tantou did the same, hurrying to the rail, not to succor his frightened mount but to climb up on the stanchion.

"What are you doing?!" Harry shouted, moving aside as three sailors came running by on the canted deck.

"I'm going to swim to shore," said the Métis.

"No! No! Wait!"

"Wait to die?"

"Wait! Do nothing more."

Making his way to the corner of the bulkhead, Harry looked up along the deck toward the bow. There was confusion and panic aplenty, but no smoke or flame.

"It's all right," Harry said. "We are safe."

The steamboat heaved again, sending him sprawling once more, scraping his knee on a protruding bolt. Raising his head, he turned to port to see the remnants of the Confederate craft go careening downriver in a mass of broken wood and iron. There was what looked to be a torpedo, canted at a high angle.

When this wreck was fairly downstream of them, the steamboat crew fired two shells from the small field gun that was secured to the upper deck. The first round overshot, but the second struck the derelict squarely on what remained of the aft deck. There was a small explosion, and then a mammoth one that showered them with splintered wood. In a moment, there was nothing on the water where the wreck had been but smoke.

GRANT'S tent was only a few hundred yards from Halleck's, but Grant refused to make the short journey. The commanding general had not responded to any of Grant's communications, and until he did, Grant saw no reason to indulge him with the social niceties. He contented himself with his cigars and his correspondence, writing letters to Julia and his brother in Galena. The latter had been seeking government leather contracts in his name. Grant was asking him to desist. He had problems enough.

Sherman, his bowler hat pulled down low over his brow, came riding up about midafternoon.

"Set your camp up already, Grant?" he said, accepting a cigar.

Grant lighted one for himself. "Never broke camp. I don't think I'm any farther from our front line than I was at daybreak."

"Maybe here on the right, where Halleck stays," said Sherman, pulling up a camp chair and dropping into it. "But John Pope's been moving forward on the left. 'Reconnaissance in force,' I think he calls it. Anyways, he's got his main body at Seven Mile Creek and threw a division over toward Farmington. They must be four or five miles from the Rebs' outer defenses at Corinth."

Grant puffed, showing little reaction to Sherman's news, though it did interest him greatly. "Halleck will only call him back. Set him to entrenching."

"Not if there's a fight."

"Most particularly if there's a fight. He'll want a realignment, anchored back here. I tell you, Bill, this man will advance only when the enemy's people are in retreat."

"Won't argue with that, Grant. Just hope Pope can effect that kind of movement on the left. Shake 'em up and push 'em back. Then Halleck will have to move."

"You would think he's in an office at the War Department. By jig, Bill. He sits."

"Have you pressed him on your request for command?"

"Yes. I've asked repeatedly to take over on the right. There is never an answer."

"Be patient, Grant. See what Pope can stir up."

Grant nodded. "Another day or two. But I tell you, Bill, we are wasting opportunity here—Corinth, Jackson, Vicksburg. The South could be cut in twain. I'd write to Mr. Lincoln himself if I knew the man—if I thought it would do any good. I'm prepared to resign my position here and seek a reassignment from Washington. I'd rather command a brigade or regiment than endure any more of this."

"Patience, Grant. You stood by me when I was crazy. I stood by you when you were drunk. We stand by each other. We'll get through it."

Grant smoked, nodding, but without great conviction. Sherman put his hand on Grant's shoulder, then returned to his horse.

Rawlins came in shortly after.

"Telegraph message for you, General." His stony face showed he had read it.

Grant unfolded the paper. It was from Washington. Congressman Albert E. Abbott was en route by train. He wished assistance in determining the whereabouts of his wife.

Chapter 12

HARRY picked up his card, frowning. A six of hearts. Happily, he had two sixes more. Happier still, he had two tens to go with them.

He sat back, seeing the one-dollar bet that came his way but not raising it, leaving that to the sallow-faced army major at his left.

They were playing poker around a cotton bale on the aft deck of the steamboat. Three others were in the game—two of them also army officers, the third a sutler of some sort named Fenton. The Federals had purchased from him much of the provender that was the boat's principal cargo, and he was flush with money. His raises were becoming almost a reflex, as he demonstrated again when the bet came around to him.

If reluctant to win large amounts of money from military personages in a position to do him harm, Harry was not so worried about offending corrupt-looking civilians. He bettered the sutler's raise by two dollars—hoping it would scare the three officers out.

It did. Fenton raised again, and Harry called.

The sutler had a flush. Staring at Harry's full house, he became a sadder and less wealthy man. And a more disagreeable one.

"Is gambling your main trade, friend?" he asked. In Richmond and Washington that had been true enough, though the fellow could not have known that.

"Just a way to pass the time," Harry said, raking in his winnings. "Mostly I sell horses to the army." That was true as well.

"That one-eyed bone bag your stock?" He gestured at One-Eye, who was at the opposite rail, tied up next to Tantou's horse.

The Métis was on the upper deck, sleeping in the sun.

"He's proved a worthy mount. I acquired him in New Mexico, and he's made the journey since then without complaint or fault."

"Curious that I've not won a hand since you got in the game," said the sutler, getting finally to his point.

"I did not mean to end your luck. If you like, I'll drop out." Harry was sixty-two dollars ahead.

"No need to do that, Raines," said the sallow-faced major. "This is a friendly game."

Chastised, Fenton took out a large flask from his coat and drank generously from it, wiping his lips afterward. "Very well. Stay in the game—the better I can watch you." It was his deal. He called five-card stud.

Harry stayed in. He decided not to alter his play—lest it look as though he was manipulating the game to allay his fellow civilian's suspicions, as though for some nefarious purpose.

Consequently, he won the next two hands. The sutler threw down his cards and took up his remaining money, glowering at Harry from under thick eyebrows. "If we ever get to Natchez," he said, "I should like a game with you 'Under the Hill.'"

When Harry had visited Mississippi with his father as a young boy, they had stopped in Natchez. His father had whisked him past the whorehouses, gambling dens, and whiskey stores that made up the "Under the Hill" section of the town that lay at the foot of the bluff along the river. They'd gone directly to the respectable precincts of the town above.

"I'd be obliged," said Harry, tipping his hat and then raking in the rest of his winnings.

As he was pocketing the money, there came a sudden lurch forward as the powerful steamboat clunked to a stop. The vessel's captain had halted both paddle wheels this time.

Harry went to the rail, looking upriver, fearing the Rebel fleet. Instead, he saw only the flotilla of Union boats they had joined the night before, the lot of them stopping. The ironclad frigate that was the flagship of their river fleet was turning.

"What's wrong?" said one of the army officers at the cotton bale.

"The Reb flotilla?" asked another.

"Don't know," Harry said. "Excuse me, gentlemen."

He mounted the stairs to the next deck, ignoring the slumbering Tantou and proceeding to the steps to the pilothouse, where a sailor barred his way.

"I'd like to speak to the captain, please."

"No passengers allowed in there."

"I'm military," Harry said. "Army scout."

"Don't care."

"Well, can you tell me what's wrong? Why have we stopped?"

"Whole fleet's stopped."

"I can see that. Why?"

"Admiral Farragut's orders," said a new voice. Harry looked to see a young lieutenant standing at the rail above.

"The frigate's turning around. Are we not going any farther?"

"No, sir. Heading back."

"Back to where?"

"Down to Blackhawk."

"That far? I need to get to Natchez."

"Rebel troops around there."

"I don't care."

The lieutenant looked around him and shrugged. Harry's eyes went to the eastern shore some two hundred yards distant.

"Can you make a landing here?"

"No, sir. We are obliged to stay with the fleet."

The steamboat's starboard side paddle wheel began moving. Sluggishly, the boat commenced a shift to the left.

"I'd like to swim our horses across."

"Swift current here. You could end up pretty far downstream. Or on the bottom."

"Better than Blackhawk. Could you ask the captain to stop long enough for us to get into the river?"

"You must want to get to Natchez pretty bad."

"I do indeed, sir—or to the steamer *Crawford*. If you know where that is."

Another shrug. "Upriver somewhere. I'll ask the captain."

HARRY and Tantou stood at the now open railing, holding their horses' reins and looking dubiously at the muddy water.

"This is stupid, Harry Raines."

"Only way."

"No, there are other ways to kill oneself."

"I mean to get to Natchez. If you are coming with me, you must do this."

Tantou swore in French. "*Bien.* You go first."

Harry pondered this prospect, longer than Tantou liked.

"Let go of the reins and take hold of the stirrup," the Métis advised. Harry hesitated, then did as instructed.

Tantou slapped One-Eye's rump hard, and the animal bolted into the air. Sailing along with him, Harry went underwater with a great splash, but managed to keep his grip on the stirrup.

CONGRESSMAN Abbott came to Grant's camp from General Halleck's with an escort that happily did not include the commanding general, but counted in its assemblage seemingly everyone on his staff.

The Joint Committee on the Conduct of the War, formed after the debacle at Ball's Bluff the year before, had given itself power over every aspect of the conflict. Generals could be made and unmade by its intervention. Grant did his best to stay clear of this legislative inquisition, but, like all pests, its members were peskily persistent.

"Good morning, Mr. Abbott," he said, as Rawlins produced an extra camp chair. "I hope you've not had a tiring journey."

"Not a tiring one, but a damned uncomfortable one." He settled into the chair gingerly.

Grant was surprised by the congressman's appearance. In addition to her remarkable handsomeness, Mrs. Abbott was unusually tall for a woman. Abbott was singularly diminutive—

no taller than General Philip Sheridan, the shortest man Grant knew of in the army. Exacerbating this defect—if that it was—was an ungainly slouch. The congressman had small, weak eyes and a drooping mustache much too large for his mouselike face. Every movement seemed to induce some kind of pain. He winced as he leaned back, coming forward again.

"Would you like a cigar, Congressman?" Grant asked. "Whiskey?"

"You keep whiskey?" Abbott said, frowning. Grant had expected a weak and tiny voice, high-pitched. He was surprised to hear a deep one instead.

"No, sir, I do not. But there are officers about who do."

"No, thank you. No cigar, either. Cannot abide them."

Grant had been reaching into a pocket for his cigar case. He withdrew his hand without it. "I understand that you are looking for your wife."

Abbott made no response at first—his eyes on the grass. "I understand, from General Halleck, that you were the last one in this army to see her."

Grant coughed. He truly wanted a cigar at that moment. "She came by my headquarters, seeking a pass through the lines to visit relations in Corinth."

"And you gave it to her? On the eve of battle?"

"Mr. Abbott, it is a lamentable fact that we had no notion of battle. The Confederate attack came as a surprise. This was not only in my report but also in the newspapers."

"You were aware that the enemy was disposed between your position and Corinth?"

"Yes, sir. She said it was to Corinth she was bound. I provided her with an escort down the Corinth Road."

"How far?"

"I believe to within a few miles of the town. I cannot say. The lieutenant in charge of the escort was unfortunately later killed in the battle around Shiloh Church."

"And the others in the party?" Abbott now met his gaze.

"Only one survived the engagement at Pittsburg Landing. A Sergeant Bishop. He's gone back to a hospital boat upriver. He had returned to duty, but his wound became inflamed."

"What hospital boat?"

"I am not certain. I'm afraid I've been concerned with other matters."

Abbott shifted his weight, wincing again. He looked about Grant's camp. "There seems little going on here to concern anyone."

"That is my principal concern."

"You are second in command here. The army is advancing on the enemy. You should be busy."

Grant wanted to reply that, were it not for the entrenching, the soldiers would have had as little to do as he. But it would have done him little good to complain about Halleck to a member of the all-powerful war committee. To General Logan, maybe—a Lincoln friend who had been a congressman from Illinois—but not this fellow.

"At all events, sir," said Grant, "I have no knowledge of the wounded trooper's whereabouts now—or the state of his health."

"I'll seek him out."

"He probably can be found, but it will take time."

Abbott contemplated the ground again. "The trooper doesn't matter. I'm holding you responsible for whatever has happened to my wife."

"I'm not sure that anything has happened to her, sir. I presume she is in Corinth—with her sister. We have no communication with the town, under the circumstance. But eventually that will change."

"When?"

"We've been making about a mile a day. We should be there by the end of the month."

Abbott clenched his fists several times, then stood up. "Have you any spies—any agents, any scouts—in Corinth?"

"I don't. The division commanders have been running cavalry patrols near the town."

"I mean someone behind the enemy lines, who could go to my wife's family there."

Grant was beginning to feel he lacked the authority to order his own dinner. "If that becomes possible, Congressman, I will gladly attend to it. Are you returning to Washington?"

"No. Not until . . ." He shook his head sadly. "I'm staying aboard a steamboat—one of your transports—moored at Pittsburg Landing. As soon as you learn anything, I want—I'd appreciate it if you would advise me at once."

"Yes, sir. With all celerity."

Abbott started to leave but hesitated, looking back at Grant. "Is there something else you haven't told me?"

"She said something about her sister being in trouble—in danger. I thought perhaps she might be ill."

Abbott removed his bowler hat and ran a hand over his balding scalp. He had thick dark hair on top, but it was combed over from the side. "Is that all?"

"We found what may be her cloak. A red cloak."

"Where?"

"On the battlefield—the next day."

The congressman wiped at his eyes. "Where is it?"

Grant looked to Rawlins, who hastened into the tent. He

returned with the garment quickly, handing it to Abbott gently.

"Thank you," the congressman said somberly and he walked away, his slouch more pronounced. His escort from Halleck's staff re-formed around him.

"WHAT do you think, John?" Grant asked Rawlins when Abbott and his party had gone.

"I think he will not leave this army until there is word of his wife."

Grant nodded unhappily, then lighted a cigar at last. It brought little pleasure.

Chapter 13

HARRY and Tantou approached Natchez on the Fleet Road, which angled up from the southeast. Ascending the verdant hill on which the town was situated, they came to a crossroads and turned onto a street that ran along an empty brick ruin of an aqueduct Harry remembered was called "the canal." Running parallel to it on the left, about a hundred yards back from the edge of the bluff overlooking the river, was a broad avenue with handsome mansions and gardens. Running parallel to it on the right was Natchez's main commercial street. The other streets of the town extended perpendicularly from it to the east, including one broad thoroughfare lined with luxuriant China trees. An altogether agreeable place, Natchez, were it not for the black faces seen at toil everywhere, doubtless every one of them a slave.

What surprised Harry was the remarkable lack of Rebel soldiery. Those he saw were mostly layabouts, taking their leisure rather than defending this place from the Yankee invader. He would have thought the loss of New Orleans to the Federal government would have occasioned fortifications at every worthwhile port and strong point along the river. Perhaps the Rebels hadn't the troops, and were depending on their river fleet to stop the Federals.

"I would be happier if you were of African extraction," he said to Tantou. They were riding their now weary mounts at a walk, heading for the town's main square. "We'd cause less suspicion."

"The same'd be true were you a darkie, Harry Raines."

"You don't look prosperous enough to be a slaveowner," Harry said, "as you have refused to change from those malodorous trail clothes. At all events, I've never heard of Indians who kept slaves."

"You don't know about the Cherokee? The ones who lived in Georgia before they were run off and sent across this river?"

"Know about them in what respect?"

"They wished to be left alone by the white man, so they adopted the white man's ways. They made a written language for themselves and took up the keeping of slaves. The state of Georgia tried to move them off their land, so they went to court and sued. The U.S. Supreme Court upheld their right to their own land. But do you know what happened?"

"Does this relate to something called 'The Trail of Tears'?"

"Indeed it does, Harry Raines. The chief justice of the Supreme Court wrote the decision. The great John Marshall himself. But your president back then—General Jackson— do you know what he said?"

"I presume I am about to be informed."

"He said, 'John Marshall has made his ruling; now let him enforce it.' Instead of obeying the Court, Jackson sent soldiers to Georgia to drive the Cherokee off. And your government has been doing that kind of thing regular—until this war, which distracts them from killing Indians."

"Jackson was a lunatic and no gentleman," Harry responded. "He was a Democrat as well—the party of slavery. My family were Whigs."

"But slavers."

"I'm a Republican, and we despise slavery. How is it you know so much about the Cherokee?"

"I read about it in the *North American Review*. We Métis are very interested in the fate of your Indian tribes."

"Let us not discuss such matters now. There are eyes upon us. And also, I fear, ears turned our way."

They came upon the square, riding around two sides of it and halting before the imposing brick edifice that was the Mansion House Hotel. It was considered the best in Natchez on Harry's last visit and appeared little diminished.

"If you do not mind, Jack," Harry said, "I am going to declare you my servant just the same. Then they will allow you to stay here with me."

"This is strange thinking."

"It's the South."

With Tantou following, Harry mounted the hotel's broad veranda, noting the well-dressed young gentlemen sprawled with their walking sticks in the row of wicker chairs facing the square. Some of them slept, others were reading newspapers, still others yawned at the sparse passing traffic—all of them luxuriating in their idleness. This was precisely the scene he had encountered on his first visit here, as a boy.

One or two eyed Harry and Tantou curiously, and not a little contemptuously, as they passed into the lobby.

"Sorry," said the clerk. "Full up, I'm afraid."

Harry looked at the paltry few people in the lobby and the many keys in their boxes behind the clerk.

"That's not true," he said. "There are remarkably few people in this town. Not to speak of this establishment. I suspect there's some apprehension about Yankees coming up the river." He put a twenty-dollar gold piece on the counter.

The clerk stared at it appreciatively but then looked to Tantou disapprovingly. "And this gentleman?"

"He's not a gentleman. He's my servant."

"There is a suite of rooms facing the square. As they are on the second floor, one can see the Mississippi from them as well."

"That seems agreeable."

The clerk pushed the register toward him. "How long will you be staying?"

"That depends." He took his time signing the book, scanning the pages for an entry in a feminine hand. "Has a young woman come to this town? She has dark hair and is very pretty. Goes by the name of Louise Devereux, though she's also known as the Countess de Lachaise-Valérie, and Elizabeth Mercier."

"Three names?"

"She's entitled to all three, I believe."

"No, sir. I know nothing of such a woman."

"She's an actress."

"An actress?"

"Is there a theater in this city?"

The clerk made a face. "There is. Only the one. It's to be found at the end of Main Street, on the far edge of town. There used to be companies performing there from New Orleans and New York—but with the war . . ."

"Thank you." Harry accepted his key. "You're sure there's no one named Devereux here? A recent arrival. I suspect by steamboat."

"No, sir. But there is a plantation of that name—d'Evereux—east of here, out Liberty Road."

Harry nodded, then motioned to Tantou to follow him up the stairs.

"**WHAT** now, Harry Raines?"

"Food, whiskey, and a bit of sleep. Then we'll need the horses."

"You are convinced she is in this town?"

"I don't know where else her steamboat could have gone—unless it kept on up the river to Vicksburg."

"This is a small place. Our coming will be talked about. If she hears this talk, she will leave. You'd best look for her before you take any sleep."

"Very well. I'll send for some food. Whiskey first."

THE theater was a large and handsome brick building—considerable enough to have graced a much larger and more sophisticated city. But, unfortunately, it was closed. The bill displayed in the glass case on the outside wall advertised a play performed the previous year.

The front doors were locked. Harry, impatient to find Louise and depart from this town, went around to the rear, where at length he was able to rouse the caretaker—a grizzled and unkempt old man in a tattered waistcoat and patched striped trousers.

"Good morning, sir," said Henry. "I seek an actress, name of Louise Devereux. She may have played here in the past. A very beautiful lady, dark of hair. Do you know her?"

"Yes. And well she's gone, as she's not coming back."

"What do you mean, sir?"

"She's tainted. Negro blood. So it was said. The manager found out and run her off."

"We are talking about the same woman? Louise Devereux. Reckoned a countess down in New Orleans."

"Guess so. Was here in 1860." He squinted at Harry. "What do you want with her?"

Harry thought. "To bring her to justice."

"Well, you'll not be finding her atop the bluff, I can tell you that—if she would dare at all to come near this town."

"You've not seen her in recent days? Not disembarked from a steamer called the *Crawford*?"

"Don't know nothing about the steamboats. Don't never go down there."

Harry had nothing more to say to the man.

HE had left Tantou at the hotel, to take some restorative sleep. On his own, he set out on One-Eye for Liberty Road and the d'Evereux plantation.

It was a holding of some substance, though not so elegant as his father's Belle Haven on the James. He trotted up the drive, pulling up at the front of the house as though he were an expected guest.

An African manservant in livery answered the door.

"I'm looking for a lady named Louise Devereux," Harry said. "An actress. Recently of New Orleans."

The man stared as though Harry had uttered some mystical, evil incantation. Then he withdrew. A moment later, an elderly woman in full bonnet and old-fashioned dress appeared.

"What is your business here, sir?"

"I am seeking a lady named Louise Devereux."

"Devereux?"

"She is also known as the Countess de Lachaise-Valérie. But she is an actress. She once played here."

"Devereux?"

"Louise Devereux."

The door was slammed in his face.

TANTOU was still asleep in their room and not much amenable to Harry's attempts to stir him to wakefulness—until Harry mentioned food.

Tantou sat up. "Can I eat in the dining room downstairs?"

"Most likely not. Certainly not in the manner of dress you have chosen."

"Then where are we to eat?"

Harry had already figured that out. "Under the Hill."

"You mean down by the landing?"

"It's a separate little town down there—distinguished from the respectable community here by its complete and utter absence of law."

"Maybe we should take our chances with the dining room here. If they won't let me in, you could bring me some food in a napkin."

"I've another reason for wanting to go down there."

"Louise Devereux."

"She's obviously not anywhere up here."

"That Under the Hill is no place for a lady. Isn't that so?"

"Which is why she might find it the perfect place to be, for who would look for her there?"

"I do not think that she is there or anywhere near this city.

It still belongs to the Confederates. She was on a Yankee steamer."

"That would make no difference to Louise. She would seek to gain her ends however possible."

"What ends, Harry Raines?"

"I wish I knew."

ONE descended to Under the Hill by way of Silver Street, which cut diagonally down across the face of the bluff and connected with a sort of avenue at the bottom, which ran parallel to the river the length of the district—about seven or eight blocks.

It was truly a descent into Hell. To either side was a jumble of two-story wooden buildings that housed a succession of brothels, taverns, and gambling dens, each seeming more wretched and depraved than the other. Heavily rouged ladies of small beauty leaned and leered from doorways and windows. A few ran forth and tried to pull Harry and Tantou into their dens. Harry extricated himself, but their ripe odors lingered as he moved on.

It was a noisy place, producing a continuous low din comprised of coarse music, profane oaths, laughter, shouts, a scream or two, and an unexplained gunshot. They had both loaded their revolvers, and Tantou was carrying up his sleeve his wide-bladed bowie knife. They had left their horses in the livery for fear they might be stolen down here.

There were a number of Rebel soldiers to be seen—many more than in the town proper and nearly all of them drunk—and river men of every variety and in great profusion. The levee was crowded with steamboats, which Harry gathered had put in to shore until hostilities in the area were concluded. Farragut may have gotten this far north, but it was clear he did not control this stretch of the Mississippi.

"I want to look among the steamboats," Harry said.

"It is dark down by the water and dangerous, Harry Raines."

"No more so than here."

"Here you can see the villians coming at you."

"If the *Crawford* is there I should want to know it."

"Why not look in the daylight?"

"Because it might leave tonight."

"A wise captain if it does."

"Come along, Jack. You can watch behind us."

The way to the levee was through a squalid little alley with a sort of sewer running down the middle. They kept to either side of it, which put them in unfortunately close proximity to the ramshackle structures on either side, most of which were brothels, plying their trade quite openly. It didn't seem possible that a woman of Louise's quality could survive five minutes here.

They had to go aboard one boat to make out its name, but otherwise their perusal was without incident. When they turned back toward the main street of this Sodom, Harry noted that Tantou had both revolver and bowie knife in hand. Life would be harder when he and the Métis parted company, whenever that might be. Harry hoped it would not be that evening.

The fame of Under the Hill had spread wide. Harry's fellow gamblers at Washington's Palace of Fortune had talked of it as a place to avoid. The lucky patrons of the district, they said, were those who merely lost their money.

Walking back toward the foot of Silver Street, Harry took note of some of the loungers taking their ease on the front porch of one of the gambling emporiums, recognizing two of them as dandies from the veranda of the Mansion House Hotel. If they were among the custom of this establishment, one might expect more decent treatment within. It would invite strong censure from the law if harm came to a scion of one of the first families of Natchez. Harry's was one of the first families of Virginia, though that probably didn't count for much.

He turned into the building, Tantou following unhappily.

There was a Faro wheel, roulette, and several card games in play. He went first to the bar, ordering whiskies for himself and the Métis and paying for them with a silver dollar, nodding to the bartender to keep the change. Facing the room, he glanced over the tables. All were full, with rouged ladies hovering near like predatory birds, waiting for the winners.

A seat opened up at a table in the corner—one with another of the dandies at it. Harry walked over and doffed his hat, asking in his most courtly manner if he might join the game. The dandy looked up, studying him briefly.

"Gentlemen are always welcome," the young man drawled. "They are too few in these precincts."

Harry decided to give his name. No one here would know it. "Harrison Grenville Raines," he said, pulling up the vacated chair. "Late of the Belle Haven plantation in Charles City County, Virginia, and returning to that place."

"Seems to me you got a lot of war in your way if you're meanin' to get back to Virginia," said another player, a flat-headed, squinty-eyed man who rather reminded Harry of a snake.

"Yankees're still in Tennessee," said another, this one more resembling a well-dressed tortoise. "Beauregard's got 'em held fast."

"I was in New Orleans," said Harry. "Got out just ahead of them."

"Why didn't you strike East?" said the dandy, examining his freshly dealt hand. "Why'd you come up here?"

"I was hoping to renew an aquaintance," Harry said, peering quickly at his own cards, which were not promising. "A lady friend. An actress who I believe came this way—also running from the Yankees."

"An actress?" the dandy replied. "This is a poor town for such as that."

"She's quite famous in the East—in Richmond. And New Orleans as well. Her name is Louise Devereux."

The snake man came forward in his chair. The dandy showed little reaction to the name, staring at his cards. Finally he put them down. "I'll stand pat," he said to the dealer.

Harry was that rarest of creatures, an honest gambler whose game was based largely on judgments about his tablemates. But he had seen about every variety of cheating there was, and realized that this was a game between sharpers and losers. He had thought the dandy might be one of the latter, but now thought again. Everyone else had taken three cards but Harry, who had drawn one. It was the dandy's bet, and he made it a dollar. A bluffer would have thumped down a fiver; a sleeper would have checked. The presumption here was that the fellow might have made a flush or a straight. Their acquaintance was so limited, Harry had no real idea whether either was true.

At all events, he had kept Harry, with his paltry two pair, in the game. It was against his conservative method of play, but Harry, who was to the dandy's left, put down two dollars. The man to his left folded, as did the next two players in rotation. Mr. Snake raised the bet two dollars. The dandy saw the wager but did not raise. Harry saw it, too.

"Aces and queens," he said, laying down his cards. He hoped Tantou was observing the game with his pistol convenient.

There were some hard stares, but nothing more. The dandy lay down his two pair—jacks and eights. Snake-Eyes rose and spat on the floor. "I'm to the sinks." He walked toward the back with a swinging limp.

"You have no need of your Louise Devereux," said the dandy. "Your companion this evening is Lady Luck."

"She is not known for her constancy," said Harry.

They continued the game. Harry received three sevens the next deal. After a quick glance at the malicious faces around him, he discarded one and asked for three cards.

"What's a Virginia man doing in New Orleans?" asked the Tortoise.

"Passing through," said Harry, continuing truthfully. "Returning from the West."

"New Mexico Territory?" the Tortoise pressed.

"For a time, the Confederate Territory of Arizona," Harry replied, folding his hand as the bet came around.

"That man with you. At the bar. Is he an Indian?"

"We run the Indians outa here years ago," said another player.

"He's Canadian," Harry said. "French. An Indian-fighter."

"I heard he was an Indian."

How would the man have heard that? And from whom? Decidedly nervous now, Harry wondered if his visit to this establishment was outliving its usefulness. They had not yet eaten. He should have stopped first at a tavern. But card table talk was inevitably informative.

Two more hands were played before Snake-Eyes returned. Harry noted that he pulled his chair several inches to the side before setting his bony bottom on it. A tingle spread along the back of Harry's neck. He tried to remember what was behind him. He would have to watch this fellow's every twitch, a precaution having nothing to do with cards.

Snake-Eyes did twitch, leaning to the side, his eyes careful to avoid Harry's but held in that direction.

Harry shoved himself to the side just as the gunshot cut through the smoky air, shattering a whiskey jug on a nearby table. It was followed by a fusillade, coming not from the original shooter, but from Tantou, who fired four quick shots at the doorway to the sinks while backing hurriedly to the gambling house's entrance.

"We go now quick, Harry Raines!"

Harry was not about to argue. Regaining his feet, he pulled out his own Navy Colt and joined the Métis, allowing him to exit first. The street outside was dark, but beginning to fill with onlookers, a few with torches.

"We run," said Harry.

Tantou's response was to abruptly commence doing just that, heading for Silver Street, their only way out of town, with Harry thumping along behind him. Harry had had too much whiskey and not enough nourishment, and it quickly showed.

They were being followed by the now sizable mob. Few could have had any idea of what the clamor was about, but all were intent on being part of it. At least one of them had a firearm. Two more shots came near, a goad to Tantou, a frustration for Harry, who was having trouble keeping up.

And now disaster intervened. A yellow-sided coach came rattling out of a side street, turning up the slope of Silver Street in a spray of dirt and gravel and then stopping, blocking their way. Harry looked desperately for a way around it just as the door opened. The coachman, a tall black man, leaned from his seat and shouted, "Get in! Get in! You are saved!"

Tantou flung himself through the door, attaining a seat, and then pulling Harry in behind him. The coachman cracked his whip before the door was closed, urging the four-horse team into a lunging gallop up the grade.

"Damn you, Harrison Raines. Why do you dog me so?"

She was dressed all in black, in a wide-brimmed hat with veil, but he would have recognized her from a mile. Certainly he would have done so within any earshot of her voice. No one offstage or on had a voice so elegantly sultry as Louise Devereux's.

The coach was swaying mightily in its mad ascent. Harry wished he was sitting beside her.

"It is you who seem to be dogging me at the moment," he said. "How is it you magically appear to offer succor?"

"Because I've been waiting for you to emerge from that den of iniquity so that I might deliver you from this colony of Hell. All Natchez knows of your presence here and your insistent inquiries after me. You put me at great risk, damn you. And not for the first time. What do you want of me?"

A bump caused his head to bang against the coach's wooden frame. He rubbed the spot. "An explanation, if you would. There was this deceased gentleman on my doorstep in New Orleans."

"Harry. There is a war on. People are killing other people all over the country—and I do not speak of soldier boys in uniform. 'All murder'd: for within the hollow crown, that rounds the mortal temples of a king, keeps Death his court.' "

"*Richard III.*"

"It is that sort of time, Mister Raines, and you are a fool for intruding yourself so deeply into it."

"Did you kill that man?"

Another bump lifted them all. When they'd resettled,

Louise had a derringer pistol in her hand. They had reached the top of the bluff, and the way was smoother now.

"You are staying at the Mansion House Hotel. I will take you there, by the square, and no farther. I would have had the stable ready your horses, but there was no time. You do that and then leave at once. Go to Alabama. Get out of Mississippi. This will shortly be the worst place on Earth."

"You would not shoot me, Louise."

"If I had to, I would," she said, "despite my fondness for you."

He actually believed her.

They were rattling along Broadway. At a near corner, they made a sharp turn and followed a hard-packed street with a cobblestone bridge over the defunct canal. They were almost there.

Tantou still had his pistol out.

"I do believe you are outgunned," Harry said, with a nod to his companion.

"No. She is not, Harry Raines," said Tantou. He returned the big pistol to his belt. "She is right. We must do what she says."

"I do like a man with a brain in his skull," she said. "No matter how swarthy."

The coach skidded a little as the horses halted. Tantou snapped open the door on his side and alighted silently.

"May I kiss you?" Harry said.

She shook her head as though he'd gone mad. "Harry, please. Get out."

He leaned forward, pushed the pistol aside, lifted the veil, and put his lips to hers. For some three seconds, she was utterly his.

Upon the fourth second, the derringer went to his ribs.

"Out!" she said. "I will see you when this war is done."

* * *

HE stood on the stone walk, watching the coach as it moved swiftly off. "Where can she be going?" he said.

"Wherever it is, you and me should go elsewhere, fast," said Tantou, and started walking rapidly toward the livery.

Chapter 14

GRANT used his idle time that bright May morning to ride the line and assess the ground as Halleck continued with his snail's advance. General Pope, on the left, kept pushing ahead, and Halleck continued to haul him back again to conform to the line of the rest of the army, though he never quite got him back all the way. Ever resolute, Pope had managed to get some of his forces established near the village of Farmington and within sight of Bridge Creek, a swampy stream that served the Rebels as a moat where it ran close to the foot of the bluffs on which Corinth itself stood.

The creek, however, would stop Pope. He'd have to wait for the rest of the army to pull up in line, which would take endless more days. The general would find himself as inactive as Grant, if that could be possible.

Grant had lunch with Sherman, after which they took a short walk together along a lane that led through the woods to a wide clearing that sloped south. Two batteries of field guns had been positioned at the far end.

They lighted cigars. "Be patient, Grant," Sherman said. "Like you were with your ankle. Once we take Corinth, Halleck's bound to reorganize. You'll have an independent command again."

"If I'm to wait until we take Corinth, I'll be too old to command a thing. And should we actually achieve that military feat, I've no doubt the good general will sit there for the rest of the year, preparing defenses. He won't be content until he's dug a trench from the Mississippi to the Appalachians."

"You speak to him again?"

"Written him before I set out on this ride. I hope it will bring the issue to some decision, for I cannot abide this much longer."

"What'd you say to him?"

"I fear you'll say I was intemperate."

"At this reach of events, I'd be disappointed if you weren't a little intemperate."

"I said that if he did not restore me to a command, I was requesting to be relieved of duty."

"Grant. You can't do that."

"But I did. What I said to him was, 'I believe it is generally understood through this army that my present position differs little from that of one in arrest.'"

"That is strong." Sherman lifted his head, as though seeing something in the distance Grant could not. Then his attention turned back to his cigar and his friend. "He may act on that."

"If he does not, once we take Corinth, I may go back to Illinois and let Washington settle the matter. I have the need of defending my name besides. The damned newspapers are calling me a butcher for Shiloh."

"We should hang one of those reporter bastards every

week. They're more help to the enemy than spies."

"They'd make poor spies. They get everything wrong."

Sherman clapped him on the shoulder as they turned to go back down the lane. "John may be of some help to you," he said, speaking of his brother, a U.S. senator. "You have some friends in Washington."

"Certainly I am in need of them."

"I keep telling you, Grant. Be patient. It's going to be a long war. We've learned that much well enough."

RETURNING to his camp, Grant found an uninvited visitor waiting on a chair outside his tent.

"Congressman Abbott," said Grant, nodding to the little man. "I fear I have no news. No news of any kind."

"No one has that, alas. I expect I will have none until this army takes Corinth."

"That may take a while."

"So we have discussed. General Halleck has sent scouts into Corinth but two never came back, and those who did never got into the town. The only intelligence we have from there comes from escaped Negroes."

"And what do they say?"

"They say there are many Rebels in the place and they have put many Negroes to work fortifying it."

"And it gets stronger every day."

Abbott ignored this. "They have no news of my wife or her sister."

"They would not, sir. Unless they are from your wife's sister's household."

"Can you send someone?"

Grant dropped into a chair, removing his hat. "I have no scouts. No cavalry. No one. Nothing, sir."

"You have your staff."

Grant looked about his camp. York was standing by a tree, enjoying the contents of his flask. McPherson was up on the line. Hawkins had gone to Pittsburg Landing, acquiring fresh newspapers from the newly arriving steamboats. There was Rawlins, but he would need Rawlins with him every day he remained in this war. He could not risk him on such a mission.

"None that I can spare for this."

Abbott studied Grant with watery eyes, as though about to ask him to go himself. Grant had no answer to that.

"I could go," Abbott said, "if you would give me a pass through the lines."

"I'd fear for your fate. They captured a New York congressman at Bull Run—Congressman Eli, I believe it was. Put him in Libby Prison in Richmond. He wasn't exchanged for months."

Abbott stared sadly at the ground. "What if I explained my purpose?"

"Beauregard's a gentleman. Not all of them are. I'd say you'd be taking a chance." Grant lighted a cigar. He had only one more and would have to see to replenishment. "Congressman, I accept my responsibility in this."

He had feared that, had he not granted May Abbott a pass, she would have attempted to make her own way into Corinth, no matter the peril. Better, Grant had thought, to have a pass and an escort and travel a main road. But it was hardly fitting to be making such arguments in the midst of the poor man's distress.

"I appreciate that, General."

"When we reach Corinth, I assure you that her whereabouts will be my first concern."

"Very well." Abbott wearily got to his feet. "I'm inspecting quartermaster depots and I'll be taking a steamboat to Perryville. I'll be there several days—should you be able to telegraph me some news."

Grant stood up, placing his hand on the congressman's shoulder. "I will do that, Congressman, and I will hope that it is good news."

"Thank you, General." He turned away and started toward the main headquarters camp. Passing him, a young lieutenant came striding up and saluted, handing Grant what he assumed was a dispatch, though he couldn't think of any reason he'd be receiving one.

Opening it, Grant read it quickly. "Thank you."

"Yes, sir." the lieutenant saluted again and reversed course. His uniform was much too clean for an officer in Grant's kind of army.

The general slumped into his chair again. Halleck had replied, and Grant was unsure what to make of his words.

"Your position as second in command of the entire force here in the field rendered it proper that you should be relieved from direct charge of the right wing," Halleck had written. "I am very much surprised, General, that you should find any cause of complaint in the recent assignment of commands. You have precisely the position to which your rank entitles you."

Grant let the paper fall to the ground. Perhaps Halleck had no malice toward him at all. Perhaps he simply didn't understand. Perhaps he thought Grant should spend his time in headquarters camp, sitting on his arse like the rest of Halleck's staff.

That was not how Grant intended to fight this war.

Chapter 15

THE train north from Jackson generally followed the course of the Yockanookany River and the Natchez Trace. The latter had once been considered the most dangerous road in America, for all the bandits and cutthroats who plied their trade along it. Harry did not feel much safer on the railroad. The weather had turned hot, and the windows in their coach had been opened to provide ventilation. As the car was just behind the locomotive, sparks and embers as pesky as flies kept flying through the opening. One had burned a hole in the shoulder of Harry's coat when he wasn't looking, a defect in his appearance that annoyed him more than it should have done in their circumstance.

Tantou sat stiffly, arms folded, staring forward. He was not happy.

"What's amiss?" Harry asked.

"I have never ridden on a train before."

"What? How did you come down from Canada?"

"I joined the crew of a ship in Vancouver. When it got to

San Francisco, I left it. I was on horseback from there."

"Never on a train?"

"No."

"You don't like them?"

"They go too fast. And they are on fire."

"Not really."

Tantou gripped his arms more tightly. "How fast are we traveling?"

"I believe thirty or more miles an hour."

"Thirty? *Bien sûr?*"

"Yes."

Tantou grunted. "When will we be in Corinth?"

"Tonight." Harry lowered his voice. "Confederate generals have shot engineers who failed to keep schedules. I recall that happening at Manassas."

"Manassas?"

"The first big battle—in Virginia."

They fell silent, rattling and bumping along through the cotton fields, swaying somewhat when they clattered across the wooden trestles that bridged the creeks and streams.

"What if the rails break?"

"Tantou, would you rather be back among the Apaches?"

The Métis closed his eyes.

Harry had decided not to obey Louise's instruction to head East. As soon as they'd retrieved their horses, they'd gone north along the river road toward Vicksburg. As Harry had guessed, Louise had taken that route as well, wanting to stay close to the Mississippi. And why, he had wondered, was that? To keep near Union gunboats? Was she spying on the advance of the Federal fleet?

Wherever Farragut had gone, he had not reached Vicksburg, which the Rebels were rapidly turning into a fortress. Finding Rebel soldiers everywhere there, Harry stayed clear of the riverfront battlements lest he be suspected a spy. Instead, he'd inquired at the fine hotels of the city whether a beautiful lady in a yellow-sided carriage had taken lodgings.

She'd not done that, but she'd come through the place. Residents of the town were beginning to leave for safer precincts. A groom at a livery stable had said he'd seen the yellow-sided coach heading out on the road to Jackson. And so Harry and Tantou had done the same.

In that place Harry had a very sad moment. Ascertaining that she had taken to the railroad, leaving her coach and servant behind, he realized they'd have to dispense with their horses to follow her. Harry had become extremely fond of One-Eye, but there was no way to fit him into a railway coach seat. All the livestock cars had been taken over by the military. Most of the train was occupied by soldiery. This was a civilian coach, and there were uniforms throughout.

The train was slowing. It had made several stops to take on water and wood, and Harry supposed it was doing so again. There seemed to be nothing else on this swampy, wooded landscape worth halting their progress for.

He was proved correct—but only partly. There was a water tank and woodpile, but also a sort of platform with shanty attached. On it was a small assemblage of Confederate officers in very elaborate uniforms.

They came aboard Harry's car, where there were no empty seats. Harry glanced at Tantou, who was still staring straight ahead, though they were motionless.

"High-ranking Rebs coming aboard," Harry whispered. "Are you ready for this?"

Tantou nodded.

A captain came forward, looking from side to side as he moved along the aisle. When he came to an enlisted man, he'd lean down and speak, uprooting the fellow from the seat as he might harvest a crop. By the time he reached the end of the coach, he'd deprived seven of the poor devils of their comfort.

The man's eyes swept over the interior of the conveyance again, settling on Tantou and then switching to Harry. He came toward them, full of intent.

Harry had traveled from Richmond to New Mexico with nothing more in the way of identification than a smudged letter signed by General Robert E. Lee that commended the bearer for enlistment in the Confederate Navy. The signature alone had often sufficed, and, where it hadn't, a glib tongue and a lot of luck made up for the rest.

Tantou had been far more resourceful, going to a friendly Union officer named Weimers while they were in Santa Fe and securing a pass that had been written by the actual Confederate commander in the West, General Henry Sibley, and then left behind when the Rebels had run.

It was this captured paper he now presented when the captain came up and demanded to see something that would identify him.

"Your name is Henry Frazier?" he said, squinting at the pass.

"It is," said Tantou.

"You have something to prove that?"

"You're holding it," the Métis replied.

"Your occupation?"

"Army scout. In New Mexico."

"And now?"

"He is traveling with me, sir," said Harrison. He proffered his now bedraggled Lee letter.

The captain squinted at this with less comprehension. "This is signed by a General Lee. That the General Lee in Richmond?"

"It is, sir."

"But it says here something about the navy."

Harry snatched the letter back. "And that's all you need to know."

"Where you going?"

That was obvious. "To Corinth."

"Corinth? On navy business?"

Harry heard a stamp of foot behind him. He rose. "Captain, I see plainly that your goal here is to clear sufficient seating to accommodate your general and his staff. Mr. Frazier and I gladly surrender ours, and I would suggest you not delay the good general any further with this unnecessary inquiry." He spoke loudly enough to be heard throughout the car.

"Yes. Well, thank you." The captain stepped back, coming almost to attention.

Harry and Tantou pulled their saddlebags and rifles from beneath the seat. Harry smiled, nodding, as he passed the general, who ignored him. The cocky fellow wore a plumed hat.

They went all the way to the flatcar that brought up the rear of the train. It was loaded with barrels and packing boxes and guarded with four musket-toting infantrymen, but Harry and Tantou found a couple of places to perch without too much discomfort.

A sergeant appeared from the other end of the car. "You can't sit out here!"

Harry waved him back. "We were ordered to. Had to give up our seats inside to that general who came aboard."

The train lurched, throwing the sergeant off his balance, then began to roll forward. Tantou settled onto his patch of canvas-covered crates like a nesting bird. Closing his eyes, he pulled down his hat.

He seemed to like trains better if one could ride them out of doors.

GRANT had taken another ride along the line, which had advanced the usual mile or so along the right and center and not at all along the left, because of the barrier presented by Bridge Creek, the surrounding swamp, and the fortified bluff beyond. Pope's troops might as well have been in a rest camp now. The Rebels sat in their breastworks atop the Cornith bluff and waited, with yawning patience, for the Yankee attack that never came. Pope could have held his section of the line with a few pickets and a cavalry patrol.

All of this produced an idea that began to press itself on Grant with great urgency. He came back to his own tent at a gallop, with his staff trailing well behind. Dropping quickly from the saddle, he lunged toward his writing desk, then abruptly thought better of it and remounted. His staff, perplexed, followed him in what became a mad dash for headquarters.

Grant came at Halleck's tent with such speed it must have seemed to the commander's entourage he intended to make a jump of it. Instead, he turned and stopped his mount at the last moment, thrusting the reins into the hands of a gape-jawed sergeant and striding hunched forward through the open flap.

"General Halleck, sir," he said. "We have an opportunity here."

Halleck, reclined in one chair with his feet propped on the seat of another, had been dictating something to an aide. He lifted his eyebrows at Grant's intrusion but made no other response, resuming his droning recitation. Standing there awkwardly, feeling the eyes of the general's high-ranking staff on him, Grant could do nothing but listen. The man was ordering remounts for a cavalry brigade.

When he at last finished, he lifted his head in Grant's direction and smiled, looking like a parson at a tea. "Good afternoon, General Grant. May we be of some service?"

Grant took two steps forward, snatching up a map that had been spread out over Halleck's table. Every night's entrenchment had been marked on it, giving it the aspect of some striped jungle creature.

"General Halleck," Grant said, laying the map on Halleck's lap, "we have an opportunity. Cornith could be ours by tomorrow noon."

"What do you mean, General Grant? Are the enemy abandoning it?"

"No, but we have an excellent chance of compelling them to do so. Observe." He pointed to Pope's position on the left. "General Pope has perhaps a third of the Rebel troops tied up defending the bluffs against him. He's not going to attack—unless it's part of a general assault on the Confederate works—because he has a creek, a swamp, and that high hill before him. But as long as he's there, they must man every inch of their line."

"Yes? Well?"

"They will remain in that position even if they only think he's there. General Halleck, if you would have General Pope leave a skeletal force behind and swing the major part of his troops around the center and right of our army, he could cut both railway lines and take the town from the flank—even the rear—in coordination with a general offensive by our center and right. Beauregard would have no choice but to run. We might even bag most of his army."

Halleck's pale eyes were studying him—a schoolmaster trying to make sense of a pupil's wild ravings.

"General Grant, if I may—"

"General Halleck. It's terribly clear. You must order the appropriate movements to begin at once."

"General Grant. Please do not agitate yourself. You have an interesting theory there. I would certainly commend it for a class discussion back at the Point. But my instructions are clear. We are to avoid combat if at all possible—not bring it on by attacking the enemy at the point he is most interested in defending. No, sir. I intend to take Corinth by maneuver."

"General, this *is* a maneuver."

"Well, thank you, General Grant. Now I must return to my work." He turned away, gesturing to his aide to pick up his paper and pencil.

Grant left the camp raging with a desire to somehow tear up the trees he passed and fling them behind him, but he simply trudged off, head down, shoulders hunched, into the afternoon.

Chapter 16

SOMETIME after sundown, it began to rain. Perhaps half an hour after that, the rain turned to downpour. Harry and Tantou sheltered themselves as best they could, which was not very much at all. A short while later, the train stopped. They could not have been more wet had they plunged fully clothed into the Mississippi again.

Soldiers were coming along the tracks, though it was hard to see them in the darkness. There were shouts, directed at the occupants of the cars. "All civilians off the train! All civilians off the train!"

A peculiar array of possibilities ran pell-mell through Harry's brain. There was fighting up at Corinth. The track had broken or a bridge had washed out. They were searching for someone they wished to arrest and take prisoner. They were looking for spies to shoot.

He'd heard no cannon fire, the usual presage of a battle, or even thunder. It had not been raining long enough to have washed out a bridge, and if the track was out, they'd be taking troops off the train as well.

That left arrests and spy shootings. An officer in a cape, followed by a sergeant swinging a lantern, came up to them, peering at their clothing. "All civilians off the train!"

Louise, they'd well determined, was not on the train. She was most likely now in Corinth.

"We're army scouts!" Harry said. "Heading for Corinth!"

"What's your rank?!" the officer shouted back.

"No rank!" Harry said. "Scouts!"

"Off the train!"

Tantou rose, swinging his saddlebags over his shoulder and picking up his rifle and the buffalo gun. "Come, Harry Raines. We go get dry."

THE Métis had been too ambitious. The soldiers gathered all the civilians into a sort of column, provided umbrellas for the few ladies, then led the group off through the muck alongside the roadbed at a slow, sodden, slog and shuffle. Harry put all thoughts of dryness from his mind. There was no such state. There was only cold and wet. Perhaps, in the morning, the wet would be less cold.

A small woman with a bundle in each arm was tottering along ahead of him, the umbrella the army had given her canted back so far it could not have kept a drop from her brow. Harry moved up beside her, taking the umbrella and holding it straight up above her.

She looked up at him fearfully, then put her head down and resumed her forward progress.

"Where are you bound, madam?" Harry asked.

"Corinth. Have a son in the army. He was wounded in a great battle they had up there."

"Are we near?"

"Don't think so. They said we were going to Rienzi. There's a boardinghouse there where we can stay the night."

"Did they say why we can't go on to Corinth?"

"No, sir. Maybe another fight. My son won't be in it, though. I'm here to take him home."

"You're a brave lady."

"I'm his mother."

They kept on, leaving the chuffing locomotive and its pale headlamp behind. Following a shallow curve of the track, they compressed to single file as they crossed a short trestle over a creek. At length they came to a road crossing. An officer sitting aboard a large horse directed them across the tracks to the right. Accomplishing that, they came around a bend and saw a few dim lights in the distance.

"Rienzi," said the woman.

"Is there a place to stay?" Harry asked the officer.

"Boardinghouse. Please keep moving."

There was only one such establishment, and it was already quite full of stranded humanity. Seeing the older woman and the other ladies safe inside, Harry inquired of the proprietress whether there was a Miss Devereux in residence, identifying himself as her brother.

She shook her head unhappily. "Didn't favor the accommodations here. Think she persuaded some young officer to let her on a train. There were volunteer nurses on it, going to Corinth."

"When was this?"

"Midmorning."

"Today?"

"Yes."

"Do you remember the officer's name?"

"They come and go. I'll remember hers. You'd think she

was Queen Victoria. And she's but an actress. That's what the soldiers say. It's me who ought to be lookin' dubious upon the likes of her upon my premises—even if she did decide to join the nurses."

"She is a countess," Harry said.

"What?"

"A French countess. The Countess of Lachaise-Valérie."

The woman snorted. "Good night, sir."

TANTOU had found himself a bit of shelter beneath the boardinghouse's side porch, and stirred himself from it to follow Harry with some reluctance. "Where now, Harry Raines?"

"She's left this place. I don't like it much anyway. I mean to go to Corinth."

"How far is that?"

"One of the soldiers said it was eight miles—by way of the railroad."

"Aren't no other roads. All mud now."

"Let's go find the railroad."

"The soldiers will stop us."

Harry lifted his face to the downpour for a moment. "Not tonight."

GRANT had a late-night visitor: Former congressman and now Brigadier General John A. Logan. An Illinois man, he was a political friend of the president's, though a Democrat. Politics had determined his rise to general officer, but he'd served ably in the Mexican War and had been wounded at Fort Donelson—only now returning to active duty. His brigade had been given control of the Mobile and Ohio Railroad north of Corinth.

"How are you, Grant?" he said, slumping into a camp chair. The rain was seeping through the canvas tent top, but he paid it no mind.

"Tolerable," said Grant. "We could be in Corinth now, were I heeded. But I've not been."

"That's what Sherman tells me."

"Any news of Farragut?"

"He's got a Rebel flotilla plus Vicksburg between him and us. He's somewhere below both."

"If we'd only push."

"There's been a lot of railroad traffic into Corinth," Logan said, taking out his flask. He didn't bother to offer it to Grant.

"You have scouts there?"

"No, sir. But we can hear it."

"Hear it?"

"On the rails. We listen to the rails all the time. I have men, Grant, who can put their ears to that steel and within a minute or two tell you whether a train is full or empty."

"And what do they say?"

"I think we must wait for this rain to abate, for it dulls the sound. But there have been many trains in recent days."

"Reinforcements." Grant frowned.

Logan shrugged. "Could be. Could be troops departing."

"Our commanding general's most devout wish. Bloodless victory. It has not yet occurred to him that our aim here is the defeat and removal of Rebel armies, not the seizure of names on a map."

Logan's response was cut short. An officer was standing in the tent opening. Colonel York.

"Pardon the intrusion, General," York said to Grant. "Could you spare me a moment?"

Grant thought it rude to ask Logan to leave and an imposition for himself to have to step outside. He could not imagine what York had in mind to say that required such discretion.

"I think not now, Colonel."

"Well, sir, you asked me to inform you as soon as we had word." The man looked utterly stricken.

"Word?"

"About Mrs. Abbott, sir. We've found her."

Chapter 17

HARRY and Tantou reached Corinth with the first light of day—a gray murk in the east that showed little promise of brightening. The rain had stopped, but the mist was still so thick with moisture one almost didn't notice. Where there weren't puddles, there was mud, even along the railroad right-of-way. Harry despaired of ever having his boots clean again.

There was more railroad to the town than anything else—lines coming in from the south, the southeast, and the east, expanding to several tracks across and intersecting near a round house and a wide thoroughfare appropriately named Railroad Street.

They passed only a few sentries, huddled in doorways and half asleep. None challenged them. Approaching the main depot, Harry noted smoke and occasional sparks coming from the chimney.

"They have a stove in there," Harry said. "Let us declare that our destination."

"If it is warm and dry it will be full of soldiers," said Tantou. "Do we want to be among them?"

"I can't think of a safer place."

"If they let us in."

No one stopped them. The waiting area benches and the floor around the stove were all crowded with sleeping soldiery, but they found a clear space in the far corner.

"What now?" Tantou asked.

"When in Rome," said Harry.

"Where is Rome? This is Corinth."

Harry gestured at the soldiers. "Sleep, Jack. Sleep."

HUNGER brought wakefulness. Harry sat up, surprised to see the depot now nearly vacated, though a small group of ragged soldiers was clustered near the door to the platform.

"Jack," he said, shaking the Métis. "Get up. We need to find something to eat."

Tantou did not move. "And Louise Devereux?"

"Food first."

Rising, Harry shook out his clothing, then looked for the sinks. An older sergeant was at the trough. He knew of no restaurant nearby, but said there was a grocery up the tracks where food and whiskey could be had, though at a dear price.

They found it easily. Harry ignored the large rat sitting on his hind legs just outside the door, ducking his head as he entered. There was not much stock on the shelves, but he managed to assemble the makings of a meal—the preponderance of it beans. Happily, the grocer had a fairly fresh ham under a cloth, and Harry bought several thick slices of that, as well as a demijohn of whiskey.

He could have bought a new saddle for what he paid for the groceries, but war was war.

Grocers meet a great many people. Before leaving, he asked if Louise had come into the town.

"If she's a respectable woman, she is either staying indoors or has fled the place, because it is no longer safe for such a woman here," the grocer said. "There are too damn many soldiers. We've had attacks upon women. Even murders. Corinth is dangerous. I would not let my wife out of doors."

"And if a woman is not respectable?"

"The army camps are full of such. The saloons here as well. An actress, you say?"

"Yes. Long, dark hair. Very beautiful. Louise Devereux."

"There's a saloon around the corner and up two blocks. Cassidy's. Inquire there." He turned away.

Food first. They found a place to cook in a small grove of trees near the tracks. The town had become quite busy with the advance of the day. Soldiers were forming up and marching off, mostly toward the northwest. Two trains came in during their meal, bringing more soldiers, but not many. Curiously, there were no freight trains bearing supplies. Perhaps those were coming in by wagon—or would, when the roads dried.

Tantou devoured his ham first, then turned to the beans. "We need horses, Harry Raines."

"We may have a hard time finding any. A large army like this will have laid hands on every animal."

"Then we must steal some."

"That's a less than sensible idea."

"You told me you once stole a Yankee general's horse."

"General Hooker's. Yes. But I was lucky. I did that in Washington City, which I knew well. And it was early in the war. Easier to move around."

"I wish to walk no more in all this mud."

They were so covered with it they had come to resemble the Confederate troops around them.

"Finish your food," Harry said. "I want to visit this Cassidy's saloon."

THE few customers, all Rebel officers, were at the bar, and they were a glum lot, unhappy with the army's inactivity. They talked of the situation in Corinth as though it was a siege whose end was a foregone conclusion. They spoke derisively of the Federals for failing to wage much of a fight and of their own commander, General Beauregard, for failing to seek one.

"The goddamn Yankees have taken forever to do it but now they've got their trenches within three miles of us," said one bedraggled captain with a whiskey bottle before him. "They bring their big guns up and they'll have the town under fire. Then what's it worth?"

"We can't give up the Mississippi," said a lieutenant without explaining himself. It seemed to Harry that, with New Orleans gone, the river was useless to the Confederacy.

He kept his opinion to himself. He was surprised that these men spoke so freely in front of him and Tantou without knowing anything about them. Perhaps they'd had too much whiskey. At all events, he wasn't interested in the military situation here.

"I'm looking for a woman and I wonder if any of you might have taken note of her," he said. Every eye in the place was suddenly upon him. "Her name is Louise Devereux."

"Who are you?" the lieutenant asked Harry.

"Harrison Raines. From New Orleans. Got out just ahead of the Yankees. She got out just ahead of me."

"What do you want with this lady?"

Harry thought—quickly. "She's my wife."

"Your name's Raines? And you say she's Devereux?"

"Her stage name. She is an actress."

"An actress?" said a major. "We've had no actresses here. The town's under siege. The theater's full of wounded from Shiloh."

Harry nodded. "Sorry to have importuned you."

The conversation was not resumed. It was as though they were waiting for Harry to leave. He decided to do so.

"Could you direct me to a hotel?" he asked after finishing his drink and stepping back from the bar.

"Corinth House," said the bartender, "but they've got no rooms."

WHAT the man failed to explain was that this establishment also had been turned into a hospital. As they approached, Harry saw a sad-eyed woman in black seated on the steps, a shawl around her shoulders despite the increasing warmth. The sun, thankfully, was now burning through the mist.

Harrison introduced himself.

"I am Mrs. Cumming," said the woman, with an accent Harry associated with Alabama or Georgia. "I am a nurse here. Do you seek a relative?"

Harry hesitated only briefly. "My brother. Major Robert Raines. I've had no word of him for months."

In truth, the two had not spoken since Sumter.

The woman rose, holding the railing for support. She seemed very weary—or ill. "I do not believe we have any patient of that name, but I shall check."

"May we come with you?"

She looked to Tantou, somewhat disdainfully. Harry wondered if she thought him Negro. "Yes. Of course. Follow me, please."

Tantou shook his head, and stayed where he'd been standing.

The once-grand hotel had been converted into a chamber of horrors. Even the lobby had been made into a sort of ward for the less seriously wounded. As they proceeded further within, the seriousness of the injuries and the awfulness of the smell increased, but the moans and groans diminished.

"I thought the great battle was some weeks ago," Harry said.

"They are still bringing in wounded from that—some who could not be moved earlier," said Mrs. Cumming "And there are daily skirmishes." She paused by an open door—a room with women on the cots. She smiled wanly at one and gave a little wave, then moved on.

"Who are they?" Harry said.

"My fellow nurses, who have taken sick. This hospital is full of sickness, I'm afraid. It touches all."

Passing more wards, Harry observed that most of male patients seemed to be missing portions of limbs.

Mrs. Cumming shrugged. "That's the sadness of this place. There are times when I think the fortunate are those who die on the battlefield. The wounded came here with arms or legs cut off because the bones have been shattered. Or they came with wounds that later became so inflamed that they required amputation. In either case, most of them die, taking days or weeks to do it. Those few who survive and recover are miracles to me."

She entered an office, where a male clerk was at his bookish labors. Mrs. Cumming went to his table, removing a large ledger book and opening it. " 'Raines,' you say? 'Robert Raines'?"

"Yes. My brother."

"What regiment?"

"Virginia cavalry. I've forgotten the number."

She flipped through several pages. "No. No Robert Raines. No one from Virginia."

The clerk was now very curious.

"I'm sorry to have put you to this trouble," Harry said quickly. "I stop at every hospital. As you must understand."

"Yes. I do," she said. "Can I help you in some other way?"

Harry waited until they were in the hall. "There's a woman who might have knowledge of my brother. I saw her briefly in New Orleans—before the Yankees took it. I have been given reason to believe she came here. I wonder—"

"What is her name?"

"Louise Devereux."

Mrs. Cumming stopped, her dark eyes now wary. "You know this woman?"

"I have made her acquaintance. I cannot truly say I know her." That was certainly no lie.

"She came to us only yesterday, saying she wished to help. And I will credit her with sincerity in that wish, though she was not much good at this work."

" 'Was' not, ma'am?"

"This morning she volunteered to go out with some stretcher-bearers to bring back some wounded from a skirmish. I forbade her to do it, but she was very willful and insistent. I hadn't the strength to prevent her."

"Where did she go?"

"North. Near the railroad, I think. The men with the stretchers said she simply disappeared into the woods."

"Hmmm."

"Perhaps it is just as well. She was so pretty . . . it was a disturbance to the men. Mrs. Hudson, she is the matron here, disapproved of her. I think she would have driven her away had she not run off."

"Is Mrs. Hudson here?"

"No. I would not advise your speaking to her."

Mrs. Cumming accompanied him to the front veranda. "We are in a holy cause, Mr. Raines. Yet God is trying us mightily."

" 'Holy cause,' ma'am?"

She seemed surprised. "The very same that George Washington led us in against the despot king of England. Our freedom. Our rights. Our wish to be our own people."

There were two black men laboring with shovels by the street, repairing the drainage ditch. Harry said nothing more.

Mrs. Cumming took his hand. "I hope you find your brother, sir."

"Thank you, ma'am. And thank you for all you're doing here."

"They will be moving us soon. The Yankees are near, and I don't think this town can last long."

"I hope you will be safe."

She nodded, sadly, then returned inside.

Harry rejoined Tantou, who had gone down onto the lawn. "She was here. She's apparently gone north. I believe she has crossed over to the Union lines."

Tantou looked up and down the street. A squad of infantry was marching toward them, led by a mounted officer. "We should leave here now, Harry Raines."

"Yes. But I'm not sure where to go." He fetched up his saddlebag and threw it over his shoulder. "Let us first go somewhere where this infantry squad isn't."

Tantou nodded, pushing through the gate. Harry followed after, and they started north at a brisk pace. But they were too late. They heard the officer's horse move into a trot and then the sound of soldiers at the double quick.

"You there! Halt!"

Harry glanced over his shoulder as though this was some sort of mistake, but kept walking. The officer took out his revolver and fired it once into the air.

They stopped. Harry turned with great slowness. "Sir?"

The officer loomed over him, leaning forward in his saddle, keeping his sidearm in hand. "I am Lieutenant Shakes. Is your name Harrison Raines?"

Holding their muskets at the ready, the other soldiers had caught up with their leader.

"It is, sir. May I be of assistance to you?"

"You may be of assistance to General Hindman. You are to come with me."

"General Hindman?"

"Brigadier General Thomas Hindman, C.S.A. Now come along."

THEY were brought to a boardinghouse near one of the other railway lines that ran through Corinth, this one serving as both the general's residence and the headquarters of his division. Harry knew little about these western generals—Union or Confederate—but had read about Hindman in the Washington papers, for he, too, had been a U.S. congressman before secession.

They were made to sit on a bench in the front hall of the house while the officer went to report at Hindman's office, which Harry guessed had once been the parlor of the premises. After a few words, Shakes left. Thumping down the front steps, he called his infantry squad to attention, then returned to his saddle and led them away.

The front door remained open. There was a breeze, and the air was fresh with the sweetness of the late southern spring. Here and there were dapplings of sunlight. Had they a better idea of their fate, it would have been a pleasant interlude.

There were footsteps, and the door behind them opened. Out limped a small man in the most resplendent uniform Harry had ever looked upon. It also was the tightest-fitting, giving the bantam brigadier the aspect of a circus performer. He wore patent leather shoes and a ruffled shirt, lacking only a cocked hat to complete his masquerade as a Napoleonic officer. Harry gathered he had been injured, for he used a cane.

"You are named Harrison Raines?"

Harry stood up. "Yes, sir."

"You are seeking Mrs. Mary Townsend?"

"Townsend? No, sir."

"Yes. It's been reported to me that you've been all over this town looking for Mrs. Townsend. Now, that poor woman is missing, and her husband, who is a colonel in my command, is quite distressed. Why are you looking for her?"

"But I'm not, sir. I've not heard of her before. I am seeking an actress named Louise Devereux."

"I was told it was Mrs. Townsend."

"No, sir."

"Well, I have sent for Colonel Townsend, and he will be here presently to talk to you. You sit back down and wait."

Harry did so. "Yes, sir."

Hindman took a handkerchief from his sleeve, ran it past his nostrils twice, returned it, and went back into his office, shutting the door.

* * *

TOWNSEND was a big, flush-faced man with side whiskers and large blue eyes who seemed on the verge of very bad temper. Without stopping first to pay his respects to his commanding general, he marched right up to Harry, sword clanking.

"Are you this man Raines?" he bellowed.

"I am that man, sir." Harry felt he should stand up, but he was apprehensive to do so.

Townsend reached down, grabbed Harry's coat by the lapels, and pulled him to the feet—and very close to his large, spittle-spewing mouth. "What do you know of my wife?"

"Nothing, sir."

"But you've been asking about her!"

"No, sir. After another woman. Louise—"

Townsend thrust him back down into the chair. "What Louise?"

"A Miss Devereux. I've been pursuing her all the way from New Orleans. I've never met Mrs. Townsend."

He was yanked erect again. "If you don't know my wife, how do you know her name?"

"General Hindman—"

Down he went into the chair again. "Who are you, Raines? Why aren't you in the army? Everyone's in the army."

"Sir—"

The colonel's now quite florid face came down to Harry's. "If any harm's come to Mary—if I find you've had anything do with it—I will have you shot, sir!"

He entered Hindman's office without knocking, slamming the door behind him with such force the wall shook.

"We should go now, Harry Raines," Tantou said quietly.

"I do agree." Harry rose carefully, then tiptoed to the door. There was a private standing outside, holding his musket loosely. The other soldiers in the street were paying the building no attention.

Six horses were tied in a row to the fence—no one minding them.

Harry returned to Tantou's side and leaned close to whisper. "Very well. We go now. Follow my lead. Do as I do. Do what I say."

"What will you do?"

"Shhh. Now come on."

He led his companion to the door, waited a moment, then said in a very loud voice: "Yes, General. I'll do it. And do it now, sir, as you instruct!"

Harry stepped smartly out onto the porch, ignoring the soldier, and proceeded unhesitatingly to the nearest horse, pulling the reins free. Trusting that Tantou was right behind him, he swung himself up into the saddle. The private had taken a step forward, musket held more usefully.

"General's orders," Harry said to him. "We'll be right back."

Tantou was aboard an animal, one he chose from farther down the line. Without looking back to see if Harry's was with him, he led the way down the street.

They moved at a trot, turning at the corner. Quickening the pace slightly, they kept going until they came to the railroad tracks, then turned again, heading north. After another few blocks, they broke into a canter.

HARRY hoped they might get by the troops camped outside of town without hazard, as the soldiers had been idle for some days and would have taken to the common activities of camp—gambling, drinking, sleeping, and shirking.

Up on the line, he knew, it would be different. There had been skirmishes. The Yankees were moving steadily forward. The Rebels manning the forward positions would be alert.

But they would be looking toward the Union Army, not expecting intruders from behind. Everything depended on how fast Harry and Tantou could move.

But, nearing the line, Harry stopped. They were on a road that ran next to the railroad line. Up ahead, the road seemed to disappear. There were a number of soldiers gathered on the tracks. Harry put on his spectacles. The Rebels were on the near end of a railroad trestle. He judged it crossed a stream or a creek—nothing wider—that ran through the bottom of a ravine.

"There's a stream ahead," Harry said. "We've got to cross it elsewhere."

"We've got to cross it quick," said the Métis.

Harry looked over his shoulder. There was a small body of cavalry coming up the road toward them, moving fast.

"Very well. To the right."

Harry steered the horse he'd stolen, a fine, strong animal, to the side of the road and down a steep incline to a muddy gully. Tantou followed, then moved ahead—rapidly. Harry found himself holding to the saddle pommel to keep aright.

They were approaching the line, which bordered a wide creek. There were entrenchments running between it and the watercourse, soldiers' heads visible here and there along them.

Tantou jammed his heels against his horse's flanks, goading it into a mad gallop. Harry did the same. They came upon the Rebel troops running at speed, leaping over fallen logs, startling the soldiers.

With a cry, Tantou jumped his horse over the trench and

the following mound of earth, the animal landing badly but recovering its balance. Harry managed the leap more cleanly and retook the lead, splashing into the creek, which was swollen with the recent rain.

He was halfway across before the Rebels began shooting. Ducking down, he looked back to see Tantou, looking as wild as a madman, hurrying after. Two shots sang overhead, then a third. Then a whole volley—everything passing well overhead.

The firing unfortunately drew a response from the Union side of the creek. Most of this was directed at the Confederate line, but a few bullets began singing their way.

With a lunging leap, Harry's horse attained the opposite bank and thundered onto the dry ground on the other side. He saw orange flashes in the brush ahead. Then he heard a cry. Looking behind him, he saw Tantou slump forward in the saddle, grabbing hold of his horse's neck. The animal carried him forward a few yards, dodging around trees, then abruptly halted. Tantou went flying from the saddle.

Harry dismounted and hurried to his side. As he looked to find Tantou's wound, someone came running up behind him and struck him at the back of the head with a hard object. His last conscious perception was of Tantou swearing in French.

Chapter 18

"**THEY'RE** here, General," said Rawlins. "Leastwise, one of them is. The Indian was wounded crossing the creek and a surgeon's looking after him."

Grant sat a moment, puffing on his cigar. This was a very small and mean way for Halleck to address his complaint of idleness.

"Shall I send him in, General?" Rawlins continued.

"No, no," said Grant, getting unhappily to his feet. He went to the tent opening and studied his new guest. The man had told the line company that had captured him that he was a Union Army scout named Harrison Raines, though none such had ever come into Grant's ken, and Halleck had said flatly he must be a Rebel spy. "The fellow needs tidying. I venture to say he's the muddiest man on either side of the line."

"Yes, sir," said Rawlins, with a discreet glance at Grant's own dun-covered boots. "Should we clean him up first?"

"No. Let's get on with it."

Grant went to his cigar case and took out two fresh ones, slipping them in his coat pocket. Then he stepped out into the now bright daylight.

"Good afternoon, sir," he said. "I am General Grant. I am told you are Harrison Raines, claiming to be an army scout, late of the New Mexico Territory."

"That I am." Harry treated the general to one of his Virginia gentleman bows. "At your service, sir."

"I am told that, if your explanation fails to satisfy me, I can have you shot—or hanged. General Halleck said that his preference is for the latter and that I should attend to it quickly. But I have a good deal of time at my disposal presently, and I intend to make use of it."

Harry blinked. This general he had been taken to was a curious fellow—short, and careless in dress, wearing a private's coat with major general's stars on it. He had a sharp, straight nose; a pleasant face; and clear, intelligent eyes. His voice was the calmest Harry had heard in either army.

"I certainly hope you will find my explanation satisfactory, sir," he said, "as it is the truth. I strongly suggested to the other general that he telegraph Washington for confirmation of my identification."

"Yes. You said to contact a Major A. E. Allen. That's why you were taken to Halleck."

Harry took a step closer. "Do you know who he is?"

"General Halleck has informed me. You claim to work for Allan Pinkerton."

"Yes, sir."

"He reports to General McClellan. What are you doing out here?"

"Returning from New Mexico, sir. And a mission."

"What was that?" Grant seated himself on a camp chair and motioned to Harry to take the one opposite it.

"To determine Confederate intentions in the West."

"And did you?"

"Yes. They planned to run a railway to California and establish a blockade-free port on the Sea of Cortes. As well as buy up parts of Mexico."

"But that's been made moot by the battle of Glorieta Pass."

"Yes, sir."

"Were you there?"

"Arrived too late, sir."

"So your mission was for naught."

"Yes, sir. Doesn't matter much anyway, now that the Mississippi's in Union hands."

"Well, it's not quite that. Vicksburg and Port Hudson are still in the enemy's possession. How did you get here?"

"Came through Texas and Louisiana. Got to New Orleans a few days after Admiral Farragut took the town."

"What brings you up here then? Why didn't you take ship back to Washington?"

Harry pulled a cigar of his own from his coat pocket, but it had become soggy from the previous day's rain, and pulled apart. Grant handed him one of the two in his pocket, taking the other for himself. "I've been following a woman, General. I don't know for certain. I can't prove it. But I believe she might be a Rebel agent."

Grant took from his pocket the folded piece of message paper that Halleck had sent along with his request that Grant deal with this man.

"Louise Devereux."

"Yes, sir. I've followed her all the way up the Mississippi.

She killed a man in New Orleans and left him on my doorstep."

Grant consulted the message again. "It says she claims he was a Rebel agent bent on killing her."

"You've talked to her, sir?"

"No, I have not. But others in authority here have done so."

"Well, it wasn't just that. She took from me a large sum of federal gold that I am duty bound to return to, uh, Major A. E. Allen."

Grant squinted at the message paper. "There is mention of that here. She turned a large sum of gold over to General Halleck's headquarters."

"She did?"

"So says General Halleck, and he is in command of this department."

Harry pondered the ground. "Does she claim to be a Union agent?"

"She has satisfied General Halleck in that respect, as you have not, sir."

Harry rubbed at his eyes. "I should like to speak to her, if she is still here."

"I've no idea where she is, Mr. Raines. For the moment, you are restricted to speaking to me—until I render some disposition of this matter."

"Yes, sir. Can you tell me, at least, if she is safe?"

"I gather she is very safe."

"Then I am glad for that."

"Even though you thought her a Rebel agent?"

"I am well acquainted with the lady."

Grant puffed on his cigar, contemplating this man, weighing various considerations, such as Raines's pronounced Virginia accent. To be sure, the general in chief, Winfield Scott, had one similar.

"Can you ride, sir?"

"I rode in here, at some peril, on a horse I took from the Rebels. Your soldiers took it from me."

Grant smiled. "I have no soldiers, sir. I'm deputy commander here. If I had soldiers to command in this place I would be occupied with more important matters than you and Miss Devereux."

"I can ride, General. It it perhaps my only talent."

"I'll provide you with a new mount. I want you to accompany me to a clearing in some woods. It is not far."

Harry stared at him. "Certainly, sir. Whatever you wish."

GRANT chose his roan horse Fox. He ordered up a bay stallion for Harry named Smoke, who'd belonged to a Union officer killed at Shiloh. "He's a jumping horse," said Grant.

Mounting, Harry held the reins close to the animal's neck and turned him, spotting a snake-rail fence a hundred or more yards off. A touch of heel to flank sufficed to set the dark gray horse into motion. He sailed over the barrier with a foot to spare. Harry turned him back quickly—lest someone think he was attempting escape and loose a shot at him—and then took the fence from the other side just as smoothly.

Grant appeared fascinated. "You ride well, sir."

"I raise horses, when I am not otherwise employed by the Federal government."

"You belong in our cavalry. I applied for the cavalry when I graduated from the Point. Horses were fairly much my only pleasure at the Academy."

"They turned you down?"

Grant nodded. "Sent me to the infantry."

"Sorry."

The general had thought upon the matter of where he might be now had that assignment request been granted—doubtless commanding a cavalry brigade somewhere out on the flank. "It's worked out."

WITH Harry, Rawlins, and Colonel York trailing, Grant trotted out into the clearing, walking his horse around the center for two turns until he found the spot he sought.

Harry came up beside him.

"How long have you worked for Mr. Pinkerton?" Grant asked.

"I was recruited at the time of Manassas."

"Pinkerton was a railroad detective, as I recall. In Chicago?"

"Yes, sir. That is correct."

"Have you done any detective work yourself?"

"Yes. I assisted Mr. Pinkerton in the arrest of the Rebel spy Rose Greenhow, and in some other inquiries."

"I was hoping to hear something like that from you. I have had a most unfortunate matter thrust upon me, and it requires a detective to resolve. It most definitely must be resolved. That is why I have not had you marched off to the provost marshal."

Harry tried to read the general's intent in his eyes. For all their clearness, they told him nothing. "Yes, sir."

"We have had a most dastardly murder done—the wife of Congressman Abbott and her sister, a Mrs. Mary Townsend. Both women were ladies of Corinth, and it may well be that the murder was done there. But the bodies were found here. In this very place."

Harry looked about the ground—lumpy bare rocky patches and a sweep of high grass. There was no sign of murder—or even of the war. Only a mile or so removed from the Federal line, the clearing was a place of peace and tranquillity. "Murdered how, sir?"

"Gunshot. Both of them shot through the breast. The oddity of it is that they were found together in the same coffin. Right here, on this spot of ground. They were fully clothed, the one placed upon the other."

"Found when, sir?"

"Two days ago."

"And murdered when?"

"That we do not know. Another oddity is that both bodies were embalmed."

Harry wondered if he had heard the man rightly. " 'Embalmed'?"

"Prepared as though for a funeral."

"In Corinth?"

Grant shrugged. "We have embalmers traveling with this army—and doing far too brisk a business. But none has come forward with any knowledge of this tragic affair."

"Where are the bodies now?"

"Buried, for the moment, at a church up the road called Shiloh. Congressman Abbott has been notified, and we expect he will be here shortly to claim his wife. The other lady is the wife of a Rebel colonel, whose regiment is among those arrayed against us. I suppose arrangements can be made if he finds a way to contact us."

"The Confederates' General Hindman has expressed a strong interest in Mrs. Townsend."

"Expressed to whom?"

"To me. We were briefly detained, and he questioned us about her, thinking I was asking after her, though it was Miss Devereux I was seeking."

"What did he have to say?"

"Not much. Colonel Townsend came upon the scene, and he had a lot to say. While he and General Hindman were conversing, we escaped on two of the general's horses."

"That's unfortunate."

"Sir?"

"I expect you'll be needing to make inquiries in Corinth. And this army will not be going there anytime soon."

"You want me to go there?"

"That would be my wish."

"And if I decline?"

"Then I will send you back to General Halleck. There is little time, sir, and this matter must be resolved."

"A choice between being hanged here or being hanged there."

"You seem a resourceful man, Raines. You must have been to have come all this way through Rebel territory."

Harry nodded. The general took that for assent.

"Good," Grant said, and started to turn his horse.

"General, may I have the assistance of my Canadian friend Jacques Tantou?"

"The Indian? Yes. You may have the assistance of anyone you wish."

"May I keep this horse?"

"Yes. Of course."

"And one for Tantou?"

"Yes. These things I can easily command."

Grant moved Fox to a walk.

"One more thing, General."

Grant turned in the saddle but did not stop. "Yes?"

"How much gold was it that Louise Devereux turned over?"

"I believe the sum was two thousand dollars."

Harry and Tantou had been carrying three thousand that disappeared from under the rope at the Florance House. "Thank you, sir."

Chapter 19

TANTOU had been taken to a hospital tent set by the river. He'd assured Harry that his wound was not serious, but Harry had learned from his experience in three battles that there was no such thing. Torn flesh of even the slightest magnitude could fester and turn gangrenous, admitting no solution but amputation. The mortality rate for that procedure, depending on where the cut was made, exceeded 50 percent.

Harry found the Métis curled up on his cot, seeming oddly small for a man in excess of six feet in height. He was clutching the wounded arm.

Seating himself on what little space remained on the narrow bed, Harry gently touched the man's shoulder. "Jack. It's me. Harry."

"What do you want?" The half-breed did not open his eyes.

"I want to know how you are. I hope that you are well."

"I am in pain. And I do not feel good." This was the first time Harry had ever heard Tantou complain that he hurt.

"Was the bone struck?" He looked at the bandage around the Métis' arm, just below the shoulder. Blood had seeped through it.

"No. But I have pain."

"What do the doctors say?"

"They moved on to others. An orderly told me that I am lucky."

"Can you sit up?"

Tantou lay there a moment without making reply. Finally, reminding Harry of a sick horse, he prepared himself with a quiver of shoulders and then pushed himself upright. He swayed a moment with his eyes closed and then opened them.

Harry produced a flask. "Whiskey?"

The Métis accepted it with a nod of thanks. He took several swallows before handing it back.

"Now some for your wound."

"You are crazy, Harry Raines."

"No, I am not. I have seen doctors do this. It helped their patients."

Tantou pondered this. "It will cause more pain."

"Briefly."

The Métis unwound his bandage and took back the flask. He winced but did not cry out as he splashed the liquor over the ugly, swollen wound. "It has caused more pain."

"Yes. I'm sorry."

"What do you want?"

"We're in a difficult situation," Harry said. "They have telegraphed Washington to confirm we are who we say, but I do not know how long that will take. In the meantime, there is one Union general who wants us hanged or shot and another who wants us to go back to Corinth and do detective work."

"You do not cheer me, Harry Raines."

"It's General Ulysses Grant who wants me to go to Corinth. Two women from there have been found murdered on this side of the line, and he wants me to find out why. If I go, I am going to need your help, if you're well enough."

Tantou looked to the other men in this tent, who all seemed to be taking turns coughing.

"What women?"

"They were sisters, and one of them is the wife of a congressman."

"And what is our reward if we succeed?"

"We would be under Grant's protection."

Tantou rubbed his eyes, then sat straighter. "What of Louise Devereux?"

"She has come through here. She had convinced the generals that she is a Union agent."

"Do you believe that?"

"She confuses me. What I propose is that we ignore her, and do what General Grant requests."

"Were these women shot by the Rebels?"

Harry shrugged. "Don't know. They were found lying together in a coffin, which had been left in a clearing. Each was shot through the chest. And the bodies were embalmed. That is all that I know, except that the other sister was the wife of a Confederate colonel."

Tantou considered all this carefully, then lay down again and closed his eyes. "I will help you. But not today."

GRANT had provided Harry with his aide Colonel York, ostensibly as the Army of the Tennessee's military liaison to the inquiry but in practical terms the portable source for requisitions and orders, as Harry deemed necessary.

What he found most immediately necessary was a pass that would get him to Shiloh Church without interference. Once there, he needed a written order authorizing exhumation of the two sisters. York was quite helpful, but the captain in charge of burials was something of an obstruction.

"You cannot do such a thing. It's a sacrilege. The deceased now lie in church ground. And you need permission of the next of kin."

"I have the permission of General Grant," Harry said, though the general had given him nothing that specific. "The husband of one of the victims is many miles away in Tennessee, and the other is a Confederate officer somewhere on the other side of the line. I intend no desecration. I wish merely to examine the bullet wounds. Then the corpses—the ladies—can be returned to God's good earth. I would also point out that, ultimately, next of kin will undoubtedly be wanting to move the remains elsewhere anyway."

Colonel York was looking elsewhere. The captain went up to him. "Can you vouch for what this man has to say, sir?"

York appeared extremely uncomfortable. "I can say that General Grant has sought this man's help in dealing with these unfortunate murders. Beyond that—"

Harry dug into his pocket and produced the pass Grant had written out for him.

The captain handed it back. "It doesn't authorize you to exhume two civilian corpses," he said.

"It authorizes me to do anything I damn well please. All I ask of you, sir, is that you not interfere." Bold words. Harry really hadn't the courage to back them up. He turned to Colonel York. "If you would, sir, find us two men and two shovels. I will take responsibility for everything else."

"I am a colonel," York said to the captain.

"Sir, I do this under protest."

"That will be noted."

USING York's authority, Harry had the coffin brought into the church, so that the examination could proceed discreetly. One of the soldiers who'd been detailed to assist them used a crowbar to open the lid, damaging it slightly.

Harry was stunned by the beauty of the face that was revealed to him, despite her gray pallor. He put on his spectacles. "Why weren't they buried separately? It looks like they've been left just as they were."

"That's true. General Grant thought it best. Certainly until Congressman Abbott returns and makes other disposition."

"When is he due to return?"

York spread his hands apart to indicate his ignorance. "A message was sent to him, but we've not heard back."

Harry returned his attention to the dead woman on top. "Which sister is this lady?"

"That is Mrs. Abbott. May Abbott. Beneath her is Mrs. Townsend. Mary Townsend. They were born May and Mary Sayres. They're twins. Born in Corinth. Both married politicians. Mrs. Townsend's husband was a U.S. congressman before secession. That's all I know about them."

"That's quite a lot."

"I accompanied Mrs. Abbott across the river the last night—the last night we had word of her."

Harry stepped back. "I will need the services of a surgeon. Do you suppose there is one convenient?"

"Most convenient," York said. "They tend to be employed near the cemeteries." He went to the door.

Harry nodded to the soldiers. "If you would, gentlemen,

I'd like the ladies removed from the casket and laid separately upon the pews."

The soldiers looked at each other dubiously.

"Please, men. General Grant wants this matter resolved
as soon as possible."

They did not move. Harry took a step toward the nearest
of them. "I should point out that I hold the rank of captain."

This surprised York, but he said nothing. The enlisted
man sighed and shook his head but returned to the casket,
motioning to his comrade to go to the coffin's other end.
Harry could not understand their reluctance. Moving bodies
should have been a frequent occupation for Federal soldiers
since Shiloh. Perhaps it had something to do with the
deceased being female.

Mary Townsend was a mirror image of her sister May.
Unlike her sister, she wore rouge, reminding Harry oddly of
Louise. The thought of that lady lying dead like this made
him shudder. He wished he had not told Grant she might
be a Southern agent.

He waited until the surgeon arrived before continuing
with the examination. The doctor, whose name was Horace
Schmidt, appeared displeased with this duty. He was somewhat disheveled, and his uniform was stained and muddied—
doubtless the result of his labors. Harry wished he could have
had his surgeon friend in Washington—Colonel Phineas
Gregg—attend to this task. He wondered how much this
doctor was like Gregg.

He offered Schmidt a drink from his whiskey flask,
which the officer accepted.

"It's a sorrowful task, sir," Harry said, "but I wish to examine the fatal bullet wounds and I thought it best to have a
medical man perform the task, as my knowledge is deficient."

The surgeon, a captain, grunted, then turned to May

Abbott. He looked her over a moment, then pointed to the dark, round hole burned in the fabric of her dress. "There is the wound, sir," he said.

Harry coughed politely. "This is indelicate, but I think it will be necessary to partially undress her so that we might actually see the injured flesh."

Another grunt. Harry proffered the flask again. After taking another, larger swallow, Schmidt bent to his task, pausing first to contemplate the woman's face—as though asking her forgiveness.

After that, he was all business. Undoing the buttons of her blouse, he then raised her up slightly as he pulled the garment off her shoulders and down to reveal her upper chest. Gently lowering her to the pew, he turned back the unbuttoned bodice to reveal her breast.

It surprised Harry that there were no undergarments—though that could have been the work of whoever had performed the embalming. She had a full bosom. The bullet had struck just above the left breast, apparently missing the ribs and passing through the vital organ that was the heart. He asked the doctor to confirm that.

"Yes. Precisely there," said the surgeon.

"If you would, sir, may we determine whether there was an exit wound?"

Schmidt raised her up again, pulling the blouse down further as he looked at her back. Harry came nearer, taking note of a much larger hole between the spine and the left shoulder blade.

"Thank you, sir. And now, the other lady."

The procedure was repeated. Like her sister, Mary Townsend was wearing a dress, but no undergarments. The doctor pointed to a larger opening in almost the same place her sister had been struck.

Harry pondered the difference in the diameters of the two perforations. "Dr. Schmidt, may we now look at her back as well?"

The surgeon, less gently now, rolled the woman onto her side, and then pulled the dress top down a good ten inches. There was nothing—no perforation, no mark upon the skin. He continued to pull down the clothing until he had bared her back to the waist.

"No exit wound," said Harry.

"No, sure ain't," said Schmidt.

"That's peculiar, for the weapon used was of a large caliber."

"Maybe it was a weak powder load," said York, who'd followed the proceedings with great fascination.

"The bullet lies still within the body," said the surgeon.

"Yes," said Harry. "I'd like you to remove it."

The doctor expressed his distaste by spitting on the church floor. "I've enough such work to do on the living."

"These women were murdered, Dr. Schmidt. They deserve justice. That bullet may lead to it."

Schmidt motioned to one of the soldiers to bring forth his instrument case. Taking forth a scalpel, he estimated the round's path into Mrs. Townsend's body, then rolled her onto her back. Probing the wound, he dug deeper and deeper, without success.

"I shall have to go in the other way," he said.

"If you would, sir."

Once he set about it, the grisly business did not take long. He held up the spent round to the light, then handed it to Harry. The much-misshapen object was stained dark with now dried blood.

"I make it to be of .44 caliber," Harry said. He started to hand it to York, but the colonel shrank from it—not unreasonably.

Harry pocketed it. "Thank you, Doctor."

"You want no further examination?"

There were things he might learn from that, but he deemed them not worth any further violation of the women's dignity.

"They should be returned to the grave until the arrival of next of kin."

"See to it," York ordered the soldiers.

"**BOTH** shot through the heart?" Grant asked. "That's strange."

"Not as strange as finding them both in one coffin," Harry responded. "The bullet that killed the one passed completely through and struck the other sister, Mrs. Townsend. We were able to recover the round." He held it up, offering it to the general's closer observation.

Grant declined. "No, thank you. No need."

They were seated in Grant's tent, with Harry, York, and Rawlins in a semicircle of camp chairs facing the general.

"They were both wearing dresses, but nothing underneath," Harry said.

"That's strange, too," said Grant. "What do you make of it?"

"The bodies were embalmed. Whoever dressed them afterward may have been in haste."

"I'll leave it to you to answer that puzzle. What will you do next?"

"There's much I don't know about these sisters. Is Congressman Abbott expected soon?"

Grant shrugged. "I still cannot say."

"Then I should go into Corinth. With your help, sir, I think there's a way." He briefly summarized his idea.

"General Halleck will never approve of that."

Harry stared at the ground. "Then what are we to do?"

"We will not inform General Halleck," Grant said. He bent forward. "But what you see of the enemy in Corinth, this you must report to us."

"Yes, sir."

"That requires your coming back."

"Unless your army captures the place while I'm there."

"We could be another month in accomplishing that."

"I trust you don't doubt that I intend to come back?"

Grant spoke through a veil of cigar smoke. "Let us say I am hopeful of that prospect."

Chapter 20

"YOU'RE sure you're well enough to do this?" Harry asked Tantou.

By way of answer, Tantou mounted his horse, sitting in his saddle as straight as ever, though he held his injured arm at a crooked angle. "Let us go now, Harry Raines."

The Métis had removed the bandage that had been wound around his arm, for it would have given the game away. This had caused a bit of bleeding, which was all to the good. He could claim a fresh wound.

Mounting the animal he had stolen from General Hindman, which the Union Army had since returned to him, Harry nodded to the lieutenant leading the cavalry troop that had been assigned to accompany them.

"Which way do you want to go?" the cavalry officer asked.

"Whichever way affords the least danger of getting shot by Rebels as we cross the line."

"That'll be around our right flank. It'll take a while."

"The 'while' I can handle. It's the bullets I want to avoid."

The lieutenant waited for Harry to draw up next to him, then moved his mount out, the rest of the cavalrymen following. Tantou rode at the rear of the column but seemed able to keep up.

"I haven't told my men what's afoot here," the lieutenant said. "General Grant said the fewer to know the better."

"A sensible fellow, the general. But what is it they think they're doing?"

"Escorting a scouting party."

"And when the time comes?"

"I'll explain matters otherwise."

"And the shooting?"

"I'll commence that a minute or two after the time comes, but you'd better make good use of the time."

"Don't worry about that."

"It would be more convincing if you fired a shot or two back at us."

"I suppose it would."

"Are you good at missing?"

"Without my spectacles, I am among the best."

THEY made their turn south too close to the Rebel left flank and so encountered pickets while still riding as a group. One of the Rebels stepped out from behind a tree in the woods ahead and loosed a round in their direction, aiming far too high. Harry saw no choice but to bolt from the Yankee cavalry troop at that moment, though this gave him no opportunity to reconnoiter the ground ahead and the disposition of the Confederate troops arrayed before him.

He feared Tantou had not been paying attention, but was happily surprised to note the Métis coming up behind him.

Glancing back, he saw the Indian holding his seat well while guiding his mount with one hand.

They were covering ground fast, yet the Union cavalry troop had not yet stirred. Harry took out his Navy Colt and sent a round in its direction, aiming high.

Too high. He struck a tree branch some twenty-five or thirty feet above ground. It cracked and fell on one of the troopers, prompting the lieutenant to commence the Union's part of the charade.

"After them, men!" A bugler commenced a call Harry did not recognize.

Harry fired one more revolver shot, again high, and then concentrated his attention on the Rebel soldiers ahead. Only a few were visible. Though the picket who had shot at them was busy reloading his musket, the others were staring dumbly, trying to make sense of the little drama.

The Yankee cavalrymen now added their weapons to the fracas, prompting the gaping Confederates to see to their own defense. Weaving back and forth, Harry continued pounding hell-bent for the south. There was quite a lot of gunfire now, which he could only hope would find no human mark. He certainly didn't want to be responsible for any injury to the Northern cavalrymen.

Once past the pickets, assured that Tantou was keeping up, Harry bore right into another patch of woods, charging on through the trees and brambles and out onto a wide, undulating meadow beyond. Jumping his horse over a shallow stream, he urged it up a small rise that followed, finding himself on a railroad bed with two tracks. Reining in the animal to wait for Tantou, he looked to the north. There was smoke, but not from any approaching train. The Union Army appeared to be burning something a mile or two up the line.

He would not dally to find out what. "I want to get these

horses back to Hindman's headquarters, where we took them," he said. "Can you manage that?"

"If they don't shoot us on the way in."

"Then we must move fast."

ON the outskirts of the town, the Rebel army had set a sort of breastworks across the tracks, as though they feared the Federals would attack by train. Harry thought of dodging off back into the woods to avoid this barrier, but feared he'd only draw deadly fire. He needed to establish his bona fides as one of them.

Slowing his horse to a trot, he raised his right hand. Several soldiers stood up, aiming their muskets, but Harry kept on, easing now into walk. A sergeant wearing a dress sword and hefting a large dragoon revolver stepped out from behind the logs.

"I'm Captain Harrison Raines," Harry said. "I'm a scout for the army, and I have information for General Hindman. I must get to his headquarters."

The sergeant took a step closer. "Where's your uniform, *captain*?"

"It proved an inconvenience." Harry leaned down from the saddle, pulling a folded paper from his pocket and gesturing with it. "Now, look you here. I must get this information to General Hindman. I have a troop of Yankee cavalry after me, and my servant's been wounded."

Tantou obligingly gripped his injured arm.

"What kind of scout has a servant, *captain*?"

"I am a *gentleman*, sir. Now let me pass so that I may report to General Hindman." He pointed to his horse's brand: *C.S.A.* "This is the general's own horse, damn it. Allow me to bring it back."

A young lieutenant now appeared from behind the logs, looking nervous and apprehensive. He walked up to Harry's horse, squinting at the brand.

"Take these men to General Hindman, Sergeant," he said. "Under escort."

Harry stole a quick look back at the artillery massed behind the breastworks as they left. They were Quaker guns, logs painted over to look like cannons.

HINDMAN, dressed this day in a cavalry officer's short jacket, tight pants, and a red ruffled shirt, rose from his desk, astounded. "You've come back?"

"Yes, sir," said Harry, standing at attention. Tantou went to a side chair, still holding his arm.

"But you stole my horses. And you came back?"

"We borrowed your horses, sir—but only to prove our worth as army scouts, for I feared you were not believing me."

"What are you talking about?"

"I have important intelligence here, General," Harry said, handing over the paper he had exhibited to the sergeant. "The current positions of the Yankee army."

Hindman made no move. "Truly?"

"As best as we could scout 'em."

Grant had seen to the careful preparation of the map. It showed the Union left where it actually was along Bridge Creek—as the Confederates already very well knew—but it showed the center and right elements placed much closer to Corinth than Halleck had allowed them to progress, and in far greater numbers than actually existed on the ground. He'd also mixed up the divisions, moving Sherman and Lew Wallace on the map to places where they were not.

Hindman spread out the map, flattening it with his hand.

"If this is true, they're much nearer than we thought. Have they brought up artillery?"

Grant hadn't thought of that. "Yes," Harry said. "In haste, I failed to note it." He pointed on the map to where he'd seen the rising smoke. "They've put some in here."

Hindman peered more closely. "You must have ridden through the entire Yankee army to learn all this. How'd you manage that?"

Harry moved to change the subject. "I also have news of Mrs. Townsend."

The general's head snapped up. "You do? He has been asking."

"Yes. I recall that from my earlier encounter with the colonel."

"Well, what is it?"

"She and her sister, a Mrs. Abbott, were seen together in a clearing near the Corinth Road."

"Within our lines?"

"No, sir. The other side. They were also seen at a church. Shiloh Church."

"There? The fighting was terrible around there."

"Yes. This was after the battle, sir."

"Any word of them since?"

"No, sir."

"So they're on the Federal side of the line?"

"I believe so, sir."

"Why would Mrs. Townsend cross over to the Yankees?"

"Perhaps to meet with her sister."

"Yes," Hindman said. "Of course."

"My man Tantou, sir. He was shot by the Yankees. In the arm, sir."

Hindman gave the Métis the merest glance. "Take him to

the surgeons. I want to show this map to General Beauregard."

"Yes, sir. Could you write us a pass? We were detained once trying to come into the town. Almost shot by our own side."

The general scribbled something on a piece of notepaper, signing his name with a flourish. "Report to me later."

"Thank you, sir. And horses?"

"You will walk. This is a small city."

THE Corinth House hospital was in fact not far. They set off down Railroad Street, which had the main commercial establishments of the town on one side and railroad tracks on the other. They kept close to the tracks, wishing to avoid whatever trouble might lurk among the townspeople passing on the opposite side. It was hot, without any hope of more cooling rain.

They passed many railroad passenger cars on the tracks, all empty—most with the windows standing open.

"Your arm?" Harry asked.

"Still there," said Tantou.

"Still hurt?"

"Yes."

"At the hospital, we shall put some more whiskey on it. You have seen what can happen to people whose wounds are ill attended."

"What I see now is that General Hindman does not trust you."

"What?"

"We are being followed."

Harry stopped and put on his spectacles, pausing further long enough to note that the Lieutenant Shakes who'd pursued him on his earlier visit to Corinth was now doing so again, making the same pace and in company of four infantrymen.

"It's all right," Harry said, resuming their walk. "We are going where we said. I doubt they'll interfere."

KNOCKING at the hospital door, they were greeted by two female nurses, who identified themselves as Beth Howard and Kathleen Jurgensen. Bowing, Harry asked if he might speak to Kate Cumming.

"Oh, no sir," said nurse Howard.

"No, I'm afraid not," said nurse Jurgensen.

"She's not ill?" Harry asked.

"No, sir," said nurse Howard. "She has removed to Okolona."

"Is that a hospital?"

"No, sir," said nurse Jurgensen. "It is a town. South of here. South of Tupelo. They are moving many of the wounded there."

"Why? This seems a perfectly good hospital."

"It is, but they are moving the southern wounded away from here as quickly as they can," said nurse Howard. "They're leaving the Yankee patients behind—except for those only lightly wounded, those well enough to walk. Those, they're sending south as prisoners."

Harry glanced behind him. Lieutenant Shakes and his men had taken up station in the street, waiting and watching. "Actually, ladies, I'm inquiring after a woman—a lady—who might have been a nurse here. She's missing, and many are trying to find her, including General Hindman."

"Who is that, Mr. . . . ?" said nurse Jurgensen.

"Captain. Captain Harrison Raines. I'm an army scout.

So is my associate, Mr. Tantou. He's been wounded, shot by the Yankees, and I was hoping to find a surgeon."

"Oh, yes, Captain," said nurse Howard. "Come in. There is still a doctor on the premises."

They opened the door and stepped to either side. Harry entered first. Tantou followed, gripping his arm and grimacing. Shakes and his men remained outside.

Turning down a corridor Harry had not noticed on his earlier visit, the two women led them to a sort of waiting room, where a medical orderly sat dozing in one of the uncomfortable-looking wooden chairs that lined the walls.

"Wait here and I'll fetch Dr. Morgan," said nurse Howard.

Nurse Jurgensen remained behind, however. Ushering Harry and Tantou to two chairs, she sat down on a third.

"The lady you were inquiring after, Captain Raines?"

"A Mrs. Townsend. An army officer's wife. She—"

"Oh, yes. Poor Mrs. Townsend. Mary Townsend. She's a nurse, yes, indeed. Many of the ladies of Corinth have volunteered. But she was assigned to another hospital, a smaller one, in the Baptist church. It's said she went out to tend the wounded during the big battle. She never returned. Do you suppose the Yankees took her prisoner?"

"As she was a noncombatant, I should certainly hope not."

Nurse Howard appeared in the doorway. "Dr. Morgan is busy amputating a Yankee soldier's leg. But he says he will attend to you in a few minutes. Would you like to wait in his surgery?"

"But you said he's—"

"He has another surgery where he doesn't do amputations. It's just down the hall. I'll leave you with another nurse there."

"We're off duty," said nurse Jurgensen. "We were just leaving when you arrived at the door."

Harry stood up. "Thank you, ladies. You've been most gracious."

"This way," said nurse Howard.

She led him now back into the land of moans and groans, though they were fewer than on Harry's first visit. Nurse Howard indicated a room on the left. This time Harry let Tantou enter first.

Another nurse was at a cupboard, filling a shelf with clean rolled bandages. She had long, dark hair and wore a stained apron over the skirt of an expensive dress.

"Lie down on that table," she said over her shoulder. "Be with you in a moment."

Tantou did as commanded, rolling up his sleeve. Harry stood next to the table, certain of his perceptions, but waiting to make sure.

Finally, after nurses Howard and Jurgensen bid farewell and left, the other nurse turned around, evidencing no surprise, except to see which of them was on the table.

"I thought you'd be the wounded one, Harry," she said.

"If I'd known I'd be nursed by you, Louise," he said, "I would have seen to it."

Chapter 21

THE surgeon made no appearance. Perhaps he felt any procedure less than dismemberment a nuisance not worthy of his time. Louise tended to Tantou's injury herself, cleaning the wound and then winding a fresh bandage around it. Bidding him wait, she suggested to Harry that they repair to a more suitable location for discreet discourse.

It proved to be a place where Harry certainly had no wish to go—the yard behind the hospital. Enclosed by a picket fence, it was strewn with every imaginable kind of refuse, from rotting garbage to piles of bloodstained bandages and clothing. A number of empty coffins had been stacked by the back porch. There were no corpses, but a large, open-topped crate stood filled with dismembered limbs, including a leg that was dripping fresh blood over the side.

"What a romantic bower," Harry said.

"No one comes out here if it can be avoided," she replied. "Come. You must look as though you are helping me."

She went to a well that stood improbably at the rear of the yard, lowering a bucket in practiced manner.

"You make a lovely drudge," he said.

"Cease your flippancy, Harry. We have little time. Why have you come back to Corinth?"

"Orders from General Ulysses Grant. Do you know him?"

She shook her head. "Only that he won a victory up in Tennessee."

"Well, he knows you."

"He commanded at Shiloh. I know that, too. Did he send you down here to capture me?"

"You are not the object of his interest. There were two women of this town—twin sisters—a Mrs. May Abbott and a Mrs. Mary Townsend. They are his preoccupation."

"I know of them. Why do you say 'were'?"

"You mustn't say anything. No one in Corinth seems to be aware of it, but they are dead. Murdered. General Grant has taken it upon himself to discover why, and I am his instrument."

"But what of me? I never met them. I've not been here long. I only know that Mrs. Townsend was socially prominent here, and that she had worked as a nurse, like so many."

She began hauling up the bucket.

"You can help me," he said. "Ask among your fellow nurses in town if Mrs. Townsend had enemies, and when she was last seen. I'd be particularly interested to learn if she had talked about her sister to anyone and if the sister ever reached Corinth."

Louise set the sloshing bucket on the edge of well wall. The sleeves of her dress were rolled up, exposing her lovely arms. He remembered well the soft, fine hairs on the back of them.

"Why should I do this?" she asked. "It is none of my concern."

"Do it for General Grant. You claim to be working in the Union cause. Perform a service for it."

She snorted. "You should not be obstructing my work with matters that have nothing to do with me."

He looked about the yard. "What is your work? Nursing Rebel soldiers back to health so they may continue the war?"

"Don't be such a dolt, Harry. There is no better place to pick up information than a hospital. And most of the patients here now are Federals."

"And you are learning things from them?"

"Stop it, Harry. You are vexing me." She brushed a strand of her long hair away from her eye, revealing a tear, which she wiped away as well.

He stepped closer. They had been out here too long, but he didn't care. "When this is over, I thought I might ask you to marry me."

"And the fair Caitlin Howard?"

He reached to take the bucket from her. "I can only marry one woman at a time."

"Let us talk no more of this, please." She started back across the yard.

"I've persuaded General Hindman here that I am a Rebel scout, but not all here believe that," he said.

"That's because you're a terrible actor—though I know you pride yourself in that talent."

"No matter. I have a pass from Hindman and will continue my inquiries. I will come by here tomorrow—to learn what you have learned."

"I may not be here."

He paused, taking hold of her arm. "Louise. There's something else. You've crossed the battle line twice now, with apparent ease. What route do you take? I came down the Memphis and Charleston Railroad line and was lucky I wasn't killed."

"It is well you are so lucky, Harry, for you are a fool. Corinth is an exceedingly dangerous place, and you should not be here. You treat everything as some boy's adventure— a lark. Death is no lark, Harry."

"You told the Federals I was a Rebel agent."

"No, I did not. I suggested that as a possibility, hoping that would detain you and thus end your harassment of me."

"General Grant, happily, did not believe you," he said.

"More's the pity."

"What route?"

"The Tuscumbia River. West of town. Stay close to its banks. That will hide you from view."

"Miss Devereux!"

They both froze. On the porch steps, her arms folded belligerently, stood a large, middle-aged woman with a face as fiercely ugly as her disagreeable voice. As if she weren't formidable enough, behind her stood a black manservant with huge shoulders.

"What is it, Mrs. Hudson?" Louise asked softly.

"You know very well what it is! I have instructed you not to consort with the patients. You have only been here a few days and I have had to tell you this repeatedly. Nothing could be more detrimental to the good order and moral standing of this hospital. Now I find you in the yard with one—unchaperoned!"

"This man is not a patient," Louise said. "He brought a comrade here and was helping me with the water."

"I watched you. You were at the well for an unseemly time with him." The dreadful-looking woman drew herself up. "I am dismissing you, Miss Devereux. We can do without your services."

"You haven't enough nurses to cope with things as it is."

She swept by the woman, jarring her aside somewhat, leaving Harry standing there with the bucket.

"I'll just bring this in," he said.

"You shall not!" said the woman. "Set it down!" He did so. "Now remove yourself from the premises!"

"I cannot, madam. I have left a friend in the surgery."

"You will inquire after him later!" She extended her long arm, pointing to a gate in the fence. "Now go!"

HARRY simply went around to the front of the building and, with a nod to the still lingering Lieutenant Shakes and his men, ascended to the veranda to wait for Tantou. He remained there an irritatingly long time, but forbore reentering the establishment for fear of another encounter with the formidable Mrs. Hudson.

The Métis emerged finally, looking haggard and spent. "I am sorry, Harry Raines," he said. "I was sleeping."

"Sitting on that table?"

"Louise Devereux put me in a ward."

"Why?"

"To attend to me."

"Are you worse, Jack?"

"No. I am better. But she wanted to attend to me until that wolf-voiced woman went away."

"And did she?"

"Yes?"

"And Louise?"

"She went away also."

Returning to the street, they moved off as briskly as Tantou could manage, wanting to get some distance ahead of Shakes and company. This was easily done, as the lieutenant took time to get his men into marching order first.

"What now?" Tantou asked.

"We go to the Baptist church hospital."

"What will we do there?"

"You will wait outside this time, and give the alarm if anybody dangerous comes by."

"In this place everybody is dangerous, Harry Raines."

"So Louise did tell me."

HE was greeted at the church by a very plain-faced woman with a kindly disposition named Mrs. Oates, who invited him in as she might into a humble dwelling.

"Are you looking for a wounded soldier?" she asked.

The church was small and functioned as a single ward. The pews had been pushed to the sides, and most of the patients lay on cots or pallets on the floor. There were two other women present, neither of whom Harry recognized.

If he claimed to be in search of a patient, his justification for being here would be quickly exhausted. The men here were mostly Union soldiers who'd been wounded at Shiloh. He would have no acquaintance with any of them.

As Mr. Pinkerton always said, the truth is the best lie.

"I am Captain Harrison Raines," Harry said. "I've come from General Hindman. He's asked me to inquire into the disappearance of a Mrs. Mary Townsend. I believe she was a nurse here?"

"Yes." The woman gave a nervous glance to the other nurses. "How may I help you?"

"To begin with, I've no exact knowledge as to when she disappeared."

"I'm not sure anyone has. It was at the time of the Shiloh engagement. We were very crowded with wounded then. There were injured men waiting outside on the ground. We needed every nurse, and she failed to appear when expected."

"Did you go looking for her?"

"We sent one of the darkies to her house. Her husband was there—Colonel Townsend. He said she had left for the hospital earlier that morning."

A nearby patient gave a loud groan. One of the other women came over to him with a damp rag and began wiping his brow, speaking quietly to him.

"She had a sister, a Mrs. Abbott," Harry said. "I was told she was headed—that she may have visited Corinth recently."

"Yes. May. I was at school with both the Sayres sisters."

"And was she here?"

"No. She is married to a Yankee congressman. She lives up North."

"No one here has seen her?"

She shook her head, then turned to her companions. They both looked at him blankly. "No, Captain Raines. I've had no encounter with May since her marriage." Her lip began to tremble. "Do you think some evil has befallen Mrs. Townsend?"

Here a lie was called for. "I should hope not, Mrs. Oates." There were no black faces to be seen in the church. "Did Mrs. Townsend have a servant?"

"She has many servants."

"I mean one who went about with her—accompanied her here, perhaps. A personal maid."

"Yes. Alva. She went with her everywhere."

"Have you seen her since Mrs. Townsend's disappearance?"

Mrs. Oates put a hand to her mouth. "Why, no. Perhaps she is keeping to the house."

Tantou stuck his head in the doorway. "Harry Raines. Danger comes."

"Where is the Townsend house?" Harry asked, ignoring the warning.

"It is the largest house in Corinth, two blocks west of the square. A white house. You will—"

The door slammed open thunderously. Looking like some fiendish apparition in her dark dress and bonnet, Mrs. Hudson surveyed the interior with stark disapproval. But this time she kept her grating voice low.

"You will remove yourself from this hospital, Mr. Raines," she said. "I have dismissed Miss Devereux. I would drive you both from Corinth if I could." Her voice grew louder now. "And perhaps I can!"

Before Harry could move, Mrs. Oates stepped up. "I'll see him out, Mrs. Hudson," she said. She hurried him along past the angry crone and out onto the front steps. "I'm sorry, Captain Raines. Another time."

Harry took that as an invitation. "Thank you, ma'am."

Tantou fell in behind him.

AT the next corner they decided to split up, hoping to confound Lieutenant Shakes by making him divide his forces. The gambit failed, as Shakes and his little band just kept on after Harry, but it was useful knowledge that he would do this.

Harry went directly to the front door, knocking on it

sharply. After a long interval, a black woman responded, opening the door only far enough for Harry to see one large, apprehensive eye. "Yes?"

"I'm Captain Raines. I need to speak to Colonel Townsend."

The door opened perhaps two inches wider. "The colonel, he ain't here."

"I've come from General Hindman. I must speak to him."

She took note of Lieutenant Shakes and friends on the walk behind Harry, their presence ironically providing credence to his story. "He won't be back until suppertime."

"When's that?"

"Seven o'clock."

"He always takes his supper here?"

"Yes, sir. Every night. When he can."

"Is Mrs. Townsend here?"

He could see both eyes now. The apprehension now increased. "No, sir, she sure ain't."

"When we will she return? Suppertime?"

"Don't know."

"What about her sister Mrs. Abbott? Is she here?"

"No, sir. She bin gone as long as Mrs. Townsend."

"Are you Alva?"

"No. Alva, she's gone, too."

"My respects to Colonel Townsend, then," he said, retreating a step. "I'll call upon him later."

HARRY waited for Tantou to rejoin him, then led his odd parade back to Railroad Street.

"Where are we to stay tonight?" Tantou asked.

"The hotels are full," Harry said. "We'll have to camp in the woods, like the army scouts we're pretending to be."

"And where do we eat?"

"We shall repair to that grocery where we bought food before. But after dark."

Tantou rubbed his arm. "Why so late?"

"Scouting to do. I'd like you to make your way back to the Townsend house. Ascertain if the colonel does indeed come back. See if you can find out how many black people are at that residence, and what the rear of the house is like."

"What it is like?"

"Whether I might get into the house that way."

"I will do it, Harry Raines. But I'm hoping you will buy much food and whiskey at the grocery. I will be hungry, and thirsty for whiskey."

"All we can carry."

"Where will you go?"

"To the mortuaries. We've passed three, and they're all humming like factories. I shall make some inquiries."

"Won't General Hindman wonder why your search for Mrs. Townsend takes you to embalmers?"

"I hope to keep them all wondering."

There was the screeching sound of a train whistle behind them. Harry and Tantou turned to see a locomotive chuffing onto a siding, spewing sparks and a black, sooty cloud of smoke that darkened the clear, late afternoon sky. Hissing steam came from the side as it passed, slowing. It was hauling three cars—all empty.

"We will leave this place tomorrow," Harry said, raising his voice over the rattle of the cars.

"To go back to General Grant?"

"Yes. Louise told me of a way."

"I will bet you it's over the edge of a cliff, Harry Raines."

"We part at the corner. I'll see you at the grocery."

THERE proved to be more than a dozen mortuaries in Corinth. Two were proper establishments long predating Sumter. The others had sprung up to deal with the war trade as the Union Army pushed it the town's way. Harry started with the respectable places.

The first did not seem so respectable inside. It had been overwhelmed by death. The proprietor was wearing an apron and stained gloves.

"Good afternoon, sir," Harry said. "I fear I shall be needing your services."

The man leaned back against the desk he'd been standing near. "Hope it's not tonight."

"No, sir. Tomorrow, I think. An army officer has died of wounds out in the field. They'll be bringing him in tomorrow."

The other removed his gloves, wiping his brow with the back of his hand. "Well, he will not be the first. Who is this officer?"

Harry hadn't thought of a name—and so he did, seizing upon one he remembered distastefully from his last visit to Richmond. "General McCubbin. Nestor McCubbin. A very large man, I'm afraid. Extremely large. Weighed in excess of three hundred pounds."

"And still does, I presume."

"Yes. We shall be requiring a very large coffin—one that might otherwise handily accommodate two persons."

The undertaker blinked. "I've not heard of this general. And he's a field officer?"

"Up from Alabama," Harry said, as though that explained everything. "Have you such a coffin?"

"No, I do not."

"Could one be built by tomorrow?"

"Not by this establishment, sir. We have too much business before you."

"Can you think of another place where I might obtain one?"

"Masterson's, over on Bunch Street. He's my main competitor. I know that he has dealt with such custom—an outsized deceased of remarkable proportions."

"Yes?" Within the past few days?"

"No, no. Two years ago or more. It was before the war."

"I thank you, sir. I shall seek elsewhere."

The man pulled on his gloves. As Harry had not noticed before, there was a dead soldier, still in uniform, lying on a cloth upon the floor.

He made the mournful rounds of all the other such establishments he could find—with no success until he came to a long shed near the tracks that distinguished itself from a mere hovel with a sign saying, "Thomas O'Toole, Esq. Expert Embalming. Low Rates for Soldiers."

It was turning dark now. Hunger had captured his attention. Thinking that no one involved with such fine ladies as the Sayres sisters could possibly have any connection with so disreputable an enterprise, Harry thought of heading directly to the grocery without further digression. But something stayed him. Entering through the squeaking slat door, he was assailed at once by a noxious smell that seemed to combine the chemical and the natural process it was intended to retard.

"Good evening, sir," he said to a wormy-looking fellow who looked as though his previous job had been cleaning up in such establishments. "I am in need of a casket."

"I ain't no carpenter. I buys 'em myself."

"It's perhaps something you have in stock. A very large casket, for a very large gentleman—so large that a coffin that would accommodate him would accommodate two other people."

The man was sitting on a board table, eating a large chunk of bread. "Had one like that. Made for a fat man like yours. But it's been bought, some days ago."

"By whom?"

"Is that your business?"

Harry smiled. "I am Captain Raines, army scout, and I am doing this on behalf of a fallen high-ranking officer. If I can find this outsized coffin, then my mission is fulfilled and I can return to my regular duty."

The man swung his legs back and forth a few times. "The army builds coffins—any size that's needed. If you're with the army, why'nt you have 'em build one for you? Army's been making coffins since Donelson."

"None has been conveniently obtained," said Harry. He reached into a pocket and gave the man five dollars of Mr. Pinkerton's gold. "Just tell me who bought it."

"Don't know her name."

" 'Her'? A woman bought it?"

"One of the nurses. We got so many in town now."

"Where did you send it? One of the hospitals?"

"Didn't send it. She had a black man come around with a wagon."

One last question occurred to Harry. "Was she pretty, this woman?"

"Couldn't say that. No, sir."

"Thank you."

* * *

COLD beefsteak, beans, corn bread, and whiskey was the menu for dinner. Harry and Tantou had certainly dined on less in New Mexico Territory, and were happy to have so ample a repast in a city so filled with hungry soldiery.

They had made their camp at the railroad yards, between two tracks bearing two idle trains minus their engines. The two of them were hardly noticeable with so many soldiers in bivouac around them.

Tantou reported that Colonel Townsend had come home to his house. After his meal, the African women retired to their quarters, leaving the colonel in his study. Tantou had waited until he saw the man put aside his papers and go for his whiskey, then left.

"Do you know now who killed those women, Harry Raines?" he asked.

"No, Tantou," said Harry between chews on his meat, which was tough and stringy. "But I think we have narrowed the possibilities."

The Métis stared at his tin plate. "To what?"

"You mean 'to whom?'" said Harry.

Tantou grunted. "Talk how you like. Who killed them?" He drank hard from the demijohn of whiskey Harry had bought. Tantou seemed bent on getting drunk, and Harry was of a mind to join him.

"Don't know," said Harry, taking back the jug. "But I have narrowed down the whys."

"How many whys are left?"

"Maybe a dozen."

"Have more whiskey, Harry Raines."

He did. "I need to get into the Townsend house, Jack."

"I told you. Colonel Townsend is there. He had dinner. He is probably in bed now."

"You didn't tell me why you think that."

"I don't want to."

"Why not?"

"Because he had a guest to dinner, and she hadn't left when I departed from the backyard."

"Who?"

"I shouldn't tell you."

"Damn it, Jack, why not?"

"It was Louise Devereux."

Harry chewed down a large bite of meat. "Did she come through the front door, or the rear?"

"That house has two front doors and three rear ones."

"Which did she use?"

"One of the rear."

Harry put aside his memories. "Did she leave?"

"Not before I did." He leveled his gaze at Harry's coat pocket. "Have you cigars?"

Harry removed his case, taking out two long, thin cylinders of tobacco leaf, handing one to Tantou. "Do the black people sleep in the house?"

"No, Harry Raines. There are cabins behind the kitchen. The slaves sleep there."

"Do you think I could enter that house now without being noticed?"

"No, I think the colonel's a man who shoots before he thinks."

"Hmmm." Harry watched the smoke from his cigar rise into the black, starry sky.

"Is there some way we could make them leave the premises?"

"Yes. A fire. But it would either burn up what you are looking for inside that house or it would go out and they would come right back."

"I need to talk to General Grant. We can go north. Around

the lines. Louise said we should take this river that runs to the west of the city."

"I can find it."

"We'll leave before dawn."

"Good. I want to leave."

"Will you wake in time?"

"I will wake before you, Harry Raines."

$\mathbf{A}\mathbf{S}$ they completed their preparations for departure in the darkness, it occurred to Harry that he had neglected something basic to their needs.

"Horses," he said.

"What about them?" Tantou said, taking the opportunity to relieve himself by the side of one of the railroad cars.

"We don't have any."

"There's a horse line on the other side of the tracks. It will be easy, Harry Raines."

$\mathbf{T}\mathbf{H}\mathbf{E}$ mounts were indeed easy. Saddles were not. Harry and Tantou approached them slowly along the railway tracks, talking casually as they drew near, pretending to belong in that vicinity. They walked along the line in that manner, all the while looking for tack but finding none.

"What have they done with it?" Harry asked quietly. "These mounts have only halters."

"It's all they will need," Tantou said.

"What do you mean?"

"On the trains."

They walked on a few paces. Finally Harry stopped, looking back down the railroad tracks, which were choked with passenger and freight cars.

"I see what you mean," Harry said.

"What shall we do?"

"Can you ride bareback?"

"I can ride any way there is to ride."

"We have only this way."

"Then let us go." The Métis observed their surroundings a moment. "We walk them out. Into the trees."

"Yes. Best way. Take from the middle of the line."

No one was watching them. There was a noisy card game at one end of the row, a sleeping sentry at the other. Certainly there was no need for further hesitation. Their situation could get no better.

"Pick a dark horse," Harry said.

Tantou gave him a disdainful look. "Would I take a white horse, Harry Raines?"

"Sorry, Jack."

THEY led their purloined mounts between the railroad cars for perhaps half a mile, then cut into the woods just outside the town. There they waited for any sound of alarm.

But there was no outcry. Harry could scarcely understand the laxity that had overtaken this place. The Confederates seemed to have tired of Corinth. The Union was not giving battle. There was consequently no reason to be there. It seemed almost that the Rebels were abandoning the war.

"Let us mount up," Harry said.

THEY struck out due west, expecting to find the Tuscumbia River in short time, but they were more than two hours getting to it. Following the watercourse in the dim moonlight, taking careful note of the path of that celestial orb, Harry came to an unfortunate realization.

"It's no wonder there are so few soldiers here," he said. "This river runs northwest. It goes miles to the left of the Federal positions. It'll take us forever to get back to Grant."

"Not if we ride fast."

Harry pulled back on the halter line, pulling his mount's head to the side and slowing it to a halt.

"That is not fast, Harry Raines."

"I want to stop here and light a fire."

"Why?"

"I want to write a note to Grant, and I need light to do that."

"Why do you need to write to Grant if you are going to see him?"

"I'm not going to see him. Not yet. You ride to his camp. I am going back to Corinth."

"You are crazy, Harry Raines. This will be the last of you."

"Maybe not. At all events, this is what I am going to do."

Chapter 22

HARRY turned away from the river too soon on the return ride, and got lost. It was nearly morning by the time he reached the outskirts of Corinth, there abandoning his stolen mount. Sentries had been posted at both the roads leading into the town from the west, but he found a way between these guard stations that kept him from their view. A dim gray light was entering the sky in the east by the time he reached the Townsend home.

The kitchen was a separate building in the rear, not far from the slave quarters. Harry avoided both, going to the side gallery. He suspected that the front door would be bolted and had no wish to expose himself to the view of any provost guard patrols who might be coming down the street. But the windows were open. He eased himself through one and found himself in a side parlor.

He stood listening to the sounds of the house, all seeming normal and natural, including snores decidedly male. He could make out the shape of a table against the wall. As he hoped, there were candles on it. Lighting one, he held it as a torch before him, setting forth.

The central hall led to a wide, curving staircase. A door to the left opened into a much larger parlor. A door a short ways farther on the right opened to what Harry sought: the study.

There was a large desk at one wall and a much smaller writing desk in the opposite corner. He went to the latter first, judging it to have belonged to the mistress of the house. Opening the lid carefully, he was greeted by a number of drawers and pigeonholes. Finding three separate sets of letters, he simply shoved those into his coat pockets for later perusal. The drawers yielded little else, though he was surprised to find a small percussion cap pocket pistol in one. It was loaded. He put it in his pocket as well.

A sudden noise at the rear of the house made him reach for his own Navy Colt, but listening, he realized it was made by servants readying the separate kitchen for the morning labors. He still had time, but not much of it.

Ignoring the colonel's desk, he returned to the hall and began a slow, careful ascent of the stairs, heading for the snores. Pausing before an open door, he pushed it fully open, noting the large form of Colonel Townsend lying crosswise on an enormous canopied bed. To the left was a mirrored clothes rack, with his resplendent uniform coat on it. Moving nearer, Harry noted the man's sword and, on the other side, a wide belt and a holster, from which the grip of a large pistol extended. This was all he sought.

Pulling it forth, he caught the front sight of the weapon on a leather strap, causing it to fall to the floor with a loud thump.

The snoring ceased. Harry shrank back to the side of the rack, holding his breath as he waited for Townsend to react. All the man did was roll on his side. Harry retrieved the pistol and stuck it in his belt, then moved to the doorway, pausing again.

Do the guilty sleep so easily, unconcerned? Pinkerton had told Harry that Abraham Lincoln and Jefferson Davis shared an inability to sleep because of the massive number of deaths for which they and their policies were responsible. What of a single death? Or two?

Townsend rolled back and recommenced his snoring. Harry was out of the house within a minute.

HE headed for the camp he and Tantou had established along the tracks, astonished to find the railroad and its workers in motion. Trains were being organized and coupled— locomotives chuffing backward and connecting to their burdens with loud clangs.

Waiting for a train with five cars as it pulled out, he stepped across two sets of tracks and then turned south, coming upon the food and drink they'd temporarily abandoned. Dogs or some sort of other creature had been at it, devouring the meat but leaving most of the bread and all of the whiskey. Mentally pushing back his fatigue, Harry picked up the demijohn they'd left behind. It would have to do for breakfast.

More than sustenance, he needed sleep. None of the rail cars parked along these tracks had moved. He guessed they would not be soon. Entering one of them, he lay down on a seat. The upholstery was torn and smelled oddly, but it was all satin and goose down to him.

HAVING nothing to do after lunch, Grant allowed himself a short nap in his tent. The respite proved shorter than expected. He had just dozed off into a dreamy state when he felt his shoulder being shaken. He opened his eyes to see Major Hawkins standing over him.

"Scout's come in, General. Has a report for you."

"What scout? I have no scout. I have no troops."

"It's the French Indian, sir. The one who came in with that Virginian."

Grant sat up, rubbing his eyes. "Yes. Very well. Where is he?"

"Just outside. Colonel York's talking with him."

"Raines did not come back with him?"

"Guess not, General."

"'Spect I'd better find out why." He rose, surprised at how fatigued he felt.

York was haranguing the Indian, leaning into him in intimidating fashion, though the other remained unfazed, staring back hard.

"Why are you being so uncivil to this man, Colonel?" Grant asked, trudging up.

"He has a written message and won't hand it over."

The Indian turned to Grant without changing his stern expression. "Harry Raines said I should give this to you." He did so.

Grant went over to a camp chair to read it, lighting a cigar. Before commencing, he looked back to Tantou. "How'd you get through the lines?"

"Went around them. West of here."

"Hungry?"

"Yes, General."

Grant's eyes went to York. "Get him some grub, Colonel."

"Yes, sir."

The note had been written in pencil, and in some haste. A few words were smudged and unclear, but enough was legible. "Where's McPherson?" he asked Major Hawkins.

"Reconnoitering the line, sir. Your orders."

"Yes." He went back to the message, reading it twice. "Has there been any word of Congressman Abbott?"

"No new word, General. He is supposed to be on his way."

"Have a telegraph message sent again—throughout the department. He should come now. He should make haste."

"Sir."

"I'm going over to see General Halleck."

THE commander had somehow augmented his already enormous staff, and the mob of officers was standing around him as he sat at a table set up outdoors, studying a map. Grant had seen it before, amazed at the richness of detail as concerned the Union side of the line and the lack of it about the Confederate positions.

"My apologies for interrupting your contemplation, General Halleck," Grant began.

"Glad you're here, General Grant. We are making plans for our defense."

"Defense, General?"

"On the left. Beauregard has had time to reinforce his position there and I expect that he will shortly move against our works. His hope will be to separate us from the river, just as they've been trying to do all along. If we can repel them vigorously, perhaps they at last can be induced to retreat from Corinth."

"But General, that's the news I bring you. The rail lines in town are full of empty cars. They've been coming in empty and leaving with soldiers. The sick and wounded first, but now the able-bodied under arms. If we move now around the right, we can cut off their rail lines on the south. Will have Beauregard in a bag, sir."

"You'll just have another bloody battle on your hands, General Grant. Maybe worse than Shiloh. As I said, they're being reinforced. And they've been bringing up heavy artillery. The bluff above Bridge Creek fairly bristles with it."

"I have news about that as well, General Halleck. Those are 'Quaker' guns. Logs painted to look like cannons. They've got them throughout their defenses."

Halleck's beaming relish at more trenches to dig now turned sour. "How do you come by this 'news,' General?"

"Scouts, sir. One has just come in from Corinth, using the Tuscumbia River route I keep urging you to let our army take."

"How is it you are deploying scouts, Grant? You have no direct command. You are my deputy."

Some of the staff officers were eyeing this exchange with embarrassment; others; with anticipation.

"These are the men you sent to me. The men I've employed in my inquiry into the fate of Mrs. Abbott."

"I sent them to you to be interrogated, General. To find out what they might know of the reasons for her death, coming up as they did through Corinth. I wanted them arrested—and possibly hanged as spies. The one's a Virginian with Confederate officers in his family. The other's both an Indian and a foreigner. You would have me move this army on their word?"

"I've had word from Washington over the telegraph, General Halleck. They know nothing there of the Indian, but the Virginian is bonafide. An intelligence agent under General McClellan's command."

"I don't know how anyone in Washington can be so certain about a Tidewater Virginia man who comes to us out of Texas by way of the Mississippi delta. Safer to arrest him, I say. I will not move on his word."

"Then send out your own scouts, General. They will confirm what I have said."

"I have sent them out, sir. They report the enemy position reinforced with heavy artillery."

Grant stood a moment, mulling over his choices. Then he saluted. "Thank you, sir."

"I expect we may be attacked in the morning, General Grant. Please join me in that eventuality."

"Yes, sir. If we are attacked, I shall definitely want to be involved."

THE Indian and Colonel York were waiting for Grant when he returned.

"You have been fed?" Grant asked.

"Yes."

Grant dropped into a camp chair. Oddly, his ankle was hurting him again. "What will you do now? I would advise you to leave this area as soon as is convenient. General Halleck has persuaded himself that you are a Rebel spy."

The Indian seemed to think on that. "I would like to. I would like to go north. But I should go back to Harry Raines. With your instructions."

"My instructions?"

"About Mrs. Abbott and her sister. What he should do."

Grant dug the message from his pocket, reading it once again. "He asks me to check the contraband camp here for a black woman named Alva who was a slave owned by Mrs. Abbott's sister. He says we should inquire after Mrs. Abbott's own maid, though he does not know her name."

"Yes. That is what he asks. I read the message."

"That will take time. I will detail one of my officers to see to it. In the meantime, I would like him to inquire as to how Mrs. Abbott and her sister were regarded in Corinth. I suspect each sister may have brought trouble on the other."

"You want me to go back there."

"Yes. Please. And take the same route. I would like to know more about it."

"I need horses, General. Harry Raines says he would like the horse you loaned him the other today."

"Yes. Of course."

"And our rifles. They took them from us. There's a long-barreled buffalo gun."

"I'll see they're returned to you. Cigar?"

Tantou shook his head.

"Tell Raines to be careful. I will need his testimony if I'm to resolve the matter of those poor women."

THE railway car in which he was blissfully slumbering was violently jarred, causing Harry to fall from his seat to the floor. As he tried to sit up, there was another great lurch, this time in the other direction, and his head struck the sharp-edged wooden base of the seat. Pulling himself up, finally, he put his hand to his head. It came away with a smear of blood.

Glancing out the window, he thought at first the line of cars on the next track had begun to move, then realized it was his own conveyance. Sticking his head out the window to see where the train might be bound, he noted a large mob of soldiery waiting along the track. He had only a few seconds to remove himself from the railcar if he did not want to make the acquaintance of a great many fellow passengers.

Struggling to the rear end of the car, he flung himself onto the platform and then down the steps. The speed of the train seemed much greater from this perspective. Hanging out a little, he saw a band of horsemen up this side of the tracks. He could wait no longer.

His goal was to land running, but he was not quite fully awake and he landed clumsily, twisting one ankle and driving into the rocky ground with the knee of his other leg. Rolling, his arm got wrenched beneath his back. When he finally ceased all this unintended motion, he hurt in fairly much every quarter.

The horsemen appeared not to notice him. Taking a few deep breaths to calm himself and prepare for his next exertion, he got awkwardly to his feet and, when the way was clear of his departing train, hobbled to the line of still idle cars. Crawling under one, he crossed an adjoining road into the trees and paused to lean against one.

His knee was bloody, his ankle swollen, and there were nasty scrapes across the back of his hand. He had no idea of where he could now go. Then of a sudden he did.

THE backyard of the church was as cluttered with medical detritus as the larger hospital, though it lacked the otherwise ubiquitous piles of sundered limbs. Finding the back door open, he entered to find Mrs. Oates and a black woman laboring at a large wooden tub.

"Captain Raines! What has happened to you?"

"A nasty encounter while on scout duty, ma'am. May I rest here a few minutes?"

She came to his side. He was in truth so pained and weakened by his walk from the railroad he wasn't certain how much longer he could stand.

"You may rest here as long as you need to, Captain. Doctor Haynes has left for the day, but I can attend to you. There's someone here who would like to speak to you."

"Miss Devereux? Is she here?"

Mrs. Oates attempted to mask the offense she had taken, but failed. "Miss Devereux has not been seen today. I expect she is keeping clear of Mrs. Hudson. I will attempt to treat your injuries as well as she might."

Harry smiled, though with difficulty. His head was hurting badly, and his vision was getting a little blurry. "I am sure you are by far Miss Devereux' superior at that, ma'am. It's just that I have a message for her."

"Do you wish to leave it with me?"

"No. No, it's—" Harry collapsed.

When he awoke, he was lying on a pallet in the main room of the church, not far from the altar. His coat had been removed and his pants leg cut away. His head, hand, and knee had been bandaged.

Mrs. Oates was not in view. Turning on his pallet to ease his pain, he found himself looking into the staring eyes of the man next to him—a Union soldier who appeared to be still recovering from a wound to the chest. The man was hearty of color and frame, though. Death had not yet begun to hover over him as it had the others.

Perhaps the soldier would recover. At the Battle of Ball's Bluff in Virginia the year before, Harry had seen a young officer from Massachusetts named Oliver Wendell Holmes take a round through the chest. He was back with his company within weeks and, as far as Harry knew, still in the army.

"That nurse put you here for a reason," said the soldier, his eyes still fixed on Harry's. "I asked to speak to you."

"Why is that?"

"You were here a day or two ago, asking after a woman named Townsend, and another named Abbott."

Harry sought a more comfortable position but supposed there wasn't one. "I was. They're sisters who are missing, and I'm trying to find out what happened to them."

"Are you kin to them?"

"No. I was asked by a general to find out what I could."

"A general on which side?"

Harry studied the man's broad face, searching for any hint of guile, but finding none.

"You may not believe me, but the true answer is on both sides."

"Mrs. Oates says you're a Rebel captain and maybe some sort of spy."

"I am a scout."

"Mrs. Hudson says you're one of us—a Yankee spy."

"I do not like that woman."

"Neither do I." The man extended a hand. "I'm George Meehan, a trooper with Ingersoll's cavalry brigade. We provided the escort General Grant ordered for the Abbott woman."

"My name is Harrison Raines. All I am at liberty to say is that my loyalties are not the same as my family's, and I come from Virginia. You were part of the escort?"

"No, sir. But my friend Donlon was. Volunteered. They all volunteered, except Lieutenant Riordan. He was ordered to the detail."

"Have you something to tell me?"

Meehan rolled onto his back, looking up at the vaulted ceiling. "I don't know. Donlon told me about it when they got back."

"Told you about what?"

"This strange thing. It was all of it strange—this lady wanting to go through the lines on such a night and the general allowing it. But when the escort got down the Corinth Road as far as Waldron's Creek, she bade them turn back. They took her across the bridge, which neither side was guarding that night, then left her there."

"What was the strange thing?"

"Coming back across the bridge, Donlon saw a man on horseback waiting in the trees to the side of the road."

"A sentry?"

"I don't think so. Seems like he followed them there and was waiting for them to leave."

"No one spoke to him?"

"No. Donlon said Riordan was in great haste to get out of there—though a man must wonder why. He only got himself killed the next day."

"And this mounted man?"

"He crossed the bridge, following after the lady. Don't know if he meant her ill or well, but he seemed bound to find her."

"No one spoke to him? Recognized him?"

"It was night. Very dark."

"Was he tall? Short? Fat?"

"Can't say. Wasn't there."

They lay there without speaking for a long moment. Harry felt embarrassed to be among these men, having suffered only these small cuts and bruises. "Thank you for telling me this, sir."

"I am but a private."

"But a valuable man, sir. I am obliged. Are they treating you well here? One hears stories."

"These ladies, the nurses, they are as well disposed toward

us as they have been to their own, but it's a hard place, this town."

"The Rebels are leaving it. You will soon be among your own."

Private Meehan closed his eyes. "I rejoice to hear it."

"Say nothing more about me, if you would, sir. Not to anyone."

"I will not."

AFTER a while, Harry began to get used to the coughs, groans, and wheezing. He was brought a meal of fresh bread and a thin soup made with a curiously rubbery meat. Feeling somewhat restored, he was of a mind to get up and seek out Louise, as it seemed clear she would not be making an appearance here. But he quickly changed his mind. The front door to the church was rudely swung open and Mrs. Hudson entered, in yet another black dress, accompanied again by the muscular black servant.

Happily for Harry, she kept her eyes from the patients, striding along the aisle between them and turning with a swish of many skirts to head for the back room. In a moment, her dreadful voice was being raised against Mrs. Oates.

Dreadful as it was, it carried news. The Rebel army was pulling out of Corinth, heading for Tupelo, fifty miles to the south. Mrs. Hudson was asking for nurses to go as well. The evacuation was to be conducted throughout the remainder of the day and the night. All were to be gone by the next morning.

"I cannot," Mrs. Oates said. "We have seriously ill and wounded patients here. And Corinth is my home."

Mrs. Hudson raised the volume of her voice still higher.

"These 'patients' are nearly all Yankees, lately employed at killing our own blood. And of what worth is your 'home' to you if it is taken by the enemy?"

"Nevertheless, I cannot go with you. My place is here. I am not under military orders."

"If you are here, you are under my orders! I am matron here. And if you don't obey them, I'll run you off."

"As you did Mrs. Townsend and now Miss Devereux. It's a wonder we've been able to care for anyone."

"The train that's been assigned departs at seven o'clock tonight. I will expect you to be on it."

The door opened and slammed shut as Mrs. Hudson came back into the ward. This time she stopped halfway up the aisle to survey the patients, as though making sure they were all Federals. Harry had been able to count only three Confederates, all so badly off they couldn't be moved.

Feeling her gaze on him, he rolled over, pulling the slight blanket he'd been given over his face. When he looked again, she was still staring at him, but she then abruptly left, without a word to anyone.

MRS. Oates came quickly to his side. "I do believe, Captain Raines, that it would be wise for you to depart from this place, if you are able. Mrs. Hudson is aware of your presence here, and disapproves of it."

"She did nothing about it."

"Not yet."

Harry sat up. He felt much better, but did not want to leave this place. "Very well, ma'am. I appreciate the warning."

"Make haste, Captain. Find somewhere to hide. The

Yankee army will be here soon. Then you'll be safe."

Harry let that pass. He gestured to the man on the pallet next to his. "Take good care of Private Meehan, here."

"Captain Raines, we take good care of all who enter here." She helped him to his feet. "I'll get you a walking stick—for your ankle."

At the back door, he lingered a moment. "Can you suggest a hiding place?"

"Many of the residents of Corinth are leaving, too. Seek an empty house—away from the square."

"Why are you being so helpful when you think I'm a Yankee?"

"I don't think you're a Yankee. I think you're a Southerner who is helping the Union cause. And I hold no blame against you for that. After Shiloh, after all the horrors we have seen just in this little church—I want the war to end, Captain. I want that soon. And I know that will not happen until the Confederacy surrenders. The politicians say the rule of Washington is tyranny, but I would rather that than any more of this slaughter. I would see every Negro free if it would spare the loss of another single soldier."

"Have a care to whom you speak such thoughts, ma'am."

"That I do, Captain, but there are many people here who think them." She opened the door. "Good luck to you."

Harry went to the edge of the porch, looked both ways, then cautiously descended the steps. He had limped along only a few feet more when he heard a sharp voice behind him.

"Not an inch farther, 'Captain' Raines, or I shall put a pistol ball right through you."

It was Lieutenant Shakes, this time with about a dozen men. He had a revolver in hand. Three of the soldiers had leveled their muskets.

"Where's your horse?" he asked Shakes.

"In front, sir. I shall ride, and you shall walk. And it is a long way to the provost marshal's."

"What is this about?"

"You're under arrest, sir, for espionage. I expect they'll be hanging you by the morning."

Chapter 23

THEY took Harry's Navy Colt as well as Colonel Townsend's pistol, which Harry had already determined was a rare .44-caliber Lefaucheux revolver. Imported from France, they were the only weapons in either army using pinfire cartridges instead of percussion caps. One saw them only in the possession of officers, almost always wealthy officers. Stonewall Jackson, though no aristocrat, had one—a gift bestowed on him by his men.

Harry had removed one of the cartridges, but they had taken that, too. Happily, they had left the letters he'd stolen. There was little light in the cell into which they'd tossed him—a tiny, barred chamber in the basement of the courthouse—but enough to make out the writing.

They were love letters, written with great discretion, yet clear in the ardor of their message. Addressed simply to a "C," they were signed "M." As in "Mary." It was doubtful that they'd ever reached their destination. Townsend must have had them intercepted.

Harry had read five of them by the time a grumbling warder appeared at his door with a noisy ring of keys. Opening it, he stood there, staring—a scraggly old man with a uniform that seemed from another war. "Are you Captain Harrison Raines?"

"Yes."

He motioned for Harry to come forward. "You're to come with me."

The old man was shoved aside by a burly sergeant. "On your feet, Raines. March!"

A stagger was all Harry could muster, moved along by jabs of the sergeant's pistol barrel. At the top of the stairs they entered a large hall, which was busy with soldiers and clerks filling boxes with papers. Harry was shoved into an office and the door locked behind him.

Only a moment later, it opened again, admitting Colonel Townsend. He seemed as full of rage as before, but when he spoke, it was quietly.

"You are a Yankee spy, Raines. And we have proof." He stepped closer as two men entered behind him—an officer Harry had not encountered before, and General Hindman, wearing a white ruffled shirt.

"You have the pistol?" Townsend asked the other officer.

"Yes, Colonel." He produced the Lefaucheux revolver.

"And it was found on his person?"

"That it was. Along with a Navy Colt."

Townsend took the French pistol from the other, brandishing it at Harry. "Here then is proof, General. He broke into my house last night, taking this weapon and some important papers. Search him further."

The officer shrank back from Harry—as Harry supposed he might do himself—and summoned the sergeant, who made a more thorough perusal of his belongings, pulling out the letters at the last.

Townsend snatched them away. "You see! My letters!" He shoved them into his own pocket. "I say he is guilty. A spy, claiming the rank of captain, but caught in civilian clothes. Hang him, General. As soon as is convenient."

The sergeant dug further, removing the pocket pistol Harry had taken from the colonel's desk.

"See!" thundered Townsend. "He stole that, too! He would have shot us all where we stand. We should hang him at once!"

"That will have to wait for the morning, Colonel. I've too much to do right now."

"At dawn then."

"Sir," said Harry, before they could depart, "your pistol, the Lefaucheux, it is of .44 caliber."

"Yes. So?"

"This is unusual. Most of the officers' sidearms in both armies are of .32 or .36 caliber."

"This is a special weapon. I have had it since First Manassas."

Hindman took out his own pistol. "You're wrong, Raines. My Kerr revolver here is of .44 caliber. And there are many of them in our cavalry."

It occurred to Harry that this was true. He pressed on, regardless.

"Were you in Corinth the night before the battle at Shiloh Church, Colonel?"

Townsend seemed offended by the question. "I was with my regiment, you Yankee bastard. Where else would I be when the army was on the move and preparing for a fight?"

"That's true," Hindman said. "He dined with me that

night, and in the morning he and his regiment were among the first to attack."

"Why are you asking?" Townsend said.

"I fear I have bad news for you, Colonel." Harry hesitated, wondering in what manner the man would react—and wishing he had not left all the other rounds in the pistol. "Your wife is dead."

"What?" said Hindman. "How do you know this?"

"I was behind Federal lines for a time. She and her sister May, the both of them shot to death with a .44-caliber pistol. The bullet that killed your wife, Colonel—it was recovered."

"What were you doing behind enemy lines?"

"Scouting." Harry kept his eyes on Townsend, who stood gape-mouthed. "Inquiring after Mrs. Townsend's absence, as General Hindman ordered."

"She's dead?" Townsend asked, as though he didn't quite understand the words.

"Were they were caught in the battle?" Hindman asked.

"No, sir. I believe they were in Corinth at the time of the battle. Or near it. They were murdered. Shot at close range."

Townsend went for Harry, grasping him by the shoulders and making him hurt everywhere. "Who did this? You? With my revolver?"

"It didn't happen last night, Colonel. It was many days ago. They were found in a casket, their bodies embalmed."

"This is extraordinary," said Hindman.

Townsend went to a chair and slumped into it, dropping the pistol to the floor. He put his face into his hands and began to weep. Harry judged him in the wrong calling. Such an emotional man should have been on the stage.

"Take him away," Townsend said finally. "His fate is decided."

Hindman nodded. The sergeant took Harry by the arm.

"Give him whatever he wants," said Hindman. "It's a while before dawn."

HARRY did indeed receive something he strongly desired that night, though the treat was not requested and took him by great surprise. He had finished a very good meal of ham, gravy, and peas, and was enjoying a fair brand of whiskey when his cell door opened, admitting first a lovely scent and then a lovely lady.

"Louise, are you going to be popping out of doorways the rest of my days?"

"For that to happen, you would have to be very lucky indeed, Harry. And I see you are no longer lucky at all. Besides, you haven't many days remaining. I'm told less than one."

"How did you learn of this?"

"I have become acquainted with General Hindman, but the whole town knows of it. Someone informed on you to the provost guard."

"I fear my only hope is for a Union attack, but the commanding general over there doesn't think soldiers should be used for such a purpose. How did you get in here?"

"I am now very well acquainted with General Hindman." She sat down on his cot, looking with a mixture of horror and amusement at his appearance. "Did they beat you?"

"No. I fell off a train."

She took his injured hand. "Poor Harry. You are at once the most pathetic and most ridiculous figure I ever saw. It will be most demeaning, going to your death with just one pant leg."

"I will try to think of a way to avoid that embarrassment."

"I came back to Corinth to warn you, though now it makes no difference at all." She kissed the hand she held. "Poor, poor Harry. I wonder if it is my fault you are here."

"Warn me of what?"

"I should have told you of this long before. I had no idea you would dog my steps all the way up the Mississippi."

"Louise. Please. Of what?"

"There's a murderous gang."

Harry withdrew his hand, then put his arm around her shoulders, as he might a naive child he was trying to explain some complex matter to. "My dear. There are great battles raging over this land that daily take the lives of thousands in the awfulest manner imaginable. Why should one worry about mere murderous gangs?"

Her voice went soft. "They're after people like you."

"Virginia gentlemen?"

"This is not such an amusing matter, Harrison Raines. I don't how high up in the Confederate government the official sanction comes from, but they have it, these gangs. They travel behind the Rebel lines, looking for Union agents or anyone they think might possibly be a Union agent. Then they kill them."

"Kill."

"Yes. Kill. Murder. 'An honorable murderer, if you will; for naught I did in hate, but all in honor.'"

The quotation came readily to his mind. *"Othello,"* he said. "But you say these are 'honorable murderers'?"

"I'm saying they're official murderers—executioners, if you will, government assassins, who ply their trade without benefit of trial or verdict. Their toll in New Orleans was prodigious before the Federal army came, and they added to it afterward."

"And the man you left on my doorstep?"

"You thought he was a Yankee agent who was after me. You erred, sir. He was one of these thugs and he was after *you,* not me."

"Are you saying you cut his throat?"

"Not me. An associate. My manservant, Jules."

"And these fiends are in Corinth?"

She moved away from him slightly. He supposed he did not smell so good. "They are up and down the Mississippi. And they are here."

He removed his arm from her shoulders, yearning for a bath. "As you say, 'Countess,' it matters little. General Hindman and one of his colonels have me bound for the gallows."

"I saw no gallows erected here."

"They mentioned a rope. Perhaps they'll just make do with a box to stand upon."

She became sad, which unnerved him. "I know." She took his hand again and then gave him a dazzlingly theatrical encouraging smile. "I will think of something. I always do. In the meantime, there is this." She reached within the bodice of her dress and pulled forth a very small single-barreled derringer pistol. "Hide it."

Harry put it in a pocket. "What would you have me do, Louise, shoot that poor old man out there who's the warder?"

"I would have you shoot whoever it's necessary to shoot." She gave him a quick kiss on the cheek and stood. "But I will think of something. You just stay alert and watch for an opportunity. I will do my best to provide you one."

"But why aren't they after you, if you're one of us?"

She gave him another smile, this one enigmatic, then called for the guard to let her out.

* * *

HARRY finished most of the bottle of whiskey, managed a few hours of fitful sleep, and awoke after four o'clock to the dread realization that no opportunity of any sort had been provided. It was altogether possible now that he was as close to doom as any soldier rising to charge the enemy. Whether hanging was pleasanter than having one's head blown off by solid shot he did not know. He suspected not.

For a moment, he considered writing letters to his sister Elizabeth, and to Caitlin Howard, once the object of so much of his passion, though now beginning to fade into the graveyard of mind where memories of lost loves are laid. He supposed he might give them to Louise, who might keep her own fair neck out of a noose long enough to get back to Washington.

But such an act would be surrendering to his fate, which he still declined to do. And it would bring on more melancholy than he could possibly bear.

He concentrated on how he might escape. A breakaway as they exited the courthouse? Taking a hostage with the derringer? Luring the old warder to the cell and shooting him for his keys? He thought upon it hard, drinking the remains of the whiskey.

HE dozed off, awakening to the clang of the door and the sight of first light in the high cellar window. The warder was there, accompanied by the burly sergeant and four soldiers with muskets. Two of them entered the cell and bound his wrists.

Harry had learned a little trick from his Secret Service colleague Joseph "Boston" Leahy: If someone attempts to tie your hands, turn the wrist ends onto each other as the rope draws tight. This then requires only a slight rotation to loosen the bond.

He attempted it. The soldier noticed and set the wrists right again, pulling the rope tight. Then he shoved Harry out the cell door.

They'd neglected to tie his ankles, as was done to prisoners at the military hangings he'd witnessed. He could only wonder at the portent this might bear.

He found out as they emerged onto the courthouse veranda. A group of soldiers had gathered beneath a large oak tree on the lawn. A horse had been brought to it—a rope with a well-knotted noose dangling just above. The mount had a bridle but no saddle.

Harry stood a moment on the courthouse steps, looking to the other side of the lawn, where some officers were standing. General Hindman was there, as was Townsend. Hindman waved to Harry, who politely nodded.

He looked up and down the street for some sign of Louise. If she had not been able to provide an opportunity, as promised, he might at least have a lovely female face to gaze upon as he left this life. But she was not in view. No woman was.

What he did notice was that there seemed to be very few soldiers in the town. He'd heard numerous train whistles and chuffing throughout the night.

Another prod from the sergeant and he descended the steps, wishing he was better dressed. He looked less a Virginia gentleman than some drunken vagabond. His head was aching badly from the whiskey.

They lifted him onto the horse's back. He was a nervous animal and he stepped to the side, prompting one of the soldiers to go to that flank to hold him still, lest he run off before the noose could be placed and tightened.

The sergeant took hold of the rope and reached to put it around Harry's neck.

Harry closed his eyes. If he could not look upon Louise in person, he would seize upon a remembered image of her for his last moment.

The shot that came next sent a large piece of metal whizzing very near him.

Chapter 24

HARRY'S only real conceit was that he might well be the best horseman in Virginia. Perhaps not so good as his cousin by marriage, Belle Boyd of Martinsburg, a horsewoman of such accomplishment he had seen her ride her horse Fleeter at full gallop while standing on the saddle. But he could take six-foot jumps with ease and keep his seat upon the most troublesome mount.

Every bit of this skill was required now.

The bullet that had been fired hit the sergeant with a whumping sound as loud as his cry. He fell backward, letting go of the noose, which fell partially over Harry's head. He managed to toss the rope off and kick the nervous horse hard enough to make it bolt, pulling free of the startled soldier holding the bridle and pounding off across the lawn, gathering for a jump over the fence.

Harry had taken plenty of jumps bareback but never with his hands tied behind his back. All he could think to do was lean forward and clench his teeth upon some thick strands of the mane, while gripping the animal's rib cage as tightly with his legs as he could manage. It was the worst possible way to take a horse over any kind of obstacle, and Harry was certain he and the animal would part company upon landing, if not before.

He lurched to the side and almost pitched over the horse's right shoulder, but regained his balance with a sideways lunge to the left. He could barely maintain his painful grip on the bitter-tasting mane, but it kept his head down, making him much less of a target for the soldiery who were now firing their muskets at him.

Unless, of course, they were smart enough to aim for the horse.

Careening along the sun-hardened dirt of the street, he was at the least grateful that the musket fire was driving the frightened horse exactly where Harry wanted to go, which was in the direction from which the shot that struck the Rebel sergeant had been fired.

He had to assume that shooter was a friend, unless the bullet had been intended to kill him before the rope did—and missed.

His back and legs were now hurting beyond all tolerance from his contorted position. He could only hope this presumed rescuer would come to his assistance soon. Otherwise he would shortly fall into the street and his poor, bruised, ill-clad body would quickly grow heavier with the weight of musket balls.

Holding fast somehow for another agonizing block, he was relieved at length to see a large dappled horse with a brown-jacketed rider swing out from some trees and gallop onto the roadway behind him. He needed now to slow his own frantic mount so the other could catch up.

Pulling the mane to the left and digging into the ribs on

the animal's right side with his knee, he steered it toward a line of empty wagons parked along some storefronts on the left side of the street. The animal succumbed to this instruction, but, drawing close to one of the wagons, turned at the last moment and stumbled slightly. By then the other rider had reached him.

It was Tantou, not an apparition. Grim-faced, the long buffalo gun slung over his shoulder and bouncing, the Métis pulled his horse ahead and then reached down to grab the bridle of Harry's frightened beast. Turning both of them at the next corner, he proceeded a few yards down it and then brought both animals to a sudden halt.

Harry went flying off, landing on his side. Tantou dismounted quickly, swiftly cutting the rope that bound his friend's wrists. Harry sat up, rubbing them, and then his shoulder.

"Can you ride this horse, Harry Raines? We must go."

"Yes. If you'll help me back on."

Tantou locked his fingers together and held his hands out as a sort of stirrup, giving Harry a boost.

"What were you trying to do back there, shoot the rope in two?" Harry asked as he took the bridle in his hands.

"That would be stupid," said Tantou, getting back aboard his horse. "Who could shoot so good as that? I was trying to shoot the man who was putting the rope around your neck."

"I think you killed him."

Tantou made a face at him. "If we do not go now we will be killed, too."

THEY galloped on to the end of the street, crossing yet two more sets of railroad tracks and trotting behind a line of freight cars. Farther down the right-of-way he could see other trains loading up with passengers and freight. In the distance was the smoke of a train heading south, out of town.

"Wait," said Harry, pulling up.

"We must go back to the Union lines, Harry Raines. The Rebels will be searching for us through all the town."

"I don't think so. You can see the Confederate army's pulling out. I think most of it's already gone." There was not a single soldier to be seen along this shunting.

"The party that was trying to hang you—they will be looking."

"Maybe. But I want to stay in Corinth. And I think the Federals will be coming soon now."

"Maybe not soon. They move slow. If all U.S. soldiers moved this slow most of America would still belong to the Indians."

"How did you know where to find me, Jack?"

"I went to the hospital. The big one where Louise Devereux took care of me. They told me."

"Was she there?"

Tantou shook his head. "Mrs. Oates. She told me they were hanging you."

"We must wait," Harry said.

"Wait where?"

"I want to go to Colonel Townsend's house."

"That is crazy."

"No, it is not. No one will be there. It is a good place to hide and wait."

"There may be the black people there."

"I shouldn't think they'd cause any problem. If they're loyal to the Confederacy, they will be leaving Corinth with the rest."

"What if the colonel comes there?"

"All the better, for I would like to capture him. But he must still be at the courthouse."

"When should we go?"

"Now."

THEY made their way through back streets to the other side of the town, then doubled back and approached the Townsend house from the opposite side of the square. It unnerved Harry a little to come so near the scene of his intended doom—upon the horse that was to have been the instrument of his execution—but he took reassurance from the presumption that his persecutors would not expect to find him in such proximity.

An alley led behind the Townsend home to a gate and a stable. Opening its door, they quietly led their horses into it. There were six stalls—two occupied by what looked to be a carriage team. A black youth was in the corner, forking hay. He stopped, motionless, and speechless, too.

Tantou looked to Harry, who stared at the boy for a long moment, then stepped toward him, compelling the youth to stumble backward.

"Don't be afraid," Harry said. "We're scouts from the Union Army. The rest of the soldiers will be along soon. They will be occupying Corinth and you will have nothing to worry about. You will be free."

Harry actually was not certain of this. The youth appeared not to comprehend.

"All you need to do is stay here and tend to our horses," Harry said. "Say nothing to anyone about our being here. Not even to your master." Tantou reached into his money belt and removed a five-dollar gold coin. "If you do as I say, you may keep this," Harry continued. "If you disobey me, my Indian friend will take that long gun of his and shoot you. Do you understand?"

The boy nodded vigorously. Leaving the buffalo gun slung on his shoulder, Tantou took out his large saddle pistol and waved it slowly at the black youth for emphasis. The groom nodded again, even more emphatically.

Harry went to the door leading to the garden, which was bordered by the slave quarters, the kitchen, and the rear of the main house. There was no sign of any activity. "Do you have another pistol, Jack? They took mine."

"No."

If the colonel was now at home and saw their approach through a window, they'd find themselves welcomed by the .44-caliber Lefaucheux.

"Perhaps we should wait for tonight."

"You said now, Harry Raines." Tantou gently moved him aside and went through the gate, pistol to the fore.

Harry followed, glancing to either side as they crept forward. The garden was well trimmed and full of flowers, though one long bed near the wall was barren, reminding him of a freshly dug grave.

Tantou disappeared into the small building ahead. There were no gunshots.

THEY found two black women in the kitchen. Taking them in tow, they discovered another—a maid—in the main house. Having ascertained that neither the colonel nor any other white person was at home, Harry brought the women into the front parlor. He went through the same routine as with the boy, asking them to stay in the kitchen, threatening to have Tantou shoot them if they tried to leave the property, and offering them each a five-dollar gold piece if they would do as he said and wait for the Union Army.

He was sure Mr. Pinkerton would approve this expenditure of Federal exchequer. The chief was not only an ardent abolitionist, he also viewed the black people of the South as the very best intelligence asset the Union had, and worth every penny of whatever sum was used to recruit or reward them.

The young maid was not so cooperative, however. "Colonel Townsend, he whup me if I help you Yankees."

"I'm not a Yankee. I'm a Southerner who doesn't believe in slavery."

She looked confused.

"Don't worry," Harry said. "We're here to talk to the colonel. No harm can befall you while we're here, and we'll stay until the Yankee army comes." He pressed the coin into her hand.

"Dat for me?"

"Yes." He patted her on the head as a sign of amity, but this seemed to afright her, as she ran from the room. He heard the door close. Going to a window, he calmed himself as he saw her disappear into the building housing the kitchen, instead of heading out through the garden gate.

"I'm going upstairs," Harry said to Tantou. "Keep watch for Townsend—or anyone."

"You going to sleep, Harry Raines?"

"No. I'm going to commandeer a pair of Townsend's trousers. I weary of looking like some wretched deckhand off the *Pequod*. I may borrow a clean shirt as well. Would you like one?"

The Métis sniffed himself, then shook his head. "If I steal a shirt, I will steal one of General Hindman's."

Harry hurried up the stairs. The house appeared not to have been cleaned in some days. The banister was dusty, and there were dead insects here and there on the floor.

He went first to the colonel's room, happy to be able to peruse its contents at some leisure. First he attended to his wardrobe, finding in the colonel's armoire a suitable pair of gray trousers and in a neighboring chest, an abundance of laundered cotton shirts. The fit was loose in both respects, but adequate. He thought a moment of helping himself to one of Townsend's fine frock coats, but figured that would amount to outright theft. The pants and shirt were simply necessary forage. He set another of their five-dollar gold pieces on the colonel's dresser as compensation. If he did not leave this house soon, there'd be none of Pinkerton's gold left.

Harry had been in enough ladies' boudoirs in his time to see that this was solely the colonel's room, lacking the slightest hint of a lady's residence or visitation. He went through it quickly, hoping to find his navy Colt. A dresser drawer yielded only a fully loaded .36-caliber Griswold and Gunnison revolver, which Harry elected to commandeer as well. The memory of the rope was doing more to assuage his guilt than the five-dollar gold piece. On further thought, he snatched back the heavy coin.

Moving down the hall, he passed a child's room, clean and neat and full of toys but looking much abandoned. Puzzled, he crossed to a bedchamber at the head of the stairs. Here, he was certain, was the domain of Mary Sayres Townsend.

The maid had tidied it, but not much. What looked to be riding clothes had been thrown over a chair. A small, open portmanteau was on the floor beside it. Harry went through the bag quickly, finding nothing but a few delicate female garments, all neatly folded.

He searched the drawers of the night table, a dresser, and

a mirrored dressing table in the corner of the room, his reward only more predictable items. Turning away quickly from the reflection of his marred, tired, dirty face in the mirror, he sat a moment on the upholstered bench, wondering where else to look—and for what.

His gaze fell to the carpet. He found himself staring at it as though mesmerized, realizing that it wasn't the rug that had caught hold of his mind but the realization that he had overlooked something. Getting down to his hands and knees as best he could with his injured leg, he examined it carefully but failed to find what he sought.

Returning to the rooms he'd already visited, he performed a similar exercise in each. A fourth bedroom, at the rear of the house, yielded the same unproductive result. It was sparsely furnished, with a washstand but no other convenience. The bed had been slept in but not made. There were some women's undergarments on the floor beside it. Harry gingerly examined one item, swearing as something sharp pierced the palm of his right hand. Taking the garment out again, he found a gentleman's stickpin in the folds of it. Holding the item closer, he took note of a diamond on the end.

More carefully, he wrapped the pin in the clothing, and folded that into a square, returning it to the pocket.

He pondered. There were three female servants still in this house, including the young maid. Why had this room not been cleaned?

A separate corridor led to another two chambers, one completely empty and another a sort of library, but with few books. Both had rugs on the floor—dirty, but not stained.

He finally found what he sought in a side parlor on the main floor. The carpet here had been removed, leaving a large square of less varnished wood in the center of the room. A circular table, devoid of objects, stood in the center of it.

Harry knelt beside it, putting on his spectacles and then moving around the rim. The surface had a tiny bit of dust on it but recently had been cleaned and polished.

The curving side of the table was another matter. Just beneath the edge of the tabletop were some dried runlets of a dark stain. Following the rim around, he found more. To make certain, he used the sheath knife he kept in his boot to scrape a few flakes off the wood into the palm of his hand. He held them up to the light.

Now he was certain. The color was right.

Going to the doorway, he took from his pocket the Griswold and Gunnison revolver he'd acquired upstairs. He aimed it toward the table first from the hip, moving from side to side. Then he raised the weapon, sighting carefully from several angles.

Returning to the table, he knelt before it and turned back to the doorway, imagining the scene. As he did so, shifting one knee, he winced from a sudden pain. He had knelt on something sharp. It was a military button, made of highly polished brass. It was altogether logical to find a uniform button in the house of a colonel, or would have been had not it belonged on a Federal uniform.

"Harry Raines." Tantou was calling from the front parlor.

"What is it?" said Harry, putting the button with the stickpin. "Is Townsend coming?"

"No. But riders are."

"In uniform?"

"No. Come here, Harry Raines."

He did so, pistol still in hand. The Métis was at the window, standing by the curtain, his eye on the street outside. Joining him, Harry saw two horseman riding their mounts

at a slow walk down the street, the men's heads turning
back and forth as they passed the houses to either side.

"You're right, Jack. They're not army. So why should we
fret over them?"

"Look at them close."

One was stout and dressed in a green-checked suit. The
other was tall and slim, his clothes those of a gentleman.

"We have seen them before," Tantou said.

"Yes, but where?"

"The fat one on the riverboat. The tall one at a card table,
in Natchez."

Harry squinted. As best he could determine, Tantou was
correct. "Why would those two be together? The one's just a
traveling peddler, and with the Union Army for customers.
The other, he's a gentleman—and I daresay a Rebel."

Tantou stepped back. The riders had stopped. "They
know each other well, I think."

"Maybe they're on our side," Harry said. "If they were
Rebels, why would they be coming into Corinth just when
the Yankee army is about to do the same thing?"

"They haven't explained themselves to me," said Tantou.

The riders moved on, turning at the corner. Harry crossed
the hall into the dining room, whose windows faced the side
yard. Crouching down, he watched the two men continue
on, paying no further attention to the Townsend house.

"I should truly like to know why they are here," Harry
said as Tantou came up behind him.

"You said you wanted to capture Colonel Townsend."

"Yes, I do."

"Then we should stay here."

Harry stood up. "Unless he left with the rest of the army."

"Harry Raines, we should wait here."

"Very well. For a while."

Tantou lay down on the floor beside the table. "I will sleep. You keep lookout."

The windows rattled an instant before the whump of an explosion jarred the street. It was quickly followed by another, and then a third. In the distance, in the fading daylight, Harry could see the rising smoke over the trees. Then came a flickering, orange glow.

"What is it, Harry Raines?" said Tantou without rising.

"They're blowing up things."

"Buildings?"

"No. I think locomotives. It's happening over by the tracks."

"Locomotives cost money. Why would they blow them up?"

"They must have needed repairs the Rebels don't have time to make. So they're blowing them up to keep the Yankees from using them."

Tantou rolled over. "This is a very strange war."

HOURS passed. They changed watch. When Tantou awakened Harry from his own turn at slumber, it was nearly dark.

"No sign of the colonel, Harry Raines. I think maybe he has gone south with the army. A Rebel cavalry patrol came by, but they kept going."

Harry stretched and rose. "I think you are right. Let us get something to eat."

There was food in the kitchen—a ham, fresh bread, and a bowl of boiled eggs. But the black women had gone. A better word was "fled."

"I don't think they went to the colonel. He would have come at us by now if they had," Harry said.

"Maybe they told him we were waiting to bushwhack him and he took that as a reason to stay away."

"I simply cannot comprehend how any person of color could perform such a service for an oppressor."

"Maybe they are afraid, Harry Raines."

Harry stopped in midchew. "The horses."

THE stable groom was still on the premises, asleep on some hay in one of the empty stalls. Their mounts were where they'd left them, munching some hay the boy had provided for them. Harry stroked the neck of his, still marveling at the remarkable manner in which the animal had been acquired. Then he went to the tack room, deciding to liberate one of the colonel's fine saddles. He doubted he could bring himself to ride bareback ever again.

"I think we should leave now, Jack," he said, settling the saddle on the animal's back.

"I would say this is now the safest place we could be in this town."

"Maybe so, but we're not accomplishing anything for General Grant."

Tantou considered this. "How does he know what we are accomplishing?"

"He doesn't, but he will soon."

"Where do you want to go?"

Harry pulled on the cinch strap, shoving his hand beneath the leather to make certain it was tight. "To find a card game, Jack."

"You looking to meet up with those two who rode in today?"

"They came all the way up here for something. I'd like to find out what."

"But what do they have to do with the dead sisters?"

"Nothing. But I don't think they're here to advance the cause of the Union."

"They could be here looking for you, Harry Raines."

Harry nodded. "So I shall save them the trouble. But let's finish eating first."

THE streets were quite desolate with so many darkened houses. They moved toward Railroad Street at a slow trot, pausing at intersections to make certain the way was clear of possible trouble. They encountered none. Dogs barked. Cats and rats loitered by some of the wood lot fences. A wagon of some sort rattled along one of the side streets, and on one corner they saw two improbable ladies standing with parasols. When one of them called to Harry, he realized that the prostitution so rife in Washington and Richmond had come to this once quiet and respectable community as well.

The presence of the bawds suggested that a saloon might be open.

Turning into Railroad Street, which had a macabre aspect from the light of the still-burning railroad cars, they found one—a large, noisy place opposite the railroad depot. Harry pulled up several buildings short of it, tying Hangman, as he now called his horse, to a hitching rail. Tantou dismounted and did the same.

"You just going to walk in there?" he asked.

"Yes."

"You remember what happened in Natchez?"

"Someone fired through a window at me."

"Yes, while that tall one you call a gentleman looked on."

"You backed me then. Can you now?"

"*Bien sûr,* Harry Raines. I will follow you in and move to the right. Find a place to sit where I can watch everything."

Tantou had tied the buffalo gun across the rear of his saddle. It was an unwieldy weapon for such close quarters.

"And now, *mon ami,*" Harry said, "some diversion and refreshment."

THE saloon was fairly crowded for a town that otherwise seemed a graveyard. Most of the patrons were Confederate shirkers and deserters, waiting for the Yankees to come take them away from the war. A few railroad workers were at the near end of the bar. Pausing just inside the doorway, Harry took note of two ladies in the commercial way, then moved to the bar and ordered a whiskey. Turning to face the room as he sipped the drink, he saw Tantou in a corner, leaning against the wall with arms folded, pretending to watch a dice game. At the rear of the room, a card game was in progress.

Harry put on his spectacles. He was either very wise, or very lucky. The sutler and the dandy were in the game.

He came and stood behind the dandy, who was examining a freshly dealt hand.

"Good evening, sir," Harry said. "May I join you?"

The dandy carefully set down his cards, smiling as he looked up at Harry. "Do I know you, sir?"

"Harrison Raines, of Charles City County, Virginia. I made your acquaintance briefly in a game down in Natchez."

The smile dwindled, and then was gone. "As I recall, sir, your departure was sudden. What are you doing up here in Corinth?"

"Same thing I was doing in Natchez," said Harry, pulling

up a chair and setting it to the dandy's right. The man moved over.

"Looking for a lady, as I do recall," he said. "Did you find her?"

"Yes."

"Where is she?"

"I don't know. I lost her again."

"Is she in Corinth?"

"Possibly. I do not know."

"We are speaking of Louise Devereux?"

Harry stiffened. "How do you know her name?"

"You spoke of it all over Natchez."

Harry nodded. "Shall we play?"

The sutler sat opposite, watching the exchange like a badger peering from his den. Harry ignored him, setting down his whiskey glass and waiting for the deal of a new hand.

"Weren't you supposed to be hanged today?" It was the sutler, Fenton, speaking this time.

"Some thought so. I didn't."

"One of those who thought so got killed, I hear. A sergeant."

"That was unfortunate."

"But you escaped."

"That was the fortunate part," said Harry. "Three cards, please."

The dandy was paying no attention to Harry's conversation with Fenton. He'd drawn only one card, and was staring at it bemusedly.

"If you're on the run, how is it you're still in Corinth?" the sutler said.

"It's the Rebel army that's on the run. I like it here." Harry had three kings. The dandy bet a dollar, and Harry saw it.

"You like it here because the Yankees are coming?" said Fenton. "As I recollect, you were on the *Crawford* coming upriver. That's a Yankee riverboat."

"And you were on it as well, sir. Holding a Yankee contract for provender."

"Doing business with 'em don't make you one of 'em."

"I know. I sell them horses—when I'm back East."

"That where you're headed? Back East?"

"Can we play cards, damn it?" grumbled one of the other players.

Harry lost to an eight high straight. He tossed his cards. "Not headed anywhere tonight," he said to the Fenton.

"You remaining here in the hopes of another encounter with Miss Devereux?" asked the dandy.

"As the gentleman said," said Harry, " 'Can we play cards?' "

He won the next hand, and the following one. The other players, who included one of the Confederate deserters, began to indicate some unhappiness with Harry's intrusion, but the dandy and the sutler simply played on, saying nothing more. Harry glanced over in Tantou's direction, distressed to find him gone from the corner. All Harry had in the way of weapon was his sheath knife and the Griswold and Gunnison, which was in a pocket of his coat. It would be awkward trying to make use of it.

"Actually, gentlemen, I'm in Corinth because I'm looking for a Confederate officer. A colonel named Townsend."

"Like you say, friend," said the sutler, "the Rebel army's gone. Why would he still be here? You don't see any fancy colonels in here, do you?"

"He lives here."

"If the Yankees catch him, he'll be living in Camp Douglas in Chicago."

"That may well be why I am having difficulty locating him."

The bartender came over, though no one had summoned him, and set two fresh bottles of whiskey on the table. The dandy nodded, shoving money toward him.

"Deal me out this hand," Harry said. "I'm going to the sinks."

THERE was a drunken old man asleep on the dirt floor. Two wobbly-looking shirkers, leaning on each other for support, were at the trough. Harry waited for them to conclude, then stepped forward as they departed.

As he hoped, Tantou slipped from the shadows and came beside him.

"I know why they haven't yet tried to kill me," Harry said. "They want something from me."

"The gold?"

"No. Louise."

"What do they want with her?"

"They did not say. I am hoping she is someplace far away, though I suspect she is still here."

"Why is that?"

"Because those two still are."

"Should we leave now, Harry Raines?"

"I want to play a few more hands."

"Why?"

"I can't decide whether these men are working for the Rebels or the Federals. I'd like to find out."

"Maybe they are bounty hunters, working for themselves."

"Five more hands, another glass of whiskey. Then I go. When I've played the fourth hand, you leave. Go to the hospital. See if you can learn something of Louise's where-abouts. Then meet me at the Townsend house."

"What if you run into trouble?"

"You run for the Union lines. But I should like to find her, and get her out of here. If these two are looking for her there are probably others."

"I think you will run into trouble, Harry Raines."

"Go, Jack. Good luck."

SHERMAN had posted his division for the night on the extreme right and, after a brief discussion with General Thomas, came by Grant's tent for a visit.

"Damnation, Grant," he said, pulling up a camp stool, "I think tomorrow we'll be in a fight. Halleck's astir as I've never seen him."

"Could be just that Washington has telegraphed him asking why he's not been stirring," Grant said. He handed Sherman a cigar and lighted one for himself.

"Pope says he's been hearing trains all day. Something's up."

"Stopped now, though. Right?"

"Haven't heard any along my front tonight."

Grant grinned and puffed. "Bill, I shall be greatly surprised if we stir anything more deadly tomorrow than shovels."

"Can't dig another trench. Our forward line now is almost on top of the Reb pickets. That's why I think there'll be a scrap. Slow as we've been, we've had to bump up against them sometime, and I think this is it. Halleck's ordered up additional ammunition. More artillery, too. We could be in Corinth tomorrow."

"I may well sleep through this great battle of yours, as I doubt it will disturb me much."

They were interrupted by the sound of a rider arriving in great haste. There was an exchange of words outside the tent, and then Major Hawkins stepped inside. "Forgive my intrusion, General Grant. There's a courier here for General Sherman."

For a fraction of a second, Grant had actually believed Halleck might be communicating with him. "If he has a dispatch, fetch it in here."

Hawkins performed this duty quickly. Sherman read the message. "It's from Halleck, all right."

"Promising a fight?"

Sherman read it aloud. " 'General Pope advises me, 'I have no doubt, from all appearances, that I shall be attacked in heavy force at daylight.' Be prepared, General Sherman, to reinforce him if necessary."

"And bring your shovels," Grant said.

Sherman stood, clamping his cigar in a corner of his mouth as he pulled on his riding gloves. "Where'll you be tomorrow morning, Grant? Want to position yourself near me?"

Grant put his hand on the other's shoulder. "Thanks, Bill, but I'd better tag along somewhere near 'Old Brains'— in the odd event he should actually need me."

They were interrupted by Colonel York, who apologized for his intrusion and hastily withdrew.

"I'll be going then, Grant," Sherman said. "Think I'd better put out extra pickets tonight."

"Tomorrow's June first. It's been almost two months since Shiloh."

"Patience, General."

When Sherman had gone, Grant looked outside. "Come back here, York. You have something to report?"

The colonel came forward, as though reluctantly. He waited until he was fully inside the tent before speaking. "I do, General."

"Well, then, can I hear it?"

"Yes, sir. I detailed a party to the contraband camp to look for those Negro servant women you asked about. One of them, I believe, was named Alva."

"Indeed. And?"

"They found them. It took a while because they looking among the living. They turned up among the dead."

"The dead?"

"Casualties are pretty heavy in that camp, General. Almost as bad as the military hospitals."

"They died of disease?"

"No, General. They were slain."

Grant took a long puff of his cigar, then squinted at his subordinate through the smoke. "You're not going to tell me they were both shot through the heart?"

"No, sir. Through the head."

Chapter 25

HARRY moved down the street at a trot, crossed the tracks, then slowed to a walk. Only the burning railroad cars cast light into the darkness. He wondered if there was an inhabited house left in town.

Looking back, he saw no one following, and stopped. There was no light at the far end of this street that would silhouette him, but anyone turning into it from the railroad would have the glow of the smoldering fire behind him.

Or her. He wished against all logic that Louise might now come trotting up to him with Tantou, ready at last to flee this place and her mysterious avocation. They could be on a train to Nashville and the East within two days.

But General Grant might not appreciate that. Neither would the spirits of those two beautiful dead women he'd so rudely disturbed. He had to see this through.

Harry put on his spectacles again, in time to note a flicker of movement—a silhouette, quickly joined by two others: riders coming around the corner at a walk.

The man on the left was tall, and for a second or two Harry thought somehow it might be Tantou. This was nonsense, of course. His brush with hanging that morning must have jumbled his senses.

He clicked his horse forward, keeping it to a walk, proceeding another two blocks and then looking back at his leisurely pursuers, finding them content to match his pace. At the next corner he steered his horse left, moving a little closer to the plank sidewalk. Stopping a block farther, he waited, and was not disappointed. The three riders, barely visible, made the turn as well.

Now he moved forward at a jangling trot. One block. Then another. Then another turn.

If nothing else, Hangman was a good bolter, as he'd proved on the courthouse lawn. Harry halted him again, this time dropping from the colonel's excellent saddle. Taking out the Griswold and Gunnison, he whacked the animal with the butt on its hindquarters. As it cantered down the street, Harry flung himself over the picket fence of the house on the corner, dropping quietly and staying low.

As he expected, the trio came by dead set on the runaway, first at a trot and then in a canter. He recognized the shape of the sutler, trailing a bit behind the other two.

When they had passed, Harry crept around the other side of the house, vaulted the fence again, and then took to the cross street, walking as fast as his various pains and injuries would permit, heading for the big white house just two blocks away.

THE black women had come back. Despite the hour, he could hear them in the kitchen, though he could only wonder what they were preparing and for whom.

There was window light on both floors of the house—as he recalled the arrangements, lamps in two of the bedrooms and the front parlor. He sought a darkened window to make his entrance, pushing in an interior shutter and pulling himself over the sill.

He landed in what proved to be the dining room. His arrival on the floor had been with a thud he feared could be heard upstairs. But there was no response. He sat perfectly still, waiting and listening. He heard no footsteps, but there was a cough—from upstairs.

It occurred to him that this encounter might prove easier than he expected. Taking up the gentleman's Griswold and Gunnison, he moved toward the sound, halting at the foot of the stairs. There was another cough. He set foot on the first step and started up.

Townsend was in his bedroom, at a small writing desk in the corner by a window overlooking the street. Harry entered the room with the pistol cocked and aimed.

"Good evening, Colonel."

"Thought you would have been in Yankeeland by now," Townsend said without looking up.

"As your army has departed it, I expect Corinth will be Yankeeland itself pretty soon."

The colonel put down his pen, blew upon the letter paper, and then folded it and set it aside. Only then did he look up, turning in his chair. Harry of a sudden feared the man might fly into one of his spectacular rages, but he kept his calm.

"Why have you come to my house, Raines?"

"I might ask the same thing of you, sir. You run the risk of becoming a prisoner of war if you linger here much longer."

Townsend rubbed his chin, as though thinking about

some other matter having no relation to what Harry was saying. Then he sighed, a seeming sadness coming into his eyes.

"I have remained behind to attend to my late wife and her proper burial here in the town of her birth. I must assume that those in command of the Federal army are gentlemen, and that they will allow me to perform this unhappy duty. Yes, I would hope for the courtesy of a parole. If I don't get that—well, I must attend to my poor wife no matter what."

"That's commendable, Colonel. Now, before we continue with this conversation, I would appreciate it if you would hand over your weapons. I'll return them to you when I leave, but I would feel much more comfortable in the meantime if I could have possession of them."

Townsend sighed again, then opened a drawer of his writing desk and took out what Harry recognized was his Navy Colt. He brought it to Harry, and then also surrendered his Lefaucheux revolver from his holster. Holding them clumsily with his left hand, Harry stepped back, gesturing to the colonel to resume his seat.

When he had done so, Harry went to an armchair, setting the Griswold and Gunnison pistol on the floor, sticking the Lefaucheux in his belt, and taking up his still-loaded Navy Colt as his instrument of persuasion.

"I would be sorrier about this intrusion, Colonel, were it not for your participation this morning in my happily unsuccessful lynching."

"It is common practice for both sides to hang spies."

"I did not come here as a spy."

"You deny that you're a Yankee agent?"

"I came here in search of a friend. My reason for staying here is that I have been asked by General Grant of the Federal army and your own General Hindman to determine how and why and by whom your wife and her sister, Mrs. May Abbott, were killed."

Color came to Townsend's face. "I'll attend to that myself. I don't need your help. Sir."

"I have not undertaken this effort for you, sir, though you have my sympathy for your loss. I gave my word to both General Grant and General Hindman that I would do this."

"Raines, I wish the event this morning had proceeded as planned."

Harry raised the barrel of his pistol, aiming it generally at Townsend's head. "But it did not. You'll have to deal with the present circumstance."

"You hold a gun on me. What do you want?"

"I want to know what you know about this. May I assume that Mrs. Abbott and your wife met their unfortunate fate in this house?"

"Why in hell do you think that?"

"As it happens, I've already determined that fact."

"You think May was here?"

"Was she?"

Townsend looked away. "I was with my regiment. After Shiloh, we were deployed east of here until a week ago. When I returned, my wife was gone. Her sister was not here."

"You didn't ask your servants what happened to your wife?"

"Of course I did."

"And they didn't tell you Mrs. Abbott was here?"

"Very well. They did. But they were excitable. You can never believe them. It seemed unreasonable to believe May had gotten through the lines."

"What about your brother-in-law, Congressman Abbott?"

"You imagine him here? Should I suppose Abraham Lincoln is in Corinth as well?"

"It's easier to come and go through the lines than you might think, Colonel."

"You've proved that, sure enough. You Yankee spies seem to be everywhere."

"I told you, I came here to find a friend. Her name is Louise Devereux. She is also known as the Countess de Lachaise-Valérie. Do you know her?"

"I know her to be a Yankee spy, just like you." His rising color was visible now. "The title of countess is spurious, no doubt."

"Not at all. There are many such in New Orleans, from the French days."

"She is not a respectable woman."

Harry had lowered his pistol. He raised it again for emphasis. "Where is she?"

"How in hell would I know that?"

"She said she made the acquaintance of General Hindman. You have been much in his company."

"She was a nurse. I visited the wounded of my regiment at the hospital. I may have met her."

"Louise is one of the most beautiful women you and I will ever meet. You would have remembered."

"Very well. I remember. But I do not know where she is. She was only there a few days. There are not many nurses left. Most of them have gone with the Confederate wounded to Tupelo."

There was a crash of glass downstairs. Harry got up, hesitating. "Stay here if you would, Colonel. I'll see what this is about." He lingered in the doorway to make certain that Townsend was not moving, then took to the stairs.

Tantou was standing in the downstairs hall, holding the buffalo gun and another rifle, his eyes a little wide.

"What did you break?" Harry asked.

"The window beside the door. It was locked."

"You might have tried another way."

"No time, Harry Raines. They're hot after us."

"Who?"

"Friends of your two card players. We escaped them, but I think maybe not for long."

" 'We'?"

He nodded to the front parlor. Harry descended the rest of the stairs and went to the room. There, lying on a horsehair sofa, was Louise.

"She's been shot," Tantou said. "I don't think bad."

Harry went to her side, happy to see her smile.

"Hello, Harry. We meet in the strangest places."

"Where are you hurt?" She was wearing a black dress, and he could not make out any blood. "What happened?"

"Somebody followed me," Tantou said. "I found her at the hospital, with Mrs. Oates. When we left, we were shot at. Miss Devereux got hit."

She had taken his hand. Harry squeezed hers reassuringly. "You were on horseback?"

"On my horse. I put her behind me. I wish I hadn't done that, Harry Raines. *Bien sûr,* I wish I hadn't."

Harry ran his hands down Louise's sides. His right one came away wet. "I fear I must remove a portion of your clothing, Louise. I must look at your wound."

"You will see nothing you haven't."

"Alas, the circumstances are different." He unbuttoned her dress, pulling the top part aside. The white of camisole was stained crimson, but not as much as he had feared. Taking out his sheath knife, he cut away the cloth that covered her injury.

The bullet had dug a canal across her flesh along a rib. Though this deep trough welled with blood, he could see a bit of bone. Examining the swelling around the wound, he judged the rib had been cracked, at the least.

Louise of a sudden sat up. Appearing magically in her hand was a derringer pistol. Aiming it over his shoulder, she fired it once, the report deafening Harry's left ear.

Reaching for his own pistol, Harry turned to see Colonel Townsend standing at the bottom of the stairs, holding a pistol. He did not appear to have been hit by Louise's shot, but it stopped him where he stood. Harry had always judged the effective range of a derringer to be about six feet.

"Don't just stand there," Harry said. "Help us. Miss Devereux has been shot."

Townsend remained motionless. Then he began to edge away.

"Damn it, sir!" Harry scolded. "Do you call yourself a gentleman?"

Tantou had quietly moved to the side, presenting Townsend with two targets instead of one—presuming he really was of a mind to employ the gun. Harry brought his Navy Colt to the fore, but kept the barrel low.

The colonel carefully put his revolver in his holster and came forward, entering the parlor. Standing before Louise, he bowed. "How can I help?"

Except for a bit of horse doctoring, all Harry knew about medicine was what he had learned from his chess-playing friend Lieutenant Colonel Phineas Gregg, the army surgeon in Washington who had taught him the curative powers of liquor, applied liberally, externally as well as internally.

"I need whiskey and some clean cloth. A lot of it, to bind the wound. And if those kitchen servants of yours are still on the premises, I should appreciate some hot water."

"I'll go with him," Tantou said.

Louise was beginning to show signs of pain now. Harry lifted her legs fully on the sofa, then placed a cushion under her head. "You have a nasty wound, but the bullet struck nothing vital. I think you have a broken rib."

" 'A hit, a very palpable hit.' "

"Hamlet."

She coughed, then smiled again. "You actually listen to the words, do you? You don't just sit there in the stalls hoping for a glimpse of the actresses' ankles."

"Your beauty is a powerful distraction."

"Was I not a good Ophelia?"

"The best."

One night she had played Ophelia, while Caitlin Howard had performed Queen Gertrude. He would not have admitted this to himself at the time, but he had been far more attentive to Louise.

"Why were you at the hospital? Why haven't you gone north?"

"Haven't finished my work."

"What work? You came here with Tantou."

"He told me you were in trouble and needed to talk to me."

"Turns out to be true." He looked again at her wound. It was oozing rather than flowing blood, but there was no way of knowing how much she had lost. She was very pale. He began to fear that she might die.

But he reckoned he was being overly worried. The bullet had not penetrated her body. It had only torn the skin and scratched a bit of bone.

He kissed her hand.

"Here's what you asked for, Raines." It was Townsend, carrying a bottle of whiskey and followed by the two black women—one carrying a steaming kettle and the other a bundle of sheeting. "Now I must ask you—gentleman to gentleman—to let me go."

Tantou stared at the colonel as though he were daft.

"I thought you wanted to wait for the Federal army—because of your wife."

"Hooligans have taken over this town—as the injury to Miss Devereux attests."

"Shoot him, Harry," she said. "He's a Rebel officer. He tried to hang you this morning."

Shooting was the only real means at Harry's disposal to stop the man from leaving. But he didn't want that. He certainly did not want a lot of bullets flying about the room—with Louise lying here helplessly.

"I think you should stay," Harry said. "Corinth will fall. The South will lose the war. You know that."

"Good night, sir. I'll do my best to see that no one molests you here." He stood a moment, reassuring himself that Harry would not put a bullet in his back. Then he vanished.

Harry held Louise's hand as he cleaned the wound with the warm water. She clenched his tightly but made no sound. When he poured the whiskey, however, she gave out a shriek, rising up and holding him fast. He waited until she at last relaxed, then offered her the bottle.

"How inelegant," she said, but she drank.

Setting the whiskey aside again, he had her sit upright, and then began to remove her clothing down to the waist. "I'm sorry. Has to be done."

She smiled in reply, then looked to Tantou, who was watching, but without expression. Harry wondered at all the extraordinary things the Métis' eyes had looked upon.

When he had disrobed her, he began winding the sheeting around her as closely as he could, as much to protect her rib as the wound.

"Too tight?" he asked.

"I'll bear it."

"When the Union Army comes, we'll get you to a surgeon."

"And when will the Union Army come?"

"I would hope very soon, but they have a peculiar commanding general."

A shot. Then two more. Broken glass flew through the air seemingly from every direction. Harry flung himself on Louise, pushing her down on the sofa, then dragging her with him to the floor.

Tantou was at the side of the door, aiming his buffalo gun at something in the darkness. Its report caused the glass of the hall chandelier to rattle.

The fire was returned from outside, shattering more window glass and pockmarking the wall with puffs of dust and wallpaper.

Harry took Louise by the hand. "We have to leave, quickly."

Tantou had put aside the buffalo gun and taken up his other rifle. Aiming it, he hesistated, then fired. A wailing cry followed the echoes of the shot.

"Where do you want to go, Harry Raines?"

"Out back. The stables."

"Okay."

Holding both rifles in the crook of his left arm, Tantou fired off two rounds from his pistol, then moved back along the hall. Harry pulled Louise along with him.

"Can you walk?" he said.

"Yes. Of course. I just hurt." She got to her knees, then rose to a sort of crouch.

They reached the rear door, flung it open, listened a moment, then crept out onto the house's back porch. The garden, illuminated faintly by the lamp in the bedroom above them, seemed to be clear of intruders. Harry took Louise by the waist, only to have her cry out. He gripped her hand instead.

"Can you run?"

"No, Harry. You ask too much."

"I'll go ahead," said Tantou. "If something moves, shoot at it. I will try for the stable wall."

He crept forward to the edge of the porch, stepped down into the garden, and moved left. Harry saw a flash from the darkness beside the stable building. Tantou went low as the bullet whipped into the wall of the main house behind them.

"Into the kitchen!" Harry said. He fired two pistol shots in the direction of their assailant, then pulled Louise across to the doorway to the kitchen building. It was a brick structure, built against fires, with one window looking out upon the garden. The black women had left, but there was still a fire glowing.

"Stay down," he said to Louise. Going to the window, he fired another shot into the blackness, hoping to draw fire away from Tantou. He succeeded. A bullet struck the exterior wall. Another chipped a piece of brick from the window frame.

Tantou came rolling through the doorway. He'd dropped his rifles but still had his revolver.

"Shut the door!" Harry said.

"No, Harry Raines. We need it open to shoot at them."

He moved to the side of the doorway. Louise crawled to beneath a large wooden table. Harry went to the window. He had the Lefaucheux, fully loaded, in his belt, but guessed that would not suffice, and so he took the time to reload his Navy Colt.

He had rammed paper and ball cartridges in only three of the chambers when the ghoulish form of a tall bearded man appeared at the door, guns blazing. Tantou put two rounds in the man from the side, then hit him hard on the head with the butt of the weapon.

As he fell, another man appeared, behind him. Harry snatched up the Lefaucheux and aimed at his chest. The round made him fly backward.

There was still the third man. "Jack. Fire out the window. I'm going after the last one."

Tantou did as instructed, saying nothing. Harry leapt over the two dead men, bringing up both the revolvers. "Again," he said.

"I have only one round left."

"Shoot it."

Tantou did so. As Harry hoped, their remaining assailant fired back, the flash marking his location in the brush beside the stable.

"Reload," Harry said, "then let him have every chamber."

Harry counted every second it took the Métis to complete the task. When Tantou finally had done so, emptying his pistol in a quick fusillade, Harry moved forward at a rapid crouch. When the return fire came, it was from a nearer place—a tree by the long, barren flower bed. The shooter was aiming at the kitchen window.

Continuing on, Harry circled around the far end of the garden, coming back upon the man from the rear. He could only hope that Tantou was not preparing to fire again. Given that possibility, he had to move quickly.

He didn't want to shoot this last intruder. He certainly didn't want to kill him. He'd no idea how hard to hit him on the head to render him insensible without causing fatality. He did his best.

The man groaned after he was struck. Slumping to the ground, he groaned again.

"Don't shoot!" Harry shouted to Tantou. "I have him!"

They dragged him back to the kitchen. "It's the gambler from Natchez," Harry said.

"He lost this hand," said Tantou.

Harry heard a moan, but it wasn't the dandy. It was Louise.

He hurried to her side. She was taking short breaths, and crying out between them. She was clutching her other side. She'd been shot again.

MAJOR Hawkins shook Grant awake. "What is it?" asked the general. "Are we under attack?"

"No, sir. It's—"

"Is Halleck finally moving on Corinth?" Grant sat up. There was a dim light outside from a lantern, but little of the illumination filtered into the tent.

"No, sir, I'm afraid not. It's Congressman Abbott, General Grant. He has arrived."

"What does he want with me? Halleck's in command."

"He said he was told you now know what happened to his wife."

Chapter 26

AT Grant's request, Colonel York saw to the congress-man's comforts for the remainder of the night. Grant returned to his own tent and his too often disturbed sleep, hopeful of being able to continue his slumbers well into the morning, as Halleck would be waiting for an attack that would never come.

Grant reminded himself that he had thought the same thing back up the river by Shiloh, and had been rudely surprised. But Pierre Beauregard was no Albert Sidney Johnston, and those Corinth trains had not been bringing reinforcements. Grant went to sleep thinking he might be able to make use of Congressman Abbott—if not to secure another command, at least another assignment. Maybe over in Missouri or Arkansas. He could not abide much more of this.

HE was awakened in the morning by an excited Captain Rawlins. "General! It's happened!"

Grant succumbed to a yawn. "What is it, John. I can't believe we're actually being attacked."

"On the contrary, sir. Corinth is taken."

"Truly?" Grant sat up.

"Yes, sir. Pope's crossed Bridge Creek and is on the bluff. Sherman's in their works, too. He pushed his pickets out early this morning and they encountered nothing. Quaker guns. Everywhere. But nothing else. The Regs took every cannon and bullet with them. The town's deserted."

"How do we know this?"

"Sherman sent a dispatch, General." Rawlins handed the paper to him.

Grant read it over quickly, then folded it and put it in his pocket. He lighted a cigar and began pulling on his pants.

"No time for breakfast," Grant said. "Get the rest of the staff together. I'm going to ride right in."

"What about Congressman Abbott?"

"Wake him. I want him with us."

GRANT'S party, which included his Fourth Illinois Cavalry escort and a somber Abbott, approached the town by the Corinth Road. As they neared the now deserted Confederate battle works, Grant saw that they were less fortifications than instruments of a masterful duplicity. As the scout Raines had first reported, the fearsome-looking artillery that had so intimidated Halleck were indeed Quaker guns, painted logs mounted on carts and wagons. Set here and there along the line were straw-filled sack-cloth dummies dressed in Rebel uniforms. Some had smiles painted on their faces. One that Grant stopped beside had two bullets through the head.

"They disturbed that fellow not at all," he said.

"I saw an actual dead man like that at Shiloh," Rawlins said. Hawkins added nothing to that remark. York was riding back with Abbott and paid no attention at all.

The general moved on. Pope had been the first to enter Corinth, but Sherman's division, which Grant was trailing behind, had come in not much later. Grant found the general on foot, standing with his staff on the lawn of a Methodist church.

"Say what you will, Grant," Sherman said, coming to his friend's stirrup, "it's a brilliant victory. The most important rail junction in Mississippi ours without firing a shot."

"It's ours because of Shiloh," said Grant. "A shot or two were fired there."

"Well, that's true, I suppose. But it's still a happy occasion. If we keep pushing the bastards, we'll be at the Gulf of Mexico in no time."

"The Gulf, maybe, but we won't have the river. Won't have Vicksburg. Not going to take that place without a shot."

"Don't be a grouch, Grant. Hop down and join me in a little celebration."

"I'll join you presently, Bill. I want to see what the Rebels left in the way of stores. And I suppose I'd better find Halleck."

"Suit yourself. Join me for dinner then."

"That I will." Sherman touched his hat, and Grant did the same. Then, pressing his heels to Fox's flanks, Grant moved on.

He came upon Lew Wallace on the courthouse steps, talking with officers of Halleck's staff. When Grant dismounted, Wallace came forward, all serious, and drew him aside.

"They left us nothing, General," he said. "The Rebs took it all, except for a few locomotives and railcars they blew up or burned. There are a lot of stray dogs and cats around, but damn few people. I think only two or three diehard families have stayed. Everything else—everyone else—all gone.

"No prisoners?"

Wallace looked across the square toward some railroad yards. "A few deserters and stragglers. Pope has sent cavalry patrols down the Tupelo road, but I doubt they'll find many Rebels. We've given Beauregard so much time, his army could be in Jackson by now."

A novelist's exaggeration, but true enough.

"What about their wounded?"

"Took them along, too. Most of the nurses as well. I tell you, General, Corinth was not captured. It was abandoned to us."

"I'll not dispute the assertion, General." Grant glanced toward the courthouse door. "I'm taking dinner with Sherman, Lew. Why don't you join us—if our commander allows."

"I should be delighted, General." Wallace bowed.

Halleck and his staff were inside, occupying the main courtroom until the general decided upon a headquarters. He was seated at a long table presumably used by lawyers in normal times. Halleck seemed surprised, and not a little apprehensive, to see Grant before him.

"Good morning, General Grant. I am glad to see you well."

"Hard to sustain an injury, sir, sitting on a camp chair."

Halleck ignored this. "Take a look at the map, if you would."

Spread out on the table before him, it was finely rendered, drawn by a practiced cartographer. But it bore no sign of troop positions.

Halleck joined Grant, leaning close over the chart. "Beauregard evidently distrusts his army," he said. "Otherwise he would have fought."

"Your entrenchments, General. They must have dissuaded him."

"Of course they did!" Halleck took a deep breath, as though he'd been through some exertion. "Always entrench." He frowned, his eyes following the line of railroad on the map.

"Tupelo's where they are," Halleck said.

"Seems to be. We should pursue Beauregard with the utmost celerity."

"Pursue?"

"Yes, General."

"We have just taken Corinth. We cannot abandon it to the enemy."

"If we keep our force between Beauregard and here, we abandon nothing."

"No, General," Halleck said, his frown now seeming a permanent fixture of his face. "We must fortify."

"Fortify?"

"Fortify. And entrench."

Grant wished he'd stayed with Sherman. He stood a little straighter. "Have you orders for me, General Halleck?"

"Assist in the defense, General."

"Very well. Thank you, sir."

Once again on the courthouse steps, Grant motioned to York.

"Yes, sir?"

"The scout Raines. He must be here in Corinth. See if he can be found. I'd like to talk to him."

"Who shall I send, General? We really haven't any troops of our own to command."

"Take some of my cavalry escort. And direct the search personally."

"Yes, sir. Do you suppose he's still alive?"

"I very much hope so, Colonel."

* * *

THE nurses had placed Louise on a pallet off in a corner of
the hospital that had been converted from the Baptist church,
and Harry had spent the remainder of the night beside her.
Early in the morning, a Union Army surgeon had stopped by,
appalled to find a woman on the premises and promising help
at once, but an hour or more had passed and there was no sign
of it. When the door did open again, it was Tantou.

"You are supposed to be guarding our prisoner," Harry
said.

"He is in the cellar of the Townsend house. I have tied
him up well."

"The servants may come back and free him."

"I do not think so, Harry Raines. I left the bodies where
they fell outside the kitchen. If the servants come, they will
go away again very quickly."

Harry sighed. "More dead."

"You can say that every day in this country," Tantou said.

Harry looked about the room. A Union soldier had died
during the night. The sergeant Harry had spoken with
while briefly a patient here was gone.

He turned to Louise. She was in pain so severe it had
dulled her senses. Her second wound had been serious, the
round penetrating and exiting her left side just to the side
of her stomach. Harry wasn't sure what vital organs were
near there, but there had to be some. He was thankful that
Mrs. Oates and another nurse had managed to stop the
bleeding. Still, a doctor was needed. Louise's hand had been
struck as well. One finger looked mangled. Mrs. Oates had
wound a bandage around her entire hand.

"I will go wait outside," Tantou said. "We may have more
enemies."

"Thank you," Harry said.

Louise turned her head toward him. Her eyes were clearer now. "Harry? Am I going to die?"

He kissed her hand and then smiled. "No, Countess. We won't let that happen. But I fear you'll have to endure some unpleasantness."

"Is the bullet still in me?"

"No. It went on through. That was fortunate. You won't have to fear any doctor's digging."

"If I live, it's because of you." Her voice was faint. Harry supposed the pain was rising again, coming in waves. He wondered why she did not cry out.

"I wish Tantou had not brought you to the Townsend house."

"No. That was right. I was in danger." She coughed, which increased her hurt, twisting up her face. He wanted to hold her, but that would make matters worse.

"Raines!"

Harry looked up, hoping it was the doctor. There instead, standing by the front door, was Colonel York. He came forward, ignoring the many other patients in the room. "Are you wounded?" York said.

"No," Harry said. "My friend Miss Devereux is. We're waiting for a doctor."

York took off his hat. "My apologies, ma'am. Sorry to disturb you." He looked to Harry. "General Grant would like to see you."

"I cannot leave her."

"This is General Grant, the deputy commander in chief. If you're in the Federal service, as you say, Raines, you cannot ignore his instruction."

"I understand that. But you do not understand the severity of this situation."

York frowned, finding in Louise's stricken face the truth of Harry's words. "I can't go back without you, Raines."

Harry gently slipped his hand away from hers and carefully got to his feet, moving York away.

"Get an army surgeon over here, at the double quick. More, if you can find them. Some of the men here are in a very bad way. But she must have attention. I won't leave her until she does."

"Very well. I'll send someone. The doctors are all over at the big hospital. I'm not sure they know about this one."

"See to it, please, Colonel."

"As you command—Captain." He said that with a grin.

"Wait. How did you find me?"

"Your Indian friend is standing out by the steps—so tall and straight you'd think he was a cigar store Indian."

"I'd advise you not to say that to him."

"Yes. Well." He stepped away. "I'll see to that doctor."

THE surgeon who came, a doughty-looking fellow with gray muttonchop whiskers and an air of concern, knew nothing about the physician who had first stopped by and had no excuse for his continuing absence. He asked Harry to step away while he examined Louise and then commanded Mrs. Oates to acquire a blanket and hold it up as a screen.

When he was done, he frowned. A sensation like icy water ran down Harry's back.

"She is lucky to be alive," he said. "She's still in a serious way. What happened? I thought the Rebels left without a fight."

"This was a dangerous place in the time between their leaving and your arriving. We took refuge in a house near here and were set upon by brigands. We drove them off, but there was shooting."

"Dreadful. Dreadful." He paused. "Colonel York said you were in the Federal service."

Harry lowered his voice. "That's correct, but nothing I wish to advertise."

"Yes, well. Hmm." He turned back to Mrs. Oates. "Madam, we cannot have this woman here among all these men. There are empty houses all over this town. I want her taken to one and attended to. If not by yourself, by another nurse. I have orderlies who can take over here."

"It seems strange you are so concerned about a Southern woman," Mrs. Oates replied. "We've heard stories—"

"We are not monsters, madam. We attend to all who require it." He looked around him. "These are men from Shiloh?"

"Yes, sir. Federal soldiers. From the first day's fighting. I fear there are fewer than there were."

"I'll send for help."

Harry leaned close to the doctor. "My friend? Will she live?"

"Who can say in this damnable war? The wound is not as bad as it looks, but it is bad enough. I'll see she's comfortable."

"I can tell you General Grant will appreciate that attention."

"Grant?"

"Yes. I am going to see him now."

"We'll take care of her."

Before leaving, Harry knelt by Louise again. "They're going to move you to a house."

A faint smile. "I can hear, Harry. I was not struck in the ear."

"The doctor seems sanguine."

She shook her head. "He doesn't know."

"I know." He kissed her brow. "I must go to General Grant. I'll return as soon as I can."

"'I would have thee gone; and yet no further than a wanton's bird, who lets it hop a little from her hand.'"

"You were a marvelous Juliet." He squeezed her hand and stood. Two soldiers with a stretcher entered as he went through the doorway.

York, looking impatient, was waiting at the sidewalk. Tantou stood with him. Harry spoke to him first.

"They are taking her to a house, Jack. You are not my servant, but I would appreciate it if you would stay with her."

"I would do that if you did not ask me."

"I mean stay with her constantly."

Tantou's expression did not change. "I know."

"We're off to General Grant, then. Thank you."

"Good-bye, Harry Raines."

"ODD fellow," said York. "I don't believe I've ever been in so close a social acquaintance with an Indian before."

"He's half French," said Harry.

"Yes, well." He took a flask from his pocket. "Will you have a sip?"

"I will," said Harry. The colonel had excellent taste in whiskey. "I do believe we have met before."

"Oh? Where would that have been?"

"In Washington City, when you were a congressman. Rose Greenhow was a friend of my family's."

"Rose Greenhow the Rebel spy."

"She was then the leading hostess of Washington. I do believe you were often in attendance at her receptions and soirees."

"Well, I was. But I do not recall you, sir."

"I believe your attention was taken by the ladies."

AS York had failed to readily produce Raines, Grant had taken Halleck at his word and gone off on an inspection of Corinth's periphery, accompanied only by Rawlins and half a dozen troopers from his cavalry escort. The Confederate works were so extensive and came so close to encircling the town that there seemed little need to add to them. There would be no need at all if Halleck would listen to reason and keep the Federal army moving toward Tupelo.

Arriving at some woods on the northern outskirts of Corinth, Grant decided to make his small headquarters within them, and ordered the pitching of tents. Nearly two hours later York and Raines came in, the latter riding the dark jumping horse Grant had loaned him. York must have made a present of it.

Grant offered the scout a cigar and a chair, both of which the Virginian happily accepted, though he winced from pain seating himself.

"You all right, Raines?"

"Passed an uncomfortable night, sir."

"He was with Louise Devereux, General," York said. "They came under fire from stragglers, and she was shot. She's badly wounded. We've been at the hospital. The reason for the delay, sir."

"Unhappy news. How near are you to concluding the matter of Mrs. Abbott and her sister?"

"Very near, sir. But I fear I need just a bit more time."

"And why is that?"

"Colonel Townsend, the husband of Mrs. Abbott's sister, got away from me and I believe has left the town."

"He's a colonel in the Confederate Army. I shouldn't expect him to wait around to greet us."

"I had him as my prisoner last night, but I was distracted in caring for Miss Devereux, and the colonel departed."

"By train?"

"No, sir. By then, all the trains still in working order had left Corinth. They blew up the rest."

"We heard them. If he's on horseback, our cavalry patrols may turn him up. What do you want with him?"

"Some explanations. I have determined that it was in his house that the ladies were killed."

Grant pondered this. "Take some of my cavalry escort and look for him. But please don't go behind the Rebel lines again. You're a marked man, I'm told. Nearly hanged you, they said. If they capture you and finish the job, this enterprise will be concluded unsatisfactorily."

As would Harry's life. "I might not be back until tomorrow, General."

"Very well, but I don't want you behind the Rebel lines."

"I understand, General."

"I gave you a good horse, Raines. Now, please be about your business. I have promised Congressman Abbott an answer."

Chapter 27

"I am, it seems, at your disposal again, sir," said York after they had mounted. "Where would you like to go first?"

"The Townsend house. I wish to speak to my prisoner."

"Very well." York pulled his horse around to the right, then stopped. "Where is this house?"

"Continue as you have, Colonel. To the right."

"Thank you. Captain."

THEY entered the grounds through the garden. York was quite disturbed to see the bodies, which were marked by clouds of flies.

"Who are these men?" he demanded.

"Our assailants from last night. The fat one was working as a sutler for Farragut's river flotilla, but I think his true employer wears a Confederate uniform. The bearded gentleman is not known to me. One of them shot Miss Devereux. I am not clear as to which."

York gulped. "So you killed them both?"

"We shot them because they were trying to shoot us and were doing an excellent job of it. If this offends you, sir, look upon it as a miniature of one of your glorious big battles. Shiloh come to mind. Surely you have seen dead men before."

"Surely I have." York summoned two of the cavalry escort forward. "Bury these men, please. Doesn't have to be deep. Just quick."

"We have no shovels, sir."

"There must be some in the stable."

"Wait," said Harry. He went to the bodies, waving some of the flies away, then knelt by the fat sutler, averting his eyes from the man's face.

The pockets yielded a small folding knife, a short-barreled pistol, a bloodied handkerchief, a whiskey flask, a deck of cards, a folded map of Corinth and surroundings, and a large wad of U.S. greenbacks.

"How can you stand the smell?" York said.

"I can't," Harry said. He moved to the bearded man. This search was performed much more quickly, as he had nothing in his possession but a folding knife and five twenty-dollar gold pieces. "You are a gentleman, Colonel. Are you a man of means as well?"

"Not particularly."

"Your father?"

"He owns a mercantile firm in Philadelphia. And a few ships."

Harry handed York the money. "This will be safe with you then."

"Should I turn it into the provost marshal?"

"No. It is evidence."

*　*　*

THE Natchez dandy had been tied very securely. The ropes that bound his wrists and feet were looped fast around two beams, suspending him above the ground in the manner of a hammock.

"This is rather cruel," said York.

Harry took out his sheath knife, slicing the rope at the man's feet first and then sawing away at the other. He tried to catch him when it parted but missed. The dandy fell with a nasty-sounding thump. He glared at Harry like a trapped beast waiting his chance.

"Tantou is very fond of Miss Devereux," Harry explained.

"Would you like water?" York said to the prisoner.

The dandy smiled. "If you would be so kind, sir, I would appreciate it."

York went back outside. Harry came nearer his prisoner. "What is your name?"

"Stephen Gillette."

"Are you from New Orleans?"

"I am from Natchez, sir. Where we met, as I do believe."

"You are very civil today. You were not last night."

"Just a soldier, sir, doing his duty."

Harry took out his Navy Colt. "I do believe, Mr. Gillette, that you and the other two gentlemen are assassins who have gone about the South hunting suspected Federal agents and killing them, as you tried to do to me last night."

"And I do believe you are a Federal agent, Mr. Raines."

"I am an army scout. More to the point, sir, you have been captured and made prisoner while not in uniform. You know what that means."

"I am not a spy, Raines. Whatever I've done, it's been within Confederate lines."

"You are not in uniform, and you are now behind Union lines. I am in a position, sir, to decide whether you are to be treated as a spy, and at some point hanged, or should be considered a member of some sort of irregular militia, and therefore to continue your status as prisoner. Right now my leanings are toward 'spy.'"

York returned, bearing a tin cup and canteen. He poured water and placed the cup in Gillette's hand with great gentleness. "Can we not undo his bonds?"

"Not just yet," Harry said. "Why did you come after us, Mr. Gillette?"

"Orders."

"Whose orders?"

"I cannot say. I was told to come here and . . ." He stared hard at the rope around his wrists.

"And kill me."

Gillette's eyes fell to his wrists. He was perhaps wondering if it would make any difference if he was free of the rope. "Yes."

"And Miss Devereux?"

"Not initially."

Harry stepped away, going over to an upended trunk. He lay it on its side and sat down on it. "Who told you I was a Yankee spy?"

"The word came from New Mexico, by way of Texas, and then New Orleans. We were told you'd have some strange French-speaking Indian with you, and a uniquely long rifle."

"Buffalo gun."

"I've no familiarity with those animals, but I believe that is what this sort of weapon is called."

York poured the man more water, then capped his canteen and moved to the side, following the exchange as though it were a theatrical piece.

"Who is the fat man in the checkered suit we're burying out there?"

"His name is Hannibal Fenton, as you know. He followed you from New Orleans. Used to be a drummer, but signed up with us when the Federals got close to New Orleans."

"And the bearded man?"

"He's local. His name's Silas Granger. He was a paddy roller before the war."

"What in blazes is a paddy roller?" York asked.

"Slave-hunter," said Harry grimly. "They go after run-aways for a fee. They carry studded wooden clubs they called 'paddles,' employing them to subdue and discipline the slaves they caught, before marching them back home. The Negroes call them paddy rollers—after these 'paddles.' "

"What barbarism."

Gillette glowered at the officer. He'd probably taken him for a friend, but now found him to be a Lincolnite abolitionist.

"Did you take your orders from Silas Granger?" Harry asked.

Gillette observed him coolly for a moment. "Sir. I am as much a gentleman as you. Do you think I would accept a man like that as a superior?"

"Then from whom?"

"I was sent here by Colonel Jenkins in Natchez. He told me to find you and Miss Devereux."

"For what purpose?"

"To apprehend you."

"Meaning, to shoot us?"

Gillette turned away, silent.

"This man should be turned over to the provost marshal," said York.

"No," said Harry. "I don't want him put with the other prisoners. Can you assign a man to guard him?"

York shrugged. "You seem to be giving the orders here, Raines."

"Then assign a reliable man to him and let's be off."

"Where?"

"South. I'd like to renew my acquaintance with Colonel Townsend, if that's still possible."

As they followed the road out of Corinth, York at his side and the five Illinois cavalrymen trailing behind, Harry began to have a sense of the true nature of this war.

It was a war of roads. Rivers of mud in the rain, corridors of choking dust in the dry heat, they crisscrossed every reach of the South. Generals moved troops along them; dug troops in along their sides. They were a major element of every strategy, every tactic. It struck Harry that the war would not be won until the Federal armies had marched down every Southern road, but, oddly, jangling along this one toward the town of Rienzi, it seemed to him that this particular road—slicing straight through soft fields bordered by cottonwood trees—might somehow be the magical one that led to victory and an end to the fighting.

It led to Jackson, and thence to Vicksburg. The fighting in the East was about armies. The place names were almost irrelevant—merely focal points for maneuver in the great wrestling matches between the great forces sweeping back and forth across the countryside.

Here in the West, it was all for places: New Orleans, Island No. 10, the Mississippi; Fort Donelson, Nashville, Shiloh, and now Corinth. The Union Armies were clumsy and often ill-led—as this lunkheaded Halleck daily demonstrated—but, overall, they were resolute, inexorable in their forward push, tearing chunks off the Confederacy as they went along—as they would do again as they rose from their entrenchments and took to this road.

"I don't think we should go much farther," York said.

"Colonel, we're not two miles outside of Corinth." Harry looked to the distant point where the road disappeared at a line of trees and sky.

"Yes, but the same may be true of the Rebels," York said.

"We're supposed to have set up prisoner camps for the Confederate stragglers. We've yet to encounter any."

"Very well, Captain. You have General Grant's authority. I do not."

"Not at all, Colonel. We share it. Now, everything depends on our recapturing Colonel Townsend, and I intend to find him."

"You should never have let him go."

"As I've said, I had distractions—Miss Devereux the chiefest."

"I suppose."

"Have you never been confused by the company of a beautiful woman, Colonel?"

" 'Confused'? What do you mean?"

"Made to act irrationally."

"No," said York, spurring his horse forward.

THEY passed an encampment on the right side of the road and then another on the left. A mile or more beyond, a cavalry patrol was spotted coming toward them from the south, signaled by dust.

The lieutenant in charge saluted York, eyeing Harry with curiosity.

"Any Rebels?" York asked after returning the salute.

The younger man shook his head. "We went down five miles. Not a mule. When they skedaddled, they kept at it."

"Have you seen any Secesh prisoners?" Harry asked. "I'm looking for one."

"I think they have a few in those camps back up the road. We've seen none. We've seen no one."

"Very well," said York, evidencing some relief. "We'll accompany you back to Corinth."

"No," said Harry. "I want to go on."

York swore. It was the first time Harry had heard him do that.

WITH the colonel becoming increasingly disagreeable, they advanced another three miles or so, encountering no Rebels, uniformed or civilian. No Africans either. The slaves had either been taken down to Tupelo with the Confederate Army or had somehow made their way to Federal lines. As he hadn't seen any on the road, Harry could only presume the former.

The top of a small rise gave view of a farmhouse and barn. Harry parted from the others and trotted up to the house. He halted his horse before the front door, waiting, for something about the place gave the sense of human occupancy. Finally, a small girl came and stood in the brightness of the sunlit doorway, peering up at him. Her mother joined her, but stayed in the shadows.

"Are there any Confederate troops nearby, ma'am?" Harry asked.

"Who are you?"

"Army scout. We're not looking to do battle."

"None here. None comin', I don't think. Long gone."

Harry surveyed the horizon. Nothing moved. "Thank you, ma'am."

As he turned his horse, she asked: "Are you a Yankee?"

"No, ma'am. Just a traveler trying to find his way home."

THEY found a major back at the encampments who took them to where the Rebel prisoners were being kept. There were perhaps a hundred men there, all but two of them in the enlisted ranks. A captain, covered with dried mud and apparently captured trying to cross a stream, was the highest-ranking officer. He had no knowledge of Townsend. He asked for whiskey, giving Harry the idea that he'd stayed behind mostly to sleep off a bender. None of the Union men felt inclined to indulge the fellow. As he thought upon it, neither did Harry.

THEY returned to Corinth at dusk. York stopped at the courthouse to inquire after the latest orders. Harry waited outside with the Illinois cavalrymen, idly listening to their soldiers' jokes and complaints while fixing his mind on matters of more moment.

York came down the steps, slapping his gauntlets against his legs.

"Damnation," he muttered, mounting his horse. "Not a Rebel in miles and we're digging gun emplacements."

"What are your orders?"

"Are you done with me?"

Harry thought upon this. "I should like to return to the Townsend house and check on my prisoner. If you would oblige me, I would appreciate your taking him to General Grant's camp and putting him under guard for the night."

"Where will you go?"

"To the hospital."

"I understand that, right enough." He gave Harry a salute and prepared to move on.

"A moment, sir. There is something else I need. Have you some dispatch paper?"

York provided a sheet and a pencil. Harry wrote on it quickly. "Tomorrow," he said, handing York the sheet of paper, "I shall require the use of the Townsend house—and the presence of the people on this list."

York frowned. "You have put my name here."

"Yes, I have."

"For what purpose?"

Harry considered this. "To deal with contingencies, Colonel." He saluted the colonel, then trotted away in the other direction.

TWO ambulances were standing in front of the hospital, which the Union Army had taken over in a very major way.

He stopped a surgeon just inside the door. "Excuse me, sir. I'm looking for a woman patient. A gunshot victim. Louise Devereux. She was taken to a house near here, but I don't know which one."

The doctor contemplated Harry sadly. "That poor creature, yes." His eyes narrowed slightly. "Are you kin?"

"A friend. A very close friend."

"My regrets, sir. Our troops are instructed not to molest civilians. I'm so sorry your friend was injured."

"This was done by Confederates. Where is she?"

"Let me see to one of the men here, then I'll take you there."

"How is she?"

"I will take you there, sir."

*   *   *

IT was a tall house, with five gables and three chimneys. Tantou stepped out of the darkness as Harry approached.

"She's alive?" Harry asked.

"They say so," said the Métis. "They will not let me go inside."

"We'll see about that." Harry mounted the porch steps quickly, slipping at the top and banging his shin.

Mrs. Hudson answered the door. She appeared to be alone. "You are not welcome here," she said, starting to close the door once more.

Harry put his shoulder to it and pushed it back, nearly toppling the woman, who appeared now ready to shoot him if only she had a gun. He wondered if she did.

The surgeon followed him inside, lending some authority to his intrusion. "Where is she?" Harry asked.

"I will not tell you."

He pulled out his Navy Colt, pushed her back against the wall, and waved the barrel in front of her nose. "Where?"

"You are a damned ruffian!"

Harry feared her black retainer would leap upon him from behind, but there was nothing. "My apologies, madam," he said. "But I mean to see her, and will do so now."

"She is in a bedroom to the rear," said the surgeon, moving on in that direction.

Harry released Mrs. Hudson as he might a growling dog, following behind the doctor.

It was a small, dark room, illuminated only by a single candle. Louise lay face up on the bed, covered only by a sheet. Mrs. Oates sat in a chair in the corner nearest the door. The nurse smiled at Harry. "She will be happy to see you," she said.

Harry nodded to her but went quickly to Louise's side, sitting carefully on the bed. "Louise?"

Her paleness was evident even in the dim candlelight. When she did not respond, he took her hand in his and repeated her name again. At last her eyes opened. Her lips made the form of "Harry," then her eyes closed.

Kissing her hand, he gently lowered it to the bed and stood up, turning to Mrs. Oates. "If you will excuse me, Mrs. Oates, I'll attend to her now."

The older woman rose. "I do not think that can be permitted, Captain Raines."

"If you please, Mrs. Oates." He took the chair she had vacated and dragged it to the side of the bed. Seating himself, he took revolver to hand again, resting it on his lap. Mrs. Oates and the surgeon left, closing the bedroom door quietly. From then on, Harry concentrated solely on listening to the worrisome sounds of Louise's troubled breathing.

Chapter 28

HARRY awoke to find himself being shaken by the surgeon from the evening before.

"You must leave now, Mister Raines. We are going to examine the patient."

Rubbing his eyes, Harry ignored the command. Looking past the doctor, he noted the kindly Mrs. Oates standing on the other side of Louise's bed.

"Is she well?" Harry said.

The doctor appeared gloomy. "I don't know. She has a fever. I must examine her, and I would like you to leave, please."

Harry stood. "Louise?"

She paid him no attention. Her eyes were open, staring up at the ceiling. He took a step toward her, but the surgeon barred his way with an open hand.

"Please, sir."

*   *   *

TANTOU was seated on the porch, looking sleepy. Harry settled in beside him. "She's not doing so well."

"If she dies, we go kill that gambler."

"Let us not talk about that just yet."

Harry's attention was drawn to the street, as a group of cavalry jangled up to the house, Colonel York in the van.

"My compliments, Captain Raines," he said, dismounting. He approached the porch in parade ground fashion. "I come directly from General Grant. I am to inform you that he would like the matter of Mrs. Abbott and Mrs. Townsend resolved as soon as possible. He has given you everything you asked to assist in this enterprise, and wishes you would now make haste. Congressman Abbott would like to return East. And the general has plans as well."

"I think I can now accommodate him." Harry stood up. He needed to visit the privy. "I would appreciate having some of these cavalrymen accompany us to the Townsend house."

"What for? Captain."

"Among other concerns, for a grave-digging detail."

York took a step backward, as though Harry had said something shocking. "Have you killed someone else?"

"You recall that next to the two graves your men dug there's a long flower bed that looks like it might also be a burial mound?"

"Yes."

"I think that's what it is. I would like to know who it contains. And I would like to see the people whose names were on that list gathered at the Townsend house as well."

"We have brought them to the courthouse."

"To the Townsend house now, please. I trust General Grant and Congressman Abbott will be in attendance as well."

"Why should they do that?"

"Because I am about to resolve this matter."

The colonel returned to his horse. "It has been a pleasure serving under you, Captain. I look forward to the morrow, when our ranks shall assume their natural state."

HARRY waited until the doctor emerged from the house. The man seemed inclined to ignore him and pass by, but he stopped, reluctantly.

"The fever continues high," he said. "I am concerned about her hand. One finger is badly damaged. The other is in a dreadful state. I am going for my instruments, and then I intend to amputate."

"Doctor, she's an actress. She—"

"One cannot quote much Shakespeare from the grave, sir."

"What do you mean? Will she live?"

"That is my hope, but the finger is beyond saving."

"Her other wounds?"

"We'll do what we can." He hurried on.

Harry turned to Tantou. "Will you join me at the Townsend house? I'm not sure what I will encounter today."

"What of Louise Devereux?"

"We'll have to trust her to the doctors."

"You trust too much."

TWO men from York's cavalry escort had preceded them to the Townsend house and had begun digging at the long flower bed. Harry's greeting to them was not returned as they sweated at their labors.

Passing the three juxtaposed cabins that were the slave

quarters, Harry led the way, stopping in first at the kitchen. He kept his eyes from the wall where Louise had shed blood, but gave the room a careful perusal. The large ham that had been there the day before was still beneath its cloth. He uncovered it, finding it still fresh, if smaller than he remembered. He found three eggs in a lidded jar.

"Let's have a fire and breakfast," Harry said.

"You want me to make it?"

"I will make it if you like, but I want to do some looking around first in the house. Then I will prepare breakfast."

"No. I will do it."

Leaving Tantou to his chore, Harry went into the house, visiting every room he had searched before. The spare bedroom seemed different than he remembered. It was something to do with the bedclothes. They were still in disarray, but in a different arrangement. Mrs. Townsend's bedroom had that aspect as well, as did the colonel's.

He went to the writing desk there, but it appeared to be the same—the writing paper just as he had seen it when Townsend had been at his correspondence. Then Harry noticed the armoire. The door was ajar. Opening it fully, he found a dirty cotton shirt rolled into a ball at the bottom. Within it was a set of men's underclothes and some recently worn socks. Dropping the clothing, he turned and hurried downstairs.

Tantou had set out two plates and was frying the ham and eggs together.

"Come with me a moment," Harry said, poking his head inside the doorway.

"Why do you have your revolver out?"

Harry placed a finger to his lips. "Come."

"No. Breakfast first."

Harry sighed. With a quick glance at the digging cavalrymen, he entered the kitchen and seated himself. "Let's be quick about it."

It was a very good meal, and there was coffee, too.

"There is more meat," Tantou said, wiping his mouth with the back of his hand.

"There is, but not so much as there might have been."

"What do you mean, Harry Raines?"

"Someone's been eating the ham."

"When?"

"During the night." Harry rose. "Let us save what's left for our friends with the shovels. And I think we may have an additional guest before General Grant and the others arrive here."

Tantou rose and took out his pistol. "Where?"

"I think one of the slave cabins. Be careful."

They found him under a rope bed in the last cabin, lying very still with hands folded over his chest.

"Come along, Colonel. Breakfast is ready."

GRANT had left two letters on his camp desk—one addressed to the general in chief, Winfield Scott, and the other to Halleck. The contents were largely the same. He was resigning his meaningless post here in Mississippi and going to St. Louis, where he hoped another assignment could be found for him. He was holding off mailing the letters until after his session with Harrison Raines. If Congressman Abbott was happy with the result, Grant would press his case on him. If he was not pleased—or worse, if he was compromised by it—well, St. Louis it was.

That he was having to subject himself to this kind of

indignity angered Grant. He was a good soldier. He knew how to win battles, defeat adversaries, destroy enemy armies. This war was being run by fools, and he was not sure whether Abraham Lincoln was one of them. If Halleck continued much longer in this command, he'd be certain of it.

"Are you sure this gathering is necessary?" Congressman Abbott asked, bouncing along on his horse at Grant's side. The general had moved his horse Fox to a trot as they approached Corinth.

"I think it will be useful," Grant said. "I am hopeful you will be able to return East with the knowledge that we attempted some justice here."

"You will not detain me any longer when this is done?"

"Congressman. You are in no way under my supervision. Quite the contrary."

Abbott's hat began to slip from the bouncing. He had the poorest seat when posting at the trot Grant had ever seen. The general reined Fox back to a walk.

The congressman was grateful. "You're not happy with your present situation, are you, General?"

Grant had promised himself he would speak no ill of Halleck, no matter how pressed. "I think I provided better service at Donelson than I have at Corinth." He didn't bring up Shiloh.

"Something can be done about that," Abbott said.

"The only way to win this war is to get on with it," Grant said, speaking more to the world at large than to the congressman.

"The quicker I get back to Washington, the quicker I can attend to this matter."

"We will not keep you long, Congressman."

*   *   *

SEVERAL horses were tied up along the fence in front of the Townsend mansion, including half a dozen cavalry mounts from the Fourth Illinois.

York was standing at the gate. "Good afternoon, General. Everything has been done as Mr. Raines wished." He held Fox's reins as Grant dismounted.

"Where is he?"

"In the rear, sir. They've dug up a Negro who was buried back there."

Grant clamped a cigar between his teeth without lighting it, then mounted the stairs. Inside the house, he noted a gathering of people in the parlor to the right—an odd collection: a slave woman, a black stable boy, a Confederate officer, a dour woman in nurse's garb, a shabby civilian in funereal clothes, and an elegant fellow who might have been local gentry. Two of the Illinois cavalrymen stood as though on guard at the doorway, carbines in hand.

"Hello, General," said Raines, coming down the hall. "I believe we are ready."

"This seems all very irregular," Grant said. He lighted the cigar.

"It's the best I could do under the circumstances. Would you mind stepping in here? Raines gestured to an open door on the left. Beyond was a well-furnished study. "This the house of Colonel Townsend, C.S.A., who, as you know, is the husband of Mrs. Abbott's late sister. He is the officer you saw in the parlor."

Grant looked about the room. "What have you in mind here, Raines?"

"If you would seat yourself at Colonel Townsend's desk, sir. I'm not proposing anything like an official proceeding, but I would like to interrogate the people we have waiting in the parlor and do it before you—one at a time. When I'm done, I think you will have a clear idea of what must have happened to those unfortunate women, and why. And I think you will be able to satisfy Congressman Abbott on that question."

Grant took the chair. "You don't mean to make me a judge here?"

"No, sir, but I think it's important for you to hear everything."

The general leaned back, contemplating his cigar. He sighed. "Very well. I'd like to have Rawlins in here as well, and Congressman Abbott. Oh, yes, and Colonel York."

"I'm afraid, sir, that Colonel York is one of those I mean to interrogate."

"Does he know that?"

"I'm about to inform him—if this procedure meets with your approval."

"It mystifies me, Raines. But go ahead."

HARRY asked York to accompany him out to the back, where they found the cavalrymen at rest, having completed their labors. In the opening they had made in the flower bed, one could see a very dark face. Harry turned away.

"You understand that I'm going to bring people individually before General Grant?"

"That's what you said."

"You're going to be the first."

"Now see here, Raines."

Harry drew him aside. "I do not wish to harm your career, Colonel. I'd not deny the Union cause an able officer if it can be avoided. But I need some truthful answers. If you'll oblige me, we'll find a way to work around General

Grant. If you won't, then I'll have no choice but to inform the general that you and Mrs. Abbott were lovers, and that she came into General Grant's headquarters with the express purposes of enlisting your assistance in getting through the lines to her sister's house in Corinth. And that you may have had an assignation with her before she died."

York's blasé expression suddenly hardened. "That's nonsense—damned nonsense!"

"As I said, Colonel, I remember you from evenings at Rose Greenhow's in Washington. I encountered you at her house one evening in the company of Mrs. Abbott. I recall it well. I was reminded of it when I first looked down on her in that coffin."

"I think you are exaggerating a simple friendship."

"A very close friendship. The night she came to Grant's headquarters at Cherry Mansion, you accompanied Mrs. Abbott deep into Rebel territory after she and her escort had parted company. A mounted officer was seen crossing a bridge after her. I have a button from your uniform that must have fallen from her own clothing."

"Enough, Raines. Are you going to ask me about all this in front of the general?"

Harry heard flies. He called to the two cavalrymen by the flower bed to put some sort of cover over the exposed dark dead face. Then he returned his attention to the much-troubled colonel.

"I will ask you only whether you accompanied Mrs. Abbott further than the cavalry escort had taken her, and whether she told you she was going to the Townsend house because she feared her sister's jealous husband might kill her because he had discovered her sister's own indiscretions."

York took a deep breath, exhaling slowly. "It's the truth."

"Then it should be easy for you to answer."

"No. Not easy. Her sister's indiscretions had been with me, Raines."

"There were letters. I think he may have found one of them."

"Both sisters?" York nodded. "I recall that also. At Rose's. A sister on each arm."

"You don't understand."

"Neither, I'm sure, does Colonel Townsend. He did find letters. But as you were careful enough to use only your initials, I don't think he knows it was you."

"How can you be sure of that?"

"Because he would have killed you by now."

"YOU did *what,* York?" Grant asked.

"I accompanied her farther than the cavalry escort did, sir. There were a lot of Rebel units in the area, and I feared for her safety." York looked to Congressman Abbott, who sat glumly by Grant's side.

Grant was on to a fresh cigar. "You asked my permission to do that, Colonel, and as I recall, I declined." He struck a match.

"Yes, sir. But the situation appeared dire. The enemy pickets—"

"Those weren't pickets, Colonel. That was the Rebel army moving out in force—as we discovered so rudely in the morning. You might have informed me of their presence."

Rawlins, seated on Grant's other side, interceded. "I'm sure Colonel York would have informed you if he had made it back in time. As you recall, sir, they started their attack before you'd hardly had a bite of breakfast."

"Were you aware of the enemy moving out of Corinth in full strength?" Grant asked.

"No, sir," said York. "I was concentrating wholly on Mrs. Abbott's safety." He gave another glance to Abbott, who simply stared.

Harry could have interjected that Mrs. Abbott's safety had not been well attended to that night by anyone, but instead stepped forward, saying, "Mrs. Abbott told the general she needed to pass through the lines because her sister was in danger. Did she by any chance explain to you the nature of that danger?"

York struggled to indicate to Harry that he felt grievously betrayed by this question, without indicating the same thing to Grant. "I believe this is a very personal manner that for the sake of the lady's reputation I should forbear discussing."

"Which lady?" asked Abbott.

"Mrs. Townsend," said York.

"Colonel," said Harry, "the lady is dead. We are trying to ascertain the cause. Justice must trump discretion."

York composed himself, then spoke slowly. "Mrs. Abbott told me that her sister Mrs. Mary Townsend was romantically involved with a Union officer and that this had been discovered by Colonel Townsend. She said he was a hot-tempered man who was singularly jealous and possessive and that Mrs. Townsend had written her that she feared for her safety in her own house."

"Did she say which Union officer?" Grant asked.

"Someone in General Halleck's army, sir. I haven't the name. She said there were letters, but they used only initials."

"I have no more questions for you, Colonel," Harry said. He looked to Grant, who shook his head. Rawlins took out a small notebook and wrote something in it.

"You may go, Colonel York," Grant said.

"Who shall I send in?"

"No one just yet," Harry said. When York was gone, he turned to Abbott. "I have a question for you, Congressman."

"Is this necessary?" Abbott asked.

"Very irregular," said Grant.

"It's a simple one," Harry said. "Did you wife accompany you out here, or did she come on her own?"

"On her own."

"Did you pursue her here?"

"I'm here on official business—an inspection tour."

"But your tour took you near to where your wife had gone?"

"What are you insinuating? I hoped to meet with her while I was out here—hoped we might return together."

"Was there a letter—mailed to Washingtom—from her sister?"

"Yes. I believe so. She would not tell me its contents. I don't want to answer any more questions."

"I have no more for you, sir. I'm going to bring in your brother-in-law now. Have you any objection?"

Abbott sat back, wiping his face and the top of his head with a handkerchief. It was already a hot day. "No, Raines. Proceed. I will be interested in what he has to say."

TOWNSEND was escorted into the room by one of the cavalrymen, a gesture the Rebel colonel did not appreciate. Brushing off his sleeve where the soldier had held his arm, he went to a chair on the other side of the room from the desk and sat back, stiffly. He made no effort to extend any military courtesies.

"I resent your occupation of my house, General," he said. "I resent being held prisoner in it and demand to be sent to a prisoner-of-war camp and exchanged according to commonly agreed practice. I also would request that you allow me to see to a proper burial for my wife."

"Your protest is duly noted, Colonel. I am not here in the capacity of jailer. Mr. Raines, here, is conducting an inquiry into the murders of your wife and her sister, and since you are in Federal custody as a prisoner of war, we'd hoped you would cooperate in it."

"There is little I can tell you about my wife's death. I was away with my regiment when it happened. By the time I returned after the second day of the battle, she and her sister had disappeared."

"Have you proof of your whereabouts?" Rawlins asked.

"Yes. I was in the fight at Shiloh. You captured one of my captains—and I think a colonel of the Alabama regiment next to us. If they haven't been shipped off, you can ask them."

"Can we ask them?" Grant asked Rawlins.

"They could be up at Cairo by now, General."

"General Hindman did say Colonel Townsend was at the battle," Harry added.

"My regiment is part of General Hindman's division, General Grant. He would know whether I was on the field."

"You served in Congress together," Harry noted.

"Never mind that, Raines," Grant said. "I know Hindman. I'll take his word on this."

Harry moved outside of Townsend's immediate reach. "Colonel, I mean no offense to you, but we've been given reason to believe that your wife may have been guilty of an indiscretion with a Union officer."

Townsend abruptly came forward, hands on the arms of his chair, as though he were about to leap at Harry, in the manner of a wild animal seeking a bite of throat. He restrained himself, but not by much. "You trespass on my wife's honor, sir. Were we in different circumstances, I would call you out."

"Nevertheless, were you aware of such a liaison?"

"Damn you! I will not allow you to speak of this!" A plea to Grant. "This is outrageous, sir!"

Grant gave Harry a reproachful glance, waving his hand as if to shoo the subject from the room.

"Very well, Colonel." Harry crossed to a bookcase, where he had left the Lefaucheux. "When I found this in your bedroom upstairs, five of the six cartridges had been fired. At what, sir?"

"Why are you such an idiot? I was at Shiloh! I fired them at Yankees, like you!"

"I am a Virginian, sir. Not a Yankee. I have one last question for you. We found a man—a black man—buried in your garden. Can you tell me who he is, and why he is there?"

"No, I cannot. I was told my wife's maid and her sister's were shot while in Federal custody. These are murderous times—I would say especially for the Negro."

"This man was killed fairly recently. Well after Shiloh. Well after you returned to Corinth."

"I have spent my days with my regiment, returning home only at night. I've no idea what went on in my absence. Union agents have been agitating among the Negroes. I'm not surprised some of them have gotten killed."

"But why buried in your garden?"

"Who knows? You yourself had two men buried there."

Grant and Rawlins looked to one another. Abbott seemed lost in his thoughts—or his sadness, if that's what it was.

"Thank you, Colonel," Harry said. The cavalryman opened the door and moved toward Townsend, who pulled his arm away when the soldier tried to grip it.

The colonel strode out of the room, his boots sharp against the floor.

THE cook was summoned next. She'd been found in the contraband camp, though the scullery maid who worked with her in the Townsend kitchen had not been located. The cook was wide-eyed with fear, exacerbated by Townsend's booming from the parlor: "I'll not be compromised on the word of a Negro!"

Harry shut the study door and offered her a seat.

"What is your name, ma'am?" Harry asked. His courtesy confounded her. He gestured to her to respond.

"I'se Lucy."

"You're the cook here?"

"I'se whatever dey wants, but when dey wants to eat, I'se the cook."

"When did you last see Mrs. Townsend?"

"The night her sister May come visitin'."

"Did you cook for them?"

"Nossir. I acks Mrs. Townsend if she want to eat somethin', but she said no and tol' me to go back to bed."

"Were they alone—Mrs. Townsend and Mrs. Abbott?"

"Nossir. Dey had a genl'man guest."

"Did you see him?"

"Nossir. But I heard him. Dey was joyful."

"Joyful?"

"Dey was happy, the three of them."

Grant was not. Harry began to fear he'd be given insufficient time for this.

"Do you remember anything else?"

"Nossir. I goes to sleep in my cabin. Jessie, de scullery maid, she sleeps dere, too. But den I wakes up because dere's dis mighty screamin', and den I hears dis gunshot."

"You're sure it was a gunshot?"

"Yessir. Nowadays we all knows what dey sound like."

"And then what?"

"Dis big black man comes up to de door to ma cabin and tells Jessie and me to stay in dere."

"Did you recognize him?"

"Yessir. He de man from de hospital."

"And then what happened?"

"Ah pokes out ma head a li'l later and ah sees him loaded somethin' into a wagon out by de stable. It's a wagon wid a canvas top, from de hospital."

"Ambulance?"

"Yessir."

"And then?"

"He drives off. I goes back to bed, but when I wakes up, everybody but Jessie and Toby, de stable boy, dey's gone. Miz Townsend, Miz Abbott, de genl'man caller, Alva and Miz Abbott's maid, dey's all gone. De side parlor carpet, it's gone, too. Colonel Townsend he comes home late in de day, toward sundown, an' he throws a fit. He calls in de army police—"

"The provost guard."

"Yessir. Dey looks all through de house and de kitchen and our cabins and de stable, but dey don't find nothin'."

"And then?"

"And den Colonel Townsend he gets real drunk and de next dey he goes back to de army. And den nothin' much else happen until you and dat Injun show up and den de Yankee army comes."

"How did you get to the contraband camp—the place where we found you?"

"Jessie and me, we runs away, but the Yankee soldiers find us and take us to de camp. Dey tell us we's free, but den dey bring us back here."

"You are free," Rawlins interjected. "When this is done, someone will take you back to the camp."

Grant made no objection. Abbott was staring in apparent amazement at the entire proceeding.

"While you've been in the camp, have you encountered anyone who saw Alva and Mrs. Abbott's maid while they were there?"

"Yessir. A preacher man. He's a black man, but he's de boss man kinda of de camp."

"Did he say what happened to them?"

"He say dey was kilt."

"Did he say by who?"

"Nossir. But only black folks in dat camp."

"Thank you, madam."

LUCY was replaced with Toby the stable hand, who told a similar story, confirming that the wagon seen that night was an ambulance.

"He brings out two long sacks—like eleven-foot cotton sacks, only dey's heavy."

"Is that all he put in the wagon?"

"Nossir. He brung out Alva and the free woman who's maid to Miz Abbott. He tells dem he's taken dem to de Underground Railroad so dey can go north and be free. But he tell dem dey must never come back to Corinth, lessen dey want to be slaves de rest of dere lives."

"Did you know this man?"

"Don't know him. But ah seen him plenty. He be a slave, but he somethin' like a free man down at de hospital, workin' with all dose women."

"Did you have a close look at what he was loading into the wagon?"

"Nossir. I stays in the stable, outa de way. Can I go now?"

"Stay in the parlor with the others awhile. You'll be free to go in a bit."

"Yessir." He was out of the room like a rabbit.

HARRY'S next performer in this peculiar recitation was the scrawny undertaker, who introduced himself as Elias Mason. He told those assembled that he would be glad to answer their questions, provided he receive in return permission to continue doing business in the town, with whatever custom the hospitals and the Federal army might provide.

"Such matters are not my responsibility," said Grant quietly.

"I'll write a note to the provost marshal," said Rawlins, and he commenced to do so.

Harry sat down. Every one of his various pains, aches, scrapes, and bruises was revisiting him. "Mr. Mason," he said from his chair, "you are acquainted with a gentlemen in your trade named O'Toole?"

"I am, sir. He operates the undertaking concern down the street from mine."

"He has an assistant—a black man?"

"Yes, sir. Joseph. He's a freedman."

"And where are both of these gentlemen now?"

"In my establishment, sir. I found it necessary to embalm them, as they were discovered in O'Toole's place dead. Shot dead, the both of them."

"Has anyone been apprehended for this crime?"

"No, sir. The sheriff, before he departed the town, said he thought it might have been done by robbers. Mr. O'Toole came into a sum of money recently. Bought himself a new hearse and several suits of excellent clothing."

"When was this?"

"Right after the battle at Shiloh Church," the undertaker said.

"Was this sudden wealth due to the increase in custom from the dead soldiers being prepared for shipment home?"

"I don't think so. We all got pretty well busy, but the payment comes from the families, and it's slow in coming, usually."

"But Mr. O'Toole, from somewhere, acquired a lot of money, and in a very short time. He wasn't stealing from the bodies he took in?"

Mason squirmed a little. "I won't say there's not an undertaker who might find a place for something that's of no earthly use to the departed on occasion. But the personal possessions are supposed to go home with the remains. And it's a hanging offense to be caught stealing. So I don't think so. O'Toole was what you might call low end, but not so foolish as to be taking that much money from dead soldiers."

"So how do you think he got it?"

"Someone gave it to him."

"For services rendered?"

"There's only one kind of service he performed."

"And just now he and his assistant have been shot dead."

"Yes, sir. And no one has claimed them, or stepped forward to pay my bill."

Harry had no doubt Mason would find a place for some of Mr. O'Toole's possessions that were no longer of earthly use to him—including perhaps especially the brand-new hearse.

"Thank you, sir," Harry said. "Your services are no longer required here."

"I should hope not," Grant said. When the undertaker had departed, he asked, "How many more?"

"Just two." Harry went to the door and paused. "I should like my Indian friend Tantou present when we talk to my next guest, General. Tantou seems to have an intimidating effect on him, which is well, as the fellow is a professional assassin."

"Assassin?" said Abbott. He looked frantically about, as though for some means of escape.

"I'll explain in due course."

Gillette was brought in with hands bound in front of him. Tantou followed after, bearing the buffalo gun. He seemed a man to intimidate an entire brigade.

"Please be seated, Mr. Gillette, and tell us where you're from."

"Natchez, Mississippi, in the Confederate States of America." He slouched back in the chair, as he might have done taking his leisure on the veranda of one his city's finer hotels.

"And what is your occupation?"

"Gentleman."

"Are you also a gambler?"

"Yes. As are you."

"Do you not have an additional occupation? Are you not a sort of bounty hunter, paid by your government to track down Federal agents operating within Confederate lines?"

"I am a deputized Confederate States marshal, sir. It is my duty to apprehend enemy spies and saboteurs, just as it is for my counterparts in your country."

"In 'our' country, as you put it, sir, enemy agents are

apprehended and jailed, but then they are accorded the nicety of a trial—not gunned down in back alleys."

"We are at war, sir," said Gillette. "Gunfire is a commonplace. Spies tend not to want to be apprehended. They try always to escape. As you should know."

"Why did you come to Corinth?"

"I was ordered here, along with Fenton."

"For what purpose?"

"To assist the people here in apprehending you and Louise Devereux."

"You consider Miss Devereux a Federal agent?"

"Yes, I do. As I consider you."

"Mr. Raines is a scout with this army," Rawlins corrected sternly.

Gillette shrugged. "My orders were to assist with your arrest."

"You spoke of no arrest when you came upon this house in the dead of night. You came at us with guns blazing."

"You won that scrap. Quit complaining."

Harry went over to the window. He could see the courthouse over the trees, and a church steeple. The house where Louise lay was nearby. "Who were the people you were sent here to assist?"

"I don't think I'm required to answer that."

"I know who they are. They both lie dead in the garden, along with that man Fenton you came up from Natchez with. I want you to tell the General."

Gillette apparently decided it would be useful to seem cooperative when speaking with Major General Grant. "One is a black man named Long Tom. The other is a former slave-catcher named Granger. We were told to report to them."

"Which one gave the orders?"

"The Negro."

"Does that not seem a little unusual for the state of Mississippi?"

"Orders are orders. Granger didn't seem to cotton to it much, but I didn't mind. He was just passing them on."

"From who?"

Gillette hesitated. "I cannot say."

"Because this person is still alive?"

"I cannot say."

"What if it means your life?"

Gillette looked to Grant. "Does it?"

"This is not a judicial proceeding," Grant said. "But an answer would be appreciated."

The dandy stared down at his bound hands. "I cannot say."

"I do not believe you," Harry said, leaning back against the windowsill. "Is not the person sitting just across the hall in the parlor?"

"No."

"Can we get on with this?" said Abbott. "I have much melancholy business to attend to."

"Is there anything else you would ask this man?" Grant asked Harry.

"No. There is only the woman left."

QUEEN Marie Antoinette could not have gone to her scaffold with more injured dignity than Mrs. Hudson displayed entering the room. All the men stood, waiting for her to seat herself, which she defiantly refused to do.

"Please be seated, madam," Grant requested.

"I shall not. I shall stand my ground proudly before you barbarians."

Grant was flustered. "Madam, I wish to conclude this business and get on with my own. If you will not cooperate, I'll have you locked up."

She glared at him, then went to an armchair, alighting in it with a harrumph and folding her arms across her chest. "Let me tell you, General, I consider this an outrage. I have stayed behind in Corinth when my own people have abandoned it, solely to continue caring for your soldiers, and my reward is to be dragged here at gunpoint and subjected to the vilest humiliations."

"Madam, we only want to ask you a few questions," Grant said, trying to sound kindly.

"That you could have done at the hospital—without bayonets."

Harry doubted that considerably. "Mrs. Hudson, are you acquainted with the Negro man named Long Tom?"

Her arms went higher on her chest. "Of course I am. He works with us in the hospitals."

"And do you give him orders?"

"Of course I give him orders. I am the matron there. I give them all orders."

Harry walked over to stand directly before her. "You are acquainted with the late Mrs. Townsend, and Miss Louise Devereux?"

"Why do you ask me that? You know very well that both of them worked for me as volunteer nurses there—Miss Devereux only briefly, Mrs. Townsend for many weeks."

"Do you believe both of them are Federal agents?"

"Sir. Mrs. Townsend is the wife of an officer in the Confederate States Army. She gave unstintingly of herself in the work at the hospital. Would that all the nurses followed her fine example. As I say, Miss Devereux was with us only a few days. I found her work and deportment unsatisfactory. I believe she is a woman of low moral standing."

"Would it make any difference if I told you that, in France, she holds the title of countess?"

"None whatsoever."

"Or that she has at times been in the employ of the Confederate government in Richmond?"

"That matters not. She was flirting with those poor wounded men—torturing them in their last hours with salacious excitements. Her conduct was in violation of every rule and regulation."

"And she's very pretty." Harry inwardly chastised himself for that ungentlemanly snipe, excusable only because he meant to break her composure.

"That has nothing to do with anything—except for the deleterious effect upon the wounded and dying."

"What do you suppose would move a black man to do odious work on behalf of the Confederate government that enslaves him?"

"He would do it because he is a slave. It is custom. I do not believe in it—the peculiar institution—but there it is."

"Is that what induced Long Tom to become a government assassin? Along with Mr. Gillette and Granger, the former bounty hunter?"

"I do not understand you, Mr. Raines."

"Mrs. Hudson, Mr. Gillette, and the late Mr. Fenton traveled here from Natchez to assist Long Tom and Granger in hunting down and killing me and Mrs. Devereux. This was an assignment, given them by someone here."

She stared at him blankly.

"I believe that someone is you, madam," Harry concluded. "I believe you are in charge, not only of the hospital, but also of the hunt for Federal agents in this area. You gather information from the wounded. You placed a Confederate soldier in Northern uniform among them. He talked to me at length, professing friendship."

The blank stare remained. At length, it gave way to indignation. "You are reprehensible, sir. Because I chastised Miss Devereux for her behavior with you, you would now have revenge on me by accusing me of crimes before these Yankee officers?"

"Only because I believe you are guilty. These men acted on your orders."

"Preposterous!"

"They were all carrying substantial sums of money, Mrs. Hudson. Money you paid them."

"I did not. I have no money. I am a widow. My husband was a preacher."

"I saw you give Long Tom money. Right there in the hospital. I was there—as a patient. I saw it."

"Of course I gave him money. It was to buy supplies."

"Raines," said Grant. "Have you any proof of this accusation?"

Harry thought upon this. "If you would accompany me out to the garden, sir."

HE had the soldiers bring Gillette, Lucy the cook, Toby, and Mrs. Hudson to the opened gravesite. Grant and Rawlins stood to the side. York lingered back on the rear porch.

Long Tom looked peaceful, despite the large bullet hole above his left eye. It was an exit wound. He'd been shot in the back of the head.

"Is this the slave Long Tom you worked with?" Harry asked Gillette.

"I thought we'd established that fact."

"Lucy, you know this to be Long Tom?"

"Yessir. Dat him."

"Toby? This is the man you saw putting the big bundles in the ambulance?"

The boy nodded.

Harry turned somberly to Mrs. Hudson. "There you are, madam. This man accosted Mrs. Townsend and Mrs. Abbott in the side parlor of this house, killing the two of them with one bullet. I believe that happened only because Mrs. Abbott stepped in front of her sister, trying to protect her. He was only interested in Mrs. Townsend, because he had been told she was an enemy agent, but May Abbott stepped in the way."

Mrs. Hudson's malevolent eyes had grown very large. Then she closed them, shaking her head sadly. "She was an excellent nurse. It is sad."

"Confess your part in this, Mrs. Hudson. You cannot escape the fact that this man was your slave."

Now she seemed totally bewildered. So did Lucy the cook.

"Long Tom ain't belong to Miz Hudson," she said. "He belong to Mrs. Oates."

Harry stood motionless, his eyes on Long Tom's sleeping face. The kindly Mrs. Oates had placed him next to the very healthy wounded 'Yankee' sergeant. Mrs. Oates had taken such a keen interest in him—and in Louise.

"Excuse me, General," Harry said. "I must go."

There were at least a dozen horses tied along the fence in front of the house. Harry leaped aboard the nearest—a tall bay with a Federal saddle on him—and whipped him into a mad gallop down the street.

Rounding the corner near the church, he saw the surgeon

walking along toward the big hospital. The doctor, head
down, took no note of him—his mind on other matters.

There was no time to stop and ask after Louise's well-
being. That was something Harry would have to deal with
personally—and fast. Pounding on, he took the next corner so
swiftly he nearly came out of the saddle himself. Regaining
his seat, he finished the next block as though in a race. He
could see flames in the front window as he pulled up.

The front door was locked. Harry moved to the window
beside it and kicked it in. He had to kick several times more
to clear the wooden frames. Then he made his way inside,
into a smoky room.

He was able to make out the hallway. The bedroom was
at the rear of the house. Putting his head down and a handkerchief over his mouth, he lunged on toward the bedroom.

Flames were curling up from beneath the door. It, too,
was locked. Moving at a run, he hit it with his shoulder,
rebounding in pain but budging it not at all. Recalling suddenly how his friend and fellow intelligence agent Boston
Leahy dealt with locked doors, he backed up and kicked it
hard just beside the latch.

It gave way, revealing a chamber bright with fire.

Chapter 29

HARRY lunged into the room, trying to keep low. The counterpane had begun to catch fire at the foot of the bed. He flung it off and onto the floor, then went to Louise's side. Her eyes were closed. He was unable to tell if she was breathing. Her skin was warm, but that could be only from the heat of the fire.

Coughing, he started to lift her from the mattress, halting when he looked behind to see that the open doorway leading to the rest of the house was now closed by a curtain of flame. He might be able to leap through that himself, somehow, but not with her in his arms.

Gathering her up again, he staggered through the smoke toward the room's only window, finding it closed. Holding her close to him with one arm, he tried to open the window with the other, but it would not budge. He tried kicking at it, but had lost his strength. The smoke was too much.

He lowered Louise to the floor, then returned to the challenge of the stubborn sash, shoving hard twice with no result but a hard pain in his shoulder. The window had somehow been locked or blocked.

The heat was so intense he wondered if his back was on fire. His breaths were little more than occasional interruptions of his coughing. Whatever he was going to do, he had only a few seconds remaining.

There was a sudden crash of glass and wood, and then another, and then another. Something cut his face, but that didn't matter. Squinting through the smoke, he saw the windowpanes and frame rapidly disappearing as a great stick was repeatedly smashed against them.

It wasn't a stick. It was a rifle—the buffalo gun.

Harry leaned out over the windowsill, filling his lungs with clean, clear air. Then he knelt back on the hot floor and took Louise into his arms again, lifting her to the window. Strong, waiting hands took her and pulled her out through the jagged opening, ripping part of her nightdress. Harry reached beneath her legs, raising them over the shards of glass and splintery wood until she was clear of the sill and the room.

"Get her away!" he shouted. It was all he could manage.

Tantou took the still-unconscious Louise in his arms and backed away. "Get out now, Harry Raines! The whole house is burning!"

Harry could not recall how far the drop was to the ground, but he hurled himself through the window without regard to it. He landed on his painful shoulder, having inflicted a ripping cut across his knee from a sharp piece of glass. Lying there on the grass, he saw flames coming out of the window he'd just left and the one just above it. Filling the sky above was thick, black smoke.

He shoved himself backward a short distance, then somehow got to his feet. For a moment he couldn't find Tantou, but at last he did. The Métis had taken Louise to the vegetable garden of the house next door, laying her on the soft, freshly planted soil. Harry came near and heard a delightful sound: she was whimpering. Her beautiful eyes were open. She was alive—though there was no telling for how long.

"We have to get a doctor," Harry said.

"I will stay with her."

"Wait." Harry stood straight, looking about. "Mrs. Oates. Where did she go?"

"I don't know, Harry Raines."

"We have to stop her. But wait here. I'll get a doctor." Limping, he started around to the front of the burning house, dodging a sudden shower of sparks that spewed down from the roof.

Soldiers were standing in a clump by the front gate. He recognized them as Illinois cavalrymen, and the jerking, thrashing form in their midst as a now-captive Mrs. Oates. It took three of them to hold her. Colonel York was one of them.

Harry saw more soldiers coming from the direction of the courthouse. None was carrying anything that might be employed to fight the fire, which was now beyond extinguishing except by its own accord. One of the soldiers was an officer. As he came nearer, Harry saw that he was the surgeon.

"Is she . . . ?"

Harry pointed to the house next door. "In the garden. With my friend. Please hurry."

Wide-eyed and wheezing, the doctor did so. Harry wanted to go back with him, but there was Mrs. Oates.

He stepped before her but could think of nothing to say. She had stopped struggling, and contemplated him quite calmly.

"I am a woman," she said. "You cannot hang me."

Harry struggled to control himself. "If Louise dies, madam, I will gladly shoot you."

York pulled him aside, ordering the cavalrymen to take the prisoner to the courthouse. "A military tribunal will deal with her," he said, leading Harry even farther away, so that no one could hear them. "General Grant had to leave. He would like to speak with you later, if that's convenient."

"Yes. Of course."

"He has questions."

"I have one myself. For you."

"Sir?"

"What will you do?"

York seemed astonished. "What do you mean? I shall continue as aide-de-camp to General Grant, if he'll have me."

"That's another question. He may not take kindly to your having gone all the way into Corinth, returning with no useful military intelligence—and hours late to the field of battle."

An ambulance rattled around the street corner, its team coming toward them at a trot. A man in civilian clothes dodged out of its way. It was Congressman Abbott.

"He said nothing about that," York said. "Nothing at all. I told you, Raines. I saw little of the enemy, not until I neared our own lines. I know nothing of Corinth."

Harry produced the diamond stickpin and handed it to him. "You are singular among your fellow officers in the elegance of your cravats, Colonel."

York studied the object, then placed it in a pocket. "Thank you for retrieving this."

"You were in Corinth, at the Townsend house. And you returned to your army disguised as a woman."

"Sir?"

"No one in Lieutenant Riordan's unit found May Abbott's cloak. You had it all the time. She loaned it to you, to wear coming into Corinth, and leaving. You brought it back neatly folded—and unsoiled."

York scuffed at the grass with his highly polished boot. "I would call that surmise."

Harry dug into his pocket, retrieving the uniform button he had retrieved from the Townsend house. "I believe this is yours also, sir. It must have come off your tunic. You perhaps removed it in too much haste."

York colored. A portion of the burning roof abruptly sagged, then gave way, falling into the flames that were consuming the second floor of the house.

Abbott was almost upon them.

"Now you insinuate, sir."

"You loved them both, didn't you?" Harry said.

"We should not be discussing this with Mr. Abbott about to join us."

"What I mean to say is that you loved them both together—at the same time. And they reciprocated in like manner. Both of the sisters loved you."

"Please, sir. Not now. I will discuss it with you later—over a glass of good whiskey."

Abbott stood before them, breathing deeply. His eyes went from York to Harry and back again. "I am not stupid, York. I listened to every word back there. It all comes together now. I understand."

"Congressman, I would urge you to calm yourself," Harry said.

York began backing away, but it was too late. A pocket pistol came into Abbott's hand. He raised it quickly, before Harry or the colonel could wrest it from him, and fired twice into York's chest.

Chapter 30

DAYS passed without further word from Grant, which was just as well, as Harry was in no mood to be distracted from his principal concern, which was Louise. Using Grant's authority, though he was not sure he was still entitled to it, he commandeered another house for her, and this time he and Tantou performed the role of nurse, with one or the other of them always at her bedside.

It was not a seemly business, but Harry was no stranger to it, having seen his other actress love, Caitlin Howard, through several sweaty, delirious bouts of overindulgence in the opiate laudanum.

Louise was holding her own. She was young. Her wounds had been kept clean. No bone had been struck but for the glancing blow to the rib. The smoke from the house fire had a lingering effect on her, but her flesh had been barely singed. There was much that augured well. Still, Harry had seen too many young and healthy soldiers appear to recover from wounds and then perish in a single night. Most of those dying in this war were not the victims of shot and shell at all, succumbing instead to the maladies of camp and the march.

She spoke to him from time to time, in little more than whispers but always clearly, even when she was merely speaking aloud the lines of plays. She seemed to marvel at his presence every time she took note of it.

" 'As constant as the northern star, of whose true-fix'd and resting quality, there is no fellow in the firmament,' " she said, blessing him further with a sweet smile.

He touched her cheek and found it hot, yet the flesh of her good hand was cold.

With his dying breath, with an odd grin, Colonel York had bequeathed Harry his silver flask. He'd not touched it nor any spiritous liquors since the fire, but now he did, leaving Louise to more sleep and going out onto the porch. Tantou, who'd been sitting out there, rose morosely silently and went into the bedroom.

Harry drank, then sighed. He sat down on the steps and drank again, wondering what lives might have been led by all the people involved in this bizarre affair had there been no war.

A rider approached the house at a trot, a young Federal officer Harry had not encountered before. "Captain Raines?" he asked, pulling up at the gate.

"That's me."

"General Grant's respects, sir. He wonders if you would find it convenient to meet with him at his headquarters."

"Certainly. When would he find it convenient?"

"Immediately."

THE tents at Grant's little compound had all been struck, and his writing desk and other furnishings were being loaded onto a wagon. The general had retained one camp chair and was sitting in it, puffing a long cigar as he attended to correspondence. He looked up, his clear blue eyes friendly, but his expression blank, as though his thoughts were still on his writing. As Harry dismounted, Grant at last rose, setting down his notebook.

"Good morning, Raines. Thank you for coming."

"You're leaving, sir?"

Grant looked about him, as though confirming the observation. "I am. I'm going to Memphis." He started to walk away from his laboring soldiers, heading for a meadow beyond the trees with a patch of wildflowers at the center. "I can scarcely believe it, but I've been restored to an active command. Halleck has given me the right wing—the Army of the Tennessee. We're into the business of protecting railroads now. General Buell's Army of the Ohio has the Memphis and Charleston. Pope's Army of the Mississippi protects the Corinth railhead. I have seven rail lines between here and Memphis, which will be my headquarters. I leave for there directly."

Birds were singing in the branches. It was a singularly peaceful place.

"You asked to see me, sir?"

"Indeed. Sorry I've taken so long in doing so. The imperative in this matter was to satisfy Congressman Abbott that justice was being done for his wife. I daresay he's satisfied now, the poor devil." He took two long puffs on his cigar. "I'll confess it. I had hoped he might be of some help to me in rescuing me from my enforced idleness, but now it develops such help wasn't necessary at all."

The general began a slow perambulation of the greensward, one hand held behind his back.

"What will happen to him?" Harry asked.

"As Colonel York was a serving officer, he'll go before a military tribunal. I presume he'll plead the unwritten law concerning his wife's infidelity."

"Do you believe she was unfaithful, General?"

"You were very skillful if very discreet in your presentation, Raines. We all caught on quickly. Abbott perhaps too quickly. A civilian jury would likely let him off. A military panel will be harsher, but Abbott has friends still on the Joint Committee on the Conduct of the War, so they'll be wary. Perhaps he'll get off still."

"I liked York, sir, but there was some justice in what happened."

They walked on several yards more. "They hanged Gillette this morning as a spy. I had not a thing to do with it. Provost marshal's doing. He telegraphed your boss, Mr. Pinkerton. Seems he has a policy toward the murder of his agents. Eye for an eye. Justice in that, too—for what they tried to do to you."

"Actually, hanging me would have been all proper and legal."

"Shooting Miss Devereux wasn't. How is she?"

"Improving—slowly. We're hopeful."

"Good. You need anything, go to Sherman."

"We'll be leaving as soon as she's well enough to travel." That was a presumption. Harry hoped he wasn't tempting fate with such optimism.

"Going back to Washington?"

Harry nodded. "Near there." He stopped. "There's one matter I didn't adequately clear up, General. I've no doubt that this man Long Tom killed the Sayres sisters and their maids, and did so on Mrs. Oates's orders."

"That's been proved beyond a shadow."

"But what I failed to prove is why Mrs. Oates ordered the deed."

"I saw the look on Townsend's face. He was a man undone."

"I guess he could not bring himself to kill his wife, so he persuaded Mrs. Oates she was a Federal spy, and sealed her fate. Conveniently, he was leading his troops to battle when the murders were done."

"Yes. All that's very clear." Another puff. "The Oates woman was more than the chief of an assassination ring. She had spies under her command as well. Odd that a woman like that could be involved in such deadly mischief."

"Rose Greenhow ran the Confederate spy ring in Washington, and there is a woman in Richmond of my acquaintance who serves the Union cause there in like manner."

Grant stopped. "There is? What is her name?"

"I should not say it, sir."

The general moved on. "Do you think Townsend killed Long Tom and the undertaker?"

"Yes, sir. And the undertaker's assistant. He may have been so frightened of being found out that he was planning on eliminating Mrs. Oates as well. I'll wager that was why he was lingering in Corinth when he should have been skefdaddling with the rest of the Reb army. But I haven't proved any of this. So he goes free."

"He's on a train, heading for Chicago and Camp Douglas."

"The prison camp," said Harry.

"Not a nice one."

"But he'll be exchanged. There's no justice in that."

Grant altered course to head back for his little command. "I strongly disagree with the practice, Raines. We exchange them on parole and they're back in the lines shooting at us before we can turn around. The North has a huge numerical advantage over the foe. Their ranks diminish with every battle. Yet we foolishly reinforce them with these continual exchanges. If I am ever in a position to do so, I will have them halted for the duration. But for now, I'm going to start with Colonel Townsend."

"Sir?"

"I have numerous friends in Illinois. The commandant at Douglas will be informed that Townsend is not to be exchanged. Never to be exchanged."

"And after the war?"

"Those are hard places, those camps. Not every prisoner is going to survive the war." Grant dropped his cigar end on the ground and crushed it out.

When they reached the campsite, everything had been packed and loaded. Grant's horse was saddled and waiting.

"Will you be leaving him behind?" Harry asked.

"What do you mean, Raines?"

"When you take the train to Memphis."

"I'm not taking the train."

"But it's a hundred miles or more."

"It's June, and lovely weather. I'm going to ride Fox all the way."

Harry surveyed Grant's party. With aides and staff and cavalry escort, there weren't fifty men there. "General. The Confederates will be prowling the country between here and the Mississippi."

Grant pulled himself into the saddle and reached for a fresh cigar. "You are a good scout, Raines. I had thought to ask you to join my command in that capacity. But I fear you have made your occupation too well known in these parts. You'd be a marked man. I think you have compromised yourself badly. I wonder how much service you can be to Pinkerton in the Eastern Theater."

"That won't matter, sir. I'm going to leave his service."

"What? Resign?"

"Yes, sir. I'm quitting, and I'm going home. This war is barely a year old, General, and I have killed already four men with my own hand. And I wear no uniform. It is enough."

Grant lighted his cigar. "I understand. I was ready to do the same thing a few days ago, though for a different reason. But the war won't go away just because you do."

"I'll just do my best to keep out of its way."

"Very well, Raines." He took up his reins. "Myself, I expect I'll now see this thing through to the end." Rawlins walked his horse up beside the general's—waiting, but not patiently. "I am appreciative of your efforts here," Grant continued. "Most appreciative."

With that, shoulders hunched, he headed out of the woods and onto the road, his aides and escort following. Harry went to his own horse and mounted, sitting still a moment to watch Grant's departure, wishing the general were not traveling west, but east.

Chapter 31

THEY rattled along the curving railroad roadbed, a limestone cliff and well-treed mountain slope to the left, the C & O Canal and the shimmering Potomac River on the right. They were in Maryland, but the river curved so much that they kept crossing over wooden trestles into Virginia.

"Where are we?" Louise said softly. She sat close, swaying against him with the motion of the train.

Harry bent forward to look forward out the window. "As memory serves, about an hour west of the Paw Paw tunnel."

Tantou, in the seat opposite, comfortable now aboard a railroad train, grunted. "So you are home now, Harry Raines."

"Oh, no. A long way downriver yet."

"You are home. You know where you are. You remember the trees."

"I remember the hills."

They passed a canal boat heading downstream with a load of coal, its mule on the towpath slogging along with head down. Rounding a curve, they came upon a group of

Union soldiers camped under some trees. Two of them, little more than boys, waved.

The sight of them stirred Louise. "Are there Rebels here?"

"Nearby, I'll wager," said Harry. "But there can't be many. This part of the country has small fondness for slavery. Few here would go to war for it."

"But this is Virginia."

"The war divides the state."

"How long will it go on, Harry? Till the last man falls?"

"Sometimes I think that may be so. But not for us. The war is over for us."

She came close to him, and took his hand with her right. Her left was in a black glove, with stuffed cotton taking the place of her missing finger. "How very strange that we should be here on this train together, Harry, going back to the place from which you helped exile me a year ago."

"A very different time."

"I suppose Washington is very different now."

"Dirtier, unhappier; more crowded, more expensive."

"More dangerous?"

"Doubtless."

"What are we to say to Caitlin?"

"If she is there—and not touring with John Wilkes Booth."

"If she is there, what will we say about us?"

"We are all friends, Louise. We've been through much together."

"So very strange." She rested her head against his shoulder, curling strands falling across his chest. "I am so grateful to you."

"And I to you."

"Whatever for?"

"I find myself unexpectedly very happy."

"I am a lagniappe, *comme on dit à New Orleans.*"

"Yes. A lagniappe. The most delightful to ever come my way."

"Tell me about your farm."

"It isn't much, but it's everything to me. It lies on a low hill that runs down to the Potomac a few miles upriver from Harpers Ferry. There are some beautiful mountains near. I have a large house with a porch on three sides, and two barns. I had nearly a hundred horses on it, though they may be gone. There's an apple orchard, too."

"It sounds lovely, Harry. But will I be happy in such a place? I want to be back in Washington. I want to go back on the stage. I mean to. I will, Harry."

"Yes, and I'll be in the front row. But that will have to wait. The capital's full of Rebel agents, and I expect some of them will be looking for us."

A familiar mischief came into her voice. "And what if it turns out that I am one of them?"

"Then I would be devastated, for now I can never think of you as an enemy."

"Nor I you. Never again. 'Under the greenwood tree, who loves to lie with me, and turn his merry note, unto the sweet bird's throat. Come hither, come hither, come hither; here shall he see, no enemy, but winter and rough weather.'" She kissed his cheek. "It is July, and sweet weather."

"You have not recovered fully, or even half, Louise. You must not think of going to Washington, or anyplace else. Not for some time. Please."

"Very well. Not until I grow stronger."

He kissed her hand, ignoring the stares of a woman across the aisle who reminded him slightly of Mrs. Hudson. "Thank you."

"And it's peaceful there—on your farm?"

"Oh, yes."

"Far from the war?"

"There's nothing there to fight over. Down the road is a pleasant village called Shepherdstown. Across the river from it is another, called Sharpsburg. I will take you picnicking there. I know of a special place. There's a wide, clear-running creek that winds through some lovely foothills west of South Mountain. It's the most peaceful place I know of on Earth."

"What is it called?"

"The creek? Antietam."